Praise for Jo

"Gripping. . . . With a convincing backdrop of Prohibition-era New York, Green carefully weaves historical detail and complex relationships into a tense narrative that doesn't let up till the close. The author's fans won't be disappointed."

—*Publishers Weekly* on *The Metropolitan Affair*

"In this new series starter, Christy Award–winner Green (*Drawn by the Current*) offers details of Egyptian art, a rich cast made vivid by small details, plenty of historical references, and a plot full of red herrings. Classified as Christian fiction, this involving blend of historical crime story, family saga, and romance will please a range of readers. Suggest it beyond its BISAC category and put it on reading lists of cozy mysteries and gentle romances too."

—*Library Journal* on *The Metropolitan Affair*

"A captivating, multilayered mystery . . . with exciting clues and shocking revelations, this is an uplifting story of faith with many intriguing twists and ever-raising stakes, all leading to an unexpected conclusion."

—*BookPage* on *The Metropolitan Affair*

"[A] captivating tale . . . Green presents the perfect combination of well-developed characters, sweet romance, a glimpse into history, and a fascinating, well-researched mystery. Fans of Elizabeth Camden and Elizabeth Peters will be delighted by the start of this new series."

—*Booklist* starred review of *The Metropolitan Affair*

"*The Metropolitan Affair* is a second-chance love story set amid the glamor of New York City during the Roaring Twenties. The novel weaves historical mysteries with a fascinating behind-the-scenes look at museum work and the problems of art fraud. I loved the fast-paced jaunt through elite museums, Jazz Age parties, and antique-filled mansions on Long Island's famed Gold Coast. With smart leading characters, a compelling storyline, and a deep dive into Egyptian antiquities, this novel is a richly layered delight."

—Elizabeth Camden, RITA and
Christy Award–winning author

"A splendid and fascinating world is captured both in the golden age of the Met and through Green's marvelously painted New York. With a dash of Elizabeth Peters's Amelia Peabody that is sure to delight fans of *Miss Fisher's Murder Mysteries*, *The Metropolitan Affair* finds Jocelyn Green at the top of her game as one of the reigning queens of inspirational fiction."

—Rachel McMillan, author of *The London Restoration*
and *The Mozart Code*

"As always, Jocelyn Green pens a novel rich in history, character, and meaning. A complex exploration of family and loyalty lends depth to a thrilling mystery and a swoony romance. Steeped in fascination for ancient Egypt and 1920s New York, *The Metropolitan Affair* delivers on all fronts! Savor every word."

—Sarah Sundin, bestselling and award-winning author
of *The Sound of Light* and *Until Leaves Fall in Paris*

The
HUDSON
COLLECTION

BOOKS BY JOCELYN GREEN

ON CENTRAL PARK

The Metropolitan Affair
The Hudson Collection

THE WINDY CITY SAGA

Veiled in Smoke
Shadows of the White City
Drawn by the Current

The Mark of the King
A Refuge Assured
Between Two Shores

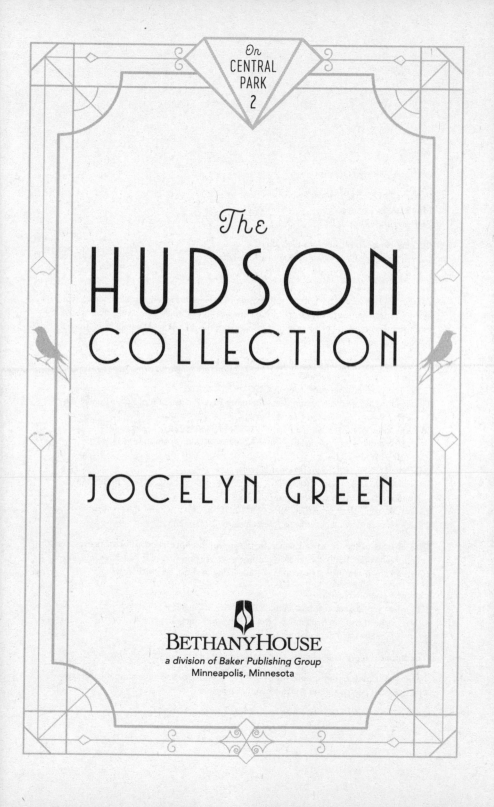

On
CENTRAL
PARK
2

The
HUDSON
COLLECTION

JOCELYN GREEN

BETHANYHOUSE

a division of Baker Publishing Group
Minneapolis, Minnesota

© 2024 by Jocelyn Green

Published by Bethany House Publishers
Minneapolis, Minnesota
BethanyHouse.com

Bethany House Publishers is a division of
Baker Publishing Group, Grand Rapids, Michigan

Printed in the United States of America

Library of Congress Cataloging-in-Publication Data
Name: Green, Jocelyn, author.
Title: The Hudson collection / Jocelyn Green.
Description: Minneapolis, Minnesota : Bethany House, a division of Baker Publishing Group, 2024. | Series: On Central Park ; 2
Identifiers: LCCN 2023058234 (print) | LCCN 2023058235 (ebook) | ISBN 9780764239649 (paperback) | ISBN 9780764242786 (casebound) | ISBN 9781493445196 (ebook)
Subjects: LCGFT: Christian fiction. | Novels.
Classification: LCC PS3607.R4329255 H83 2024 (print) | LCC PS3607.R4329255 (ebook) | DDC 813/.6—dc23/eng/20231221
LC record available at https://lccn.loc.gov/2023058234
LC ebook record available at https://lccn.loc.gov/2023058235

This is a work of historical reconstruction; the appearances of certain historical figures are therefore inevitable. All other characters, however, are products of the author's imagination, and any resemblance to actual persons, living or dead, is coincidental.

Cover by Laura Klynstra
Cover image of mansion from Natalia Sobańska / Arcangel
Cover image of woman from lldiko Neer / Trevillion Images
Frame elements from Shutterstock

The author is represented by the literary agency of Credo Communications, LLC.

Baker Publishing Group publications use paper produced from sustainable forestry practices and postconsumer waste whenever possible.

24 25 26 27 28 29 30   7 6 5 4 3 2 1

CHAPTER

1

NEW YORK CITY
MONDAY, AUGUST 23, 1926

S orry," Elsa whispered, though she knew full well the bird splayed on its back on the metal table was past feeling any pain. She pushed her glasses up the bridge of her nose, then reached for the scalpel. Having already stuffed the bird's throat with cotton, she separated the feathers down the midline of the breast. "Here we go."

"Talking to yourself again?" Her colleague approached before she had a chance to make the first incision. "Or are you talking to a dead bird while you skin it? Which is rather worse, if you ask me."

"No one asked you," she teased.

He grinned. At the age of twenty-eight, Archer Hamlin was two years older than Elsa and yet retained his schoolboy charm. She had proved immune to it, however, which made their camaraderie easy and light. He worked in the Department of Preparation, painting dioramas for habitat displays, but found reasons enough to visit her fifth-floor office. "Admit it," he said. "You're so lonely back here you've gone batty."

Batty? Never. Lonely? Maybe.

7

Definitely.

"Lauren left for Egypt last week," she told him.

"Your cousin and roommate, Lauren? Say, didn't I dance with her once? As I recall, you refused me, and she stepped in to save me from embarrassment."

"I refused you because I don't dance," Elsa reminded him with a tap to her leg. She still couldn't decide if Archer's oblivion to her limitation made him a terrible observer or a steadfast friend. "If she saved anyone from humiliation, it was me."

Archer folded his arms and leaned a hip against the table, watching her work. "You have another roommate, though. Her name is Ivy, right? Are you looking for a third to help with rent? I know a guy. He's looking to move out of his parents' house. Very tidy, very clean, upstanding and respectful. He just hasn't found the right real estate yet. He's not bad to look at, either."

Suppressing a smile, she shook her head. "You're full of applesauce." Not that she minded right now. Her work at the American Museum of Natural History was mostly done alone. Even before Lauren had taken leave from the Metropolitan Museum of Art for a six-month survey of ancient Egyptian art, Elsa had been lonely at work.

As a research assistant in the ornithology department, preparing bird skins was part of her job, and she was good at it. In fact, with her small hands and natural perfectionism, she performed the task better than anyone else in the department. That didn't mean she loved doing it.

"If you're here to rescue me from my isolation," she told Archer, "at least step out of the light for the rest of the procedure."

He shuddered. "I'm not staying. I've just been consulting with Chapman on a project. He said he wants to see you."

"Now?" She was hoping to get the bird stuffed before leaving today.

He looked at his watch. "More or less."

While Archer whistled along the corridor, Elsa covered the bird and her tray of tools and limped to the sink to wash her hands. Ignoring the ache in her leg, she made her way to her boss's office.

"You wanted to see me?"

"Please have a seat, Miss Reisner." Frank Chapman, head of the ornithology department, gestured to the chair across from his desk. The bookcase behind him held mounted birds from his many expeditions; stacks of *Bird-Lore* magazine, which he edited for the Audubon Society; and eighteen books and field guides he'd authored himself.

Elsa took the offered chair. "Can I help you with something? Have more shipments arrived from the South Seas?"

Mr. Chapman's mustache twitched in a brief smile. "You most certainly can help, but it's nothing to do with the South Seas expedition. Do you recall patrons of this museum by the name of Van Tessel? Linus and Bernadette van Tessel?"

She did. Linus had passed away two years ago, and his widow, who went by the name of Birdie, was now seventy-five years old. "I spoke with Mrs. Van Tessel at the fundraiser last summer but haven't seen her since."

"I don't think anyone has. She became something of a recluse after that. She recently passed away in her sleep at her estate near Tarrytown, about twenty-four miles north of here. Her executor called me in to hear the reading of her will last Friday. Poor woman. Her husband had been a wealthy explorer in their earlier years together, but when he died, she was saddled with his debts. Turns out, no one had been managing his investments for years."

A pang of sadness pricked Elsa's chest for Mrs. Van Tessel. She hadn't known the widow well, but even in their brief interaction, it was clear she'd been a sweet soul, and warmer than Elsa's own mother, at any rate. At least her death had been a peaceful one.

"Linus van Tessel accrued an expansive collection of birds,

and according to Mrs. Van Tessel's will, we are welcome to it in its entirety, no strings attached," Mr. Chapman went on. "But I'd rather not pack and ship everything here without knowing if we even want it all. I need someone to go examine the Hudson Collection—named for the river which flows next to the estate—to see what condition the birds are in. Do we have use for them, either here or to loan to other museums or schools? For the birds to have any value to us, we need to know when and where the specimens were captured. I want them all cataloged properly before entering the museum."

Crossing her ankles, Elsa adjusted the skirt of her drop-waist dress so the pleats ran straight over her knees. It sounded like a massive undertaking. "Are there field notes?"

"Supposedly. That's what I need someone to find. Someone thorough, with meticulous attention to detail."

"And that someone is me?"

He smiled. "None other. The will stipulates that the museums get first pick of any assets. So I imagine you'll run into other local museum staff while you're there."

"So I won't be alone." She wouldn't mind a change of scenery, and the Hudson River valley was a lovely place. But the idea of going through a dead couple's dead birds on a dusty Gothic estate in the middle of nowhere seemed macabre. A bit of company would be welcome.

"Not at all. In fact, the relatives are allowed to go in and take whatever the museums don't want. They've been asked to stay out of the way for a few days, except for a Mr. Guy Spalding. He's the nephew who inherited the land and property. He'll be your contact should you need anything there." He stood, and she took the signal to do the same. "What are you working on now?"

"A group of warblers arrived from some vacationers who wanted us to have them," she reminded him. "I'm preparing the last of them today."

"Very good. Finish that, then begin at the Van Tessels' estate tomorrow. Elmhurst, they called it. Plan to spend two or three days a week there until the project is done, which I anticipate will take a couple of weeks or so. That's the goal, anyway. I still need you reporting to your office here on the other days to keep up with your regular work. Besides, Spalding declared at the reading of the will that he would donate the entire estate to the county to avoid paying the taxes on his inheritance. He was keen to put that plan into motion immediately, but I don't know when that hand-off is. Oh, and Miss Reisner, I'd advise wearing sensible shoes at Elmhurst." He glanced at the Mary Jane heels she'd changed into after walking to work in flats. "You'll have a lot of ground to cover, including plenty of stairs."

"Yes, sir." She would not point out that a good pair of shoes would only take her so far.

CHAPTER

2

Y ou're sure this is where you want to be, lady?"
Elsa peered out the window at the turreted Gothic mansion. It was only two miles from the Tarrytown train station, but it might as well have been twenty for how remote it felt. If she didn't know better, she could imagine she'd stepped into a fairy tale set in medieval Europe.

"I'm sure." Paying the driver his fare, she asked him to return for her at four o'clock.

Pebbles crunched as the taxi rolled away, leaving Elsa on the circular drive. Slinging her bag over one shoulder, she tipped her head back, trying to take it all in. Above the veranda, sunshine washed the stone walls in oyster pink. An arched window with ribbing made the house look like a cathedral. The roofline, interrupted by a four-story tower, had steps up and down, like a fortress wall. It was difficult to believe this had also been a residence, and for only two people, as the Van Tessels had no children.

It was so quiet here. All she heard was the rush of wind through the trees. Mr. Spalding was likely inside.

A German shepherd came bounding toward her from behind the house.

"Shoo!" She held out both hands to slow his advance. Mud coated his paws, and yet the dog seemed to be in a state of absolute bliss.

"Stay down," she tried.

He did not stay down. Instead, he stood on hind legs and planted front paws on her royal blue skirt. She could feel the wet cold seep through the fabric.

"Down!"

The animal's tail wagged so hard it swayed his body. He seemed to have no intention of leaving her be. With grim determination, she tugged off the white cotton gloves she wore and stuffed them in a pocket before taking his paws and shoving them away. "You really need to work on your manners, pooch. Coming on strong is no way to treat a lady."

Her hands now as filthy as his paws, she headed toward the closest door to the mansion. "Mr. Spalding!" she called out, hoping he was near enough to hear. "Your dog is loose, Mr. Spalding!" And he trotted right alongside her, tongue lolling from a grin, tail beating against her thigh as if they were in cahoots or something.

"Barney!"

The commanding voice stopped her before she reached the veranda. Turning, she watched the dog run to his owner, who was dressed far more casually than she'd predicted for a man expecting a meeting. The trousers were fine, she supposed, but he wore no jacket, and his shirtsleeves were rolled to his elbows. He hadn't even bothered to pomade his brown hair, and a thatch of it fell over his brow. As the man approached, Barney stayed obediently at his side, ears pricked up, tail still wagging.

"Sorry about that, miss. Barney never met a stranger."

Elsa squinted at the sun over his shoulder before a cloud diffused the harsh light. She stifled a gasp. A long scar slashed the left side of his face from the top of his cheekbone to his jaw. A smaller scar marred his square chin. A gust of wind lifted his hair, revealing a third mark on his brow. If she'd met him in a dark alley, she would have turned tail and run.

Snapping her attention to his deep grey eyes, she stuck out her hand, hoping that she hadn't stared for more than a fraction of a second. "Elsa Reisner," she said. "I'm here from the American Museum of Natural History, for the bird collection."

He looked at her hand and, instead of shaking it, placed his handkerchief in her palm.

Of course. The mud.

"Thanks." She wiped between every finger, then pressed the handkerchief to the pawprints on her skirt. At least she couldn't fret about her first impression with Mr. Spalding since it was his dog who had sullied her.

He extended his hand, and this time Elsa shook it. His grip was firm and calloused. "I'll pay the dry-cleaning bill."

"That isn't necessary, but thank you." Returning the handkerchief, Elsa shifted her gaze to Barney. Now that he was sitting and leaning against his master's leg, she could appreciate that the animal just loved people. So did she. "I'm very sorry for your loss, Mr. Spalding," she added. "Your aunt was a fine woman. I didn't know her well, but we shared a love of birds. We at the museum are honored by her bequest."

When he frowned, he looked downright foreboding. "You misunderstand."

"Do I? Which part?" Remembering her gloves, she pulled them out of her pocket and back on her hands, feeling only slightly less exposed. The handkerchief had been no help in cleaning the dirt from beneath her nails.

The door opened onto the veranda, and a man of middling years in a three-piece suit filled the frame. After a moment's hesitation, he left the house and joined them.

"Miss Reisner?" Beneath a closely trimmed beard, his face was narrow, and somewhat pinched. The smell of Brilliantine from his light brown hair competed with the fresh air.

"Yes," she said, looking between the two men.

Turning, the scarred man walked away, and Barney went with him.

"Well." The newcomer eyed her mud-smeared ensemble. "Guy Spalding. I was watching for a professional, not a schoolgirl."

Heat flooded her face. She knew she looked younger than her age but couldn't do much about that. "Then who was that?"

"The man of few words? That's Luke Dupont, with Dupont & Son, the architectural salvage dealer. His company is removing and purchasing some architectural elements from me. The county plans to tear down this monstrosity once the transfer of ownership is complete, so I might as well get some cash out of it first. Now, Miss Reisner, aside from those spectacles, you're far too pretty to be a researcher type. I thought girls like you didn't get up until noon."

She bristled. "Blondes, you mean? I certainly hope you haven't formed your opinion based on the novel *Gentlemen Prefer Blondes*. It's a bunch of applesauce, if you ask me. For all of Lorelei's talk of brains, she sure didn't have any. Some of us do. Even if we are blond."

"My daughter is blond," he told her. "But I see you're not cut from the same cloth."

With no reply to that, Elsa straightened her jacket and began walking toward the mansion.

Mr. Spalding's eyebrows lifted as soon as he noticed her limp. "Ah, that explains a lot."

Elsa stopped short. "Excuse me?" She and Mr. Spalding were not getting off on the right foot. If she didn't turn this around, working with him wouldn't get any easier. She needed to try this again. "Mr. Spalding, I'm very sorry for your loss. Your aunt was a wonderful woman. If there's anything I can do for you during this time of mourning, let me know. Otherwise, I will do my work as quickly and efficiently as possible. If you'll kindly point me to the collection and the field notes, I'll keep to my own work and let you get on with yours."

The sooner she could start, the sooner she'd be done with this lonely place, where the friendliest beast was a dog. She didn't even like dogs.

———○———

Inside the mansion, Elsa followed Mr. Spalding through the vestibule and into an octagon-shaped parlor with floor-to-ceiling windows that faced the Hudson River. Birds were everywhere. Not only did they sit upon each horizontal surface, but some had been clipped to the draperies, while canaries and parakeets perched in Victorian birdcages. Elsa spied warblers, flycatchers, finches, a sandgrouse native to Africa, and an imperial pigeon that had to be from the islands of Papua New Guinea.

"They're all yellow," she observed.

"Naturally. This is the yellow room." Mr. Spalding huffed a laugh and gestured to the gold drapes and papered walls. "Every room has its color. You'll see. On some fanciful whim, my aunt had her maid rearrange all the birds a year or so ago. If Uncle Linus had still been alive, he never would have allowed it."

At the museum, birds were grouped by habitats. It made the most sense, especially once they'd started creating dioramas with lifelike flora and fauna in each display case. This way, visitors could see the birds in their proper context.

But here, birds collected from all over the world mingled. Elsa's palms began tingling as she counted more than a dozen species spanning eight genera, seven families, and four orders. The habitats represented here came from five different continents. It defied all scientific logic, mixing them together like this. It was disorienting. Even as a child, she had cut pictures from *Bird-Lore* and pasted them into scrapbooks according to their place in the animal kingdom.

Elsa set her shoulder bag on the writing desk next to a stack of notebooks. Turning the cover, she cringed at the careless handwriting. There were protocols in her line of work. Block letters only, very neat, no abbreviations. The point was for anyone to be able to understand. "These are the field notes?" Such amateur recordkeeping would slow her down.

"The ones I've come across, yes." Mr. Spalding unbuttoned his suit jacket and slipped a hand into his trouser pocket. "The will mentioned that there are notes for every expedition, so there must be more than this, but I've no time to hunt for them. In fact, I've no time to show you the rest of the mansion. Should you finish here, go ahead and move to another room. There are no locked doors, so help yourself."

"Are all the skins stuffed like this?" she asked before he could leave. When he hesitated, she clarified, "Are all the birds mounted with stuffing inside them? Or did the Van Tessels leave bird skins—perhaps in drawers or boxes somewhere—that were empty?" If she found anything valuable for the museum's collection, she'd stuff them herself.

"If there's a cupboard full of skins somewhere, I hope I'm not the one to find it. You're on your own, Miss Reisner. Good luck to you." He started toward the door, then turned back to her. "As you are searching for bird skins and field notebooks, if you come across a medieval aviary, please set it aside for me. It's quite valuable, and I haven't been able to find it yet."

"You mean an illuminated manuscript with illustrations of birds?" she confirmed.

"Yes." He looked at his watch. "You'll know it when you see it. I trust you'll bring it to my attention when you do. For now, I must be off."

She agreed, and he left.

Elsa slid into the chair for a brief respite. Quiet pulsed around her, a dense but tangible thing. A taxidermized *Onychorhynchus coronatus* stared at her from the corner of the desk. She smiled, enchanted by the Royal Flycatcher's crown. Above a yellow body, bright orange feathers tipped in royal purple fanned across its head. As the only species in its genus, Elsa knew Mr. Chapman would want to add it to the museum collection, so long as she learned when and where it'd been collected.

Pulling from her leather bag, she spread out a handful of field labels and opened a fresh notebook to the chart she'd already prepared for the Hudson Collection. For each bird, she'd need to record on the label and in the notebook a catalog number, the species, the sex, the locality where the bird was found, and the date the bird was taken.

She stared at her beautiful chart. If she listed the birds in the order she found them—by color—her documentation would be as disorganized as this house was. The only solution she could think of was to write on only one side of each page, then when everything was accounted for, cut the chart into rows and rearrange them by species, genus, family, and order, and then transcribe it all again.

What a headache.

There was no use tagging this Royal Flycatcher until she found more information about him. It must have been caught in South or Central America, so she looked through the notebooks Mr. Spalding had gathered, hoping to find them labeled by expedition.

They were labeled by year.

So much for shortcuts.

No wonder Mr. Chapman had assigned this job to her. No one else on staff would have the patience for this.

Leaning one elbow on the desk, she rested her chin in her palm for only a moment before correcting her posture. She may have a limp, and she may not have the physical stamina of her peers, but thanks to her mother and strict teachers, no one could say her spine wasn't straight, for all the good that did her.

Alone with her posture and a few dozen dead birds, she reached for the oldest notes, dated 1871. Birdie would have been twenty years old, and her husband, Linus, twenty-eight.

The first entries were written by Linus and mostly described the hassle of the voyage to certain islands in the Pacific and the process of obtaining a special license from local authorities to hunt birds and bring the skins back to America. Apparently, he'd had a servant or assistant with him named Geoffrey—no surname recorded. From what Birdie had told Elsa at the fundraiser where they'd met, Linus had been independently wealthy and wanted to make a name for himself by amassing a collection of rare finds fit for a museum, including bird specimens, art, and artifacts. But instead of sharing with an actual museum while he was alive, he kept it all in their mansion.

Elsa's eyes glazed as she scanned line after line about setting up camp, venturing out, getting blisters, bruises, and dysentery. It seemed that poor Geoffrey bore the brunt of the work while Linus stayed in camp to heal after cutting his foot on a rocky trail. The few birds that were caught Elsa recorded in her chart. If she found them in the mansion, she'd create matching field labels to tie on their legs.

Halfway through the field journal, the handwriting changed from masculine printing to curving script as a new expedition was recorded in 1876.

Well, it's time to truly live up to my name. People shortened my full name of Bernadette to Birdie when I was too young to have a say in the matter. For as long as I can remember, people thought it a lark (pun intended) to give me bird-themed gifts for birthdays and Christmases. I've always enjoyed bird-watching, but now Linus says it's time to take it further.

To be a true life partner to him, he says, I must partner in his work, too, searching the world for fine-feathered friends to take home with us. He says my retching over the side of the ship will be worth it. Yes, it will be. But the reason I lose my breakfast is not from motion sickness. I'll let him believe as he likes though, until I can be sure.

Elsa sat forward, her interest spiking. The field journal had taken a turn toward diary. But . . . Birdie was pregnant? The Van Tessels had no children. Maybe Birdie was mistaken about her condition. Or she might have lost the baby on the expedition. How very sad.

Then again, maybe Elsa had been the mistaken one. She settled back in the chair, thinking. As far as she knew, the Van Tessels had no living children now. That didn't mean they had never lived, just that they hadn't lived as long as Birdie.

But the notebook ended with that entry, and the next one picked up years later. The third one Mr. Spalding had found chronicled one of Mr. Van Tessel's expeditions before he and Birdie married.

A flutter of movement at the window drew her attention.

Ready to stretch, she went to the double doors facing the Hudson River, which was about a hundred yards from the mansion and partially screened by elm trees. On the other side of the doors, a courtyard featured a fountain in its center, with concentric circles of benches, potted boxwoods, and other flowers radiating from it.

Mesmerized, Elsa watched as a little girl, likely around twelve years old, raked the pebbles covering the ground with deliberate strokes. Shoulder-length brown hair pinned at the sides hinted at a mother's care. A ruffled pinafore over a yellow dress remained as white as her socks. Elsa, too, had taken great care to remain clean and tidy ever since entering boarding school. She'd learned the hard way that the consequences of anything less hadn't been worth it.

She smiled at the girl, lifting a hand in friendly greeting. With no response, she unlocked the door, stepped outside, and relished the damp breeze coming off the river. Clouds muted the sun that had speared through the trees only hours ago.

Elsa wove through the maze of benches and planters until she was a few yards from the charming little girl with a grown-up rake, and grown-up concentration to go with it. She hadn't looked up, though she must have heard Elsa's footsteps.

"Good morning," she tried.

Still, the girl didn't respond. She didn't even look at her as she continued to rake in a circle around the fountain. She did, however, study the sky as though she could hear thunder that hadn't reached Elsa's ears yet.

"I'm Miss Reisner," she said as the girl approached. "Will you tell me your name?"

"Yes."

A pause followed. Elsa studied the girl's methodic movements, waiting, but nothing followed. "What is your name?" she tried again.

"Danielle." She remained focused on pulling the rake behind her, drawing neat parallel lines over the tracks she'd made.

"It's nice to meet you, Danielle. I'm here from a museum to take care of the bird collection inside."

"Miss Birdie is gone," Danielle murmured. "Miss Birdie is gone." Thunder rumbled in the distance.

"Yes, she is. I'm so sorry. Was she your . . . ?" Elsa wondered if Danielle was the daughter of a servant or of a relative who was supposed to wait a few days before coming to claim Mrs. Van Tessel's belongings. "Are you here with your mother or father?"

Danielle stopped short, looked at Elsa's shoes, frowned, then peered into her eyes for the first time. If those deep blue pools were the windows to her soul, they were locked tight and the shades were drawn. All Elsa could see was disapproval.

At once, she realized why. "Oh, pardon me. I'm in your way, aren't I?" Taking a step back, Elsa sat on a bench and let her pass with the rake. "Is this better?"

Danielle raked over the slight impressions Elsa's shoes had left. She reached the place she'd started in the circle and noticed her own footprints again. Danielle's eyebrows knit together as she looked behind her and before her, as though she were trying to work out how to rake them away without stepping on the lines she'd already drawn. Her knuckles went white on the tool's handle. Elsa didn't know why the lines in the pebbles were so important, but it was obvious that they were critical to the child, at least for this moment.

"I have an idea," Elsa said. "Why don't you step over here, and then we can reach over and connect the lines from here. What do you think?"

Without meeting her gaze, Danielle followed her suggestion. When she struggled to reach the rake far enough without it dropping, Elsa held out her hand. "May I try?"

She surrendered the rake, and Elsa managed to complete the task. "Better?"

Insects rattled. Danielle's attention snapped sideways, and Elsa followed it. A chickadee had landed on the edge of the fountain. He dipped in and out of the water and shook his wings.

The girl mumbled something, and Elsa asked her to repeat it.

"Oh! *Poecile atricapillus*. That's right!" Elsa corrected Danielle's pronunciation, but the child had gotten the scientific name right. She'd probably read it in a book and had to guess at how to say the Latin. "You're a girl after my own heart. I've loved birds since I was your age, and younger, too."

Another bird cheeped, and then another. Without looking for either, Danielle said, "*Cardinalis cardinalis. Agelaius phoeniceus.*"

She had identified a northern cardinal and red-winged blackbird based on their sounds alone. Remarkable.

At last, the girl took the rake back from Elsa, her gaze swiveling to the mansion. "Those are Miss Birdie's birds. You can't take Miss Birdie's birds. They don't belong to you. They stay here, like me. We stay." She thumped her palm to her chest as she said this, then pointed to Elsa and motioned toward the road.

Rain began to fall. Danielle took her rake, climbed onto a bench and hopped from one to another, careful not to disturb the pebbles, then leapt from courtyard to lawn and dashed away.

Elsa slipped back inside the mansion and closed the door on the strengthening rain and wind. After drying her glasses and replacing them, everything came back into focus. Silver braided streams ran down the windows and poured from gargoyle downspouts. The grooves Danielle had traced into the pebbles shone with collected water. The girl had left a trail of questions in Elsa's mind. How well had she known Birdie? If she lived here, where were her parents? She was clearly determined to stay, but what would they do once the county took over the estate? Regardless, Elsa hoped she would see Danielle again.

Chafing her arms, Elsa sneezed, and the sound bounced off the vaulted ceiling. She reminded herself she wasn't alone here. It only felt that way.

It was not a feeling she cared for. At the museum, she often worked on her own, but she could always take a break and stroll through the galleries. Mingling with patrons always eased the tension in her shoulders. Interacting with them refueled her before she returned to her office.

"No offense," she muttered to the yellow birds in the parlor. "But you aren't much for conversation."

In truth, she wasn't convinced that Mr. Dupont would be much better. But if he was tearing the mansion apart, he might have seen more field guides. She couldn't begin tagging birds without the details within those pages.

Leaving the parlor through the rear hall, she crossed into the adjacent room and found herself in a dark, wood-paneled library. Floor-to-ceiling cases held leather-bound volumes, and crown molding rimmed the ceiling. On a table between two wingback chairs was a camera, a floorplan drawing of the room, a note-book, and two of the largest tape measures she'd ever seen. But there was no sign of man or beast.

Exiting the library, Elsa followed a marble hallway through the empty dining hall and into the four-story stair tower. Her leg ached just looking at the winding steps.

"Mr. Dupont?"

No answer.

She summoned her strength. She had climbed stairs before, for goodness' sake. She could take it slowly.

By the time she reached the second floor, however, her lungs bothered her as much as her leg. Anger flared, but it wasn't strong enough to mask the dread that sparked it. This was ridiculous. She couldn't be getting worse.

After a few moments to regain her composure, she continued her search on the second floor, determined to focus only on finding another human being. "Hello? Is anyone up here?" Still slightly out of breath, her voice didn't carry like she wanted it to, but she resolved to ignore that fact.

Through one grand bedroom after another—each with its own color theme and matching birds—Elsa searched. It felt like a game of hide-and-seek, with a niggling suspicion that she was the only one playing.

When she reached the art gallery, she rested on a bench and stared at the stained-glass windows, if only to anchor herself in the present time and place. She was no longer the child she'd been at boarding school, trying to keep up with the other girls and failing, laughter ringing in her ears. She had been playing hide-and-seek with her classmates, only to realize they'd broken the rules and left the agreed-upon boundaries. They left her alone to wander in vain until her weak leg collapsed. The matron had sent her to bed, where she'd stayed for three days to recover. Three more days alone when she desperately longed for companionship. Her parents, who lived less than five miles from the school, did not come to visit her, either.

Elsa would search no more today. Drawing a fortifying breath, she stood and went back to the stairs. Going down would be easier.

Wind buffeted the stone tower. Beyond the windows, lightning forked. Thunder clapped, and she took the stairs a little faster.

"Mr. Dupont? Barney?" Boy, she must be really desperate to want to locate a dog. But having a friendly canine at her side had its charms right about now.

She tried a light switch, but nothing happened. Either the power had gone out from the storm, or Mr. Spalding had already had the electricity shut off. She normally enjoyed a good summer storm. But being here alone when she hadn't expected to be . . . It was all too Gothic for her taste.

Her mind played tricks. Was that a person or the wind? Then the moaning stopped, and shouting took its place. The tone held not anger but fear. Urgency. Someone was in distress.

At the bottom of the tower, she hurried along the corridor as much as she dared, looking and finding no one. Then a flash of lightning illuminated the silhouettes of two men outside on the covered veranda. One smoked a cigarette between words frayed with shredded nerves. The other voice held steady. She'd heard him speak this morning, but barely. She must have been so preoccupied with the scars and the dog that she hadn't noticed how rich the sound was.

She couldn't see their faces with their backs turned to the

window. But as Mr. Dupont soothed the other man, he didn't sound scary. He sounded like . . . well, like someone you'd want by your side in a storm, whether it raged in the sky or in one's soul. Clearly he'd weathered his own.

Thunder rolled, and rain blew sideways, spraying the windows. Baskets of ferns swung wildly from the veranda's ceiling.

The man with the cigarette was shaking. "I want to go inside," Elsa heard him say.

"That's a good idea, but you can't smoke in the house," Mr. Dupont told him. "So you either stay out here and get wet or come inside out of the storm. It *is* just a storm, Tom. It's 1926, this is New York, and we're on a job. You're safe now. You're safe."

"No." Tom shook his head. Thunder boomed again, and he sank to the floor, covering his head with crossed arms.

In a flash of fur, Barney bounded onto the veranda, ran to Tom, and nudged under his arms to lick his face.

Mr. Dupont waited until Tom buried his fingers in Barney's fur, returning the affection.

"Come on." Mr. Dupont took the cigarette and smashed it in a planter. "You don't need that." With a hand to his elbow, he helped him up. Barney placed his head beneath Tom's palm. This time, the dog's tail wasn't wagging.

Elsa backed away from the windows and watched the trio walk toward the door. When they came inside, she was waiting by one of the fireplaces in the library.

Both men stood straighter when they saw her. Barney pressed against Tom's side.

"Hello again," she said to Mr. Dupont. "I'm afraid we didn't have a proper introduction this morning. I'm Elsa Reisner," she added for Tom's sake, then explained why she was here. "Mr. Spalding told me you're salvaging some of the architecture for Dupont & Son, correct?"

"That's right. I'm the son in that equation—Luke Dupont—and

this is Tom Lightfoot, assisting me." He rolled down sleeves that had been pushed to his elbows and buttoned the cuffs.

"It's a pleasure to meet you, Mr. Dupont, Mr. Lightfoot."

"Oh, please, none of that for me. Tom'll do fine." A dimple appeared as a smile formed and then faded. Dark blond hair was pomaded back from a smooth face that would seem boyish if not for the sunken cheeks.

"And just Luke," added the man whose voice ran deep. He was only an inch or so taller than Tom, but his presence felt far more solid. Tom held his shoulders slightly forward, creating a hollow in front of his chest.

Elsa smiled, happy to shed the stiff high-society manners with which she'd grown up. "All right, then. Let's dispense with formalities all around, or at least between the three of us. Mr. Spalding mentioned something about you working in here, but he hasn't told me much else."

"Anything we can help with?" Luke asked.

"Possibly. I'm looking for something you may have come across."

"Is this about the aviary?" Tom asked. "Mr. Spalding already mentioned it. He thought it would be here in the library, but we never saw what he described."

"Ah. He asked me to keep an eye out for that, too, but I'm on my own search for field notebooks. They are basically journals or logs kept on expeditions to collect birds. Have you found anything like that?" She explained why she needed them to complete her assignment.

They said they hadn't but promised to let her know if that changed.

That settled, Elsa mentioned encountering Danielle in the courtyard. "Do you happen to know who she is, where she lives?"

Luke hooked his thumbs into his beltloops. "Likely the gardener's daughter. Mr. Spalding mentioned they'd be about. His own children are older."

Lightning flashed, illuminating a stained-glass window Elsa hadn't noticed before. "Are any other servants still around?" she asked.

"Not that I've seen." He flicked a glance to the rain pelting the windows. "The place seems pretty deserted."

"So I've noticed." Elsa also noticed Tom petting Barney and growing more at ease by the moment. "What exactly are you two doing in here?"

"We're deinstalling this library and will assemble it again in our warehouse on Long Island." Luke snatched a short pencil from behind his ear and tucked it into his pocket. "Our clients often want to purchase entire rooms either for their own homes or for houses they are building for their clients. Tom's helping me take down all the measurements, photograph from every angle, and label every single thing we move—and I mean every panel, shelf, every piece of crown molding, even the floorboards and books. Then a contractor and his crew will come in and start dismantling. At that point, I'll go through the rest of the mansion and salvage whatever else I deem worthy. Door fixtures, chandeliers, fireplaces, things like that."

Elsa hadn't expected to hear so many words from Luke all at once. He seemed more comfortable half-hidden in shadows than he'd been in glaring daylight. She hoped she was wrong about that. How sad that would be. Yet an aversion to exposure was a feeling she understood.

After inquiring a little more about the process, she asked, "Were there any birds in here when you arrived? I've seen them in most of the other rooms."

"There were," Tom volunteered. "We heard someone was coming from the museum for them and didn't want them to get dusty while we were working, so we moved them. Much to Barney's regret. Right, boy?" Smiling now, he rubbed the dog between the ears.

"Thank you for that." Elsa tried not to wrinkle her nose at the wet smell coming from Barney's fur. She spotted a narrow door beside the fireplace, most likely a closet for storing firewood, which would make it empty this time of year. She pointed to it, and Tom nodded.

It was too dark to see inside properly. "Did either of you find a kerosene lamp about, by any chance?"

"Tom did. Spalding insisted on shutting down the electricity to the estate before we got here, to our great annoyance. Natural light isn't always enough for good photographs, and we need good photographs. Gobs of them."

"I imagine. Would you mind terribly, Tom?" Elsa asked.

Tom fetched the lamp and turned the knob. Amber light radiated from the hurricane as he crossed to the fireplace and set it on the mantel.

Thanking him, Elsa walked to the closet. The door budged open with a squeak. Crammed onto the shelves inside were birds to match the library: a great green macaw, an African emerald cuckoo, European greenfinch, a mitred parakeet.

"Shrapnel?" Tom asked.

She turned around. "Pardon me?"

He nodded to her leg. "Were you a nurse over there? Red Cross? Was your hospital hit?"

She shook her head, realizing they'd seen her limp for the first time. "I'm afraid it's nothing so courageous as that. Just polio."

Luke frowned. "*Just* polio?" His grey eyes assessed her, seeming to look past the flippant comment. The dim light, storm, and remoteness of the place had cast the three of them into an unintended closeness. But she hadn't come here to talk about the disease that wasn't through with her yet. Compared to going to war, this was nothing. She didn't want pity, but neither did she feel qualified to accept the respect in their expressions.

"I would have counted it a privilege to serve, but no one thought I'd be much good as a nurse given my physical limitations."

"It's better you weren't there with us." Tom fished a Lucky Strike from his front pocket.

Luke took it from him and slipped it right back where it came from.

"Count yourself lucky you didn't go." Tom stared at his now-empty hand. It trembled.

"I count myself fortunate that brave men like you did." Elsa took his hand in hers and shook it. "You gave up more than we can ever imagine. Thank you." The tremor faded in her grip, and Tom's cobalt gaze met hers. The corner of his mouth tipped up, and the dimple flashed once more.

She didn't know many veterans of the war, though it was her generation that had fought. Archer hadn't joined up, and neither had his friends. She had the utmost respect for those who had.

Luke turned to the crates on the ground. "How about we move the birds to the dining room for you?"

"That would be lovely. The table in there will make a better work surface than that small writing desk I've been using in the parlor. Handle them by the mounting bases rather than touching their bodies, if you please."

As the men fetched the birds, Elsa brought her things from the parlor to the dining hall. Cobwebs stretched across the chandelier and netted the crown molding at the ceiling. At one end of the room, an arched window held stained glass in shades of red and burgundy. But the colored glass had broken in places, and water damage stained the wall below it.

Luke set the last two birds on the table. "Thanks, by the way, for how you were with Tom. He feels overlooked most of the time. It's nice for him to be seen by someone other than me."

"Oh." Surely she didn't deserve praise for such a small inadequate thing. "I—of course. I meant what I said, and that appreciation extends to you, too. That is, if you also fought in the war?"

"Safe assumption," he said. "I did."

"Thank you."

"You're welcome." Outside the sky flashed again, lighting every scar and angle of Luke's face before casting it back into shadow.

"You'll make sure your dog doesn't get in here and steal one of the birds, though, won't you?"

"Barney won't leave Tom's side until Tom's nerves settle down, which will be after the storm. And then we'll send Barn outside again."

Elsa raised an eyebrow. "The dog is that smart?"

"You'd be surprised." Luke smiled for the first time in her presence and was utterly transformed.

Nothing in this place was as it seemed.

CHAPTER

3

NEW YORK CITY
WEDNESDAY, AUGUST 25, 1926

E lsa stood on the east steps of the American Museum of
Natural History, her gaze winging over the street and into
Central Park. Not that she could see all that much from here.
The fall migration had started, and she was itching to spend time
deep in the park's Ramble with the seasonal visitors.

The only birds she saw at work were dead ones.

She buttoned her knit cardigan. Taxis and buses motored past,
with commuting autos in between them. Exhaust fumes rode the
breeze. After checking her watch, Elsa glanced to the right and
spotted her roommate Ivy, on her way home from working at
the New-York Historical Society on the next block over. Their
apartment was a mere tenth of a mile from here, and they almost
always walked to and from work together.

"Good day?" Elsa asked, meeting her on the sidewalk.

"So much fun. Friday is the 150th anniversary of the Battle of
Brooklyn, so we've been getting ready for the commemorative
event." Ivy paused, placing one Oxford pump on the second
step to retie the laces. "If people thought our giant July Fourth
bash was the end of our celebration of the American Revolution,

they're about to find out it was only the beginning." Straightening, she beamed.

Ivy had earned a master's degree in American history from Bryn Mawr outside Philadelphia before moving to Manhattan for a fresh start. All these American Revolution anniversaries were totally her cup of tea.

Elsa linked her arm through Ivy's and started walking. "Will the society be commemorating every significant date for the next seven years, ending with a party for the peace treaty?"

"I wish!" Ivy laughed. "Our plan is to at least honor the meaningful ones for New York State, but rest assured, I'll be honoring every moment in my heart. Prepare to hear about each one." They sidestepped a boy hawking the evening news. "How about you? How did it go working through those field notebooks you brought back from Elmhurst?"

Elsa's nose wrinkled. "I didn't get as far along in them as I would have liked. More boxes arrived from the Customs House, and those don't wait." As she spoke, they passed a pair of starlings eating the remains of a soft pretzel on the ground.

"Who at the Customs House is sending you packages?"

"We have patrons who sometimes send us birds or bird skins from overseas, and those have to go through customs first."

Ivy frowned. "As in, they go on vacation and decide to kill birds for the museum while they're at it?"

"Something like that. At least most of them have a handbook on how to prepare the skins, thanks to one of my colleagues, Mr. Griscom. You wouldn't believe what we were getting a few years ago. But some people still don't follow directions. In one of the packages today, birds were shipped in the flesh—that means they didn't just send the skins but the entire bodies—and they hadn't been fully dried first. They used a wooden box instead of tin, and insects destroyed them. Mr. Chapman still wants to use the skeletons, though."

Ivy cast her a sidelong glance. "Let me guess. You have to clean the remaining flesh from bone?"

"I'll spare you the details. You're welcome."

Ivy shuddered, and sun winked off her dangling earrings.

Elsa laughed. "I'll go through the Van Tessels' notebooks over the weekend, and hopefully I'll find more next Monday when I go back. I wish you could come with me and see what it's like."

"I'd like that, too. I was so excited when I learned Mrs. Van Tessel bequeathed her paintings by John Audubon to the society. I volunteered to go collect them, but I'm a librarian, not a curator. Still, I'd love to see the estate *and* Tarrytown. Did you know that British Major John Andre was arrested as a spy near there on September 23, 1780? His capture exposed Benedict Arnold's plan to surrender the fort at West Point. Plus, *The Legend of Sleepy Hollow* was set just north of the town. The Headless Horseman lost his head during one of the Revolutionary battles." She wiggled her dark eyebrows. "You haven't seen any ghosts on the estate, have you?"

"You'll have to come see for yourself," Elsa teased. The Hudson River valley was famous for its supernatural legends, none of which fazed her.

"Let's plan on it."

"Speaking of plans, you don't have any for this evening, do you?" Elsa asked.

Ivy swept her black bangs to one side. "I don't know. Do I?"

At the corner of Eighty-First Street, they waited for autos and cabs to pass. Half a dozen sparrows perched on the street sign, watching. A smile tugged Elsa's mouth. "We've been invited for dinner with Archer and a friend of his. And when I say 'invited,' I mean begged. Practically coerced. At least he promised that dancing won't be part of the evening. It's a weeknight after all, and everyone has work in the morning. But as Archer says, we still have to eat. Shall we go?"

"Is this the same Archer Hamlin who dressed up as the mummy of King Tut for that Halloween party you took us to last fall?"

"The same. And his friend played the role of Lord Carnarvon."

Ivy laughed. "I'd love to go out tonight. Friday I'm busy with the Battle of Brooklyn event, anyway. Where are we going?"

"The Ritz-Carlton."

Ivy turned to Elsa and gaped. "I'm pretty sure I can't afford to breathe the air in front of that place, let alone eat their food." She may have a graduate degree from a prestigious all-girls school, but what she couldn't fund herself was provided by scholarships and a personal benefactress. Ivy had never been wealthy.

"We wouldn't be paying, they would be," Elsa said as they hurried across the street to their hotel-apartment complex, the Beresford. The doorman greeted them each by name as they entered.

"I don't know," Ivy murmured. They crossed the lobby to the elevators and waited for one to open. "It sounds thrilling, but I wouldn't fit in with the Ritz crowd."

"You got that right. I consider that to be one of your finest qualities."

The elevator arrived, and they stepped inside and requested their floor from the operator. Once the door opened on their floor, they thanked him and headed down the corridor. Ivy still looked thoughtful. Ever since illness stole her family when she was only fourteen, she'd earned her own way by becoming a widow's companion and personal secretary. She would never spend gobs of money on a gourmet dinner at a fancy hotel restaurant when she was already paying for dining room meals that came with living in a Beresford apartment.

Honestly, Elsa didn't fit in with the Ritz crowd, either. She'd been to the Ritz, and to The Plaza, and to Hotel Astor, most often as a guest attending with her parents the debutante balls of her peers. She never danced, of course, but it wouldn't do to decline the invitations. And so she'd sat on the edge of those parties, her back flawlessly straight, while her parents waltzed with the rest. Those nights would have been torture without her cousin Lauren there to keep her company.

"We don't have to go." Elsa unlocked the apartment door and waited for Ivy to enter before she closed and locked it behind them. "I don't want you to feel uncomfortable."

"I wouldn't if you were with me." Ivy hung her purse on a hook on the wall, then propped a fist on her hip. "To tell you the truth, I've always wanted to see what all the fuss was about the Ritz. And you and I don't pay?"

"Not a dime."

"But what would I wear?"

Elsa smiled. "I'll help you choose."

Inside the Ritz-Carlton Hotel foyer, Elsa untied the silk scarf she'd worn to protect her hair. Archer and his friend, Percy Osborne, had picked her and Ivy up in Archer's white Rolls-Royce Phantom convertible, which made for a windblown twenty-minute ride.

From the foyer, they passed directly into the Palm Room, where potted palm trees soared beneath a glass ceiling. At the far end of the room, an orchestra played from a gallery.

"Well, this is the berries. I knew I wouldn't be fancy enough for this place," Ivy whispered as she tucked her own scarf and dark glasses into her purse. Couples sat at small tables, drinks in hand. Judging by their formal dress, they'd be heading to the theater, opera, or Ziegfeld's Follies tonight.

"You look stunning, as always," Elsa told her friend. Ivy's sleek black bob was a striking contrast to her perfect creamy complexion. The curvy figure beneath her sheath dress may not be the current fashion, but she was oblivious to the admiration she drew. "And if by 'fancy,' you mean entitled, arrogant, and grossly wealthy, then fancy is not a trait you ought to aspire to, anyway."

Archer laughed. "That's a bleak picture of our set, isn't it?"

Elsa didn't enjoy being lumped together with the people who frequented the Ritz. "Let's call them our parents' set, then, but not ours."

"And yet here we are," Percy quipped, "right along with them. Would you prefer a hot dog from a pushcart in Central Park?" His brown eyes sparkled behind round tortoiseshell-framed glasses.

"I gather you've never *had* a fresh hot dog in Central Park." Ivy twisted a rope of beads around one finger. "They're delicious!"

Percy huffed. "I'll take your word for it."

Archer chuckled and led the foursome through the Palm Room and Oval Restaurant, then up two flights of stairs to the outdoor Roof Garden. Heads turned, ever so slightly, as people noticed Elsa's limp and then pretended not to.

By the time they reached their round table for four, Elsa's leg ached, and her breath came quicker than it should. It was a silent throbbing that whispered to her, *You're different. You're weak. You're a burden to be cast off as soon as you slow them down.*

She stuffed the voice into the dark corner of her mind from which it had escaped. Laughter rippled from a table nearby, and she glanced at the two couples enjoying some joke she'd missed. She wondered if they'd left children home with a nurse or governess, as her parents had so often done, or if they'd sent them off to boarding school for the fall semester yet. She wondered if they ever thought of the little ones when they were out of sight, or if it was only children who longed for a ray of warmth from their parents.

Turning away from them, she relished a cooling breeze. Baskets of pink roses gently swayed from the tented canopy made of green-and-white-striped silk.

"Almost as good as eating at the park, eh, Ivy?" Archer winked at her.

"It's lovelier than I'd imagined," she admitted, though Elsa noticed she didn't point out that these were not food cart prices. In fact, the prices weren't even listed on the menu.

After the waiter took their orders, Percy drank from his water goblet, then swiped a thumb over the condensation beading the glass. "You can't persuade me that standing in line with the peasants for a paper boat of greasy food and then sitting on a hard bench—or worse yet, the ground—is better than being waited on like civilized human beings." Brilliantine shone on his chestnut hair. The tidy mustache countered the boyish effect of a faint spray of freckles over his flaccid face.

Archer clapped him on the back. "Percy was born with a silver spoon in his mouth."

Percy grunted. "So were you. And from what I understand, so was she." He nodded toward Elsa.

"Ah yes," Archer said, "but the difference is that she has spit hers out, and so have I. Or, at least, I'm trying to."

Elsa glanced at Ivy, wondering if her roommate was silently writing off these two young men as rich snobs. "What does that mean, Archer? You're *trying* to spit out the silver spoon? You mean you paid for that Rolls-Royce yourself?"

Archer pulled an emery board from his pocket and began filing his fingernails. "That was a gift from my father, and a fella doesn't turn down a gift like that. It has a self-starting engine, for heaven's sake, no more hand-cranking. But like I said, I'm moving out of my folks' house on Fifth Avenue as soon as I can. I'm going to stand on my own two feet. I'm forfeiting my allowance and proving to my father that I'm man enough to live on my own."

"Why now?" Elsa asked. She applauded the principle but didn't understand the delay. She'd permanently moved out almost as soon as she turned eighteen. Then again, her parents' house hadn't felt like a true home since before she contracted polio. After her hospitalization, it had shrunk to a convalescent room, and then to the place she visited on breaks from boarding school and holidays from Vassar College.

Archer sent her a sheepish grin. "Wealth is seductive. It took me a while to realize that freedom and independence are even more valuable. I was serious when I told you I was in the market for a good apartment." He tucked the emery board away.

The waiter returned with a dish of caviar served with a stack of blinis. Percy scooped some of the sturgeon eggs onto one of the small buckwheat pancakes and popped it into his mouth.

Ivy wrinkled her nose. "I don't see how you can eat fish eggs."

"It's an acquired taste. Most of the finer things usually are. Shows class to enjoy it."

Elsa wasn't convinced but didn't argue.

"How about you, then?" Ivy asked. "Do you still live with your folks?"

"Not on your life." Percy's gaze flitted to an attractive woman passing by. "I have an apartment of my own on Fifty-Second Street, between Fifth and Sixth Avenues."

"Your apartment is paid for by your grandfather," Archer added.

Percy shrugged. "It's true. My parents are gone, my grand-father pays my rent and expenses." He topped another blini with caviar and ate it.

Ivy frowned. "You don't work?"

"I write. That's work. As soon as I sell a few pieces, I'll be set for a year. And I'm working on a novel, too, a real crowd-pleaser for the masses. How's this for a title: *Death by Romance*? Would you read something like that? You would at least pick it up and read the first page, wouldn't you? Besides, I stand to inherit a great deal when Grandfather dies. But am I just sitting around, waiting? Of course not."

Elsa raised an eyebrow. "I see. Maybe we'll all learn to love hot dogs as Ivy does and cut our expenses considerably."

Percy cracked a smile. "There's more than one way to balance the budget. One of our buddies has a suite upstairs. Friday nights, he hosts high-stakes games—"

"That's not for me, not anymore," Archer interrupted.

"What's this?" Percy asked. "Since when?"

"Since I resolved to only bet my own money, not my allowance from Daddy. Losing hurts. You have no idea how many weeks I'd have to work to make up for one night of bad luck. Count me out, Perc."

Elsa gave him an approving nod, glad to see he was showing signs of maturing. Gambling was a foolish waste, even if one had cash to spare.

"Are you pulling my leg?" Percy's voice began rising. "Everyone will be there."

"Don't cast a kitten," Ivy said. "Broad is the path that leads to destruction and all that jazz, you know."

Elsa chuckled and agreed. "You might try the straight and narrow one, Percy."

He smirked. "Now, there's an acquired taste if I ever heard of one."

Their server returned with everyone's entrées. Once the food was placed before them, Ivy silently blessed her meal, and Elsa did the same.

"Bon appétit!" Archer picked up his fork with undue fanfare and dug into his duck and peaches.

Elsa's plate of lobster medallions was so artfully arranged with the asparagus tips she almost didn't want to ruin it by taking a bite. But she did, and it was worth it. The Beresford dinners were good, but the Ritz had earned its reputation.

"How's your shrimp scampi and bean sprouts?" she whispered to Ivy.

"Another acquired taste, perhaps? But hang on a minute." She swirled another bite through the coriander dressing and tried again. "Yep, I'm acquiring it."

Percy lifted a blini and said, "To acquired tastes."

"To the straight and narrow," Elsa added.

Archer raised a glass toward her and then to Ivy. "To my collective conscience."

CHAPTER

4

TARRYTOWN
THURSDAY, AUGUST 26, 1926

On the bright side, at least Elsa knew without any doubt that she was not alone in the Van Tessel mansion, thanks to the hammering in the library.

She hadn't seen Mr. Spalding today, but he'd left two more notebooks on the table for her along with a note that he'd come across them yesterday. Perhaps he'd been looking for that aviary again. Regardless, she was delighted that the first one she opened was Birdie's continued account of the expedition during which she'd suspected herself pregnant. Specimen data was mixed in, and that would be useful to cross-reference Linus's notes for the same information. But it was clear she used this space for personal journaling and didn't intend it as the scientific record her husband kept.

Not long into reading it, the racket from the adjacent room got the better of Elsa's curiosity. She went to the doorframe to watch.

Luke sat on the floor before one fireplace, and Tom sat at the other, on the opposite wall. They must have brought in a larger crew yesterday, because the crown and baseboard molding were completely gone. The bookshelves, too, had been moved out.

Barney rested on the bare floor in a patch of sunshine, but when the dog noticed her, he roused himself.

She extended her hand, mostly to keep him from getting past and disturbing the birds on the dining room table behind her. Misinterpreting her gesture, he pushed his head under her palm and wagged his tail.

Luke turned and stood when he saw her, then pulled cotton from his ears. A pencil poked up from the pocket of his shirt.

"You've made remarkable progress in here," she said. Dust swirled on sunbeams and itched her throat. "What's today's project?"

Luke stepped closer, likely to be heard over Tom's hammering. He angled himself so the scarred side of his face was less visible, and she wondered if that was intentional. She hoped it wasn't.

Pointing to where Tom worked, he said, "You see all of those tiles surrounding both fireplaces? They've already been spoken for by one of our clients, an interior decorator."

"So soon?"

He nodded. "She saw a photograph and decided these were exactly what she needed. Only, she doesn't want the fireplaces they're attached to. We've got to chisel each one out of the wall and label the backs so they can be reinstalled in the right order."

Some tiles were spread on the floor already. She moved toward the fireplace to inspect them. They were not identical squares but had been painted with an intricate pattern of peacock and ostrich feathers that stretched from one tile to the next. "Now, that's painstaking work. What happens if you break one?"

Luke winced, his gaze darting to a broken tile on the floor near where Tom knelt, the cotton in his ears obviously doing its job.

"Oh. Oh dear," Elsa said.

"It was bound to happen. But we contract with some of the best conservators in the world. They'll paint a new tile based on what we broke."

We, he'd said. Clearly, the break had been Tom's doing, and yet the way Luke spoke, he shared the blame. She wondered why. Luke watched Tom for a few moments, his expression dark.

No, not dark. Concerned. She must see past the scars that could disguise the man beneath.

"Is he . . ." Elsa lowered her voice, unsure if she had any right to ask how he fared after the terrible storm that had rattled him last week. Barney had proven a comfort, but she wondered if the effect was long-lasting or not. "Is Tom quite recovered?"

"Not quite." Luke looked about the room. "If we can deconstruct this place and then reconstruct it again to its former glory, can the same be done with people? Can people be rebuilt? If not in body, can their spirits be restored?" He didn't look at her as he spoke. If he was seeking answers, he wasn't asking for them from her.

Leaving the men to continue their work, Elsa returned to the dining hall to transcribe data from the field notes into her chart. Each expedition she'd found logs for had lasted at least six months, with the longest lasting a year. It made for a lot of reading in between each recorded specimen. The binding in one of the notebooks had rotted away, and the loose pages stuffed inside were all out of order. She had to set them back in proper sequence for her to know which entries belonged with which dates and location. Doing so took hours, with only a ten-minute break to eat the baguette and apple she'd brought for lunch.

By half past three in the afternoon, she wasn't done yet, but she'd been working at it for so long her eyes were bleary. Ready for some fresh air, Elsa decided to use the unused portion of her lunch break for a walk outside.

In the courtyard behind the mansion, Danielle was nowhere in sight, but the pebbled paths had been freshly raked, bringing a smile to Elsa's lips.

An eastern bluebird chattered from a crabapple tree. With the warm sun veiled by gauzy clouds, Elsa ventured onto the lawn and strolled toward the bird. Breathing deeply, she filled her lungs and felt the country air expand in her chest. Slowly, she exhaled. It was lonelier here than in the city, but it was also far easier to breathe without pollution.

Maybe this was what she needed. Maybe her lungs would gain some of what they'd lost if she just . . . cleaned them out a bit? Was that possible? And maybe her weakened leg would regain strength with moderate exercise here where the air was clean.

It was worth a try, and on days like this, the trying would be pure pleasure. Besides, she'd heard that physical exercise cleared the cobwebs from one's mind, and she could certainly use that, too.

Setting a reasonable pace, Elsa started down a path, destination unknown, and allowed her thoughts to wander, too. She'd read enough of Birdie's journal this morning to learn that she had definitely been pregnant. She'd been six months along before they returned to Elmhurst in March of 1877. She'd written of Linus wanting to make sure she had the best care possible for the birth of their first child.

And then, maddeningly, the story stopped, or at least the recording of it. The next field notebook was written in Linus's hand and began in September 1877. The baby would have been born in June, or earlier if it had been premature, and yet there was no mention of either Birdie or the baby whatsoever.

A northern cardinal cheeped from a nearby mulberry tree. To catch her breath, Elsa paused in the shade, where fuzzy, heart-shaped leaves cast swaying shadows on the lawn. Birdie would not have gone on the expedition with an infant, so it made sense that Linus went without her—except for the fact that Linus had good reason to stay home, too, in that case. Why would he want to miss so much of the baby's first year? Then again, Elsa's uncle had missed much of Lauren's childhood, too, trading time at home for archaeological digs in Egypt. Elsa's father had been home during Elsa's childhood, but admitted he didn't know what to do with her until she'd grown old enough to carry a conversation. Her earliest memories were of her nurse and governess, not her parents.

In the majority of species across the animal kingdom, males simply weren't part of raising offspring—which was one more reason that birds were particularly fascinating. In many cases, male birds shared the responsibility. Starling males brood during the day, while females brood at night. Double-crested cormorants take turns every hour, and African common waxbill couples warm the eggs together, at the same time, during the entire incubation. The sandhill crane male helps his partner incubate the eggs, feed the chicks, and even helps raise the young for a full year.

Not so Linus van Tessel, and most other male *Homo sapiens*.

Rested, Elsa left the shade. The path curved, and a walled Italianate garden came into view. It was cut into the bluff overlooking the river. She entered through an arch, taking the stairs down into a maze of geometric patterns. A pool marked the center, and at the far end, a pavilion overlooked the river. The sense of order here appealed to Elsa's fondness for precision.

A serviceberry tree grew outside the garden wall, and a scarlet tanager sang from its overhanging branches. But then she heard singing of a different kind. A woman hummed a tune Elsa didn't recognize.

"Hello?" Elsa looked over the garden, divided by boxwood hedges.

From behind one of them, a woman sat on her heels, her head uncovered by kerchief or hat. Through mostly grey hair, streaks of dark auburn hinted at its former color. When she saw Elsa, a smile warmed her tanned, lined face. She could be in her fifties, although it was difficult to judge a person's age when said person exposed themselves to the elements.

"Hello!" she called. "Have you lost your way?"

"No, I didn't have a way to begin with. I just came outside to enjoy the beautiful day. I'm Elsa Reisner, by the way. I met Danielle last week. Are you her family?"

"I'm her mother." The woman pushed herself up to stand and brushed the dirt from her palms. "She told me you helped her with her pebble raking the other day. Not many would do that. I thank you for your kindness."

Elsa returned the woman's warm smile. She must have had Danielle later in life. Perhaps the baby had been a surprise to the mother, but no doubt a blessing all the same. "I'm so pleased to meet you. Maybe she told you why I'm here." She offered a brief explanation.

"I'm happy to know you. My name is Tatiana Petrovic, and you must call me Tatiana. I've been the gardener here for many years, along with my husband, God rest him."

"I'm sorry for your loss," Elsa said.

"Thank you. He was the real talent with landscaping. Mrs. Van Tessel was good enough to let us stay on, even after his passing."

"You're clearly an expert at it yourself." A variety of plants filled each bed. Some of them she recognized: lavender, roses, lilies, asters. Dwarf lilac shrubs nestled between white and blue hydrangeas.

"How on earth do you keep up with all of this?" Elsa asked.

Tatiana smiled again. "Up until very recently, I had a crew of gardeners working under me. They've all gone now, seeking employment elsewhere."

"Are you able to stay?" Elsa prompted. "Even with the up-coming changes?"

A shadow passed over the older woman's face. "You mean when the land goes to the county? I confess I am still getting used to that idea, and I don't know fully what that will mean for us.

The will clearly states we can live here. 'In perpetuity,' I believe it says. And I cannot imagine leaving. This was never my property, but I was a steward of it for decades, and I feel tied to the land. Neither Danielle nor I wish to go elsewhere, and Mrs. Van Tessel knew that. She was so good to allow us to keep the cottage and live there as long as we want."

Troubled by the ambiguity in their situation, Elsa looked out at the river, framed by the wisteria-draped pergolas. A light breeze bent the fountain grass at the edge of the pool. "I can't imagine any other place could quite compare. The grounds will still need to be taken care of, no matter who's in charge of it. Whoever that is would be fortunate to have you on staff."

"Thank you, dear. Now, speaking of home, may I offer you a cup of tea? I'm finished here for now, and my cottage is a short walk. If you have the time, I'd love to have you."

Elsa accepted the invitation, adding that she ought to be back at her task by a quarter past four. Sharing a pot of tea with Tatiana would be a lovely way to spend her break. With the estate so nearly abandoned now, no wonder the woman was eager for company.

Tatiana must have noticed Elsa's limp along the way, but she didn't say so. The woman had her own stiffness in her knees to contend with, which made their pace relaxed by mutual, unspoken consent.

When they reached the cottage, the level of disrepair brought a twist to Elsa's gut. The structure must have been charming once, but the front porch sagged, the steps were cracked, and the door didn't close properly, leaving a gap for the wind and rain to reach through. Shingles were missing from the sway-backed roof. In a corner of one window, a rag had been stuffed between the pane and its frame.

"Danielle, we have company," Tatiana said. "I have invited Elsa to share a cup of tea. Say hello to our guest."

"Hello." From where she sat on the porch, the girl glanced up, then back down to the buttons she was arranging on a tray.

"It's good to see you again, Danielle."

"It's such a fine day, why don't we take our tea outside?" Tatiana asked. "I'll just be a few moments, dear."

Elsa agreed and sat in a rocker on the porch, watching Danielle. Rows of buttons lined the tray, all of them grouped by color. Then the child tipped one end of the tray so they all slid into a jumble. With impressive speed, Danielle then began ordering the buttons again. This time by size, from largest to smallest. She had a knack for classification. A passion for it, too, it seemed.

"You're being watched," Elsa said quietly, "and not just by me. *Corvus brachyrhynchos.*" An American crow had landed on the porch railing a few feet away, his shining black eyes fixed on Danielle.

"His name is George. He gave me this one." She held up a silver button, then put it back into its place.

Elsa blinked. "He brought you the button?"

"He brings me many things. He's my friend. I feed him peanuts and corn and seeds, and he brings me presents. Once he brought me a little bone that must have belonged to a mouse. I didn't keep that one. But he brings me many things."

"Really! How fascinating! Corvids are very smart. I've heard about crows bringing gifts to people before, but I haven't seen it happen myself. What else has George brought you?"

Danielle started over again with the buttons. As she described the trinkets George had brought her, another pattern emerged on the tray, according to material: wood, shell, and metal. While her hands were busy, she said far more to Elsa than she had on their first meeting. If she liked talking about birds, Elsa was delighted to comply.

"Have you heard about bowerbirds?" she asked the child.

"Bowerbirds?" Danielle held Elsa's gaze for the first time since they'd met. A light spray of freckles dusted her nose.

"Satin bowerbirds in the rainforests of Australia. *Ptilonorhynchus violaceus.*" Elsa said the Latin again, slower this time, then waited while Danielle repeated it. "For some reason we still don't understand, they love the color blue and decorate their bowers with it. A bower isn't a nest, but rather a place for courtship and mating. They build their structures with twigs, then add whatever blue things they can find to it."

"Flowers can be blue. Berries can be blue, too."

"That's right. Some have even used berry juice to paint their twigs blue. Can you guess what else they use?"

"Feathers can be blue."

Elsa confirmed it was true. "Plus bits of glass, beads, indigo-dyed fabric—anything blue, they want to have it."

Danielle's smile changed her entire countenance, rounding her cheeks and sparking her eyes. It was the purest, least self-conscious smile Elsa had ever seen. "Miss Birdie has a blue room."

"I'm sure she does. She has a room for every color of the rainbow, doesn't she?"

"Only Miss Birdie doesn't decorate with flowers or berries," Danielle added. "Mostly feathers. And wallpaper. And paint, if you count the ceiling."

Elsa tilted her head. "You've been inside?" It struck her as curious that the gardener's daughter should have visited the mansion, but then, Birdie seemed to have a special fondness for both Tatiana and Danielle.

Instead of answering the question, Danielle shifted her gaze to George as he flapped away. "Is the *Ptilonorhynchus violaceus* related to the *Corvus brachyrhynchos*?"

"Closely," Elsa confirmed.

"Here we are!" Tatiana pushed open the door with her hip and backed out of the cottage, a tray full of tea service in her hands.

"There's a table in the shade over there." She nodded toward a multitrunk ash tree.

Elsa rose and offered to take the tray from her hostess.

"Not today, dear." The older woman smiled. "The first time, you're our guest. The next time you come, you're family, and at that point you can help as much as you like. For now, it's my pleasure to serve you. Danielle, would you care for tea?"

The girl shook her head, clearly content to stay where she was.

Tatiana nodded. "As I thought."

"Nice chatting with you, Danielle," Elsa said. "Next time you see George, tell him I said hello."

"He doesn't know your name yet. That won't mean anything to him. If you see him again, I'll introduce you properly."

"I look forward to it." Swallowing a chuckle, Elsa followed Tatiana to the wooden picnic table and helped her spread a floral tablecloth over the boards. Then Tatiana insisted on pouring the steaming brew for both of them. "This flavor—rose—is my favorite. I hope you like it, too."

Elsa tasted it. "It's heavenly."

"That it is. All of this is my little slice of heaven right here. Especially when the weather is so fine."

Elsa glanced at the ramshackle cottage behind Tatiana. "Did the will say anything about repairing the cottage?"

"Oh my, no." Tatiana settled her cup back into its saucer. "Mr. Spalding explained that there was no cash appropriated for such a thing. There are debts to pay, through no fault of Mrs. Van Tessel's. She inherited them when the master died. Completely blindsided by all of it, she was." She paused, rolling her lips between her teeth for a moment. "How I do go on. You must forgive me, dear, if I rattle overlong. It's such a treat to have someone to talk to. Not that I would share freely with just anyone. But I have a gift for discerning character, if I do say so myself, and I feel instinctively that I can trust you."

Elsa smiled at the compliment. "Do you know, when I'm alone, I sometimes talk to birds, whether they're living or not? It's a pleasure to chat with both you and your daughter."

Tatiana squeezed Elsa's hand. "Then I hope you'll come visit us whenever it's convenient for you."

"I will." She drank from the teacup again, savoring the flavor. "Speaking of the Van Tessels' relatives, do you know if Birdie and Linus had children?"

A sigh lifted Tatiana's shoulders and released them. "Not that I was ever aware of. But Mrs. Van Tessel's maternal instinct was obvious in the way she treated me and Danielle."

"How so?"

Tatiana glanced to Danielle, who remained absorbed with the buttons. She lowered her voice. "Danielle didn't speak to anyone other than me until she was three years old, and many labeled her a moron, but Mrs. Van Tessel insisted otherwise. She told me to have patience. To take heart that Danielle would speak to others when she was ready. And in the meantime, Mrs. Van Tessel took her into the house and showed her all the birds and all the art on the walls, talking to her as though she were as intelligent as any other child. Danielle opened up to her—verbally—long before she would interact with anyone else. When she was four, she finally spoke to others, as well."

"So she has been inside the house. Danielle mentioned the blue room."

"Yes. My husband passed away when Danielle was only two years old, so being able to trust her into Mrs. Van Tessel's care while I worked outside was a great gift to me."

"It sounds like it was a gift to everyone concerned."

"I believe you're right. Otherwise, Mrs. Van Tessel would not have willed to Danielle the aviary book they had often looked through."

Elsa nearly dropped her teacup. "An aviary?"

Tatiana nodded. "A medieval manuscript is an odd gift for a twelve-year-old daughter of a servant, I know. But it's true. Mr. Van Tessel was quite a collector, and not only of birds and paintings. The aviary he acquired has been dated to the fourteenth century."

"What a treasure! Is this the same aviary Mr. Spalding is looking for?"

Tatiana shrugged. "Likely so. The Van Tessels only ever owned one, and it's missing."

Dismay fanned through Elsa. She hadn't given much thought to Mr. Spalding's search for the medieval manuscript. But that was before she knew it had been willed to the Petrovics. No wonder he wanted to locate the book for them. The price it would fetch would be exponentially more than the cost of rebuilding their cottage. They could live anywhere they wanted, regardless of what the county might say about keeping them on. The aviary would secure their future.

If only they could find it.

"Do you think it has been stolen?" Elsa asked.

"I don't know about that. We just don't know where it is. It used to be kept in a glass-enclosed bookcase in the library, but Mr. Spalding said it wasn't there when he looked."

The Petrovics had so little. They deserved to have what Birdie intended to be theirs. "I'll be searching through the house for field notes anyway," Elsa told her. "Mr. Spalding already asked me to look for the aviary while I'm at it, and now I know why. I'm happy to help if I can."

Beaming, Tatiana thanked her. "Now, enough about that. Tell me, dear, what made you so interested in birds in the first place?"

Checking her watch, Elsa gave her the short version of the story. During lonely months of being bedridden with polio, Elsa had watched the birds outside her window. Their songs and flight—captivating to a girl who didn't know if she'd ever walk again—had inspired the passion for ornithology that led to her job at the American Museum of Natural History.

"And now you work with birds every day," Tatiana said. "How wonderful."

A tapping sounded, and Elsa looked up to find a red-bellied woodpecker drilling into the ash tree's diamond-patterned bark. After a few moments, he flew away, and she watched him go with a smile. It had been the living, breathing, singing, soaring birds that had attracted her from so early an age.

Elsa thanked Tatiana for the lovely time and assured her she'd visit her and Danielle again. For now, duty called. A mansion full of dead birds awaited her.

CHAPTER

5

FRIDAY, AUGUST 27, 1926

Elsa returned to Elmhurst the next day but hadn't been able to leave until after her morning staff meeting. So by the time she finally reached the mansion, she found Luke and Tom in the courtyard, eating their lunches. As soon as Luke saw her, he buttoned his collar and rolled down his sleeves. Tom didn't bother with either.

Barney stretched out in the sunshine, so content with his situation he only wagged his tail when he saw her and made no other move.

"Now, that's a good boy," she said, standing over him. She was almost tempted to rub his belly.

Almost.

Tom finished off a Coca-Cola, then lit a Lucky Strike. "Take a load off."

She sat on a bench opposite them, arranged her pleated skirt over her knees, and smiled. "Just the gentlemen I was looking for."

"There's only one gentleman here," Tom told her, squinting from the sun, "and it isn't me."

"Are you some kind of a rogue, Tom?" Elsa teased.

Luke elbowed Tom in the ribs. "Don't be fooled. He's as good a man as they come." He picked up a ball, showed it to Barney, then threw it across the lawn.

"But still not a gentleman," Tom insisted around the cigarette between his lips. "Luke and I grew up together, but not in the way you might think. My pop was, and still is, the valet for Luke's father. We lived parallel lives, I guess you could say, until after—"

"Did you say you wanted to see us about something?" Luke's interruption surprised Elsa almost as much as Tom's revelation. She'd gathered the two had some personal connection but could never have guessed Tom's family had been in service to Luke's.

Barney bounded back up with the drool-covered ball in his mouth. Luke wrestled the ball from him and threw it again. "We should get back to work," he said.

"Sorry, I did want to talk to you." Elsa lifted a hand to stay them before lacing her fingers in her lap. "The last time I was here, I visited with Tatiana Petrovic, the gardener. She told me that the aviary Mr. Spalding has been looking for was willed to her and her daughter. It would make all the difference in securing their future. I thought you should know why it matters."

A gust of wind blew Luke's hair across his brow. "That's interesting. Spalding didn't mention that he didn't have any right to it."

"He could be looking on their behalf since he wouldn't want the Petrovics searching the mansion themselves," she suggested.

Luke eyed her. "Think so?"

Well, she had thought so before he looked at her like that. She supposed a man with his experiences would have trouble believing the best of people.

Tom inhaled on his cigarette and blew the smoke to one side. "Regardless, we've emptied all the cases now and never saw an aviary. If we come across it in other areas of the house, we'll give it directly to the Petrovics."

"We did find a few more field notebooks while you were out," Luke said. "I placed them on the dining room table for you."

"That's wonderful, thank you!" Rising, she dusted off the back of her skirt and followed the men inside while Barney flopped in the shade beneath a bench.

Before she reached the dining hall, however, the sound of a door slamming drew her to the entry hall.

"Good afternoon, Mr. Spalding," she greeted him.

He looked up from the clipboard he carried. "Miss Reisner. How is your work here coming along?" His camel brown suit matched his fading hair.

"Slowly but surely. I'm making progress, but I'm afraid it's a tedious and painstaking job to match up all the notes, find the birds, and tag them accordingly."

"I don't doubt it." Smoothing his necktie, he glanced at the crates of books Luke and Tom had boxed up from the library. "I hope these will be gone by tomorrow. My mother—Uncle Linus's sister—and my children are coming, eager to pilfer."

"Yes, sir, I understand these will go out by this evening. The birds will take me much longer to finish sorting through."

He waved a hand dismissively. "My family doesn't want those birds, I assure you. I trust they'll leave you alone as they search for unclaimed valuables." Leaving the entry hall, he moved through the corridor.

Elsa went with him. "Speaking of valuables, I understand the aviary was willed to the Petrovics."

He inhaled sharply, his mustache twitching. "A foolish decision made by an old woman clearly not in her right mind."

Oh dear. "But you'll honor her wishes, won't you?"

"It's a moot point since no one knows where it is," he countered, and Elsa didn't press the matter.

At the library, he exchanged a few words with Luke, then bypassed the dining hall and entered the stair tower. Rather than climb, however, he stepped outside, stationing himself in the shade of the overhang. Two museum staff exited, carrying a painting between them. Mr. Spalding stopped them to check their identification and mark something on his clipboard.

He glanced at his watch, then toward the museum staff returning to the stair tower. They nodded politely as they passed, sweat beading their brows.

"Any of those paintings Aunt Birdie donated could have gone to the family," he muttered once they were gone, "and *we* could have *sold* them to the museums—at a bargain rate, too—and made a pretty profit. I have no idea why she insisted on being generous to institutions and not to her own people. Now, do excuse me. You have work to do, and as soon as I check out the rest of the paintings slated for the museums, I'll head back to the office."

"Of course. I apologize." She turned to go but paused in the doorway. "Where is your office?" she dared to ask, wondering what kind of a living he made. Perhaps she'd been wrong to trust he wanted the aviary only to give it to the rightful owners. Knowing where he worked might help her understand his financial situation.

"Oh no. Just what I need today." Lowering the clipboard, Mr. Spalding squinted at a dark green Ford Model T that had turned into the drive and was slowly progressing toward the house. When it rolled to a stop beside one of the museum vehicles, Mr. Spalding marched out to it, holding out his hand like a traffic cop.

At the driver's side of the auto, he paused, likely waiting for the window to open. "Not today, cousin," Mr. Spalding said loudly enough for Elsa to hear. "As you can see, the museums are here collecting their acquisitions according to the will. No relatives except for myself are to be here until they're through. Be a sport and stay out of the way, will you? Play by the rules like the rest of us."

"Play by the rules? That's rich, considering Uncle Linus never did." The glare off the windshield prevented Elsa from seeing the man inside, but it was easy enough to hear him. "If only museum staff are to be present, who is that and why is she here?"

Elsa bristled as Mr. Spalding glanced her way. "She *is* museum staff. She's *supposed* to be here. You aren't." Exhaust fumes plumed from the rattling Tin Lizzie.

"It would have been nice to learn of Aunt Birdie's passing from you, Guy. Instead, I had to hear of it from the executor of her will. You couldn't spare the time for a phone call? A stamp? The executor never said anything about waiting to come, and I've driven all the way from Philadelphia to be here."

"A day, Hugh. That's all I ask. Find a room in the village and come back tomorrow, all right?"

Muttering followed. Mr. Spalding backed up, and the auto sputtered around the circle drive and back out to the main road.

A long-suffering sigh blustered from Mr. Spalding as he rejoined Elsa. "Cold Spring Harbor, Long Island."

"Pardon me?"

"I work at the Eugenics Records Office. Second floor, third office on the right, if you wanted to know that, too. Anything else I can tell you?"

Elsa suspected there was. But for now, she took her leave.

The next few hours passed slowly. Before Elsa could go through the field notebooks Luke had located, she still had to finish putting the loose pages she'd found yesterday in the correct order. When at last she finished that job, her leg felt stiff and could do with a little stretching.

Circling around to the other end of the dining hall table, she uncovered the green birds they'd moved there from the library. The closest bird to her was *Cyanocorax luxuosus*, a green jay from the woodlands of Central America. He wore a distinctive black mask and had a blue patch on his forehead. She was sure she'd already copied the details for this one into her own ledger.

Now, where was it?

She hadn't been able to alphabetize her entries yet—that would have to be done after she finished filling it in entirely—so she had to rely on her memory or flip through every page in her notebook to find the right species. It would help to recall the year of the expedition.

Oh dear. Elsa's memory was good, but not photographic. This bird came from Guatemala, but Mr. Van Tessel had been to Central America three times. During which of those expeditions had he caught this one?

Sinking into the nearest chair, she turned the pages until she found it. She checked her watch. It had taken her three minutes to scan all those columns and locate the one she wanted.

"*No bueno*, birdie," she muttered, shaking her head at the waste of time. She filled out a tag for him anyway, leaving blank the space for his catalog number, which would have to be assigned later. She tied it to his left leg.

This little exercise only confirmed what she already knew. She couldn't operate like this. There was only one way to have any hope of efficiency, and that was to finish going through all the notebooks, copying the details into her own, and then cut up the pages and alphabetize the rows. Then she'd simply copy everything onto new pages in a fresh catalog ledger.

That was a project for another day. For now, what she needed was a change of scenery. She could always hunt for more field notebooks.

After covering the birds with the sheet once again, she left the dining room and entered the stair tower. All was quiet on the second floor now, the spoken-for paintings having been claimed. Curious about which ones, if any, had been left, she decided to find out for herself.

She'd take it slow.

The last time she climbed these stairs, she'd been in a hurry, and she'd been anxious about being alone. Neither of those was true today. She could do this.

By the time she reached the second floor, she felt the exertion in her leg and lungs, but it wasn't nearly as acute as it had been before. Encouraged, she strolled through the corridor, past the bedrooms, until she reached the art gallery.

How naked it looked without so many of its paintings. A few small line drawings remained, some of them brightened with watercolors. They resembled the illustrations she'd seen in Birdie's field notes. The Latin names for the birds had been written at the bottom in her handwriting. But instead of labeling the body parts with measurements like a diagram, they were drawn and colored as though living: in flight, brooding, feeding their young, or with their little mouths open in full-throated song. The essence of life pulsed as strong as Elsa's heartbeat.

She smiled at a row of eastern bluebirds, puffed up and huddled on a branch together as though keeping warm in the winter. How lovely that Birdie chose the common over the exotic to paint and hang in the gallery. But then, just because a bird was common didn't make it any less wonderful.

Good for Birdie. If none of the relatives wanted these, the Petrovics might.

"Miss Birdie has a blue room." Danielle's voice came back to Elsa, compelling her to search for it.

It didn't take long to find a blue bedroom suite. If it had been shared with Linus before he died, no masculine traces remained. The feminine, whimsical space seemed suited entirely for Birdie. Just as Danielle had said, the ceiling had been painted night-sky blue with yellow constellations. Mounted birds of every shade of blue blended in with the floral wallpaper. Danielle had been here. Was this where they'd looked at the aviary together?

Elsa searched the space, along with the adjoining dressing room.

No aviary.

The bed creaked as she sat on the edge to think. Had Birdie purposely kept it hidden? Maybe she'd intended to tell the Petrovics where it was kept, but then forgot or simply ran out of time.

Sliding off the bed, Elsa knelt and reached beneath the mattress, feeling along the length of the box spring. When that turned up nothing, she repeated the process on the other side.

Her breath caught when her fingers touched something hard. With her other hand, she lifted the mattress and gently removed a book.

But not the aviary.

Still, when she realized what it was, her heartrate picked up. This was the journal she'd been wishing to find, the one dated the summer Birdie's baby would have been born.

Taking a seat at the claw-foot writing desk, Elsa pushed back indigo bunting and black-throated blue warbler specimens to make room for the journal. Light fell softly on the pages as she turned them.

June 2, 1877

Some days I am so ready to meet this babe inside me, and other days I nearly panic for fear of what I'll do when I meet her (yes, her. I'm sure). Today is the latter kind of day. Me, a mother? The nursery is ready, but I am not. The layette has been prepared, but what can prepare me to raise a human being from infancy to adulthood? Linus insists the job isn't quite up to me, that the nurse and governess will play a bigger role than I will. But I can't agree to this. Why should I hand over my own flesh and blood when I'm the only mother she has?

Her eyes growing hot and sticky, Elsa swiped off her glasses, and the words on the page turned into one illegible smear in her vision. She was touched by Birdie's heartfelt emotion, but what she felt was a double-edged sword. One side was the sweetness of young Birdie as an overwhelmed mother-to-be. She'd felt inadequate, but that didn't mean she was willing to relinquish her baby.

The other side, however, was pure bitterness. Elsa's own mother had been more than willing to "hand over" Elsa to a succession of nurses and governesses, before, during, and after her bout with the dreaded disease. She didn't remember much about the worst of the illness. What she recalled was waking in a dark room, alone, with no one there to comfort her or tell her what was happening. She wanted to know why she couldn't move her legs. When would she walk again?

Would she walk again?

No one had answered her. *"Don't fuss now"* was not an answer. *"You must be a good girl and rest so you'll get better"* was not an answer, either. It did imply that good girls recovered. Naughty girls did not. And naughty girls ought to be ashamed of themselves.

Elsa was. She had been ashamed as a child, and she still battled that demon now.

She remembered thinking that she must be naughty indeed, though she hadn't meant to be, because as hard as she tried to be good, as hard as she tried to make her legs work properly again, the left one stayed stubbornly weak. Her parents must not have been happy with her. Otherwise, why would they have sent her to boarding school as soon as the doctor said it was safe?

They hadn't sent Lauren to boarding school. She had become Julian and Beryl's ward after Lauren's mother died and her father was still in Egypt. Lauren had moved in when she was fifteen and Elsa was eight, and she had stayed there until she went to college.

Meanwhile, Elsa only came home for holidays.

"What did I do?" she whispered, glancing at the little bluebird staring back at her. But this time she knew the answer. It wasn't so much what she'd done. It was what she hadn't.

She hadn't been the daughter Beryl and Julian always wanted.

Enough of that. Elsa replaced her glasses and refocused on Birdie's journal.

June 10, 1877

Linus says the baby is overdue, but I remind him that she'll come in her own time. I do think it will be soon. I can feel it in my back, my bones, my everywhere. Linus seems almost as anxious as I am, perhaps even more so.

The nursery has been ready for weeks, and yet he will not give up inspecting every inch of the painter's work. The walls are painted with birds copied from a medieval aviary manuscript. Every bird has a story we can tell our little one. The dove that returned to Noah's ark with an olive branch in its mouth. The eagle that represents the strength of those who hope in the Lord. The sparrow that God has His eye upon. It's my favorite room in the house, despite the tiny flaws Linus has found in some of the paintings. Our baby won't care one whit whether the pictures on the wall match the book exactly.

Meanwhile, I continue my daily walk—or rather, waddle—in the gardens. I don't get far these days, but—

I do believe I've just had a contraction.

There the entry ended. Sketches of a dove, sparrow, and flowering vines filled the page's margins. The artistic style wasn't anything like her previous sketches in the field notebooks or the watercolors hanging in the gallery. These must have been copied from the aviary, offering a glimpse of both the book and the nursery's walls.

Elsa turned the page. A new entry dated three days later contained a single, chilling line: *No one will let me see my baby.*

An ache spread through Elsa's chest. Had the baby lived, or was it stillborn? Did she die in childbirth?

A tiny ticking from her watch reminded her that time was passing, and she ought to return to her work downstairs. She ignored it, resolving to work on Saturday to make up for this break.

Her gaze darted to the next entry.

They say they are protecting me. But who is protecting Sarah? Why won't they let me hold my baby?

Goosebumps lifted on Elsa's skin, followed by a wave of heat. If the child had died, they should have at least let Birdie hold her and say good-bye. How unjust, how unfair, to keep secrets from the mother.

The next three pages were filled with cramped lines of lament.

Linus has just been here. He looks as though someone died, but I can hear Sarah crying. The nurse tells me I'm hearing her ghost, but I know she lives. She needs her mother. Linus says that even a mother's love isn't strong enough to fix . . . but fix what? He won't tell me. He sets his jaw and flees the room, knowing I'm not well enough to leave the bed and follow. All I can do from this bed is sing, hoping my voice will reach her, calm her. She knows my voice. But now it cracks and squeezes to a whisper.

Elsa's throat tightened, horrified by Birdie's distress. Every paragraph carried more of the same. Birdie begged the servants to bring her baby, but they'd been forbidden by Linus. The doctor came and went, urging Birdie back to health after she'd almost died in labor. But he wouldn't say anything of her baby.

The entire household pretends she doesn't exist. But this morning, Linus left on a trip. By a miracle of timing, Agnes

arrived to visit me. When I told her what has been going on,
she took up my side and left the room as one prepared for battle.
Not ten minutes later, she returned with my child.

If Linus doesn't love Sarah, I love her enough for the both
of us.

Thank God Agnes came. And I thank God that she stayed
for as long as she could.

The several pages that followed were filled with drawings of
the newborn, some of her in sleep, some with eyes wide open. In
one, Sarah reached up toward Birdie's face. Birdie was smiling.

In none of the drawings could Elsa see the baby's face below
her nose.

On the last page of the journal, a small envelope was affixed
to the page. Inside, a lock of blond curls was tied with a pink
satin ribbon. Sarah's.

And none of Birdie's relatives had even known she'd been born.

No one, that was, except Linus and a woman named Agnes.

CHAPTER

6

The revelations in Birdie's diary followed Elsa home from Elmhurst and refused to leave her alone. Questions had only multiplied in her mind since she had touched the lock of Sarah's hair. But whatever had happened next was not described in that journal, if indeed it had been recorded at all.

If her work here at the museum required more thought, it would be easier to stop pondering the estate and its secrets. Aside from Elsa working alone in her office now, the fifth floor of the American Museum of Natural History was deserted, even as the floors below buzzed with the Saturday crowd.

She opened another customs box. Inside, poorly wrapped birds were stained with blood. She could use a fingernail buffer to clean that off the feathers. But the beaks and tails broken off in transit, she could not fix. What's more, they were species the museum already had enough of. These little fellas had no need to die for the sake of science.

A soft knock at the door turned her head.

Mr. Chapman nodded a greeting. "Just wanted to let you know

I'm in my office, so if you hear any noises from that general direction, it's me and not some rogue patron."

She offered a small smile. "I didn't think you worked on Saturdays." She usually didn't, either, but her tasks here had piled up while she spent time at Elmhurst.

"The Congress in Ottawa is less than a month away," he reminded her, referring to the Forty-Second Annual Congress of the American Ornithologists' Union. "I have two papers to prepare and present, on top of my regular work, which has been accumulating while I finished my eight-hundred-page *Bulletin on Ecuador.* At least you know you're not alone up here today. What have you got there?" He entered the office for a closer look.

Elsa showed him the sorry state of the birds she'd unpacked. "Mr. Griscom's guide on the preparation of birds has obviously had an impact. But people are sending specimens we simply don't need."

His mustache drooped in a frown. "Who says we don't need them?"

She stayed silent, resisting the urge to bite her lip. She'd overstepped with that last remark. She was a research assistant, not a curator, not even an assistant curator. It was her job to take notes, prepare and tag birds, organize the catalog, and assist patrons with whatever research they came here to conduct.

But surely Mr. Chapman would understand where she was coming from. After all, he'd been the one who famously started the Christmas Bird Count, a tradition of counting birds in a kind of census, to replace the long-held custom of shooting birds on Christmas Day. Apparently the Victorians believed that nothing said "Happy birthday, Jesus," like killing innocent birds. Mr. Chapman was widely credited for saving untold thousands of birds who otherwise would have perished.

She pointed this out to him, but he remained unmoved. "There is a difference between killing for science," he said, "and killing for sport with no intention of learning from the birds afterward."

"Perhaps in the next printing of Mr. Griscom's guide, we could include a list of birds we already have enough of," she suggested.

Cupping one elbow in his palm, he propped a fist beneath his chin. "The trouble is, that could change between printings. We may think we have enough African parrots for example, and tell people to stop collecting them. But then, say, the parrot specimens we loan out to other museums or schools don't come back to us, or at least not in the same good condition. Then we'll wish we had more, won't we?" He scooped up a kingfisher, leaving its long bill on the desk. "The skeleton will still be useful for study. Proceed to remove the skin and flesh."

"Yes, sir."

As they had already gone over her progress at the Van Tessel estate yesterday, there was nothing more to say. Her boss left, and with a great sigh, Elsa turned to her tray of tools and got busy.

At two o'clock, she wrapped up her work for the day. Before leaving the building, she threaded her way from the elevator through the first-floor Memorial Hall, skirting a statue of one of the museum founders on her way to the Information Bureau. Busts of American pioneers in science seemed to watch her from niches encircling the hall.

A knot of people clustered around the thirty-six-ton meteor brought back from an expedition to Greenland. Gently, Elsa pardoned and excused her way through them, reaching the Information Bureau at last. Greeting the clerk, she purchased a postcard to send to Lauren in Egypt and tucked it into her purse.

"Elsa! How serendipitous. I called the Beresford, and Ivy told me you were here. You've made it so easy to find you."

Bewildered by the sound of her mother's voice, Elsa turned to find her standing in the hall. The pearls at her neck were as white as her gloves. A simple ribbon adorned her hat, because less was more.

"Mother. What are you doing here?" Elsa pushed her glasses up her nose, then patted her cloche into place. She hadn't been prepared to see her yet. She had only dressed for working alone, not for a social call.

With a tilt of her head, Mother beckoned Elsa away from the sales desk to a quieter section of the marble hall. She stopped between two smaller meteorites on display, the obsidian rocks glinting. "I hate to tell you this, dear, but our dinner plans for this evening have fallen apart. Charles Peterson had something come up and had to postpone. Something about an issue with one of his properties in Florida that he simply had to see to himself. He's terribly apologetic about it. We'll reschedule next month after he returns."

"Oh." Elsa felt herself relax, then drew herself up again, spine as straight as she could make it. She had forgotten that her parents had invited a man she'd never met to their weekly family dinner, which made the change of plans quite palatable. "That's all right. I don't mind. Ivy and I had a double date a few days ago, anyway."

"Really? Anyone I know?"

"Archer Hamlin and his friend Percy Osborne. You might know the Hamlins. They moved onto Fifth Avenue several years ago. He and Percy took us for dinner at the Ritz." Elsa chided herself for that last remark. She hadn't meant to imply there was anything romantic between them. She'd said it only because she knew the Ritz would impress her mother, and she couldn't resist. She couldn't remember the last time her mother had been impressed with anything Elsa had said or done.

Mother's eyebrows lifted. "How lovely. His parents' names are . . . ?"

"Albert and Gloria," Elsa supplied.

"Ah, Gloria Hamlin. Yes, I know her. We're in the Junior League together."

A train of small children passed by, each one holding to a fabric strap tied to the belt of the child in front of him. The woman holding the first child's hand appeared to be the captain of a tightly run ship.

"I can still come have dinner with you as usual, though," Elsa told her mother.

The smile fell. "I'm afraid that won't be possible. Our cook is feeling under the weather, so I gave her the night off."

"Good." Elsa was glad that at least her mother had thought outside of herself in that.

"Your father and I will eat what was left of last night's dinner."

"That's called leftovers." Elsa grinned. "You're eating leftovers. Like the middle class."

"Oh, fiddlesticks. In any case, you're better off eating dinner at the Beresford. But if you aren't busy right now, I thought you and I might do a little shopping together."

Elsa eyed her, curious at the odd idea. When she was a child, a seamstress had come in and taken her measurements, and come back with tailor-made clothes. Only when she became an adult did she shop at department stores. She'd even purchased ready-made clothes off the rack, much to her mother's chagrin.

Shopping with Mother didn't sound like a pleasant prospect. And yet she could almost hear Lauren and Ivy in her head, telling her this was less about shopping and more about spending time together. They were both orphans now, while Elsa still had both parents living. She ought not take that for granted.

"I do need a better pair of walking shoes," she said.

Mother brightened. "Then it's settled! Lord & Taylor? Saks?"

"Macy's?"

"Goodman's?"

Elsa agreed. Bergdorf Goodman's department store was more expensive than Macy's but closer.

Mother smiled. "Good. Come, Reeves is waiting."

Outside the museum, Mother's onyx Studebaker shone in the afternoon sun. Mr. Reeves, the driver, held the door open while Mother slid into the back seat.

"How are you, Reeves?" Elsa asked. "It's been an age since I've seen you."

"Pleasure to see you again, Miss Reisner." Silver threaded the hair beneath his cap. He'd been the only driver her parents had employed during her lifetime, the one who had driven her to boarding school and picked her up again to bring her home.

Before Elsa bent to take her seat beside Mother, he held out a couple of Tootsie Rolls for her, just as he had on all those trips when she'd been a child, and he'd been the first and last familiar face she'd seen. "Still partial to these?"

Her heart warmed. "Who isn't? Thank you." She unwrapped a candy and popped it in her mouth as soon as she sat in the auto. "Want one?" She held out the other to her mother, who lifted an eyebrow and shook her head.

"Seeing your dentist regularly, dear?"

Ignoring the jibe, Elsa looked out the window instead of making a snappy remark she'd regret. The auto filled with silence as they rode to the luxury department store.

A uniformed doorman opened the Studebaker's back door. Elsa swallowed what remained of the Tootsie Roll and stepped out onto the sidewalk.

With a word of instruction to her driver, Mother accepted the doorman's hand and exited the auto. Oh, the regal way she moved. She made the simple act of rising from the Studebaker and strolling toward the doors look like she was royalty. *Didn't you know? Your mother is a queen,* her father had teased when she was little. *And that makes you a princess.*

It had been a long time since she'd believed that, but Mother still moved with elegance and grace, like she knew people were watching her and wanted to make it worth their while.

People were watching both of them now. Two young ladies in short dresses and long strands of pearls exited the brass revolving doors, a man carrying hatboxes behind them. Their admiring gazes swept over Mother's perfect coiffure and poise, then became open stares at the contrast in limping, bespectacled Elsa. A spark of recognition flared. Had these women been her classmates at boarding school? Or was it only the disdain in their expressions that felt familiar? Her fingers wrapping around the remaining Tootsie Roll in her pocket, Elsa wondered how good her aim was.

So much for Madame Trudeau's deportment classes.

Straightening, she marched into the store as though she belonged with the beautiful, perfect people who shopped here. As though she belonged beside her mother.

———

Bergdorf Goodman didn't have a shoe department. They had a shoe *salon*, furnished with plush sofas and chairs, potted trees, Turkish rugs, high ceilings adorned with crystal chandeliers, and mirrors that doubled the space. Elsa and her mother sat on the edge of a purple loveseat, their posture as erect as though they still stood. A saleswoman sashayed their way, introduced herself as Bette, and inquired how she could meet their needs.

"I'd like a good pair of walking shoes, please," Elsa told her. "Size seven. Nothing fancy, just something practical. Comfortable."

"But high quality in materials and workmanship," Mother specified. "A little style doesn't hurt, either."

"But of course." Bette smiled. "We have only the highest standards here. If you'll excuse me, I'll return with some selections in a few moments."

Mother nodded, dismissing her, then rose to wander about the salon while Elsa remained seated. Single shoes were displayed on what looked like multitiered crystal cake stands. She picked one of them up, a small smile curving her lips. It was a high-heeled, white satin slipper with a delicate ankle strap and gold buckle.

"Maybe they have your size," Elsa said.

"Oh no." Mother's laugh was the flutter of butterfly wings, delicate and fleeting. "I don't want this for myself. This is like the pair we bought Lauren for her coming-out ball, that's all."

Elsa's mouth went dry. "I didn't know she'd had one."

Mother returned the shoe to its place. "It was never a secret, darling, but you were not in any shape to be bothered with anything that didn't directly relate to your health at the time."

That's right. When Lauren was seventeen, she'd already been living with them full-time for two years. With Uncle Lawrence away, Lauren was like a daughter to Elsa's parents.

"So you threw her a ball when she turned seventeen. While I was confined to my bed with polio."

"Shh, come now." Mother returned to the loveseat and sat. "You make it sound as though we went behind your back to do it. We had been planning it for a year, and staying home for the evening would not have made you any better. Besides, we couldn't very well reschedule your cousin's seventeenth birthday."

Elsa heard a smile in her mother's voice but didn't look at her. Instead, she gripped her hands in her lap and fixed her gaze on that white shoe on its crystal stand, the likes of which Elsa never had and never would wear.

"Hotel Astor?" she asked.

"Naturally. It was no more lavish a party than what we would have thrown for you, too, if . . ." Her words trailed away, and yet their meaning burrowed into Elsa. *If things had been different. If you had recovered enough for a ball of your own.* "You must understand, Lauren is my only sister's only child. Of course I would do for her whatever I thought she deserved. When we began planning her ball, you were eight years old and still healthy, and I assumed we'd do the same for you. By the time the ball took place the next year, you had been sick with that awful disease for six months. You were two months shy of your tenth birthday, and I couldn't predict your future. I wondered if the ball for your cousin would be the only ball I'd ever get to throw. I didn't want to miss it."

A hard knot formed in Elsa's throat. "And you were right. It was the only ball." She could say more. She could say she hoped Lauren's ball made Mother happy in a way Elsa never could. She could say it was ironic that Mother didn't want to miss Lauren's ball and yet had no problem missing months at a time from Elsa's life.

She said nothing.

Mother fiddled with the clasp on her handbag. "You were still in the hospital at that point, and you weren't allowed visitors except on Sunday afternoons. You never even missed us, darling. You had no idea we'd had a ball at all."

A wave of heat washed through Elsa, pressure building behind her skull.

"Speaking of Lauren," Mother went on, "I've offered to help plan her wedding while she's away. She and Joe won't want to wait long after she comes back from Egypt, and you know how early venues in Manhattan are booked. Now is the time to make reservations, and not only for the venue but catering, florist, musicians, all of it."

"That sounds exhausting. Are you sure Lauren and Joe want all that?"

Mother blinked at her. "Even a simple affair requires planning and organization, and Joe has his investigations to conduct for the police. Lauren is grateful for my help, and I'm only too glad to give it."

Elsa had no doubt about that. Lauren had likely been too busy preparing for Egypt to bother with wedding planning during the months before she left. And Mother—well, if she'd enjoyed planning a coming-out ball, she would love planning a wedding even more, especially since she might not get to plan one for her own daughter, despite her matchmaking attempts.

What would Mother do without Lauren?

Elsa pressed a hand to the throbbing behind her brow. "If you plan hers, will you leave off hoping you can plan mine one day? Could we stop with the matchmaking dinners?"

Mother cut her a sharp gaze and, in an uncharacteristic show of sentiment, placed a hand on Elsa's knee. "This has nothing to do with you, Elsa. Lauren is not now, has never been, and will never be a substitute for you. Lauren is my niece. It's only right that I fill in for what my sister would have done, if she still lived. But you are my only daughter. Do you hear me?"

Elsa heard her. But the words didn't relieve the bruises inside her.

Mother removed her hand, clasping it once more in her lap. "I planned to ask if you'd like to join me in checking out the options for Lauren and Joe. I have good taste, but that isn't enough. I'll need someone to help me keep track of all the details. You do enjoy details, don't you?"

A wry smile tipped Elsa's lips. "Depends on the details."

Before they could discuss it further, Bette returned with four boxes of shoes.

"Let's see them all before we start trying on," Mother said.

Kneeling on the carpet, Bette lifted all the lids.

"Take that one away. She's twenty-six, not sixty-two."

"Of course."

"Mother." Elsa modulated her tone to push the irritation out of it. "I like that pair the best. The cap-toe Oxfords have the lowest heel, and the heels are made of rubber. That's what I'm looking for. Let's try it on, please."

Bette looked from mother to daughter and back again before Elsa added, "In case we've confused you, I am the customer, not her. I'm paying for the shoes, either here or elsewhere."

With a nod, Bette unclasped the straps on Elsa's shoes, and Elsa slid her feet into the new candidates. After Bette laced them up, she pinched at the toes, checking for fit, then rose. "Take a stroll and see how they feel."

Elsa stood. In the corner of her vision, another young woman practically waltzed through the salon, testing a gold pair of high-heeled evening slippers. Mother shifted, clutching her handbag with tighter-than-necessary force. She crossed her ankles, then uncrossed them again.

Mother was nervous.

Elsa hated that it was because of her. This was a mistake, but there was nothing to do about it now except get through it.

Lifting her chin, Elsa walked away from Bette and Mother, forcing herself to focus on how the shoes fit, rather than the embarrassment she caused her mother.

"Do you need a lift in one shoe?" Bette asked her when she returned to her seat. "If you have one in the pair you've been wearing, could you switch it out to try it with this pair?"

Elsa smiled. "I appreciate that, but no. My legs are the same length, but one is not as cooperative as the other." Her left knee didn't bend as freely with the brace on it. But that was the point. She needed the support to help bear her weight. "The Oxfords fit fine. I'll take them."

"Wouldn't you like to try anything else?" Mother asked.

Elsa assumed she referred to the three other boxes Bette had brought, but Mother's gaze had traveled back to the satin white slipper, sparkling on its pedestal. It wasn't just a symbol of that shining ball of years gone by but of a standard that Elsa couldn't reach.

"That's all right, Mother," Elsa said. "Some shoes will never fit."

———○———

The rest of the afternoon melted away under the heat of a summer that wouldn't let go. Back at her apartment, Elsa tossed a Tootsie Roll to Ivy, then ducked into her room to change into a more comfortable sundress, pairing it with canvas sandals.

"How was work?" Ivy called through the door.

"You go first." Headache still pulsing, she headed to the bathroom to wash her face and fix her hair.

Ivy came and stood in the doorway with a brief summary of how the events had gone this morning for the anniversary of the Battle of Brooklyn. Only after that did Elsa fill her in on the broken birds she'd unboxed and her conversation with Mr. Chapman that offered no hope the trend would abate.

"Okay." Ivy crossed her arms. "So what else is bothering you?"

"Isn't that enough?"

"Sure it is, only you've never slammed so many drawers over it before. What else is going on?"

"I don't know." Elsa turned from her reflection to face her roommate. "I went shopping with Mother after work."

"Fun!" Her entire countenance lifted. "I was hoping she found you."

Elsa laughed. "The most fun I had was imagining chucking my Tootsie Roll at two gawking shoppers exiting Goodman's when we arrived."

"You wouldn't."

"No, I wouldn't. But I sure did enjoy thinking about it."

"What on earth did they do to get your hackles up so? I mean, you said they were gawking. What else?"

Pressing her lips into a thin line, Elsa shrugged. "It was the way they looked at Mother, like they were totally impressed by her, and then they looked at me, like they couldn't understand what I was doing with her."

Ivy propped a fist on her hip. "So they looked at you both. And for this, you wanted to throw candy at them? Only, not like in a parade, but as in, an act of violence?" Amusement danced in her eyes.

Elsa grinned, barely containing a chuckle. "I would never do it, though."

"People have looked at you before, Elsa. Do you always want to hurl things at them?"

"Nope. Only when I'm with Mother." She unbuckled the brace from around her left knee, applied talcum powder to the skin, and refastened the brace.

"Why?"

She couldn't answer right away. When the knot in her throat dissolved, she said, "When people react—even if it's just a second look—it reminds her that I'm different. I think she's embarrassed by how I turned out. Or at the very least, disappointed. It's humiliating." And it was easier to be angry than feel that kind of hurt.

"One of my most vivid memories from childhood was when my parents took me to Coney Island," she went on. "I was ten and a half years old, so this was about fourteen months after I contracted polio. Despite my progress with physical therapy, they knew walking all day would be too much for me. So they rented a wicker rolling chair for me to ride in along the boardwalk. Oh, the stares we drew that day. Several people assumed that I had a mental disability as well as physical. The things they said within our hearing made that crystal clear. Some asked my parents what was wrong with me as if I couldn't understand them and speak for myself. I don't remember what my parents said, but I do know we didn't stay as long as I'd expected we would. I was convinced I embarrassed Mother and Father."

"Surely that's not true," Ivy insisted. "Your parents wouldn't have taken you out in the first place if that were the case. And your mother wouldn't have suggested shopping with you today if she was embarrassed about your limp."

Elsa couldn't deny that. But that wasn't all she'd been stewing over since leaving the store. "While we were waiting for the saleswoman to return, Mother mentioned that she and Father had thrown Lauren a coming-out ball while I was sick. It's not that I think they shouldn't have done it. And I'm not jealous about it—I never wanted a ball, anyway."

Ivy's brows drew together. "I didn't have one, either. But if you aren't jealous, what is it that has you upset?"

Elsa combed through her waves again, trying to dissect her feelings, which was far more complicated than skinning a bird. At length, she put the comb back in the drawer and fought the urge to knock it shut. "She said that I never missed them. She said I never knew they were gone."

"The night of the ball," Ivy clarified.

"That's what she meant, I'm sure." Elsa turned off the light and moved into the parlor, where she flopped onto the sofa. Cleo, Lauren's cat, jumped on the cushion and bumped her head into her arm until Elsa petted her. "And she was obviously right. But her choice of words fired something in me. I spent much of my childhood missing them. I did know they were gone. Or rather, *I* was gone. I spent seven months in a stark hospital room and was only allowed visitors during a two-hour window on Sundays. That was the hospital's rule, but as a child, alone and scared, I missed my parents and Lauren keenly. After I came home, it took several more months of physical therapy for me to learn how to walk again. Once I did, they sent me to a boarding school. I had no idea why. We'd never talked about boarding school before that point. I couldn't help but feel that I was being punished when they sent me away. Did they think I wouldn't miss them then, either?"

At least when she went to Vassar in Poughkeepsie for college, she had been old enough to realize it was for a good education in biology, superior to what New York City schools were offering women. Still, she had had to remind herself that she was not being sent away again. She had chosen that path for herself.

Ivy sat beside her, rubbing a comforting circle on her back, and guilt snaked through Elsa. Here she was, talking about missing her parents when she was a child, though she had more than enough attention from them now—while Ivy's parents and brother died of illness when she was a teenager.

"I'm sorry, Ivy. How petty I sound. How unreasonable. Please, forget I said anything about it."

"Sorry, no can do. I won't forget about it, and please don't apologize. I want you to always feel like you can talk to me. Is there anything that would make you feel better?"

Elsa thought for a moment. She had seen Archer in passing at the museum yesterday morning before she'd gone to Elmhurst. After she'd told him about the hunt for the missing aviary, he mentioned another hunt was taking place in Central Park. A Eurasian eagle-owl named Zeus escaped his enclosure at the Central Park Menagerie this week, thanks to some mischief-maker who cut through the mesh wire cage. Authorities were actively trying to find him.

She told Ivy about Zeus and added, "I'd really like to go looking for him in the park, too. Apparently, his former keepers don't believe he can fly or hunt for himself. But I'm rooting for him. Wouldn't it be exciting if we see him?" Zeus belonged to one of the largest owl species in the world. With a wingspan of six feet, it would be easier to spot in flight, but the owl would likely be perched high on a branch somewhere until hunting time came at twilight.

"Sounds like an adventure. Would dinner be involved?" Ivy wiggled her eyebrows.

Elsa laughed. "You mean pushcart hot dogs in the park? You bet."

CHAPTER

7

Elsa and Ivy had not spotted the Eurasian eagle-owl in Central Park over the weekend, but arriving at Elmhurst this morning at dawn rewarded her with sightings of migrating waterfowl on the Hudson. She also found Tatiana on her knees in the Italianate garden.

"Why, Elsa!" The gardener wiped her hands on a kerchief. "I didn't expect to see you this time of day."

Elsa smiled. "I figured I'd get an early start, but I should have accounted for the fact that the mansion would still be locked. Between you and me, I'm delighted to have a good reason to simply enjoy the morning for a bit."

"Well, I'm glad you're locked out, if only for a chance for a quick visit. You don't mind if I keep planting these bulbs?"

"Not at all. You're getting the bed ready for spring?" Elsa hoped that meant she'd still be here next year.

"I normally save this task for next month, but since I have no idea where Danielle and I will be by then, I thought I might give it a try early. If it doesn't work, I won't be around next spring to know it. If it does, whoever is here will enjoy them." A sad smile curved her lips. "Truth is, I'm plain restless. And right now I'd rather plant something than rip out weeds. There's something so hopeful about sowing for the next season, isn't there?"

Elsa understood that, even though she'd never been a gardener herself. While Tatiana dug holes and planted the bulbs, they spoke of nature's seasons, of dormancy and promise, of bird migrations, and of finding a home. "Speaking of which, have you been able to speak to anyone from the county yet?" Elsa asked. "About staying on after the ownership of the estate transfers?"

"Not yet." The older woman sighed. "I did send a letter to the executor of Mrs. Van Tessel's will, though. My hope is that he'll be able to tell me our home is safe, as per her wishes, regardless of what Mr. Spalding does with his inheritance."

"That's a good place to start," Elsa agreed. "Please let me know what you learn from him, won't you?"

Tatiana told her she would.

The sun peeked above the trees, turning the river into a golden mirror, and Elsa returned to the house.

By a quarter past ten, Elsa had been extracting data from field notebooks in the dining hall for more than three hours. It was time to move her legs, even if just a little. So she climbed the stairs and headed for Birdie's bedchamber to search the dressing room for more field notebooks.

If she learned more about Sarah in the process, well, she couldn't help that.

The dressing room walls were covered with framed portraits of a baby, similar to the sketches she'd found in Birdie's diary. The bottom drawer of the bureau held a stack of watercolors that were matted but unframed. Some depicted the baby featured in the framed portraits, but others showed a toddler or a child, always with her face turned away from the artist. Elsa wondered if these were true representations of Sarah, too, or if they'd been painted only from Birdie's imagination.

Fighting a sense of melancholy, Elsa shut them all back into the drawer and stood. Hatboxes lined a shelf that ran the perimeter of the dressing room. Standing on the tips of her toes, she reached up and pulled down an out-of-place object. The blue macaw made her heart skip a beat.

As much as she wished she had seen Zeus on Saturday, this find was even more rare.

No wonder she hadn't seen it before. The *Cyanopsitta spixii* appeared to have been mounted on a grapevine encircling one of the four bed posts, but the vine had broken, with a portion still clutched in the bird's feet. Holding that piece of vine, she carried it back into the bedroom and brought it to the light spilling through the window.

Commonly called a Spix's macaw, this grey-headed blue parrot from Brazil was one of the rarest birds in the world. The museum didn't have a specimen yet. Hardly any institutions did. When German naturalist Johann Baptist von Spix discovered it in 1819, he noted its rarity, then promptly shot it and brought it home to Munich. The beautiful bird had only become rarer since then, a coveted status symbol among collectors who paid tens of thousands of dollars for a single specimen.

Mr. Chapman and the rest of the ornithology department would jump for joy at this acquisition. This was one bird she wouldn't wait to bring back to the museum. She didn't want to risk anyone taking or accidentally damaging it.

"Oh! Kittens! I didn't see you there!" A wide-eyed teenager stood in the doorway to the bedchamber, a delicate hand to her chest. Blond hair was piled on her head and secured with a beaded green headband that matched her drop-waist dress.

Elsa smiled at her. "I'm sorry if I've startled you. You must be Mr. Spalding's daughter? I'm Elsa Reisner, here to collect the birds for the American Museum of Natural History. I'm very sorry for your loss."

"Thank you. Father told us you'd be here. I'm Jane. Pleased to meet you. I meant to come up over the weekend, but other plans got in the way."

"Right. I heard your father tell a cousin named Hugh he could return on Saturday to look through everything."

"Oh yes, he was here. I understand from my brother, Wesley, there was quite a row between him and my father, but that doesn't surprise me. They've never gotten along. And now Father is busy, and so is Granny, and I simply don't concern myself with Hugh's whereabouts whatsoever. So I came up with Wesley. My driver is here, too, of course. He's packing up the china on my mother's orders." She drifted to the jewelry box and swirled a finger through the contents.

"How nice. I always thought I'd like to have an older brother," Elsa offered.

"Oh, honey, this one's no treat." Jane tried on a ring. "I mean, he's twenty-seven, so ten years older than me. We didn't have many years together before he moved out. He does enjoy rebelling against our father, though, and that is entertaining to watch." Giggling, she took off the ring and held an earbob to her ear, admiring the effect in the mirror. "That's him now. You hear him?"

Elsa cocked an ear toward the door, listening. "The piano music? It's lovely!"

"That's what he thinks." Jane laughed easily. "He composed it himself when he was a student at Juilliard—although it had a different name back then. The Institute for Musical Art, I think. At any rate, he paid a piano tuner extra to come out over the weekend, and now playing it is all he wants to do while he's here. He's found his treasure. I'm still looking." Dropping the earbobs in the jewelry box, she spun around and faced Elsa. "Am I talking too much? Mother says I do, but I like you, Elsa. I make a point of making friends everywhere I go. It livens things up so much. Don't you think?"

"One can never have too many friends," Elsa replied. "Although I'm afraid I'll be quite a bore while I'm here, since my time is to be spent cataloging the birds."

She brightened at the mention of birds. "My father says the aviary is missing. I didn't think anything of it when I heard it mentioned at the reading of the will, but Father says it's very valuable, which surprised me since it was left to the gardener's daughter. Are you looking for that, too? Is that what you were doing in here?" Her eyes narrowed by a few degrees.

"I'm keeping an eye out for it, but my main priority is the work for the museum." Elsa lifted the Spix's macaw as evidence. With a few more words, she excused herself.

Cradling the macaw in one arm, Elsa used the railing as she made her way down the steps and followed the sound of that beautiful piano music. She'd rather meet the young Mr. Spalding now before she resettled into a new groove with her work. When she entered the music room, the melody dropped away.

A young man looked up from where he sat on the piano bench. Smoothing his shoulder-length brown hair behind his ears, he stood and half bowed in her direction. "Elsa Reisner, I presume. I'm Wesley Spalding."

She came forward and introduced herself, though he seemed to already know why she was here. "I've just met Jane. She tells me you went to Juilliard. You're a composer?"

He withdrew a lighter and pack of Chesterfields from a khaki suit jacket draped over a chair. "That's right." He lit the cigarette and inhaled.

Shifting the macaw in her arm, she took a step back from the smoke. Maybe it would blow out the window without irritating her overly sensitive lungs.

"But since that has failed to generate a respectable income," Wesley continued, "I've gone back to school for a second go. I'm studying economics now at Columbia." He took another drag on the Chesterfield.

"Oh! That's quite rare to have an affinity for two such wide-ranging subjects."

Wesley laughed through his nose, and smoke puffed from his nostrils. "Don't be fooled. My one talent is piano. The only reason I'm pursuing economics is so I can afford my rent."

"I see. I'm sure it will be a comfort to have this piano, though." Smoke caught in her throat, and she cleared it. Wary of staying much longer, she let him know she'd be working mostly in the dining hall for now and took her leave.

Wesley's music followed Elsa to the dining hall. She would wrap and pack the Spix's macaw into her satchel later, but for now she couldn't resist keeping it visible. It rested on the table near her while she worked on transcribing notes from another of Linus's field notebooks into her own neat chart. Because she'd been bringing his notebooks home to work on in the evenings, too, she felt near the end of this stage. Unless more notebooks could be found, there remained just one more to examine.

The rest of the morning passed pleasantly. Jane's driver, a lean, raven-haired young man named Crawford, didn't say much as he wrapped each piece of china in newsprint and set them in cardboard boxes. Aside from the near-constant crinkle of paper, his presence didn't bother her at all.

The breeze rolling in off the river and through the open window smelled faintly metallic, hinting at a coming rain. Pine trees pointed to a polished pewter sky. At some point, the piano music had ended, and Crawford drove the Spalding siblings to the village for lunch. With a contented sigh, Elsa cleared a space at the table and ate the croissant and banana she'd brought with her. The slices of cheese she'd packed, she'd eaten hours ago.

She hadn't heard a peep out of the library lately, unless she'd been too absorbed to notice, or too distracted by Wesley's haunting tunes—or Crawford's newsprint rattling. She decided to check on Luke and Tom.

At the door to the library, her jaw went slack. "What on earth?"

Barney, who had been blissfully lounging in a patch of sun, greeted her with a friendly lick on her hand, but she was too fascinated by what she saw to do more than notice. A door-sized piece of the wall hung open on hinges, and the glow of a flashlight shone from within.

She moved into the library, stepping between panels of wainscoting that lay on the floor. "Luke? Tom?"

"In here," Luke called.

She crossed to the door, noticing a small locking mechanism on each side so it could be secured from within or without, and entered the hidden room.

Grinning, Luke pointed the flashlight all around the room. "What do you think? Should we add a secret den when we reconstruct the Van Tessels' library in our warehouse?"

Tom laughed. "What is this, some kind of Prohibition storeroom or hiding place in case of a raid? It's in the right spot for smuggling by river."

Elsa had a hard time picturing the Van Tessels getting caught up in that. She turned to take in the space. With the moving beam of light, shadows shifted over a desk with one wooden chair that took up almost the entire width of the shortest wall. The longer wall was lined with shelves that held books, folders, and papers. Perhaps more notebooks and journals hid among them.

"I have the blueprints of the house," Luke said, "and this room isn't indicated. But look at this foundation." Bending, he tapped the time-blackened bricks. "I'd date this to pre–Civil War."

Elsa gasped. "The Underground Railroad. Do you think?" Ivy had mentioned that Tarrytown was on the Underground Railroad route.

Luke's gaze caught hers. "It would make sense. The house was built in 1850, the year the Fugitive Slave Act passed. If the owners had been anti-slavery folks, this would have been a logical choice for hiding anyone on their way to freedom in Canada, especially with its remote location and proximity to the Hudson."

A few moments of quiet passed, and Elsa tried to grasp the former life this room may have had. "Linus was born in 1843. I believe his father purchased this property during the last years of the Civil War. So it wasn't his family that used the room for its original purpose."

"He used it for something, though," Tom pointed out. "Right up until he died, it looks like."

Elsa had to agree. A cable-knit cardigan sweater draped the back of the chair. The desk held a mug, blotter, date book, and even a telephone, all of which were covered in dust. She picked up the receiver, half expecting to hear an operator's voice on the other end. But the line was dead. Even if it had been a separate line from the main one for the house, the company would have discontinued service when the bills stopped being paid.

Barney ambled inside the room, his claws a quiet clicking on the floor. He sat next to Luke, pressing his entire body against his leg, looking up until Luke scratched between his ears.

"So did Linus repurpose this room as his study because it was already here, or did he intend to keep the activities and files within these walls secret?" Elsa wondered aloud. She picked up a folder and opened it but couldn't see well enough to make sense of it. Maybe there were more loose pages of field notes inside. She grabbed a few more folders to take with her out into the light.

She sucked in a breath. "Did you feel that?" She looked down, and Luke pointed the flashlight at her feet.

"What is it, a rat?" Tom cried, backing away. "I don't do rats."

Barney shifted his attention to Tom, nudging his nose into the man's palm.

"No, no," Elsa said. Thunder rolled outside, but she barely registered it. "Just air." She felt the cool brush of it slipping around her ankles. "It's coming from under the desk."

"Do you mind?" Luke handed the flashlight to Elsa, then moved the chair away from the desk. "Tom, give me a hand."

Together they moved the desk a few yards away from the wall. Elsa shone the light at what they uncovered: another door in the wall, this one no higher than the height of the desk. There was a space of an inch or so between it and the floor.

Taking a knee, Luke opened it, and a rush of dank, cool air swept into the room. Elsa moved to his side, and he accepted the flashlight again, illuminating the darkness within. "Stairs. And I'll bet you anything they lead to a tunnel that goes to the river."

"Does it look safe?" Elsa asked, bending to see inside for herself. The steps looked sturdy to her. "Shall we see where it goes for sure?"

"Would you like to?" Wonder laced Luke's voice, but she didn't detect disapproval.

Elsa grinned. She would like to, yes. But could she? Should she? Those were questions he had not asked, and so she would not answer them.

Instead, she said, "A little adventure never hurts." So long as it was very little, in her case. She figured there couldn't be more steps here than what she'd already climbed in the stair tower. And from what she could see, these were quite shallow.

"I need a smoke," Tom muttered. To Elsa, he explained, "I don't do tunnels, either. Not anymore." He left, and Barney went with him.

Luke shut the small door. "I'll explore that another time, Elsa. We have no idea how structurally sound it is after all these years, so please don't go adventuring alone."

Elsa agreed, a thrill racing through her at even the thought of walking that path. Setting the folders on the desk, she helped

Luke move it back against the wall, then replaced the chair before scooping up the paperwork again.

"I'll want to come back for more of this later." She held up the folders. The stirred-up dust entered her throat and lungs, triggering a cough.

"Yes. Later. For now, it's time to go." Luke pointed the flashlight at the way out, so she couldn't see his expression. But somehow she felt that the firmness in his voice had more to do with her well-being than with his schedule.

Back in the library, she asked, "Will Tom be all right?" She supposed he was smoking outside on the porch with Barney.

Luke rubbed a hand across the back of his neck. "That is certainly my intention." He left, perhaps to follow his friend.

A few drops spattered the pane. Elsa hastened to the dining hall, dropped the folders on the table, and moved from one window to another, closing the sashes. As soon as the last one was secure, she turned around in time to see Barney snatch a bird specimen from the table and run off with it. The flash of blue turned her stomach. He had the Spix's macaw.

"Stop, thief!" she cried and gave chase.

CHAPTER

8

Elsa stole down the corridor and followed the mangy mutt right out the back door, which apparently hadn't been latched shut. Taking only an instant to secure the door behind her, she dashed after Barney into the courtyard, wondering what kind of game this was.

Could it be fetch? When Luke had thrown a ball, Barney had brought it right back to him. But the dog gave no indication that's what he had in mind today.

The sky lowered and rumbled. Clouds churned as they sailed east, and Elsa wondered if the storm would pass them by. Barney stopped and turned to face her, ears pricked straight up, tail wagging. Bright blue tail feathers speared from one side of his mouth.

Elsa halted, afraid that if she took a step, he'd run again. Why, oh why, hadn't she secured the bird so this wouldn't happen? It was likely the crown jewel of the entire Hudson Collection, and here it was at the mercy of a dog. "Good boy, Barney. Come here." If she lost the bird, or if it were destroyed under her watch, she'd never forgive herself, and neither would the museum.

His tail wagged harder, but he didn't come.

"Fine, then. Stay there. Stay." She held out her hands, palms out.

The dog dropped to his elbows in front, his rump still high in the air. He was taunting her.

The nerve.

With her next step, he charged off as though his tail were on fire. Gritting her teeth, she followed suit, running as long as she could before slowing to a fast walk. Barney circled around again and again, remaining out of reach, but leading her on, past an orchard that smelled faintly of ripe apples.

Wind whipped her skirt sideways, and rain fell at last in great, fat drops. She rested her hands on her knees, trying to catch her breath. If she had any left to work with, she'd scold the dog. But the ache in her leg had spread fire straight up to her hip, and it jumped into her lungs.

Elsa stumbled toward a tree and leaned against it with one hand, the rough bark cutting into her palm. Putting her weight on her good leg and the tree, she pressed at the place in her chest that burned. She pulled air in, pushed it out. But the space inside her only screwed tighter, tighter.

She had to recover the macaw.

But the edges of her vision darkened, either from the storm or the lack of oxygen to her brain. Barney had disappeared, and so had all the trees except the one holding her up. All she saw was the water streaming from the ends of her hair.

Minutes passed, or maybe just seconds. Time warped to the rhythm of her respirations.

Breathe in. Breathe out. Ignore the pain and breathe.

"Elsa!" As though out of nowhere, Luke was there. The scars on his cheek and jaw shone darker against his pale face. "Are you okay?"

She shook her head.

His brow furrowed as he looked her over. "Injured?"

Another shake of her head would have to do, as she didn't have the air to explain it to him.

Resolve sparked in his steel grey eyes. "Put this on." He pulled off the yellow slicker he wore and helped her thread her arms into it. She had only fastened two of the toggle buttons when, without so much as a by your leave, he scooped her up with one arm supporting her back and another beneath her knees. "There's a pool building beyond the trees. It'll do for shelter."

She wrapped her arms around his neck and held on as he carried her. Barney trotted at Luke's heels, looking worried, but with no bird in his mouth.

"The macaw," she breathed.

Luke's quiet laugh reverberated into her body. "The bird is fine. Barney brought it to me. It's safe and secure, waiting for you back at the house. I knew right away you would have run after it. Next time—if there is a next time—come to me, okay? I'll get it back for you."

"You were with Tom," she whispered between breaths. "That was more important."

He looked at her, his nose nearly touching hers. Then he jerked his gaze straight ahead again and climbed the stairs to what appeared to be a Roman bathhouse. He carried her between two pillars and through the glass door.

A glass roof over a pool allowed in natural light—what little there was of it, at any rate. With a few panes missing overhead, it also allowed in the elements. Showers sprayed into the drained pool, which still held a few inches of collected rain from previous storms. The place smelled of mold.

With care, Luke lowered her into a lounge chair beside the pool.

"Thank you," she said.

"You're welcome."

Barney loped to her and laid his head on her lap and looked up at her.

"He says he's sorry," Luke told her.

"I know." Unable to resist the animal's human-like expression of guilt, she scratched behind his wet ears. "I speak dog."

He grinned. "I'll be right back."

When he returned from his jaunt into the men's dressing room, it was with a bundle of towels in his arms. "Here. Dry off the best you can. I won't have you catching a cold on my watch."

Since when was she on his watch at all? She sent him a quizzical look, and he took a knee before her.

"The way I see it, this is my responsibility," he said. "It was my dog that made off with your bird, wasn't it? And if he hadn't, you wouldn't have run after him, wouldn't have reached right past your limits and gotten stuck in the rain. Now, you said you've had polio. What I know for sure is that weak lungs and chest muscles make it harder to cough, which means fluid and mucus can build up in your lungs, so pneumonia could set in. I won't have that."

He was exactly right, though how he knew remained a mystery she'd have to leave untouched for now, given that she still fought for breath. Gratefully, she accepted the linens, removed the slicker, and did her best to towel-dry her clothes. When she offered his raincoat back to him, he insisted she wear it again, which she did. With one more towel, she squeezed rain from her hair, then dried her spectacles and replaced them.

Torrents drummed the roof and splashed inside. "I need a minute." Elsa leaned back in the lounge chair, willing her body to reset to normal—or at least, what was normal for her.

"We aren't going anywhere till the rain stops," he said. "Take your time. Take it easy. Just breathe. Easy for me to say, right?"

She smiled at him, then squinted beyond his shoulder. On a ledge near the roof, several swallows perched, waiting out the storm with them.

Luke scrubbed his hair with a towel, then combed through it with his fingers. He pulled a piece down to cover a scar.

"You don't have to do that," she told him.

"Habit. I don't like to make people uncomfortable. This is the only one I can hide. I tried growing a beard, but the hair doesn't grow through scar tissue, so that only made these scars stand out more." He looked away, and the marked side of his profile disappeared.

"You don't make me uncomfortable. And please don't hide your face. I like it." How awkward could she get? She felt a blush heat her cheeks, and she was grateful for the shadows that muted what must be a bright pink color.

Luke met her gaze again, then dropped it to Barney and stroked his fur. "That's nice of you to say. I confess that being around you feels a little like Beauty and the beast."

That didn't make sense. Few people who knew her limitations had ever called her beautiful. Part of her wanted to crack wise and pretend he'd called her the beast, implying that he was the beauty—which he was. Handsome. The scars did nothing to diminish that. But all she could say was "applesauce," then commenced blushing again. "Did you meet Wesley and Jane?" she asked.

"Yesterday," he answered. "Briefly. There wasn't much to say."

She nodded her understanding. Several long moments passed in quiet, aside from the rain pounding the roof and into the pool. Dried leaves floated in the water collected in the deep end. She rested her hand on Barney's back and understood the comfort Tom drew from the dog's presence. He smelled, he was wet and muddy, and he was a rascal—but underneath it all, Barney made a loyal companion.

"I think it's wonderful that you and Tom are so close, given your family backgrounds," she said, eager to change the subject. "My family had servants, too, and I didn't befriend any of their children. I wish I had. I was too much a coward to try."

"How do you mean?" The side of Luke's hand brushed hers as he petted the old dog, too.

"I overhead something that was never meant for my ears."
She took a deep breath, resolving to make the story a short one,
no matter the size it took in her memory. "I was almost seven
years old and had been playing hide-and-seek with my cousin
Lauren. She had just turned fourteen and had come to Manhattan for Christmas break. I went to the kitchen and folded myself
into a cabinet. Then the cook and her daughter, Hannah, who
was my age, came in."

When Elsa paused in the telling, Luke urged her to take it
slow. "I'm in no hurry."

"I felt sorry that Hannah was working and wondered if her
mother would let her play with me and Lauren for a while instead. I hoped Hannah would play with me even after Lauren
returned to Chicago. I was lonely and thought Hannah might
be, too."

She drew in the air she needed. "But the longer I stayed in
that cabinet listening to them, the more I realized that Hannah
was happy already. She and her mother sang songs while they
worked and told stories. They laughed together, deep from the
belly, in a way I'd always been forbidden to do."

Luke frowned. "You weren't allowed to laugh?"

"Not more than a feminine titter behind my hand. Anything
else wasn't ladylike, you see."

Luke shook his head. "I'd like to hear you laugh deep from the
belly sometime. But go on. What happened next?"

She chuckled. "Lauren burst into the kitchen and asked if I
was there. The cook said no, which tickled me to no end. But
when Lauren tramped upstairs, Hannah said she used to wish
she could switch places with me. When I heard that, I was ready
to show myself, declare her my bosom friend, and share everything I had with her."

"But you didn't."

"No, I didn't. Hannah wasn't finished. She said, 'Miss Elsa

has fine clothes and a million dolls. Her hair is so shiny, and she smells like roses. But I decided for all that, I'd rather not be her.' She went on to say it was better to stay who she was and have her mother's love because she had never seen my parents hug me. Or laugh with me. She supposed they didn't even put me to bed. And she was right. That's not what we did. She said she felt sorry for me. And that was before I contracted polio."

"My parents didn't put me to bed, either," Luke offered.

"No?"

"Nope. The governess dressed me in my best clothes every evening and paraded me in to see them for fifteen minutes before they had their dinner. And then I marched out again, leaving them to dine alone."

"Yes," Elsa breathed. "That was exactly it. It never bothered me much, though, assuming that was how everyone's family was, until I heard that Hannah pitied me. After that, I wasn't brave enough to ask her to be my friend. It probably wouldn't have worked very well even if I had. How did you and Tom manage it?"

"Honestly, I didn't talk to him much before I left home for college. I didn't realize how much he'd looked up to me until his father told me after I'd graduated. If I had given any thought to his view of our family—which I can't say I did—I'd have figured he would have looked up to my older brother instead. I sure did. Then again, Franklin was usually busy training under my father to help run the business, so he wasn't around much."

"Does he still help with the business?" she asked.

Luke shook his head, and even in the shadows, she could see his expression close off, putting an end to the topic of his brother with as much finality as if he'd already changed the subject. She didn't push.

An overhanging branch swayed above the glass roof, the leaves acting like a sail in the wind. A small limb broke off and landed with a splash into the pool.

Barney lifted his head at the sound, alert enough to look around a few moments before settling back down again.

"Is Tom going to be all right in this storm without you and Barney?" She'd feel terrible if he needed their support more than she did.

"Don't worry about it. He's usually fine when it's just rain. It's the cracks of thunder and flashes of lightning that really mess with him, making him think he's back in the war."

"But it doesn't affect you the same way?"

"No." Luke buried his hand in Barney's scruff. "Our experiences were very different. I was already in France in 1914, studying architecture. I had graduated from Harvard that spring, so I was twenty-two when the war began in Europe. I couldn't sit back and watch. I joined the French Foreign Legion as an ambulance driver."

Elsa wondered if it was typical for salvage dealers to have Harvard degrees in architecture, with studies abroad to match. But all she asked was, "Is that how you know about weak chest and lung muscles?"

He nodded. "Among other things. I got to know a lot of patients that way, checking on them as I could after delivering them to hospitals. Ol' Barney here was there, too. He could run low over the ground, carrying canteens of water around his neck to soldiers we couldn't reach yet. And he found the living among the dead, men we might have missed. Saved their lives. He saved Tom's. Likely more than once."

"Why, Barney!" Elsa cupped his chin and lifted it, noting the grey hair on his muzzle. "What a good boy you are." The dog closed his eyes and rested the weight of his head in her hand. She thought she saw him grin, and a swell of emotion clogged her throat.

Luke stroked the dog down the length of his back, scratching at the base of the tail. "After a while, I felt like I wasn't doing enough, picking up the pieces of broken men. I needed to fight the men who were breaking them in the first place. So as soon as training opened to Americans in France, I became a fighter pilot. Tom signed up to fight as soon as he could. He was seventeen. He had no idea what he was getting into."

Both of them had been so young. At seventeen, Tom wasn't a child, but he hadn't yet grown into a man. No wonder the war affected him so.

"They put him in the trenches. The heck of it is, he said he joined the fight because of me. His father—my father's valet—wrote to me, begging me to promise to keep him safe. How I was supposed to do that when we weren't in the same unit was unclear. But what could I do? Mr. Lightfoot had given his entire career to my family, and now his only son had enlisted in a horrific war because he wanted to be like me. His wife had died giving birth to Tom. So what else could I do, but promise Mr. Lightfoot that whenever it was in my power, I would keep his boy safe?"

Elsa heard in his voice the heaviness of the responsibility he'd accepted. She inhaled deeply and blew out again. "Is that a promise you're still trying to keep?"

The corner of his lips hooked his cheek. "Trying, yes. I learned not to make promises ever again, I can tell you that much. Not because I don't want to keep them, but because it's impossible to know if I can."

"He's lucky to have you in his life," Elsa said.

"I don't know about that, but we understand each other. I'm trying, at any rate."

"I know you are." She leaned her head back against the vinyl lounge chair, allowing her gaze to drift on the water lining the pool. Silver reflections blinked with every drop of rain.

"Well, have I talked enough to give you a chance to recover?" he asked.

A small laugh escaped her. She'd been trying to recover for seventeen years. But that's not what he meant. "I overdid it," she admitted, since there was no point in pretending otherwise. "I still feel winded, but at least I can talk. But my leg—" She laid a hand on her knee. The brace she wore was short enough not to show under her hem. Her first leg brace went from under her ribs to her ankle. She wouldn't go back to that. "My left leg is weak," she admitted. "Weaker than usual. And now it's pretty sore."

"When was the last time you saw a doctor about it?"

She shook her head. "I'm not going back."

The rain stopped. As quickly as it had begun, the storm relented. Light fell through the glass ceiling, fractured on palm fronds, and lay in stripes across Luke's face.

"You don't like doctors?" he asked. "Neither do I. You don't want to hear what they have to say? I get that. But sometimes we have to do hard things. If you need a certified ambulance driver to get you there, I know where you can find one."

She stared at him, surprised at the sincerity in both his expression and his words, then broke from his gaze. "Thank you, but I said I'm not going. We ought to be getting back to the mansion." She pushed herself up to stand with no incident. But when she attempted the first step with her bad leg, it buckled beneath her.

Luke caught her, holding her firmly against him. "I'll get the truck."

Elsa didn't argue with that.

CHAPTER

9

'll wait for you outside." Elsa was ready to trade the dank odor of the pool building for open air and the warmth of the returning sun.

"Sure." Luke scooped her up again, as though she were no burden at all.

"Oh! I didn't mean you had to carry me." She looped her arm around his neck anyway. The rain-dampened shirt beneath her hand clung to his muscled shoulder.

"The point of me getting the truck is so you don't have to walk and further stress your leg. Where to?" Stepping outside, he squinted in the suddenly too-bright light. "That bench near the bird feeder?"

"Yes, please." If any birds ventured out after the storm, she'd enjoy observing them there.

When they reached it, Luke set her down. "How are your lungs?"

Taking a seat, she took a deep breath. "A little better."

Barney sat on the ground beside her.

Luke nodded at the dog. "Looks like he'll stay with you while I fetch your ride."

"Will he chase away the birds?" she asked. But so what if he did? They could fly out of his reach, and they could come back. An aging war dog ought to have a little fun in his retirement. Just not with her specimens.

"He's worn out from his earlier adventure. Be good, Barn. See you soon." Rolling up his shirtsleeves, Luke turned and walked away with an enviable ease and grace of movement.

She peeled off the slicker. Closing her eyes, she relished the sound of the calming breeze through the pine needles and the black-capped chickadees in the woods. What little busybodies they were, chattering about everyone else's business.

When Elsa opened her eyes, she found Danielle standing a few yards away. She was staring at the dog.

"Would you like to pet Barney? He's very friendly."

The girl reached out, and Barney sniffed the offered hand. A smile turned her serious face pleasant. "He's very friendly," she said, repeating not just Elsa's words but her inflection as well.

"He belongs to Mr. Dupont, one of the men working at the mansion. And how is George these days?"

Danielle looked over her shoulder at the pool building. A crow stood on the porch, staring back at her while remaining a safe distance from Barney. "He's fine."

"Is that him?"

"Yes. He likes to watch and see what I do."

"You are sure that's the same crow?"

The bird flapped up and flew into the trees to perch from a branch. Danielle continued to pet Barney between the ears. "He has his own way of turning his head, and there's a bend in his tail the others don't have."

Elsa was stunned. Not only at Danielle's level of observation, but that she and George maintained some kind of relationship even outside the context of the food she left for him outside her cottage. "Ever considered a career in ornithology? The study of birds?" She was only half joking. Truly, the girl was a natural.

"That's what you do."

"Yes. Listen, Danielle. Do you hear that song? 'Chick-a-dee-dee-dee . . . chick-a-dee-dee-dee.'"

Danielle cocked her head, listening. "Yes. That's why they call the *Poecile atricapillus* a chickadee. They come to feeders but never stay and eat there. They always carry the seeds somewhere else to eat or hide away."

"That's exactly right. Did you know a single chickadee can store a thousand seeds a day as he prepares for winter? And he can remember where he hid his food six whole months later. I can't remember where I've put my handbag half the time! And those little birds—their brains are only twice the size of a pea."

Danielle came and sat by Elsa on the bench, Barney following her. "Tell me more."

Elsa smiled. The chickadee was so common, people never came to the museum asking to learn about it. But it was one of her favorite little creatures. "Listen to that song again." After a few moments, she explained, "That sound is a signal that there is a predator waiting motionless nearby. Maybe perched on the roof of the pool building or on a tree limb. Even other species listen when the chickadees signal a hawk or an owl is near. Squirrels, for example, depend on their arial warning system. The number of dees in its song communicates how dangerous it is. The more dees there are, the greater the threat."

Danielle's eyes widened. "That means the bigger the predator?"

"One would think so, but in this case, no. The smaller predators are more agile and quicker and, therefore, more dangerous than bigger, cumbersome ones. These calls from the chickadees are actually recruiting reinforcements to mob or harass the predator. Let's watch and see what happens."

Sunshine warmed Elsa as they waited in silence, alert for drama and action. Her heart beat quickly, either anticipating the scene about to unfold or still recovering from her ill-advised run. She told herself it was the former.

Soon a few chickadees swarmed together and mobbed a hawk until it gave up and flew away.

Danielle laughed. "Run off by such little things!"

Elsa laughed with her. "Their size doesn't matter when they band together with friends. That's not so different from people, right? Do you have a friend you band together with when you need help?"

"I told you. I have George."

"Oh yes, of course. But I meant of the *Homo sapien* variety."

Danielle made no reply, and Elsa decided not to press. If the girl didn't have friends her age, the last thing Elsa wanted to do was pour salt in that wound by pointing it out. Perhaps there had been other children of servants who worked here, and they moved away when Birdie died. Perhaps Danielle had lost more with the old woman's passing than Elsa had realized.

The sound of the approaching truck turned her head. It rolled to a stop, the engine cut off, and Luke hopped out and walked toward them.

"Speaking of *Homo sapiens*," Elsa said to Danielle, "this is Mr. Dupont, Barney's owner. Luke, this is Danielle Petrovic. She has a crow named George. You just missed him, but he'll be back, I'm sure."

Luke approached, and Barney ran to his side, clearly eager to be with his master again. "Nice to meet you, Danielle. You can call me Luke."

She glanced up at him but didn't shake the offered hand or meet his gaze. "What happened to your face?"

Just like that, she posed the question Elsa had been wondering but couldn't justify asking. The tone, at least, had been one of innocent curiosity, not disgust or revulsion. Still, the timing was abrupt.

"Danielle—" she began.

"It's all right," Luke assured her. "It's a fair question. It happened during the war. A wounded French soldier thought I was his enemy and struck at me with the only weapon he had left—a knife."

Elsa covered her mouth, a knot pulling tight in her chest.

"He was angry at you? He tried to kill you?" Danielle asked.

"He was afraid. He thought I was trying to kill him, and he defended himself. He was confused."

The girl stared openly at him then. "Confused," she murmured, almost as if to herself. "You weren't trying to kill him. You were not his enemy. What did you do next?"

"I took his knife away, and then I put him in the ambulance and brought him to the hospital so he could get the care he needed."

Danielle studied the grooves in his face, unflinching. When she reached up toward him, he crouched. With the frankness only a child could get away with, she touched each scar in turn. "He thought you were a hawk. And he was only one chickadee with no one to help him. He didn't know you were a chickadee, too, and that's why you came in the first place. You came to band together. That's a metaphor, what I said." A rare smile flickered.

"That's right," Luke said. "I did."

When a crow cawed from a branch overhead, Danielle patted Luke's shoulder. "Good chickadee—that's the same metaphor." She rubbed Barney's head. "Good dog—that is not a metaphor because he is really a dog." She even waved to Elsa. With that, she called to George and walked the opposite direction, the crow flying along with her.

Astonished, Elsa watched them go. "Danielle is so smart," she murmured. "I'm smitten."

"I can see why. I'm glad I got to meet her. And her crow."

Luke cracked a smile and picked up the slicker off the bench. "Shall we?"

"Let's do it." This time, Elsa insisted on simply leaning on Luke's arm as she limped to the truck, the extra time to rest having made it possible to walk without as much pain. Before she could work out how to handle the running board and climb up inside, Luke's hands came around her waist, and he lifted her up. After closing the door, he let Barney into the side of the delivery truck, tossing the slicker in, too.

Once they were driving, she said, "That was so good of you to answer her questions and let her touch your face. Did it bother you?"

"No, I'm only bothered when I think other people are. She didn't balk."

"No, she didn't." Elsa shook her head, still marveling over their exchange, and over the implications of Luke's story in particular. "The soldier struck your face three times, and still you didn't turn away from him. I find that amazing."

"I don't turn away from someone I care about, and I don't turn away from a fight. In this situation, it happened to be both." He looked her over before fixing his eyes on the narrow avenue again. "You don't have a change of clothes back at the mansion, do you?"

"Nope."

"Then you'll need to borrow some. Even if you take the next train back to the city, that's too long for you to be in wet clothes. What about Danielle's mother?"

"I'm sure she'd loan me something. I'm not ready to quit here for the day yet, and I confess that being dry would be far more comfortable than my current state." The sun had helped to dry her hair, but her dress still stuck to her skin.

Elsa directed him to the gardener's cottage, then combed her fingers through her hair. The finger waves she'd so carefully arranged this morning had disappeared, and now her natural, wild-child curls were taking over as they dried. She pursed her lips, chagrined at her disrepair.

Luke glanced at her hair and smiled. "I like it," he said. "A lot. Unless it's in architecture, perfection makes me nervous."

She laughed, genuinely amused that the standard she strived in vain to achieve was the thing he preferred to avoid. "Then you'll feel perfectly at ease around me."

"More and more," he said, then slowed the truck to a stop outside Tatiana's cottage.

The gardener must have heard them coming because she was out on the porch before Luke had even come around to Elsa's side of the vehicle and helped her down.

"Why, Elsa!" Tatiana exclaimed. "Don't tell me you were caught in that storm. You'll catch your death of cold!"

"That is the general consensus." Smiling, Elsa introduced Luke and Barney to Tatiana and mentioned they'd just met with Danielle and George, as well.

"You simply must come in and trade those wet things for something dry. That is, if you don't mind wearing an old woman's practical clothing. In this case, it isn't style that matters."

Elsa agreed. "I'd be most grateful to borrow something, if you can spare it."

"Of course. Come in, come in, all three of you. Now, I wasn't expecting company, but you remember what I said last time you were here, don't you?"

"That on my second visit, I'm family?"

Tatiana grinned. Rust-streaked iron grey hair sagged in a knot at her neck. "Exactly. That means it's all right I didn't tidy up for your visit." She glanced at Luke and Barney. "If you're with her, let's call you family, too, by extension, how's that?"

"Makes sense to me. But Barney will stay on the porch." The dog shook, spraying rainwater from his fur, then sat at his master's command. Luke offered his arm, inviting Elsa to lean on him as they entered the cottage.

Concern thatched Tatiana's brow, suggesting she'd noticed that Elsa's limp was worse today. Or maybe she'd seen Elsa cringe with the pain, though she'd tried hard not to. "Well, some days these old bones don't behave, either. You hang on to me, dear, and we'll be a matched pair all the way into the bedroom." Her warm laughter was a balm to Elsa's soul. In truth, Tatiana's bones couldn't be all that old, despite the joke, which made the stiffness in her joints all the more troubling.

Elsa hobbled off with her hostess through the sitting room. On her way, she counted three pots on the floor, collecting water from leaks in the roof, and one male canary.

"Well, hello, little one!" Pausing at his cage, Elsa spoke to the small yellow bird, who gave a bright, cheerful trill in reply.

"Meet Sunny," Tatiana told her. "He belonged to Mrs. Van Tessel, but she asked me to take care of him several months before she passed."

"Really?" Elsa and Sunny eyed each other. "I imagine he was good company for her in that big house."

"Oh, he was indeed. She was sad to part with him, but her memory was slipping near the end. She kept forgetting to clean out his cage, and whenever it got dirty, he got sick. He wheezed and squeaked and had a hard time breathing."

Elsa nodded. "Yes, canaries can get asthma from unclean sur-roundings."

"Didn't Mrs. Van Tessel have a servant to do that for her?" Luke asked.

"She let most of her staff go in that last year." Tatiana went to a small bookcase and pulled a sheet from inside one of the books. "The one maid she kept had an allergy to little Sunny, so Mrs. Van Tessel took over the duty. At least, as far as she was able to. The poor dear. I can't count how many times she came to me in the garden, telling me Sunny was sick. I came in with her each time and found the same cause, and then went in and cleaned it all up myself. At last, she decided she couldn't trust herself to keep up his care and asked if I would take him. It hurt her to do that, but she'd rather be lonely than cause him to suffer. She wrote this and bade me keep it here for her to read if she came to visit later."

Elsa accepted the note, aware of Luke standing near and reading over her shoulder. The handwriting matched Birdie's entries in the field notebooks and diaries.

Now, Birdie, this is Birdie. Take a deep breath, and calm down. You may not understand why Sunny is here with Tatiana instead of back in the parlor with you, but he belongs here now. You kept forgetting to clean his cage, and he kept getting sick. He's well taken care of now, and you can visit him whenever you like. But this is his home, for his own good. Tatiana and Danielle are loving and capable stewards.

"And did she visit him here?" Luke asked. His gaze rested on the little bird, his throat puffing out in rhythmic song.

"Many times." Tatiana's eyes glassed over. "She wrote herself a similar letter to read upon waking every morning, telling her where Sunny was. Otherwise, she'd be so upset to find him missing. Either Danielle or I would go check on her during breakfast and escort her here if she wanted to come. And then one day, it was like she was meeting Sunny for the first time. She hadn't remembered he'd ever been hers."

Elsa shook her head. "I had no idea her memory had worsened to such a degree. That must have been painful to watch. Will you continue to keep Sunny?"

"Oh my, yes." The woman returned the letter to its place on the bookshelf. "Mrs. Van Tessel was so good to my family for so many years. It's no trouble at all to care for her bird. And now, dear, it's high time we take care of you!"

Elsa followed her into the bedroom while Luke waited in the sitting room. "Here you are." Tatiana laid out a calico dress that looked to be her Sunday best. The tie around the waist meant it would fit Elsa fine. "Take your time, now. Leave your dress with me, and I'll hang it on the line outside. It'll give you a reason to come back for it later." She winked.

"My reason is you, Tatiana."

The woman threw her arms around Elsa in a quick embrace. Laughing, Elsa pulled back. "Now you're wet, too!"

"Pish! Small price to pay." Tatiana left, shutting the door behind her.

A breeze swirled through a crack between the window and its pane, tickling the hairs on Elsa's neck. Paper curled away from the wall in the corners. But the dress on the bed was clean and smelled of lavender sachet, likely made from the lavender Tatiana grew on the grounds. Easing onto the edge of the bed, Elsa began changing into it. Her shoes were soaked, but she would wait until she was back at the mansion to take them off and let them dry.

Luke's low voice sounded through the door, but she couldn't make out the words. Then the sound of footfalls on the roof, followed by pounding, told the tale.

With a satisfied sigh, Elsa finished tying the belt about her waist and made her way, unsupported, out of the room. The pain was deep and throbbing, but she had to manage it. She couldn't rely on a kind soul to escort her until she recovered, it simply wasn't practical. Favoring her bad leg, she brought her wet dress outside and paused to lean on the porch railing.

Tatiana stood in the yard, watching the roof. "I'm to catch him if he falls," she said.

"So he can flatten you?" Elsa laughed.

"Good point." She cupped a hand to her mouth and called up, "You're on your own, dear!" With mirth in her voice, she clapped her hands in Elsa's direction. "Throw it here, child! No sense in wasting steps, eh?"

After wadding up her dress into a sodden ball, Elsa threw it at Tatiana, who then went only a few steps to hang it on the line, whistling as she did so. If joy was contagious, Elsa felt herself catching it from this woman, who had burrowed into Elsa's heart. Lowering herself into a rocker, Elsa considered the puzzle that was the mother and daughter Petrovic. In many ways, Tatiana had the spunk and spirit of a much younger woman, while Danielle seemed wise beyond her years. Elsa would miss them both once her project here was completed.

"Just a few more minutes," Luke called from the roof. "Do you mind waiting?"

"No," Elsa called back. "I prefer it."

Chuckling, Tatiana joined her on the porch, while Barney stayed outside in the sun, vigilant for his master's welfare. "My, that dress looks fetching on you. You have no idea what a treat it is to have you here. And I'm not saying that because Luke is fixing the roof."

"Seeing you twice in one day *is* a treat." But with the increased weakness in her leg, Elsa wasn't sure when she'd make the hike here from the mansion next. "Do you ever come up to the mansion?"

"On occasion."

"Look for me next time you do. I'm always ready for a visit from you and Danielle." If Elsa spent an hour visiting with the Petrovics, she would simply stay that much later another day. Besides, she was already working on the notebooks at home, as well. Spending time with people was too important to skip.

Tatiana assured her she'd come when she could.

"I've been asking around and looking for the aviary," Elsa told her. "I'm sorry to say I haven't turned up any clues."

Tatiana clasped her hand. "It's good of you to try. I can't say I'm surprised, though. Such an extravagant gift for Danielle was scarcely to be believed." She shrugged. "The larger concern by far is whether we'll be allowed to remain in our home. Moving would be such a challenge for my girl."

"I can imagine."

A sigh feathered Tatiana's lips. "Whatever you're imagining, dear, imagine it ten times worse."

"Pardon me?"

"Danielle has always been a special child. Change is excruciating for her. She has ordered her world around her just so, and when something doesn't go the way she wants or expects it to, she . . ." Tatiana shook her head. "She has a hard time coping. It takes much effort to adjust, and that is putting it mildly. That's why I haven't told her there's a good chance we'll have to move. I don't want to upset her yet if there's any hope we can find a way to stay." But her voice held little hope indeed. "I hope to hear back from the executor any day now."

"That makes sense," Elsa said, wishing she could encourage her more. "The executor may have good news for you, after all." And if he didn't, it would be even more important to find that aviary.

Luke climbed down the ladder, hammer hooked through a loop in a short apron tied about his waist. A handful of shingles poked out the top of the apron pocket.

"You happened to have all that in the truck?" Elsa asked.

"No self-respecting salvage dealer goes anywhere without his toolbox and extra supplies. The shingles are a bonus, though. I had these left over from another job Tom and I did on the side. So they don't match your originals up there." He wiped his forearm across his brow. "It may not look pretty, but it gets the job done."

"A roof that doesn't leak is a beautiful thing no matter what it looks like." Beaming, Tatiana rose and stretched out her hand to shake his. "I thank you. Mrs. Van Tessel had a fellow in her employ to do these kinds of repairs, but when he left, she decided it best not to hire another in his place. Finances were lean after the master died. Those of us who stayed were willing to tighten our belts to help her make ends meet on the estate. We stayed for the missus and the land, not for the pay."

"Do you know why Mrs. Van Tessel didn't sell some of her paintings instead of bequeathing them to museums?" Luke asked the other question burning in Elsa's mind.

"Oh, she did. She sold the ones her husband preferred. The ones she kept meant too much to her to even consider parting with," Tatiana explained, then added, "I've kept you too long, I suspect."

Luke was still in his wet clothes, after all, and they both had more work to be doing at the mansion.

"Thank you for the dry clothes, Tatiana." Elsa pushed carefully out of the rocker and accepted Luke's support to help her down the stairs. "We'll visit again soon, all right?"

"I do hope so." Tatiana smiled, and her eyes pinched at the corners. "Thank you all for making this a lovely day."

Elsa squeezed her hand in parting.

At the end of the day, Luke beckoned Elsa toward the truck. "How about we give you a lift?"

"To the train station? That would be great, if you don't mind. I don't know why the taxi I requested this morning hasn't come." She'd arranged for him to arrive an hour ago. At least she'd gotten more work done while she waited.

"We can do better than that. You're going our way. We offer door to door service. You wouldn't have to walk more than the distance from the curb to your building, and bingo, you're home."

Tom finished loading something into the back of the truck and slammed the doors shut before coming around to join her and Luke. Barney trotted alongside him.

"I would have offered last week, too," Luke went on, "but you didn't know us then. I figured you'd be too smart to get into a delivery truck with two men you'd only just met."

"Especially when one of us looks like him," Tom ribbed Luke, who seemed to take it in stride.

Elsa returned their smiles. By her count, today marked only the fourth day they'd all been at Elmhurst together. She still didn't know them well, yet, but she'd like the chance to change that.

As she peered through the window at the back seat, Barney jumped through the side door and stretched out on it, ears perked up, as if asking who would sit with him. She chuckled. "Are you asking me to ride in the back of your truck with that hairy, bright-eyed thief? For twenty-four miles?" She was only half teasing. "Actually, I may warm up to him yet. But I admit to being prone to motion sickness."

In answer, Tom climbed in and sat next to the dog, then patted the empty seat in front of him. "All yours, Elsa. Let's shake a leg, huh?"

She looked from him and Barney to Luke and was strangely touched by this threesome who had been through so much together and now made room for her. She could likely handle travel by train and taxi back to the Beresford even after wearing herself out today, but these men offered more than a simple mode of transit.

"I'd be foolish to refuse time spent in pleasant company," she said. "I accept. Thank you."

"Who said anything about it being pleasant?" Tom joked.

But it absolutely was. The ride home was peppered with talk of work at Elmhurst, then ventured to stories of Barney's past

adventures at other estates. She loved seeing the unlikely camaraderie between these two men.

"I never asked how inconvenient it will be for you to bring
me to the Beresford," Elsa said. "Do either of you live anywhere
near the Upper West Side?"

"We live *in* the Upper West Side," Luke said, "which means
we're practically neighbors."

Tom named a corner only a handful of blocks from the Beresford.

"That area is full of brownstones from the last century, isn't
it? What a beautiful area." Elsa remembered the treelined streets
and uniform sandstone rowhouses.

"Some parts are more beautiful than others these days,"
Luke admitted. "In fact, the place we live in now had fallen
into disrepair long before it went into foreclosure. Soon after
I returned from war, my father heard about it from one of his
real estate contacts and sent me out there to salvage for his
warehouse."

"The real estate agent didn't mind you tearing out the best
pieces?" Elsa asked. "Wouldn't that make it harder to sell?"

Luke shook his head. "Believe me, no one was going to buy
this place."

"No one but Luke," Tom said on a laugh.

A smile curled on Luke's face. "Bought it for a song. My father
wasn't too happy when I told him, either. He'd been planning
to get some original mantels, banisters, and paneled doors.
He could have made a lot of money on those if I had ripped
them out of the house as I'd been tasked to do. But I couldn't
stand the idea of gutting the old dame even further. She'd been
ill-used for years, and I knew I could fix her up, give her back
her dignity."

Tom leaned forward from the back seat. "And?"

Luke cast him a sidelong glance over his shoulder. "And I

also couldn't stand the idea of living with my parents again in their Gramercy Park home. I had been on my own for years and couldn't go back."

Elsa could understand that. Living in one's childhood home as an adult—especially after experiencing independence for years—would be a huge adjustment.

She angled in her seat to look at Tom. "You live near Luke?"

"Very." He grinned. "We're housemates. He'd already moved in by the time I got back from Europe, and he offered me a place. I couldn't pay much for rent, but he said that was no problem as long as I pitched in to help him fix the place up. I didn't know it at the time, but it turned out to be training for the kind of work I do for his father's company now. Sure kept me busy and worn out."

Luke squinted through the windscreen at the lowering sun. "All part of the plan."

His tone was light, but Elsa believed there had been purpose in that plan, indeed. Not only had Luke given the young veteran a place to land, but he'd given him work. All-consuming, virtually never-ending work that yielded tangible results, job training, a shared goal, and a way to stop the tremors, which she'd noticed he suffered from only when his hands were idle.

"Come to think of it, he *still* keeps me busy and worn out." With a crooked smile, Tom lit a cigarette.

The smell sent Elsa's stomach churning. "Oh, I'm sorry, Tom, but would you mind not smoking until after you drop me off? The smoke will make me carsick for sure."

He promptly put it out. "No problem."

Luke raised an eyebrow at her. "He doesn't obey me half so well."

"You don't ask nearly so nice!" Tom piped up from the back-seat. Barney snored beside him.

Ignoring the jibe, Luke said, "Say, you should ride along more often. How's tomorrow?"

"Tomorrow I work at the museum. But Wednesday?"

"Wednesday," he agreed. "And every day after that you need it."

Nodding, Elsa smiled at the road ahead.

CHAPTER

Coffee burned Elsa's throat on its way down, but she barely even noticed. She sat at the writing desk in the parlor of her apartment with only the ticking clock and the soft rush of traffic outside to fill the predawn quiet. Spread before her was the folder of papers she'd brought home from Linus's secret office yesterday. Securely packaged in a box on the corner of the desk was the Spix's macaw.

Leaning back in her chair, Elsa cupped her hands around the mug and sipped. Yesterday afternoon, she'd used a fingernail file and buffer to groom the blue parrot's feathers after its misadventure in Barney's mouth. Wesley and Jane had returned after the storm and noticed her change of attire. They'd been shocked she would borrow "that gardener's shabby dress" but had left her in the dining hall after that, where Crawford finished packing the china.

Elsa glanced at the macaw again, her pulse fluttering with the anticipation of presenting it to the museum. This bird and its significance, she understood.

She could not say the same about the documents in Linus's folder.

An article from the Carnegie Station for Experimental Evolution warned of the dangers of the recessive trait of the feeble-minded.

Another article tucked between advertisements for women's footwear was headlined "New Aristocracy Will Be 'Human Thoroughbreds.'" This was eugenics, the field Mr. Spalding was in at the Eugenics Records Office on Long Island. Elsa flipped to another paper and found a drawing of a tree emblazoned with the words "Eugenics Is the Self Direction of Human Evolution." At the base of the page, each tree root was labeled with a different branch of study. The largest roots supporting the eugenics tree were genetics, anthropology, statistics, biography, and genealogy. Other roots were labeled politics and law.

Elsa wondered if Mr. Spalding inherited his interest from his uncle Linus or if it was the other way around.

After swallowing more coffee, she shifted the documents and found papers full of family trees, but not like any she'd seen before. The top halves of each page were designated *Normal Line* and *Degenerate Line*, and at the bottom were totals for both.

Elsa took off her glasses and squinted to read the fine print. Smaller charts identified in each category the number of people in that line who were criminal, alcoholic, grossly immoral, feeble-minded, epileptic, insane, neurotic, died in infancy, or died young. The normal line produced a far smaller number of each than the degenerate line.

Coffee souring in her stomach, Elsa cleaned her glasses on a handkerchief before replacing them. As she browsed the files, it didn't take long to find a pamphlet with the solution for better humans: careful and deliberate marriages, sterilization of society's undesirables, and new immigration laws. "If we can breed perfection into horses, pigs, and cows," the pamphlet quipped, "why leave human evolution to chance?" Paper-clipped behind that literature was a stack of flyers from state fairs advertising Better Babies contests.

"Good morning!"

Elsa startled at her roommate's greeting as if she'd been suddenly pulled from a deep sleep. If only she'd been dreaming.

"You're up early." Ivy yawned, pushing her hair behind one ear. She'd already washed and dressed for work, and Elsa hadn't registered a single sound.

"I was too tired last night to look at what I'd brought home from the mansion, and too curious not to dive into it before work today. Listen, have you ever heard of Better Babies contests? At state fairs?"

Frowning, Ivy grabbed a mug and poured herself coffee before bringing it to the sofa in the parlor. She curled her legs beneath her and tasted the brew before responding. "I've been to a few state fairs but never saw that in my life. Is that some kind of eugenics thing?"

Elsa nodded, then began reading from the file. "'A physician scores a baby in precisely the same way as a judge of experience in livestock scores cattle. . . . It is first necessary to establish a standard and then to compare each entry or specimen with what is known as a one hundred percent, or perfect, product.'" A chill raced down her spine.

"A 'specimen' that is a 'perfect product'? Are we sure they're talking about human beings here?" asked Ivy. "And whose standard are they using, and how did they choose it?"

Elsa turned her chair around so she could fully face her friend. "According to this, infants are lined up for judging, and then doctors and nurses record each one's weight, chest circumference, and mental capacity—although how you do that with babies, I couldn't guess."

"I'm sure all the babies loved strangers doing that."

"Babies too shy to participate in the tests lose points," Elsa paraphrased.

Ivy's eyebrows disappeared behind her bangs. "You have got to be kidding me."

Elsa passed her the document. "Look, there's even a score-card printed in *Woman's Home Companion* magazine so everyone can judge babies on their own." She waited while Ivy read the parameters. Official judges used a thousand-point scale, with one hundred points for physical measurements, two hundred for mental and psychological fitness, and the rest for physical appearance. Winners at state fairs were awarded silver trophies.

"This is a scream," Ivy declared. "Did you read this part? It says, 'Underneath the inviting charm of the idea is a serious scientific purpose — healthy babies, standardized babies, and always, year after year, Better Babies.' And then there's something about Better Babies leading to Fitter Families."

"Oh, good, so you can enter your entire family into the live-stock competition, is that it?"

"That's the idea." Ivy laughed and handed it back to her.

Elsa didn't feel like laughing. She felt like she was going to be sick.

"Come on, let's hit the dining room before the breakfast crowd. Want to?" Ivy slipped her feet into her pumps.

"You go on ahead," Elsa told her. "Bring me back a blueberry muffin and cheese, though, would you?" She didn't want to admit that her interest in these files wasn't the only reason she wasn't up for breakfast today. Sparing herself the jaunt to the dining room may make the walk to work a little easier.

"You got it." Ivy left the room.

Standing, Elsa kneaded her fists into the small of her back, stretched her leg, then went to refill her coffee, all the while try-ing not to think of how she might score in a contest devoted to the perfect human product.

She shuddered.

Back at the desk, she opened the curtains before sitting again. Light spilled through the window and landed on the folders Linus had been hiding from his wife.

Elsa moved the folder from the bottom of the stack to the top and opened it to find several blank forms titled *Individual Analysis Card*. They were two-sided, with room to record medical history and physical, mental, and temperamental traits. The last section was for the description of physical appearance.

Odd.

Linus van Tessel had been an explorer and collector in his prime, not a doctor or researcher—as far as Elsa knew, at any rate. Was eugenics a hobby he picked up when he was too old to gallivant about the globe? Maybe the Eugenics Records Office, or ERO, had recruited him to gather information for their files.

With his bent toward capturing and studying birds, he had an obvious affinity for biology, and she'd seen a copy of Darwin's *On the Origin of Species* in that secret den. Perhaps his interests included anthropology, too.

Elsa fanned through the blank forms until she saw one with fields filled in. At the top of the page, Linus had written "my copy," which she could only assume meant that he'd filled in another one just like it and submitted it to the ERO. Before she had time to wonder why he'd complete one for himself, she saw the name: Danielle Petrovic.

Elsa skimmed over the first couple of sections, which contained her basic information, noting that her parents were listed as "Croatian with unknown pedigrees" and that "frequent earaches" and "visual avoidance" were recorded. Under the *Mental* and *Temperament* headings, the form contained lists of adjectives that the recorder was meant to either cross out if they did not apply to the individual or underscore if they did. But it was Linus's handwritten comments that stopped her.

*Child cannot speak at the age of nearly four years old. Fix-
ates on certain objects she must have with her at all times. Subject is painfully shy and quiet but also demonstrates episodes of
manic outbursts during which she screams, hits her head, pulls
her hair, makes repeated inhuman noises, or sustains a groan
for an inordinate length of time. She will kick and bite and has
struck her own parents with no reasonable provocation.*

*Subject demonstrates complete lack of intelligence and in-
ability to learn. Feebleminded at best, with a likely trajectory
toward insanity or even criminality, given subject's reaction to
not getting her own way.*

Burden on society.

Mother not likely to bear more children given her age.

Elsa sat back, stunned, and read the file one more time. Danielle, a burden? What did that mean, exactly? What had been
Linus's intention when he completed this form and, presumably,
sent a copy to the ERO?

Danielle was not a typical child. Anyone would notice that
during their first interactions with her. And even Tatiana had said
her younger years had been difficult and admitted she wouldn't
speak to anyone aside from her and Birdie until sometime after
she turned four. But there was no way she could be called feeble-
minded now. She was as sharp as a hatpin. So what if her interests
were narrow? And as for wanting things to go her own way, didn't
that describe all children?

Elsa glanced at the date on the form and wondered if Linus had
filled out another one later to better reflect who Danielle was, if
indeed that could be done in a reduction of phrases and multiple
choices. But no other forms in the folder carried Danielle's name.

The one on the bottom, however, held that of Sarah van Tessel,
the baby he didn't want her own mother to see.

Goosebumps lifted on Elsa's skin. Almost afraid of what she

would learn, she read each line slowly. Under *Individual History*, Linus noted that Sarah's mother, Bernadette van Tessel, had "physical defects in her family lineage, undisclosed at time of marriage." The baby's father owned a perfect pedigree.

Of course he did.

A note referenced Linus's family tree, charted in a different document.

Elsa kept reading Sarah's card. Under *Physical*, he'd written

Born with a cleft lip and palate.
Surgery unsuccessful.
Died in infancy.

The poor baby. Poor Birdie. Elsa's vision blurred as she considered the unspoken depth of grief carried between such short lines. Linus had written this of his own child years after Sarah had lived and died, but Elsa still wondered how it had felt for him to record it so clinically.

The sections for mental and temperament observations were blank. But at the bottom, two photographs had been affixed at their corners, showing Sarah only from her nose to mouth. All they'd captured was the "defect," and nothing else about this little soul, so precious to her mother, was preserved or remarked upon.

A final note at the bottom of the form read, "With proven defects in her history, the mother did not bear children again."

By the time Ivy returned with the promised breakfast, Elsa's appetite had vanished.

———○———

The tenth of a mile walk between her apartment and the museum took Elsa a little longer than usual, but because she and Ivy left early, her pace hadn't made them late.

Soon after Elsa settled into her office, Mr. Chapman called for a special, unscheduled meeting of the ornithology department. Since she hadn't had a chance to give him the good news about the Spix's macaw, she brought the box to the conference room.

She recognized Mr. Griscom, of course, whose guidebook for skinning and stuffing birds had kept ambitious patrons busy sending her their specimens. There was Dr. Murphy, who was usually working on his monograph of the marine birds of South America. Beside him sat Mr. Miller, who studied the internal workings of all birds in the flesh they received before he dissected them, then passed them on to Elsa to skin and stuff. Two other men less familiar to Elsa were there as well.

"I suppose you can guess why I've called you in this morning." Mr. Chapman beamed. "Mr. William Rockefeller and Mr. Raymond Potter have returned from their expedition to Hudson Bay. I've invited them to show us the specimens they are most excited about and share with us any new observations about their behavior and habitat."

Elsa added her greetings to the masculine rumble of voices around the table. The museum sponsored so many expeditions all over the world, she could barely keep them straight.

Grateful to be seated after the walk to work, she focused on breathing deeply while she listened. Mr. Rockefeller and Mr. Potter took turns presenting trays of bird skins yet to be stuffed.

"Excellent, gentlemen." Mr. Chapman stood at the conclusion of their presentation. "The specimens of the more northern breeding birds make an especially desirable addition to our collections, which have been, up until now, weak in the breeding plumages."

Mr. Potter smoothed down the tie behind his vest. "Thank you, Frank. I'd love to know what I've missed since we left in May. What other exciting acquisitions does the museum have now?"

Sensing the perfect opportunity, Elsa removed the box from her satchel and set it on the table in front of her, waiting while Mr. Chapman described recent gifts of a one-wattled cassowary from a generous patron and several king and Galapagos penguins that died in the New York Zoological Society aviaries.

"Marvelous!" Mr. Potter declared. "And dare I ask what treasure lies in this little lady's box? Something other than a pair of charming slippers, I hope?"

Elsa smiled when the rest of the men laughed. "I've brought it in to show Mr. Chapman, but I think you'll all be interested, as well. May I?"

Mr. Chapman nodded. "By all means."

After lifting the lid with gloved hands, she brought out the bird and removed the paper cone she'd fashioned around it, then held it up for all to see. "*Cyanopsitta spixii*. Our first Spix's macaw, the rarest macaw in the world."

Mr. Potter gaped. "A hyacinth macaw, surely."

"The hyacinth is more than twice the size of Spix's," Elsa corrected him. "And see the distinctive bare areas of greyish-black facial patches around the eyes, the cere, and the upper cheeks on this one? Hyacinth macaws are also a more royal blue, all one color." The macaw she held had a grey head with plumage of varying shades of blue.

"She's right," Mr. Chapman said. "Well done, Miss Reisner, this is a most desirable addition to our collection, indeed. I see his mount is broken, but the Department of Preparation can fix that for us. If you would deliver it to them, let them know I'll come by later with more complete instructions on how to incorporate this magnificent creature into the Birds of the World Hall."

"Where on earth did you find it?" Mr. Griscom wanted to know.

"Behind a hatbox in Bernadette van Tessel's dressing room."

After a beat of silence, the table erupted in laughter. Mr. Potter wiped at his eyes. "So you've been on an adventurous expedition of your own, have you? All the way to Tarrytown? Well, good. Let the men do the real exploring while you clean out closets on behalf of the museum."

Elsa's face burned with irritation. Why had she phrased her find that way?

"Mrs. Van Tessel bequeathed hundreds of birds to the museum," Mr. Chapman added. "Miss Reisner is performing a valuable service by sorting through and cataloging them for us. You know our collections are filled with specimens that come from all kinds of sources. I wouldn't care if she'd found this bird in a nursery wearing a bonnet and doll clothes. The important thing is that, thanks to Miss Reisner's work, we now have our first specimen of this elusive, almost mythical, macaw."

Elsa sent him a grateful smile, but her ire had not yet receded. She left before she said something she'd regret.

Elsa's breath came in hard, shallow sips as she entered the new Asiatic Hall, temporarily used by the Department of Preparation. She told herself her elevated pulse was due solely to what had transpired during the meeting and had nothing to do with the walk to get here.

Adjusting the strap of her satchel, she paused inside the hall to steady herself. Whatever the reason, it wouldn't do to be out of breath when making her request with one of the preparators. Natural light filled the long space from several floor-to-ceiling windows. Four men in neckties and white coats worked on separate projects. One carved a window screen to look like a tangle of bamboo stalks. Two others bent over tables absorbed in tasks she couldn't see. On the opposite side of the room, another painted a diorama to resemble a rolling savanna covered by thin woodland and scrub. Perhaps it was the habitat for the group of antelope staring at her from atop their wooden platform.

She looked again at the painter, whose back was turned to her, and smiled. It had to be Archer.

As she neared him, he faced her, his expression changing from one of deep concentration to one of pleasant surprise. "Fancy meeting you here." He deposited his paintbrush in a glass on a stand that held his palette of paints.

"This looks wonderful." Elsa nodded at the diorama, and he thanked her. "I'm here to drop off a Spix's macaw that needs a new mount. Mr. Chapman will visit later with instructions. For now, where should I put him?"

"Ah! From Elmhurst? That place holds untold treasures." He beckoned her to follow him, and she did so, happy to share this with her friend.

When they reached a long table, Archer cleared off a space. "Set him here for now. I'll be sure to tell Mr. Knopf as soon as I see him."

Thanking him, she pulled the box from her satchel. Linus's folders came with it, spilling all over the floor.

"I've got it." Archer took a knee to gather the documents back into the folders. "What's all this?"

Elsa set the box on the table and told him. "We found them in a secret office off the library, which I think must have been used for the Underground Railroad."

"Really? Incredible. I've got to see that house for myself some-time." Turning his attention back to the papers, he pulled out a program. "I remember this. You hadn't started working here yet, but it was a big deal." He passed her the papers.

The Second International Exhibition of Eugenics
Held September 22 to October 22, 1921, in connection with the
Second International Congress of Eugenics
in the
American Museum of Natural History, New York

Includes an account of the organization of the exhibition,
the classification of the exhibits, the list of exhibitors,
and a catalog and description of the exhibits.

Elsa flipped through the pages but quickly decided it warranted attention she couldn't give it now. Instead, she slipped it inside the folder Archer handed her and tucked everything back into her satchel. "Did you go?"

Archer rubbed a fleck of paint from his thumbnail. "I helped get the Forestry Hall ready for special exhibits of eugenics and allied sciences. You know those glass cases in the sixteen alcoves along the central corridor? We covered those up with panels and grey cloth as a backdrop for the temporary displays. I also worked in the Hall of the Age of Man, getting the space ready for exhibitors from all over the world."

"What did you think?"

He grinned. "I thought it was an awful lot of work for just one month."

Elsa swatted his arm. "That's not what I meant. Did you read the exhibits or just prep the space for them? And if you read them, what did you think?" She leaned a hip against the table, easing the pressure off her leg.

"Sure, I read some." He shrugged. "I'm no anthropologist, but it makes sense. I mean, if what they say is true, the rate of madness is outpacing the birthrate of the general population. And if we can take steps to slow down or halt the production of degenerates altogether, why wouldn't we? Those who don't contribute to society are a burden on the rest of us."

Elsa considered asking what constituted a contribution to society, but that conversation was too big for the brief moment they had. "Well, your paint is drying, and Mr. Miller is waiting for me, so I'll let you go."

Lifting the box's lid, Archer peeked inside the paper cone and whistled low. "That's a beautiful bird, Elsa."

She smiled in agreement. "This may be the rarest discovery I make at Elmhurst, or anywhere else for that matter. Although, I'm still keeping a lookout for that Eurasian eagle-owl at the park. It would be amazing to see Zeus in nature—but also a little bit like cheating to simply find him in Central Park. Spotting a zoo animal on the other side of its cage isn't much of an accomplishment."

Archer chuckled. "Speaking of rare and valuable discoveries, did you find the aviary yet? It has stiff competition, but it might beat the macaw and the owl if you find it."

"Oh." Elsa adjusted her glasses. "No, I'm no closer on that score, despite being more determined than ever." She started back through the Asiatic Hall, and he walked with her. "By the way, how did it go with Percy Saturday night?"

A frown flickered over Archer's brow. "Saturday?"

"When I saw you at work Friday morning, you mentioned you planned to spend time with him Saturday evening in an attempt to dissuade him from gambling. Did you steer him back on the straight and narrow?"

"Ah." He stopped at the diorama he'd been painting and retrieved the paintbrush from the cup. "Percy isn't a bad egg, but he is a hard one to crack. If he's just lost a game, he's desperate to win the next to break even. If he wins, he thinks he's on a lucky streak and doesn't want to quit. It's a vicious cycle."

"So don't let him anywhere near the gaming halls," Elsa said. "If you can't find a suitable distraction in New York, you won't find one anywhere."

"Ziegfeld's Follies ought to do nicely. Want to come?"

The Follies were certainly distracting. Ladies in huge feather headdresses and sequined costumes performed choreographed routines in fantastic sets to tunes like "We're Cleaning Up Broadway." It was all a bit too showy for Elsa's taste, and she told him so. "But you and Percy should do whatever you want," she added. She'd always suspected the Follies appealed more to men, anyway, with all those showgirls on stage.

"Coney Island, then." Archer smiled. "How about it?"

"Go ahead. But I'm pretty sure Coney Island has its own gambling dens." It had everything else, from rides to sideshows and burlesque girls to the famous beachside boardwalk.

"So come with us, you and your roommate. Ivy likes hot dogs so much, I'm sure she's a fan of Nathan's on the boardwalk and would jump at another chance to win Percy over to frankfurter fandom. You girls will be our better angels, all right? Please? Say yes."

"I'll think about it." The outing sounded fun but would involve a lot of walking.

"Think fast, would you? The amusement parks are only open until Labor Day weekend and then they shut down for the season, and there goes our biggest distractions. Savvy?"

Turning from his entreaty, she limped toward the elevators.

"Hey." Archer tugged her elbow from behind, pulling her a fraction off balance. He pointed to her left knee. "If that's what you're worried about, they have wicker rolling chairs there. We could take turns pushing you."

Elsa's mouth went dry. She remembered her parents pushing her in one of those chairs and could still feel the shame of it. She would not do that again. "No," she managed to say. "If I go, I won't be a burden."

CHAPTER

11

TARRYTOWN
WEDNESDAY, SEPTEMBER 1, 1926

Elsa wasn't surprised that Luke wanted to drive her directly to Tatiana's cottage this morning since she wanted to return the borrowed dress. What she hadn't expected was for the errand to turn into a social call that included Luke and Tom, too.

She ought to have, though. Tatiana was the most hospitable woman she'd ever met. And probably one of the loneliest.

"One of the Spaldings will arrive any moment to unlock the house, and then you'll be off to work," the older woman said. "But you might as well wait here with a cup of coffee rather than sit in your truck after driving all the way from the city."

"Can't argue with that." Luke turned off the engine. "I noticed ours is the first vehicle here." He checked his watch. "It's a quarter to eight. Unless they arrive earlier than expected, too, I'd say we have at least fifteen minutes. We made good time this morning."

The men and Barney exited the truck, and Tatiana warmly welcomed Tom, the newcomer. Danielle left her tray of buttons on the porch to pet the dog's soft fur. What an interesting, beautiful group of people Elsa had found herself among. Birds of a feather may flock together, but each one here was wonderfully distinct, and they flocked together just fine.

Their fifteen-minute coffee date beneath the ash tree stretched to twenty minutes when no Spalding came, then twenty-five, and no one seemed to mind. The extra time gave Elsa a chance to witness George drop off a gift on the porch railing. Danielle, who had gone back to her button sorting, held it up, announcing it was a broken piece of a pocket watch chain.

When the crow flapped away, Elsa turned her attention back to Tatiana. "Would you tell us the story of how you and your husband came to work here?"

"That old tale?" She shook her head but looked pleased to have been asked.

"I'd like to hear it, too," Luke said, and Tom nodded his agreement.

Tatiana took another sip of coffee. "Actually, it was Mrs. Van Tessel's idea."

When Elsa gaped, the woman chuckled, then continued. "Thirty years ago, Mr. and Mrs. Van Tessel had been touring the Austro-Hungarian Empire together. He was hunting for relics to add to his collection. When they visited the Franciscan monastery in Dubrovnik, she fell in love with the gardens there. She insisted upon meeting the head groundskeeper to pay him her compliments personally. That groundskeeper was my husband."

"Was he a monk at the time?" Tom asked.

"Oh no, we had been married five years already. Certainly monks helped on the grounds, but the monastery employed outside workers, too. I was present for that first meeting with the Van Tessels and still remember her lavish praise."

Luke asked if she knew English already or if there had been a translator.

"I knew enough to understand the gist," Tatiana explained. "We had been studying it with the help of a fellow gardener from

England. We loved the work at the monastery, but there was so much political and economic upheaval during that time in our country. We both wanted to be ready if an opportunity ever came to immigrate to America. We wanted to live in a place with more stability, especially if God ever blessed us with children."

With gently prompting questions, she continued the story. Mrs. Van Tessel had been absolutely charmed by the Petrovics. Tatiana was twenty-five years old, her husband ten years her senior. He'd been the son of the master groundskeeper at the monastery, so he had grown up learning the skills and catching the passion for it. A few days later, Mr. Van Tessel concluded his business at the monastery by asking the Petrovics to come work wonders at his own New York estate. He pointed out that New York and Croatia shared a similar latitude on the globe, so the climates should also be similar. The Petrovics didn't hesitate to accept.

"I always suspected Mrs. Van Tessel was behind that offer," Tatiana added. "But clearly Mr. Van Tessel admired my husband's work on the monastery grounds, as well, and wanted his expertise in his own employ. Mr. Van Tessel took care of everything necessary to bring us over. For that, I'll always be grateful."

Now it made even more sense that Birdie felt responsible for the Petrovics' well-being. It had likely been her idea to suggest the life-altering path that put an ocean between them and everything and everyone they'd known before.

A Cadillac drove slowly by on its way toward the mansion, signaling their time was over. Elsa drank the last of her coffee, grown cold by now, and stood to go.

"Tatiana," she said. "You said Mr. Van Tessel was on a relic-hunting tour. Did he acquire anything from the monastery? The aviary, perhaps?"

Smiling, the older woman finished placing the coffee cups on a tray. "Yes. That aviary is Croatian. Like we are."

No wonder Birdie thought it should belong to them.

More than ever, Elsa hoped they would find it.

———————◇———————

Elsa spent the morning in the secret den with the door propped open to the rest of the library for light. While she sat at Linus's desk and went through more of his files, Luke and Tom wrapped panels of wainscoting in protective padding, then hauled them to the delivery truck.

As Barney was banished outside in order to protect the birds in the house, Danielle had volunteered to take him for long walks through the grounds.

In the meantime, Elsa waded through more eugenics records until she found two things that actually interested her. The first was the provenance document for an aviary, which must be the one that had been willed to Danielle. Just as Tatiana said, it had come from the Franciscan monastery in Dubrovnik, sold to Mr. Van Tessel in June 1896. According to this document, the aviary had been one of many created on site in the scriptorium. This one had been completed in 1389.

The monastery must have needed the cash for them to sell such a precious book, and the fact that there were other copies had likely made it easier for them to part with it. The amount Mr. Van Tessel had paid was listed as a foreign currency, and she had no idea how that translated to US dollars. But she tucked the document into her satchel. If the aviary was found at Elmhurst, the Petrovics would need this provenance to go with it.

That was something, anyway. Perhaps the aviary was even here in this room.

With renewed energy, Elsa searched the desk and bookcase. She didn't find the aviary, but she did come across another notebook chronicling an ornithological expedition.

"Bingo!" she said, though no one was there to hear her. If the

Spalding siblings weren't here today, she would've taken it back to the dining hall to parse through it there. But the last thing she wanted was to be distracted by Jane, so she remained in the den, adjusted the knob on the kerosene lamp, and pulled out her own notebook in which to copy specimen data.

It was past her usual lunchtime before she noticed her stomach growling. As if on cue, Luke and Tom returned, carrying small packages wrapped in waxed paper.

"Ham or turkey?" Luke asked. "Or roast beef?"

"What?"

"You didn't bring lunch, or at least not enough for us to notice. Tom went to the village deli and picked these up for us. What's your pleasure?"

"Turkey, thank you." She stood and accepted the sandwich. "Lunch is on me next time. Shall we eat out in the courtyard?"

"Sounds nice." Luke unwrapped the ham sandwich he was left with. "But I'm going to finish this off in less than a minute, and then I have a date with a tunnel."

"Really?" Elsa hadn't been sure he'd really try it out, and as it had no bearing on anyone's priorities here, save her own curiosity, she hadn't planned to remind him.

"I told you I would. Might as well get it done now before you're tempted to explore it yourself while you're in here. Mind if I bless the food?" Luke said grace over the lunch, and then finished his off as quickly as he'd promised. "We'll have to move the desk again."

"Of course." Elsa moved the chair and stood back while the men carried the desk out of the way. That being done, Luke pulled a skein of rope from his back pocket and tied a loop around his waist. The other end he handed to Tom.

"This way we can measure how long the tunnel is. Plus, if there are any forks in it or I don't come out through the other side, I'll be able to find my way back."

"Oh good," Tom said. "I thought you meant for me to pull you out by the rope if you lost consciousness from lack of air."

"Well, that too, I suppose, if the rope stops moving. Or at least you could follow the rope in to find me yourself and then toss me over your shoulder."

Tom blanched.

With a wry grin, Luke clapped his shoulder. "I fully intend to walk out, one way or another. All you have to do is hold on to the end."

"What happens if I get to the end of the rope and you're still pulling?" Tom asked.

Luke rubbed his jaw. "I'll untie myself and keep going. That's better than pulling it out of your hands and moving about with a tail, I suppose."

Elsa swallowed. "If it becomes dangerous, abort the mission and come on back." He was doing this to satisfy her whim. That wasn't a good enough reason to risk his safety.

"We'll see. Enjoy your lunch. I'll be back soon, I'm sure." Flashlight in hand, he ducked into the passage and disappeared.

She held her breath, listening to his footsteps until they receded to nothing—which didn't take long. Wide-eyed, she looked to Tom, watching the rope unspool at Luke's pace.

He chuckled. "He's a former fighter pilot, Elsa. And before that, he drove ambulances over rough terrain, often under enemy fire. I don't do tunnels, but he doesn't mind them. He won't abort the mission."

Elsa had been joking when she'd referred to it as a mission. She certainly wasn't Luke's commanding officer. "But this was meant to be a lark," she said. "It doesn't matter."

A small smile curled on Tom's lean face. "It mattered to you. You going to eat that?"

She still clutched the forgotten sandwich. "I'll take my lunch break here."

The rope was still feeding into the tunnel when she finished. With nothing else to do, she turned back to the expedition log she'd just discovered and searched for relevant data.

It did not make the time go any faster.

"Long tunnel," Tom muttered. Sweat beaded his brow. "He's still going. Man, I really hate tunnels. I'm trapped in a tunnel almost every night in my dreams. Well, not a tunnel exactly. It's a trench, but I know that if I were to go over the top to get out of it, my head would be blown clean off. So I just run back and forth between bomb blasts that get closer and closer together."

"In your nightmare?"

"Yeah. It wasn't too far from what happened."

Elsa stayed quiet for a moment, out of reverence for what Tom and his fellow soldiers suffered, and for the loss of peace that haunted them still. "I can't imagine what that must have been like for you."

"Good. Don't try. And don't worry. If the rope stops moving, I would figure out a way to get to Luke if I had to."

"For both of your sakes, I sincerely hope that won't be necessary."

"You and me both." He grinned, and then the rope went slack.

Tom paled, then turned his blue eyes on Elsa. He tugged the rope a little, and there was no resistance on the other end. "Where is he?" he whispered. The tremor in his hand grew worse.

Elsa left the desk and came alongside him. "You reached the end of the rope, and so did he. He untied himself, just as he said."

But her gentle reminder seemed to gain no purchase. The young man dropped to a knee at the opening and called into the darkness for Luke.

No response. That was no surprise, given the length of rope used. But Tom called again, a note of desperation edging his voice.

Standing, he whirled away and paced the den, twisting his hands. "He could be hurt. He could have fallen and the fall jerked the knot loose and pulled the rope from his body. I can't leave him. But I can't—how can I go in there?" He whispered as if he'd forgotten Elsa was still there.

She met him where he was and grasped both of his hands. "Tom. Remember what you told me. He was a fighter pilot. He can handle a tunnel. You saw that knot he tied around his waist. It wouldn't come loose with a hard jerk, it would get tighter. So there's no reason to believe he fell. We have no reason not to believe that he did what he said he would do. He reached the end of the rope and untied himself. He'll come back."

Tom squeezed her hands until they hurt, though she knew he had no intention of bruising her. Oh, where was Barney when Tom needed him?

"Do you think I should go after him?" He cast a sidelong glance at the dark opening.

She definitely did not. "I think he's on his way back to us right now. Shall we wait here or go outside and see if we can find where he'll come out?" Maybe they'd spot Barney while they were at it.

"Wait here." Tom seemed rooted to the floor.

So be it. She would stay rooted with him. Surely Luke would reappear in a matter of minutes.

"Say, this is a prime opportunity for me to hear some of your stories," she said. "What's your earliest memory of Luke?"

"My . . . what? My earliest memory of him?" Tom's brow furrowed as if trying to call it forth.

"I'd love to hear it."

"Okay." He took a deep breath. "It must have been the day he found me in his father's stable. I was six years old, and he was fourteen. The groom was ready to take a switch to my hide, but Luke stopped him. He said that I had come to the stable for my first riding lesson."

"And had you?"

"I didn't know it when I snuck in there, but yes." Tom chuckled, and his grip relaxed, though he didn't release her. "Luke took me to the horse he'd intended to ride himself, helped me on it, and started teaching me how to ride as if this had been his plan for the day all along. I should have been scared, being up so high on a powerful animal I didn't know. But I did know Luke. And I trusted him."

"How remarkable," Elsa mused aloud. Luke had told her that he'd had no idea that Tom had looked up to him. But if this was Tom's first memory of him, she understood completely.

"Although," he added, "I did fall off."

Before Elsa had time to respond, another voice caught up to them. "Hey, what are you trying to do, make me look bad while I'm not here? I caught you before you hit the ground, don't forget." Grinning, Luke filled the doorway to the library, his hair wet and dripping onto his bare shoulders and chest.

Tom dropped Elsa's hands, a sigh of palpable relief whooshing out of him. "What are *you* trying to do, showing up half-dressed with a lady present?"

Elsa's cheeks heated, and she looked away, but not before she noticed a shirt in Luke's hand, and that he was wearing different trousers than the ones he'd had on before he left.

"Sorry, Elsa. I thought you'd be taking lunch in the courtyard, so I came around from the other direction," he explained. "I didn't mean to make you uncomfortable."

"But you mean to make *me* uncomfortable, is that it?" Tom's teasing must mean he was feeling more like himself.

"Other than having to stoop through most of it, that tunnel isn't so bad to get through, but I came out the other side dirty and smelly. So I rinsed off in the river since I was smart enough to bring a change of clothes after we got caught in that storm Monday. But I might have cut my back on some rocks. It stings a little." He turned to let them see. "See anything? I don't want to bloody a clean shirt."

At this, Elsa shed her schoolgirl shyness and directed him to step into the library, where the light was much better by the windows. She moved close enough to get a good look at the cut on the left side of his lower back.

"It doesn't look deep," she said, relieved he wouldn't need stitches. "It just needs to be cleaned and covered."

Tom fetched their first aid kit from the other side of the room.

"Figured." Luke curled an arm around and tried to reach the cut himself. "Right about there? Pass me a cotton ball, would you?"

"Nonsense." Elsa laughed, and Tom held the kit open for her. "No matter how strong you may be, some wounds we can't reach by ourselves." She cleaned the cut and bandaged it, glad to be of use. "There's no shame in letting someone help."

Luke pulled on the clean shirt he'd been carrying, then turned around to face her. "I'll have to remember that." The twinkle in his eye said, *So should you.*

CHAPTER

12

I f there was no shame in letting someone help, as Elsa had told Luke yesterday, then there ought to be no shame in visiting a doctor.

But there was, no matter how hard she tried to deny it.

For the last two days, eugenics had been haunting Elsa. She had not been born with a defect, and no one could call her feeble-minded. Polio had not been her fault, but according to eugenics, her constitution must have been weak for her to have succumbed to the disease at all.

So far, she had not been the "burden on society" that eugenics enthusiasts so abhorred. If she became much worse, however, she would be. She pictured herself in a rolling chair again, just as Archer had suggested, dependent on others to push her around. She would never go on expeditions to Hudson Bay or the South Seas. She may not even be able to walk in her own strength through Central Park.

This bleak possibility, along with her words to Luke about

allowing others to help, had driven her to make an appointment for after work today.

Still, Elsa could scarcely believe she was in Dr. Stanhope's clinic.

Her fingers drummed the hobnailed arm of the leather chair. At least this consulting room felt more like an office, and not at all like a cold and clinical examination room, or like the hospital room that had been her home for the better part of a year. On the wall hung framed degrees. In a mirror above the bookshelf, Elsa saw her reflection.

She looked small, even to herself.

She looked scared.

The last time she had seen this doctor, she'd been a child, and he was the man who always brought bad news. Whenever he came to call, Elsa didn't always know what he'd said to her parents or teachers, but she knew how she felt in his wake.

She felt the same fear now. She was afraid she wouldn't get better than she'd been feeling these last few weeks. She was afraid he would tell her she'd only get worse. That she would be a burden after all. Again.

Elsa prayed she was wrong. But she had prayed for healing before.

The door opened.

Dr. Stanhope must be in his fifties now, with white hair fanning through black. The lines bracketing his mouth were deeper, his eyes more shadowed by wiry brows and no kinder than she'd remembered.

"Miss Reisner." He greeted her, then took his chair behind the oak desk.

Her heartrate increased. He could not be taller than five feet ten inches, and yet his presence expanded to fill the room. It was as though every disappointment, fear, and sorrow that had been attached to his visits still hovered about him, taking up space, using the air.

"Thank you for seeing me." She twisted her fingers together in her lap, wondering if these chairs intentionally sat lower than normal so patients would literally look up to him. "I won't take too much of your time."

"Proceed."

She swallowed, then explained the changes she'd noticed in her condition lately. "I never got over the limp, and my stamina never recovered to the level of my peers," she added. "But now it's even worse. Both my leg and lungs seem weaker. Is this normal?" She licked dry lips. "That is, with your other patients with childhood polio, have you seen a slight decline this many years after the illness, and if so, is it temporary, or can I expect to return to at least the level of health I had last year?"

Dr. Stanhope rose and circled to the front of the desk, inserting the tips of his stethoscope into his ears. "Let's take a listen."

She stood so he wouldn't need to stoop to her level. The chest piece pressed against her dress, and she followed the doctor's directions to breathe normally and deeply as he listened to various locations through her chest and back.

"Clear," Dr. Stanhope declared, "if weak." He draped the stethoscope around his neck once more and opened the door to the corridor. "Let's see you walk. To the end of the hall and back, in your most natural gait. Don't try to make it look pretty."

Obediently, she walked the prescribed path, returning to Dr. Stanhope at the doorway to the consulting room.

The doctor cleared his throat and hugged a clipboard to his chest. "I told you not to make it look pretty for me, Miss Reisner, but perhaps I ought to have told you not to exaggerate to make a point. Aren't you wearing a brace on your left knee?"

Elsa felt the color leech from her face. "I—I did no such thing, I assure you. I'm still wearing the brace, too."

"I simply cannot believe that your limp has deteriorated this much since I last examined you, which was . . ."

While the doctor referred to his chart, Elsa supplied, "October 14, 1916. Nearly ten years ago. I was sixteen, and by that point I'd had years of training to relearn how to walk."

A sigh puffed through Dr. Stanhope's nose. "You made this appointment to consult with me. So let's consult, shall we?" He reentered the room and sat behind the desk. Elsa followed, resuming her place, as well.

The momentary shock at the doctor's insinuation fled Elsa, leaving a scalding anger in its wake. "If I had known you'd suggest I was making this up, I wouldn't have wasted time coming."

"Calm down, and we'll get to the bottom of this. It's high time, after all. Tell me again when you started noticing a decline," Dr. Stanhope said.

She told him.

He made a note. "I see. How is your family, by the way? I should have asked after them from the first."

"Fine. They are all in good health."

"Including your cousin Lauren? Does she still live with you?"

"Lauren?" The change of subject felt disorienting. "She and I were roommates, along with another friend, up until last month. She's in Egypt now and engaged to be married shortly after she returns in six months."

"Ah. A wedding, how lovely. Is your mother involved in the planning?"

"Very much so."

"I see." Dr. Stanhope leaned forward and tented his fingers on the desk. "And how does this make you feel?"

Elsa frowned. "I beg your pardon, but I fail to see how that relates to the matter at hand."

"It has everything to do with the matter at hand. Miss Reisner, when you were sick with polio as a child, your recovery was troubling. Protracted. Once you breached the turning point, it took longer for your body to heal than it should have. You had setbacks that I could not account for. Until I considered the family dynamic in your home."

Heat crept beneath Elsa's collar. She didn't want to be here anymore, but her body remained fixed in the chair.

"As I understand it, your cousin and aunt came to visit your family when your aunt was unwell. Your aunt passed away in your home, and Lauren suddenly became a permanent resident of the household. In effect, you gained a sister, and your parents gained another daughter."

"Yes," Elsa agreed. "We all loved her and were happy she stayed."

"She was fifteen and grieving. She required a lot of attention from your parents after her mother's death. Attention you craved for yourself. It couldn't have been easy for you, raised as an only child up to that point."

Elsa shook her head. "That's not how I remember it."

"Then you became ill."

"Please tell me you're not suggesting I contracted polio as a bid for my parents' attention."

"Of course not. I believe you were genuinely sick. But I also believe that after you were able to convalesce at home, you enjoyed the concern of your parents—who had hitherto been rather aloof, I'd surmise—and didn't want it to end. I understand they threw a ball for Lauren while you were still in the hospital. Most children would have been jealous."

"Dr. Stanhope, what you are suggesting is preposterous. I didn't even know about Lauren's ball until a few weeks ago when my mother told me about it. I would never pretend to be sicker than I was for Mother or Father's attention."

"I stand by my considered opinion. You dragged out your recovery to gain sympathy from your parents. It was understandable, you being a child, but that didn't make it healthy. I advised them against giving in to it. In fact, I recommended they send you to a boarding school to eliminate the temptation for both of you."

Elsa stood. "You what?" she gasped.

"With you separated from your parents, you wouldn't be tempted to act sick, and they wouldn't be tempted to reward your deception by fawning over you. We had to break the cycle, you see. Your parents argued with me, but in the end deferred to my professional judgment over their own."

She sank back into the chair, speechless.

"And now your mother is planning Lauren's wedding. I imagine that takes up much of her time."

"Mother asked me to help her with the planning," Elsa choked out. "And I've been trying to hide how I've been feeling from my parents, not advertising it!"

"Don't you find it interesting that the recent decline you've described lines up with your mother's new and critically important involvement in Lauren's life?" Dr. Stanhope went on as if she hadn't even spoken. "You might feel replaced all over again. You might even go so far as to trick your body, to trick yourself in general. Do you want more lumbar punctures? Injections of adrenaline or intravenous serum? As your current brace proves so ineffective, shall we fit you up with one that reaches your ribs again?"

Sweat pricked all over Elsa's skin as the memories of painful procedures became real to her flesh all over again. She pushed herself up to stand on shaky legs. "We're through here," she said simply.

It had been a mistake to come.

———○———

Deep inside Central Park, Elsa sat on a bench in The Ramble, watching for movement in the tree canopy, but mostly listening. After that terrible appointment with Dr. Stanhope, there was no place she'd rather be than right here. Recording in her notebook all the birds she spotted proved a welcome reprieve and distraction.

So intent was she on looking up that she didn't notice the man approaching her until he was a few feet away. "Luke!" she said. "Do you come here often?"

A smile warmed his scarred face. Hands in his pockets, he shook his head. "My doctor prescribed this visit, specifically to bird watch. He said it was relaxing. And you were the one who mentioned The Ramble at twilight as an ideal place for that."

Ah yes. She'd forgotten she'd said that. Elsa patted the bench. "I like your doctor better than mine already. Believe it or not, I've just come from seeing him."

"You did? Did someone go with you?" He sat on the left side of her. She wondered if he meant to hide the scar on his left cheek.

Elsa waved a mosquito away, then withdrew the small jar of peppermint oil she kept in her handbag to repel the pesky insects. "Ivy's busy with a class tonight, and I'd never ask either of my parents. The last thing I want to do is remind them how defective I am." She shook a few drops of oil into her palm. "Want some?"

Luke held out his palm, then rubbed the oil she gave him over his hands and patted some on his neck. "Defective? What kind of a word is that?"

"Sorry. You're right." She capped the oil and returned it to her handbag. "I've been reading Linus van Tessel's eugenics materials—those folders we found in his secret office. It's a term I've read a lot lately."

His face clouded with evident disapproval. "Eugenics is hogwash. The self-directed evolution in the quest of a 'perfect human product'? Absolute rubbish. You were made in the image of God, and so was every other person. Once you start reducing people to measurements and heredities, you strip them of their dignity. We aren't livestock. We have souls. I don't buy that eugenics garbage."

The muscles between her shoulders relaxed. She peered side-ways at him. "Tell me what you really think, why don't you?"

The lines in his expression eased into the hint of a smile. "Will you tell me what the doctor said?"

She did. The more she shared, the darker his expression became, until a vein throbbed on his temple. "I've met doctors like him before. From what you told me, he wasn't listening to you. The army doctors didn't want to believe soldiers were sick if they couldn't see the injuries or signs with their own eyes because they wanted the men to keep fighting. But what was Stanhope's excuse? If he didn't know the answers, he ought to have said so, instead of telling you the symptoms are all in your mind."

He took a breath and rubbed a hand over his cheeks and jaw. "Sorry. Tom says I can look really scary when I get worked up. He calls it Scary Face." His lips tilted in a self-deprecating smile.

"Sorry?" Elsa resisted an urge to take his hand and draw it away from his face. "I can't tell you what a relief it is to hear you say all that. It's one thing to know I'm not well. It's far worse to not be taken seriously."

Luke leaned forward, elbows on his knees. "He might not, but I do. We'll find ways for you to still experience what you love."

"Why?" The question escaped Elsa before she could measure how it would put him on the spot. But the truth was, she had no idea why Luke seemed to be taking her burden on his shoulders. She didn't understand why he'd begun referring to them as "we."

He held her gaze. "Because that's what I do for the people I care about."

"Like Tom," she said. Loyalty was what made this man tick. Anyone would be lucky to have him as a friend.

"Yes, I'm concerned for Tom. But no, it's not the same." He took off his homburg and leaned back, turning his gaze to the trees. "I don't know, Elsa. I'm not finding bird-watching very relaxing so far." He arched one eyebrow at her, and she couldn't help but laugh.

"Maybe that's because we haven't done any yet. I've been sharing so much. It's only fair that now you at least have a chance to tell me why you need to relax in the first place. Then I'll show you how birding is done."

Music floated through the trees from a street performer playing the saxophone. Luke stayed quiet as he watched the swaying branches, but she had a feeling he wasn't listening to the jazz.

"How is your work going?" she prompted. He'd certainly heard enough about hers. "Is your father happy with what you've salvaged from the mansion so far?"

He released a controlled sigh. "He's not happy that I'm the one doing it. And he never will be." When he turned to face her, his rueful smile tugged her heart. "I'm the wrong son in Dupont & Son. Franklin was supposed to be the one taking over the business. Before the war, I made it clear I wanted nothing to do with it. I was going to design my own buildings, not rip apart and resell someone else's. I said the salvage business lacked artistry, that it was a scavenger's game, and I didn't want to be a vulture. I said a lot of things—vain, prideful things I regret to this day—when I left the US to study in France."

It was the hitch in his voice that brought a lump to Elsa's throat.

"Franklin stayed home to help Dad, and I think even my mother was glad I'd gone."

"Surely, that's not true," Elsa insisted.

He held up a hand. "Her home was more peaceful without me there to get into arguments with Dad and Frank. We, all three of us, were to blame, but it only took one of us leaving for her to have harmony again. Then the war started, and I stayed in Europe, and you know the rest of that story. Near the end of the war, Franklin enlisted, too. But he died of the Spanish flu before he even left the country."

Elsa covered her mouth with her hand. "Oh no. I'm so very sorry."

A knob shifted behind Luke's collar. "Yeah. Me too. But my folks took it hardest of all. Franklin was everything they wanted in a son. Since he's been gone, I've stepped in to help in all the ways I know how, but it doesn't make up for it. It's been eight years, and I can tell it's still hard on Dad that I'm not Frank."

No wonder he hadn't wanted to say more about Franklin when he'd mentioned his brother during the storm. He had come home from war to a house of mourning, then gave up his own career dreams to work for a father so stuck in grief for the son he'd lost, he didn't appreciate the one he still had. At least, that's what Elsa gathered. She thanked Luke for sharing such a personal thing with her, and he insisted it was no more personal than what she'd shared with him. Elsa wasn't convinced that was true.

"It's nice that you listened," he added. "It's been a while since someone asked."

"About Franklin? Or about you?"

"Either. Except for my doctor, who is overly concerned with my blood pressure. Speaking of which, ready to tell me what you see up there? I ought to do at least a little actual birding."

She smiled, comfortable with this familiar territory. "Happy to. The fall migration isn't as flamboyant as the spring one, and you have to work a little harder since they aren't singing as much and their plumage has turned more subtle. Look, there's a magnolia warbler." She pointed to the little grey-and-yellow bird perched on a branch. His spritely movements seemed to fit with the saxophone music in the background.

"I don't see it."

Elsa scootched closer to him, stretching tall from the waist so she could be as near to his vantage point as possible. Luke shifted, draping his arm on the bench behind her so she could move closer still.

"There," she whispered, pointing to direct his line of sight. Warmth radiated in the one-inch space between her cheek and his. The smell of peppermint intensified. "Do you see it? Watch for a flicker of movement." She held her breath, then slowly released it, attempting to steady the flicker she felt inside herself.

"I see that." He angled slightly toward her, apparently looking at something nowhere near the warbler. She leaned out of his way, but he touched her shoulder. "What are they saying? You speak bird as well as dog, don't you?"

She heard the tease in his voice but couldn't hope to reply with his fingers still resting near her collar. Then she saw what Luke was referring to and gasped. "Luke! You found the owl!"

"Nope," he said. "I found some mad little birds fluttering around a branch."

"Those are blue jays and a tufted titmouse, and they're saying 'Scram!' to an intruder in their territory—Zeus, the Eurasian eagle-owl that escaped from the menagerie a few weeks ago! His feathers are mottled brown, so he's camouflaged really well up there." The owl turned his head, and she caught a glimpse of his bright orange eyes. "Oh my goodness, did you see his eyes? What a magnificent bird! Despite everything the menagerie officials predicted, he looks fine and quite natural living free."

By now, a few passing people paused to peer into the tree, as well. "I see it! Look, Dad!" A young man of perhaps fourteen years passed a pair of binoculars to a mustachioed man wearing a straw hat.

A woman with grey hair turned her tanned face toward the owl, grinning when she spotted him. The strong smell of citronella and camphor surrounded her.

"What's this? What have you found?" A park official in uniform joined the small cluster of the owl's admirers, lifting his own binoculars. "There you are," he muttered. To the people, he said,

"You have no idea how wily this bird has been. I can't believe we haven't been able to catch him yet."

Rising from the bench, Elsa introduced herself and learned his name, as well. When Luke stood and shook his hand, the park official flinched at his scars. Luke didn't seem to mind.

"I'm an ornithologist with the American Museum of Natural History," she added. "Can you tell me why you're so keen to capture the owl, Jim?"

He spared her only a glance before fixing his attention on the bird again. "The enclosure is all repaired and waiting for its resident to return."

"I see." Elsa spied a mosquito landing on Luke's back and brushed it off for him. "It would appear the former resident of the menagerie has a new address. One that doesn't pen him inside a space the size of a bus stop."

"Let Zeus be free!" the boy said, and the other two nodded their agreement.

"Look, folks." Jim lifted his hands to quiet them. "That owl may look all right to you now, but our concern is that he may starve to death. All he has known for the last twelve years is that menagerie enclosure. It can't fly well—"

"And whose fault is that?" the older woman interrupted. "How could he practice when he's been cooped up for twelve years?"

"Irrelevant," Jim said. "Menagerie staff have told me Zeus is not a good flier, and he doesn't know how to hunt."

"Because his food has been delivered to him for more than a decade," Luke said. "Correct?"

"I'd like to hear more from the ornithologist." The man clasped his son's shoulder and looked at Elsa. "What do you think this owl's chances are in the wild? Or at least, as wild as Central Park can be?"

A few more people joined their small cluster, spotting the owl with their own exclamations.

"I think—wait a minute, let's watch." Elsa focused on Zeus and sensed everyone else do the same.

The predator's attention was clearly fastened on some kind of prey. In the next moment, he swooped down to the ground, out of sight behind some bushes. Then just as quickly, it emerged again, a rodent in its talons. Landing on the roof of the Ladies Pavilion, the owl swallowed it whole.

The small group cheered for the owl, and Elsa laughed with delight to have witnessed such a hopeful event. "As I was saying," she said, "the owl deserves a chance to prove that he'll be all right. He may adjust far better than any of us think."

Zeus took flight again, disappearing from view within moments.

Elsa turned to Luke. "Wasn't that fun?"

"Very." He smiled. "Since nothing can beat it, how about I see you home?" He offered his arm, and she took it. "Come on, chickadee."

"Is that what I am?" she asked on a laugh, as charmed as she was surprised.

"That's the kind of bird that bands together against a foe, right?"

Chickadees weren't the only ones who did that, but she knew what he meant. He remembered Danielle repeating Elsa's lesson after the storm. Elsa smiled, filling with warmth at this man's unexpected gentleness and care. "Yes."

"Then yes, you are my chickadee. And I'll be yours." He winked, and she felt lighter than air.

CHAPTER

Fireflies blinked above the grass and against the shadows gathering among the trees. As Luke and Elsa began walking through The Ramble, she pointed out more birds. When she did, three of the people who had gathered to watch Zeus asked to walk with them so Elsa could be their guide. By the time they reached the park's edge, they'd collected more, until their little group had grown to eight people.

"Do you do this often?" asked the older woman who smelled of citronella.

Elsa smiled. "This is the first time I've led a group, but I come here quite a bit for my own pleasure."

"You're kidding." The man in the straw hat snapped another photograph. "What luck! Junior and I are in town visiting today before we head back to Indiana tomorrow. Thanks for making our romp through Central Park special."

The older woman tapped her binoculars. "Well, I'm local. I'd love to do this again if you would consider it. I've tried bird-watching here a dozen times and never saw half so much as I did with you. And what I did see, I had no idea what I was looking at."

What a shame that was! "My colleague Mr. Griscom wrote an excellent article this summer about bird-watching in Central Park," Elsa told her. "I'm sure you could find a copy at the library if you're interested. That might help you in the future."

"Maybe. But there's nothing like a personal guide, is there?"

Elsa warmed to the compliment, happy that she'd been of some service to her. "I'll tell you what. If you ever see me here again, please get my attention. I'm happy to bird-watch together."

The group disbanded, and the smile Luke gave her reflected the joy inside her.

"You were pretty great at that," he said. "Have fun?"

"And how! What a great way to end this day. Maybe it's the adrenaline, but I feel good right now. Physically. I wonder if . . ."

Luke watched the traffic, preparing to usher her across the street. "Don't leave me in suspense. I'm all ears."

"Well, the park officials and menagerie staff thought Zeus was too weak to fly because he hadn't had the space to spread his wings and try for so many years, right? So I wonder if I've led such a sedentary lifestyle that I've actually made myself weaker than I have to be. Don't get me wrong—I don't believe for one second that a secret jealousy of my cousin either made or kept me sick. But have I caged myself, as Zeus had been caged, thereby clipping my own wings, so to speak?"

He looked down at her with a tenderness that far outshone his scars. "I don't know."

"I mean, chasing Barney was too much for me, but no one could expect to run a marathon without training, and I hadn't run like that in years. Maybe what I need isn't less activity but more—just not all at once. Could a gradual conditioning be the answer? There can't be any harm in trying."

Luke placed a hand on hers as she rested it on his arm. They crossed Central Park West and headed toward the Beresford. "Very gradual, Elsa. I don't want you to overdo it in your eagerness, okay?"

"Yes, okay," she agreed, even as her mind leapt to bright possibilities. Zeus was surprising everyone with his quick adaptation to freedom. No one believed he could survive, except perhaps Zeus himself.

What could happen if Elsa believed in herself, too?

"By the way, I saw Tatiana this morning at Elmhurst," Luke said. "She told me she finally heard back from the executor of Mrs. Van Tessel's will."

Elsa nearly stopped walking, so abrupt was the change of subject and the shift from hope to dread. "And?"

"She showed me the letter. He said that since the land will go to the county, it's up to the county whether to allow the Petrovics to stay in their cottage or not."

"Even though the will clearly stipulates Birdie's wish for them to stay?"

"That's what he said. Tatiana took it on the chin, though."

Elsa swallowed a groan. This was not the news they'd been hoping for. "Do you know if she's told Danielle yet?"

"She's waiting for word from the county on what they'll decide to do."

Elsa sighed, dismay settling heavily on her shoulders. "I hope they don't make her wait too long. If they have to move, they need time to find a new situation, and Danielle will need time to adjust to the idea. The change will be enormous."

Luke agreed. "I know a little something about real estate from working with clients decorating their homes with our salvage. It takes about thirty days to close on a house sale. I'm not sure how different that timeline would be for transferring ownership of an estate as a donation. But Mr. Spalding set the wheels in motion two weeks ago, so it could be another two weeks."

"Two weeks!" Elsa gasped. "That's practically no time at all! It might take longer than that, though, right? Wouldn't the county officials need to convene and vote after evaluating whether they want to take on such an estate? If it's so beneficial for Mr. Spalding to get Elmhurst off his hands, surely there will be considerable cost to the county to accept responsibility. They'll need to do some kind of analysis first . . . won't they?"

"That would be prudent," Luke said. "The Petrovics really matter to you, don't they?"

"Yes, they really do." They reached the Beresford, but she wasn't ready for Luke to leave quite yet. She sat in the middle of a bench outside the revolving doors, and Luke joined her, choosing the left side of her again. "My job at Elmhurst involves reading notebooks and files from the Van Tessels," she went on. "I was only looking for expedition details. But I learned how close Birdie had been with the Petrovics and how they looked out for each other over the years. Linus considered Danielle defective, and even said his own wife had proven defects in her family history, hinting that she shouldn't have more children."

Luke's brow rippled. "*More* children?"

Briefly, Elsa explained the cards she'd found in Linus's eugenics files. "As an 'imperfect human product' myself—according to those standards—I'm so sad for how Linus made his wife feel. And ensuring she never bore children again—whether through neglect or sterilization—was monstrous enough without Birdie's added grief at Sarah's loss." She paused, aware she was talking too fast.

Luke pressed his lips together, the lines of his face turning sharp in the light of passing headlamps. "Eugenics." He spoke the word as if it were a curse—and maybe it was. "What does eugenics call the soldiers returned from war with tremors, nightmares, overactive nerves, or scars inside and out? I suppose Tom and I are defects, too."

Elsa's gaze softened on the man beside her. "Applesauce. You're heroes, the both of you, and if you don't already know that, shame on the rest of us for not saying so. And please don't ever let me catch you trying to hide any part of your face from me again."

In response, he angled so he sat sideways on the bench, turning to face her straight on. A taxi pulled up to the curb, its headlamps shining on him while the rider paid the fare. The homburg brim cast only a thin crescent shadow. "Better?"

"Much." With a firm nod, she steered the conversation back to the Petrovics. "I can't do anything about Birdie's suffering now, but I can try to carry out her final wishes for the Petrovics, if at all possible. Knowing about Mr. Spalding's career at the ERO makes me feel protective of Danielle and her mother. Their champion is gone, and they're in trouble. If we can at least help them find the aviary, they'll be okay."

"That's a big *if*. Tom and I moved on from the library yesterday and have been working in other rooms. Still no dice. But we'll keep looking."

Elsa thanked him for that and rose to go. "It was good to see you this evening," she told him. "Thanks for listening, and for caring. See you tomorrow?"

He stood as well. "You bet. Is seven too early?"

"Not at all. By the way, I'll be bringing some storage trays for the purpose of ferrying back some birds."

"That must mean you're finished going through the field notes?"

"At last. Tonight's task is to cut up my own chart with what I gleaned from their expedition logs, rearrange the rows in alphabetical order, and copy all of that into a fresh ledger." Not every bird in the house had data for it, but she'd managed to collect information for three hundred of the specimens.

"Sounds like you have a long night ahead of you. I'll leave you to it." He bade her goodnight.

"See you soon."

Once Elsa was inside the Beresford's lobby, she turned and waved at him through the glass revolving door. He tipped his hat, then put his hands in his trouser pockets and walked away with his head held high.

She thought she heard him whistling.

———◯———

TARRYTOWN
FRIDAY, SEPTEMBER 3, 1926

Morning arrived all too early, but it came with a surge of adrenaline. Now that all the Van Tessel field notes were alphabetized by taxonomy in her own perfect chart, Elsa could finally assign catalog numbers to the birds, tag them, and bring them back to the museum. It felt like she'd been coming here for much longer than the two weeks it had actually taken her to reach this point. And yet, now that her progress could begin taking flight, she didn't relish the thought of leaving here for the last time. Of leaving Tatiana and Danielle.

Neither did she like the idea of parting ways with Luke and Tom when all this was over. The shared lunches and rides to and from Tarrytown had brought them all closer.

But the Petrovics were the ones who stood to lose the most. Elsa was anxious to check on Tatiana after hearing her news from Luke last night.

While the men carried her storage drawers in from the truck and delivered them to the dining hall, Elsa dropped off her satchel and made her way to the cottage. Barney kept close at her heels.

Maybe she ought to go faster. After all, if she was training her body, she should push herself to exertion. Not enough to break a sweat today, but enough to at least feel her muscles.

And, boy, did she feel them by the time she reached the cottage. She half smiled, half grimaced at Barney, who for some unknown reason looked at her adoringly. Elsa rubbed his head between his ears.

Tatiana greeted Elsa from the porch, waving as though to a long-lost friend. "Good morning, dear! How are you?"

Elsa climbed the steps and inhaled, filling her lungs with much cleaner air than she got in the city. "I feel fine," she said and meant it. "Except for the news Luke shared with me about what the executor said. I'm so sorry. How are you holding up?"

"By the Lord's strength. I've sent a letter to the Tarrytown Garden Association as well as the local conservancy asking if they're hiring, but even if they are, that doesn't solve where we are to make our home."

"I'm glad you've taken that step," Elsa said. "It's wise to explore your options while you wait to hear from the county on the matter." And if the county didn't reply soon, Elsa had a mind to pay a visit in person to investigate. If only phone service hadn't been discontinued to the estate already, Tatiana would be able to make telephone calls, presumably getting her answers much faster.

"In the meantime, would you like to visit the hummingbirds?" The hope in Tatiana's eyes was irresistible.

She needed a friend right now, and Elsa had all day to catalog and tag birds. "Lead the way."

"Wonderful. Danielle is setting out food for George in little caches she's set up for him, but she'll come join us when she's done."

"I'd love to see her again."

"Count on it. Her routines do not vary if she can help it."

Letting Tatiana set the pace, Elsa enjoyed the stroll through the backyard and down a curving path she'd not explored before. Barney loped along at her side.

"Does Danielle look forward to the school year, then?" Elsa asked. Wesley had mentioned his fall semester would begin September 29. She wondered if the village school kept a similar calendar. "She must be a good student. She knows so much about birds, and she seemed quite proud of a metaphor she used in conversation."

"Did she? Oh good. We've been working on understanding nonliteral expressions." Tatiana smiled. "The bird study is all her own doing. But there is a difference between knowing *about* birds—the facts she so easily memorizes—and really knowing them. Their unique abilities, the marvelous way God created them. It reminds me of the difference between knowing what the Bible says about God and truly experiencing Him in one's own life. I'll tell you something, dear. When I am lonely or afraid, knowing God is sovereign doesn't make me feel better."

"No?" The observation surprised Elsa.

"I'm glad He *is* sovereign, and I *do* need to know that. But only when I invite Him to sit with me in my pain do I experience His presence, and that is a comfort I cannot describe." Tatiana's smile held a serenity Elsa envied.

What a radically different approach to God. Elsa had prayed for healing, to be fixed, for the pain and exhaustion to be taken away. But had she simply invited God to make His presence known to her in the midst of it? She couldn't recall ever doing so. She wasn't asking God for comfort. She asked Him for answers. And not getting the one she wanted made her want to push Him away, not bring Him close. She'd only realized it now.

"But you asked if Danielle looks forward to school," Tatiana went on. "I doubt it. I'm not sure yet what to do this year."

Elsa steered her thoughts back to the main conversation. "Does she not attend the village school?"

A breeze caught a tendril of Tatiana's hair, and she hooked it behind her ear. "She tried when she was younger, but it didn't go well. She became overwhelmed in the new environment, and the teacher declared her unteachable."

Elsa struggled to put these pieces together. Danielle had already shown herself to have a keen mind and aptitude for learning. But both Tatiana and Linus's card had also described her as atypical. She wondered how that would translate in a classroom if the child was agitated or afraid.

"Mrs. Van Tessel hired a private tutor to teach her at home," Tatiana went on. "Mrs. Morgan was a specialist with experience working with children like Danielle. She learned not just answers for tests, but how to engage more with the world around her. Now that Mrs. Van Tessel has passed away, however, I don't have the resources to hire Mrs. Morgan on my own. I'll try to teach Danielle myself this fall. We'll see how it goes. We're both still reeling from the loss of Mrs. Van Tessel. She was so much more than an employer. The hole left by her absence is large enough to swallow us."

Elsa put her arm around the older woman. "What a special relationship you and Danielle must have had with her."

"She was a special lady." Tatiana sniffed, then brightened as they neared what appeared to be an untamed mass of vegetation. "Here we are. Mrs. Van Tessel called this her secret garden because the master never came here. She loved this place, and so do I, though it's getting away from me a bit now that the landscape crew had to find work elsewhere. Come, let's sit and watch the show."

Elsa sat with her on a weathered grey bench, close to where the grass met a riot of flora. Large patches of plants crowded together with overgrown shrubs. A trumpet vine–covered wooden arbor straddled a gurgling creek.

As if on cue, a male ruby-throated hummingbird arrived.

So did Danielle, who sat next to Elsa without a word.

Elsa greeted the girl, then watched the tiny bird dart with purpose from the red tubular blossoms of the trumpet vine to magenta bee balm, to bright orange azalea, and then to several varieties she didn't know the names for.

"They always come at this time of morning," Danielle commented. "They remember exactly which flowers they've already drained of nectar, and how long they take to fill up again."

"And they don't waste time on empty flowers, do they?" Elsa

added. "With such tiny bodies, they are masters at efficiency. It takes a lot of energy to beat those wings between fifty and seventy times a second."

"And their hearts beat at least a thousand times per minute when they're flying." Danielle spoke without looking at either adult. "They eat between five and eight times an hour. They don't like to share food, either."

Elsa smiled. "I think George might be jealous you know so much about hummers."

"I know lots about hummingbirds," Danielle said. "But I have never seen a rufous hummingbird or a blue-throated mountain-gem or calliope hummingbird, except in Birdie's collection. Did you find them?"

Elsa told her she had. They'd been separated into different rooms according to their prominent colors.

"Birdie gave me a book about birds once." Danielle still didn't meet Elsa's gaze.

"Do you mean the aviary?" Elsa figured Tatiana would have asked her about this before but couldn't resist clarifying. "Is that the book of birds she gave you?"

Danielle started rocking. "No. I don't want to talk about that. The topic we are talking about now is birds." She swayed forward and backward, as though trying to soothe herself. The last thing Elsa had intended was to disquiet her.

"I already asked her about the aviary," Tatiana murmured. "She doesn't know where it is. I'm glad to have the provenance you dropped off Wednesday evening, though. Thank you for that."

"Of course." Elsa swallowed, thinking of what else she might say to interest Danielle. "I saw a Eurasian eagle-owl in Central Park last night."

Danielle buried her fingers in Barney's fur. "*Bubo bubo*. Native to Europe, Asia, and northern Africa." She'd stopped rocking.

"Yes, but this one is special." Elsa told them about Zeus and the small group of people who followed Elsa out of the park, listening to her as their guide.

"How wonderful!" Tatiana said.

"It was." Elsa smiled at the memory.

A breeze stirred the petunias and rose of Sharon. The tall spires of purple salvia bowed. "Is serving as a bird-watching guide part of your duties at the museum?" Tatiana asked.

"Oh, no, my job keeps me securely in my office. Sending me here is an exception." And Mr. Chapman thought she ought to be done by now. He'd made it clear when he'd seen her picking up the storage trays that his patience for this project was running out. The deceased Galapagos penguins from the zoological society still needed to be dissected, and Mr. Miller needed her to assist. At least they were waiting in preserving fluids so they wouldn't decompose in the meantime.

A crow cawed as it settled onto a branch of a serviceberry tree, scaring a cedar waxwing away.

Danielle glanced at him and smiled. "Hello, George." When he cocked his head at her, she laughed, as though he'd said something amusing that only she could hear. So musical was the sound that Elsa and Tatiana laughed with her.

"I'm glad I've caught you in a congenial mood."

Elsa turned to find Guy Spalding striding toward them. Wearing another three-piece suit complete with homburg, he looked all business. Rising, she greeted him. "Those look familiar." She nodded toward the file folders tucked beneath his arm.

"Yes." He cleared his throat. "I found these on the table in the dining hall this morning. I recognized one of the ERO documents peeking out from one of the folders, so I took a look. I confess there isn't much in that old house I'm interested in for myself, but these papers of Uncle Linus's intrigue me greatly. Thanks for finding them. Since they don't pertain to your ornithological work, I'm taking them."

It was certainly his right, and so Elsa could make no objection. Still, she felt uneasy that Mr. Spalding now carried a file that called Danielle feebleminded.

"I thought I heard someone say George a moment ago," he said. "Is there someone else about?"

"George is the crow," Danielle told him.

Mr. Spalding peered at George, who stared right back. "I see. At any rate, Mrs. Petrovic, I've come looking for you on a matter that concerns you. As you know, I'm donating the entire estate to the county. I've had a meeting yesterday with a Mr. Nigel Field from the county."

Paling, Tatiana stood. "I've been waiting to hear from him myself. Our cottage still belongs to us."

Mr. Spalding huffed a small laugh. "He has no interest in your cottage, I assure you."

Danielle sat on the bench again, Barney's head resting on her knee. She watched the birds, but Elsa could tell she was listening to every word Mr. Spalding said.

"In fact, in looking over a map of the estate, he's quite interested in making these sixty-seven acres a public park and thinks this spot would be ideal for a visitors center."

"But what does a park mean for their living arrangement? You can't expect them to leave their home," Elsa said.

Mr. Spalding tilted his head, regarding her from under the brim of his hat. "That's entirely out of my hands."

Danielle started rocking again, moaning at the same time. "We can't leave. We can't leave. I won't go," she repeated over and over.

George cawed again until more crows joined him in the tree.

Elsa planted a fist on her hip. "What do you propose the Petrovics do now?"

He held up his hands and took a step backward. "That's none of my concern."

"It should be your concern, if you have any respect for your aunt's wishes," she fired back. "You can't just leave them without any recourse."

"I told you, this is out of my hands. Take it up with the county, not me."

"She's been trying, but no one from their office has responded to her." The angst in Elsa's tone seemed to upset Danielle even more.

"All I can tell you is that you have until the end of the month. At that point, the county will have complete control of the land."

Danielle's rocking and moaning grew louder. Barney whined beside her, and the cawing multiplied. "You're making George angry," Danielle shouted. She pulled hair from her braids and twisted the strands around her fingers.

Mr. Spalding blinked, brow furrowed. "Are you referring to the crow?"

"George and his friends are angry! They do not want to leave their home. They do not." The girl hunched over, her hair sticking out between her fingers as she covered her ears.

"Danielle, my dear." Tatiana touched her shoulders, only to be swatted away by her daughter.

Danielle jumped up, paced to the edge of the garden and back, then began another circuit. She beat the heel of her hand to the side of her head.

"Danielle," the man murmured, then looked at the file folder he carried.

He'd read her card. He knew who she was. He knew what his uncle had written about her.

Mr. Spalding lowered his voice. "My aunt was clearly not in her right mind when she willed a medieval manuscript to that child."

"You should go," Elsa told him, unwilling for him to witness one more moment of the girl's breakdown.

He opened his mouth, but the murder of crows exploded from the tree and fairly chased him from the garden.

Leaving Tatiana to try to soothe Danielle, Elsa marched back to the mansion in Mr. Spalding's wake. Heat flared through her. Birdie would be livid if she knew what was going on.

No, Birdie would be heartbroken. Elsa was livid. They'd already known the estate would go to the county. But Spalding and Field were making plans that drastically altered the Petrovics' lives without even letting Tatiana be part of the conversation. And now they expected them to relocate by the end of the month?

Elsa crossed the drive and entered the vestibule. Piano music drifted from the parlor but ended in a discordant crash at the commanding tone of Mr. Spalding. She stepped into the golden room.

Jane leapt from the chaise lounge. "There you are, Elsa! I was so disappointed not to see you when we arrived this morning. Don't tell me you were with the gardener and her daughter again."

Speech fled. Jane couldn't really have a reason to be jealous of her time.

"Bravo, Jane," Wesley called from the piano bench. "One might almost believe you're genuine."

Releasing Elsa, Jane spun toward her brother with a scowl, then turned a pleading pout upon her father, who stood with arms crossed, blocking the doors to the courtyard. "You see? He provokes for no reason."

A throat clearing drew Elsa's attention to a sharp-eyed elderly woman tucked into a velvet armchair. A doily topping the back of the chair made a lacy corona about her white hair. "In my day," she said, "introductions were customary." She lifted thin brows at Mr. Spalding, then sent a sideways smile at Elsa, deepening the pleasant lines in her face.

"Mother, this is Miss Reisner, the ornithologist I told you about," Mr. Spalding muttered. "Miss Reisner, this is my mother. Agnes Spalding. She was my uncle Linus's sister."

Elsa's breath hitched. Could this bombazine-draped woman in mourning be the Agnes that Birdie had written of in her diary? Shock parted her anger, followed by a hope that maybe Agnes could shed some light on . . . something. Anything. Schooling her composure, Elsa came forward to shake the woman's delicate hand. "Mrs. Spalding, it's so nice to meet you." She added her sincere condolences.

"Call me Agnes, dear. There's another Mrs. Spalding, and she hates for us to get confused."

"Mother isn't here, Granny," Jane called on a sigh.

"No, she is not." Agnes brushed a stray feather from her stiff black skirt. "Even so, I wish to be called Agnes by this smart young woman, so don't cross me. I'm too old for that."

"Yes, Granny." Jane returned to the chaise lounge, where she inspected her cuticles.

"I apologize if I've interrupted a family meeting," Elsa said.

"Oh no." Wesley closed the lid over the keys and lit up a Chesterfield. "We're only all here in one room by chance. Normally we're far more careful. I was here first, by the way."

"I was looking for Elsa," Jane said.

"Right." Wesley turned to Elsa. "And what have you been looking for?" He blew smoke her way.

"Stop this foolishness at once," Mr. Spalding scolded.

Agnes tsked. The chair's upholstery shone where it had been crushed from years of handling, and stuffing tufted from a spot where a mouse had chewed through. But the way she presided from it, the armchair may as well have been a throne. "What has you all in a dither, Guy?"

"I told the gardener some news from the county, and her daughter threw a fit."

Agnes's keen blue eyes narrowed. "You mean a child reacted strongly to the news that she was about to be homeless? How strange." Irony dripped from her tone.

"You didn't see her. This was a tantrum like I've never seen." At least he hadn't mentioned her friend the crow.

Elsa folded her arms, ready to defend Danielle, but Agnes spoke up first.

"Really? Are you not aware of the royal tantrum thrown in this very room by your own daughter?" She lifted her cane and pointed at the young woman across the room. She swung it toward Elsa and then to a nearby chair in unspoken command.

Elsa sat.

Sticking the cigarette between his lips, Wesley flipped open the lid of the piano and pounded the opening measures of Beethoven's Fifth Symphony, grinning like the Cheshire cat. "Do remind us, won't you? I can't recall."

Good heavens. This pair. Elsa remained where she was, spellbound by the unfolding tableau. It was not unlike reading a novel by F. Scott Fitzgerald. It wasn't pleasant, but neither could one look away.

"I love you, Jane. You are my only granddaughter. But you have always been jealous of Danielle. It's unseemly, considering your privilege is so far beyond hers."

Through the parlor doorway, Elsa could see Luke and Tom removing the chandelier in the entry hall. Tom had his back to her, but Luke sent her a look from his place on the ladder that told her he could hear everything. She hadn't seen Crawford yet this morning, but if he was anywhere nearby, he'd be getting an earful, too.

"Yes, yes, and the fit, Granny? Leave out no details, please." Still speaking around the cigarette, Wesley played the next measures of Beethoven's Fifth with equal passion. Would he provide a score for the entire story?

Agnes pursed her lips together, perhaps to hide a chuckle at her grandson's antics. "Wesley, please. I don't fancy being interrupted. This family has enough drama without your music."

Wesley stretched out his arm and tapped ash onto the thread-bare rug.

"Wesley!" Mr. Spalding barked.

The young musician tucked his hair behind an ear. "What? Great-Aunt Birdie doesn't care, I assure you."

"Just because no one lives here anymore doesn't mean you can treat the entire place as your personal ashtray. Show some respect!"

Elsa watched the carpet for smoke, but the ash didn't spark in the fibers. By the time she released the breath she'd been holding, Agnes had begun her story.

"It was only five years ago. Jane was twelve, and I brought her here to visit her great-aunt Birdie and great-uncle Linus. When we arrived, we were brought into this parlor, and Jane was elated to see that a table had been set for a tea party."

"But it wasn't for me," Jane added. "The dishes had all been used, and there were crumbs everywhere."

"That's right. When Birdie came in to greet us, she explained that she had just finished having a tea party with Danielle, who was seven at the time. I hadn't told Birdie we'd be dropping by that day, so we took her quite by surprise. Jane was upset that the party hadn't been for her. Poor Birdie tried to appease you, offering to have a fresh party arranged on the spot, but you refused. Oh, the stomping and crying and carrying on, child! The racket! The self-indulgence!"

"Can you blame me?" Jane sat up straighter and centered the pendant on her necklace. "She'd always told me I was her favorite niece. I thought it would be grand to surprise her, but I was the one who was shocked to my core that she'd been having a fine time indeed with a servant's child who had no manners or upbringing at all. I thought I was special. I *am* special."

Wesley tickled the ivories at a pitch to match his sister's rising tone.

"That you are." Agnes lifted an eyebrow. "And so was your fit. It was such a special fit, in fact, that it brought Linus thundering in to see what was going on. Birdie and I tried to explain things calmly, but it was impossible to be heard without yelling over your sobs. And then Linus blew up at Birdie for having—and I quote—'that immigrant gardener's feebleminded child' in the house. My domineering brother humiliated and shamed his wife in front of an audience."

"Well, Danielle didn't deserve to be here. She didn't deserve to spend time with Aunt Birdie, let alone use the good china like she was *somebody*. And she *doesn't* deserve the aviary." Jane turned on Elsa with a pointed finger. "I can tell you're a kind soul, but if you've been trying to find the aviary for her—don't. I'm glad it's missing and hope it stays that way. If it goes to anyone, it ought to be family."

Elsa stood. "That choice isn't yours to make. It isn't any of ours." She paused to gather her composure. The more she learned about Birdie, the more she realized how many choices had been taken away from her, either by her husband, circumstances, or her declining health. "If the aviary is found, it belongs to the people your aunt decided to give it to, whether you like it or not."

"Hear, hear." Agnes thumped her cane on the carpet, adding an emphatic nod for good measure.

Elsa sent a subtle smile to her new ally. "Now, if you'll all excuse me. I do have work to do."

CHAPTER

14

S tifling a yawn, Elsa shifted on the front porch of her parents' brownstone, making sure the pleats on her bodice lay straight. She knocked and waited.

Sleep had eluded her last night, hounded as she was by yesterday's events. After the Spalding family reunion in the parlor, the rest of the day had been overshadowed by the uncertain future facing the Petrovics. She'd made excellent progress tagging and cataloging birds, but she had done so mechanically. Mr. Spalding had inspected Linus's secret den and carried out more of his books and papers before Elsa had a chance to explore the space any further.

All the way home that evening, she had discussed the situation with Luke and Tom, with no solutions to show for it. Tom didn't understand why she cared so much about the gardener and her unusual daughter. *"Is it even possible to develop an attachment to people you didn't know three weeks ago?"* he had asked. Luke had caught her eye and answered, *"Of course it is."*

He was right. Perhaps it was because she'd had such a difficult time making friends during childhood that she placed even more value on the few friends she had now, no matter how long she'd known them. That included Luke and Tom, but with the Petrovics, she felt a protective instinct. They were kindred spirits, and they were so alone since Birdie had died. If there was anything Elsa could do to help them, she would.

Elsa knocked again on her parents' front door, harder this time, while her thoughts remained at Elmhurst. Her middle twisted, thinking of Mr. Spalding's reaction to Danielle's outburst yesterday morning. He likely agreed with his uncle's opinion of her. Did that have any bearing on Danielle's life, or Tatiana's?

Footsteps sounded on the other side of the door. With a quick review of her skirt, Elsa plucked a cat hair from the fibers as the butler opened the door.

"Well, hello, Miss Reisner." Benson's familiar face warmed her. His back was stooped with age, his hair frosted white from decades in her family's service. "We weren't expecting you this early, but come in. I'll let your parents know you've arrived."

Elsa stepped inside. "Please don't trouble them, Benson. I've come early to look for something in my old room. When it's closer to dinnertime, I'll join them in the dining room. Or in the parlor, if they have invited another bachelor guest."

Benson's face crinkled with a grin. "Very good, miss. I'll come get you if you seem to have lost track of the time."

She wouldn't, but thanked him just the same, and made her way to the bedroom she'd had as a child. The climb to the third floor and down the hall was good for her, she told herself as she sat on her former bed to rest. Every time she stretched herself, it made her body stronger.

Only, she didn't feel stronger yet.

No matter. She would keep trying.

For now, she breathed deeply as she recovered from those flights of stairs. With one finger she traced the stitching on the pale pink counterpane. Being here felt like she had traveled back in time, and she didn't know if she liked it. Even the sound of the mattress creaking beneath her brought back feelings of coming home on breaks from boarding school. It was an awkward in-between feeling. If this place was home, why did she live out of a suitcase when she was here?

Pushing herself up, she went to the dressing room and entered. Elsa moved a footstool to one corner and climbed it to reach whatever was on the shelf. The first thing she touched was her old flute, still in its case, and a sharp edge pressed inside her throat. Before polio, she'd been a prodigy on this instrument. She'd made her parents proud.

That was a long time ago.

She set the case on the floor, then resumed her search through the contents of the shelf, shoving toys and dolls aside. At last, she found what she was looking for: a box of old *Bird-Lore* magazines and the scrapbook she'd made as a bedridden child.

She carried the box to the bed. Sitting beside it, she lifted out the scrapbook and opened it on her lap. This was the final version, of course, nothing like the original. Elsa had begun by trying to sketch the birds she saw from her window, but she hadn't been satisfied with the result. After several attempts at various species, she'd ended up tearing out those pages entirely and using illustrations from *Bird-Lore* instead. Each type of bird had its own page. In addition to the magazine illustration, she'd recorded the classification and a log of when she'd seen it. Elsa had been doing her own bird count ever since she'd read about Mr. Chapman's idea when he was the editor of *Bird-Lore.*

"There you are."

Her father's voice lifted her head. "Hi, Father. I told Benson not to trouble you. It isn't time for dinner yet, is it?" She checked her watch, then turned her bracelet on her wrist to hide the clasp.

"I would never be troubled by learning you're here. And, no, we have a few minutes yet." Father's smile was as dignified as the rest of him. Sitting beside her, he wrapped his arm around her shoulders.

Elsa stiffened at the unexpected gesture, then glanced at him, waiting to see if he would explain himself.

A lump bobbed behind his celluloid collar. Perhaps he could tell she didn't know what to make of him. "When you were a baby, your mother and I listened to leading experts in childcare because we had no idea what we were doing. The experts warned against coddling children. Which is why we were never demonstrative in our affection. It didn't mean we didn't hold you above all the riches in this world. And as you're all grown up now, I'd say the danger of spoiling you has passed. Or does it make you uncomfortable? If you mind it, you must tell me."

Elsa nearly dropped the scrapbook she was holding. Closing it, she gripped the edges. "I don't mind it."

"Good." His brow relaxed, and he folded his hands. "What are you up to in here?"

She showed him the scrapbook and the box full of magazines. "The gardener at the Van Tessel estate has a twelve-year-old daughter who has a keen interest in birds. I thought she might like to see this. She might like to create her own scrapbook with these old magazines."

"That's very kind of you."

"They aren't doing any good gathering dust here." She gestured to the dressing room. Through the door she'd left open, her flute case could be seen on the floor.

"I didn't realize you kept that," she told him.

"Ah." Father rubbed his hand over his jaw. "I suppose your mother and I thought you may one day want to return to playing the flute."

"Because I was so terrible at the piano?" Her parents had insisted that she try learning the new instrument at boarding school since it required no lung strength. She hadn't caught on to it as quickly as her instructor thought she ought to and had been called lazy and rebellious. Honestly, maybe she had been. Maybe it had been a small act of defiance against the turn her life had taken.

"I never cared a fig about the piano," Father said. "Not specifically. We thought you would be better off with music in your life again, and at the time, piano seemed like a good idea." His brow furrowed. "You didn't agree?"

Elsa caught herself before she shrugged, another lazy gesture, or so she'd been taught. "The only thing that seemed like a good idea to me then was being home." Everything in her longed to confess how lonely and miserable she'd been when she'd needed her parents the most, but Dr. Stanhope's accusations throbbed in her head.

The past could not be undone. Was she selfish to want to tell her father how she hated his choices for her? What did she think would come of it, other than heaping guilt upon the man beside her?

Was she seeking undue attention even now?

Father's chin dipped to his chest before he lifted it again moments later. "We listened to so many experts," he said. "But we failed to listen to you. For that, my dear daughter, I'm sorry."

It was the first time she'd ever heard him apologize for anything—ever. Overcome and bewildered, she could form no response except to place her hand on his and nod that she'd heard what he'd said.

"Speechless, I see." Chuckling, he rotated his wrist to hold her hand, another gesture she could not remember him doing. "I confess that watching what happened between your cousin and her father earlier this year shook me to my core. What a tragic, criminal waste. We never know how much time we have left, so I don't want to take it for granted. I don't want to take *you* for granted. Tell me, dear. You're feeling better these days, aren't you?"

Elsa sniffed back the emotion building in her throat. "I—" She wrestled with how much to tell him and what her motivations were. True, she felt like she'd been declining lately, but Dr. Stanhope clearly disagreed. So all she told her father was "I'm training myself to increase my stamina. It's all very informal and unofficial, mind you, but if I stretch myself little by little, I must see improvement."

The corners of his eyes crinkled. "I agree you must." He had not said he was proud of her for trying, but the expression he wore said almost as much.

Encouraged, she added, "That's why after dinner tonight, I'm meeting up with friends to amble along the beach."

He checked his watch. "Yes, dinner. Shall we?" Rising, he offered his arm. "Reeves can bring this box to your apartment later. I'm eager for you to meet our guest. You'll get along with him fine."

With a sinking heart, Elsa looped her hand through his elbow. She wasn't in the mood to meet a man he wanted to pawn her off on. She'd so much rather stay here and talk more with this new version of her father, the one who had just begun to open up.

"Five more minutes," she wanted to say. An echo of her childhood plea when visiting her parents before her nurse ushered her off to bed. But in this house, punctuality was next to godliness and expectations ruled.

Even at twenty-six years old, Elsa still feared disappointing her father by asking for more of himself than he wanted to give.

Fixing a smile in place, she limped beside him, careful not to lean too much on his arm.

"Archer!" Elsa laughed in surprise to see her friend and colleague with her mother in the dining room. "I was expecting a balding widower. What a nice surprise."

"That's a bit of a low bar, but I'm glad you're pleased." He was golden tonight in a beige poplin suit, white teeth dazzling, and blond hair gleaming under the influence of pomade. "Even if I didn't already know you, I couldn't have turned down the invitation from so charming a lady as your mother."

Speaking of charm.

"This was your idea?" Elsa asked her.

Mother smoothed the waist of her dress. "Inspired by you, but yes. You mentioned going out with this young man, and I know his mother. I thought it high time we get to know him."

"So you see, my dear," her father added, "the tables have turned. Instead of you meeting a stranger, it is we who have the pleasure of acquainting ourselves with a young man already your friend."

"How refreshing." Ten pounds seemed to lift from her shoulders. She agreed to these dinner guests out of respect for her parents but had yet to take any joy from the scrutiny.

Whether Archer was playing the squire or acting on genuine impulse, he pulled out Elsa's chair for her, and they sat. Father joined Mother on the opposite side, then said grace over the meal they were about to receive.

"I have another surprise for you, but I don't think you'll mind." Mother signaled to the footmen, who served four small bowls of soup to each of the four diners.

Elsa barely held back from wrinkling her nose at what appeared to be a liquid diet of child-size portions. Not much of a feast for company.

"I asked you to help me with planning Lauren's wedding, but you never quite gave me an answer. No matter." She waved a dismissive hand, her rings catching the light and casting rainbows. "I realize you're very busy at present. So I decided that we would taste-test food from the top caterers for our dinner tonight. There's more to come, so please save room. You have a lot to sample ahead of you."

"That's a genius use of time, Mother. But shouldn't Joe be here?

The groom ought to have more say in the matter than us." Elsa hated to think they were leaving Joe out. Up until last year, her parents had considered him beneath Lauren's attention, let alone her affections. He was from a hardworking family of Italian-German heritage and made his living as a detective for the New York Police Department. But she thought he'd won them over prior to the engagement.

"Rest assured, we invited Joe." Father dipped his spoon into a bowl of minestrone. "He planned to come but had to cancel due to a break in a case."

"And I'm the lucky substitute. Can't say I'm sorry about that." Archer grinned.

Elsa tasted a matzo ball soup. Delicious. "Did you offer to postpone the sampling so he could come?"

"Of course." Mother dabbed a napkin to the corners of her mouth. "But he insisted we carry on with our plans, as he couldn't guarantee he'd be able to come later, either. He said he trusts our taste, and we're to bring him a report with our thoughts later. We even offered that his parents come, but they deferred to our judgment, as well. Besides, they have their boarders to feed every night."

"I hear the Caravellos are excellent cooks. Are there any samples here from them?" Elsa asked.

"Patience, dear. Wait for dessert."

"Please tell me that means we get tiramisu for the wedding cake!"

Mother just smiled. "You'll be the judge."

Archer waggled his eyebrows at Elsa. "I can't wait."

Neither could she. It made sense that the Caravellos would offer a dessert that could be made ahead of time, but not the main courses. Greta and Sal cooked for up to twelve people at their boardinghouse off Union Square, but they weren't equipped to cater to a guest list that would reach into the hundreds.

Relieved that the Caravellos were being included as much as possible, Elsa relaxed and enjoyed the soup course. At the end of it, Father pulled out paper and a pen and passed them to Elsa to take notes of everyone's impressions.

Next came a variety of salads and vegetables, then fruit dishes. During the entrée samples, Father's questioning of Archer ventured beyond the small talk they'd enjoyed so far.

"Now, Archer, I know you work with Elsa at the museum as a preparator. What kind of education trained you for that kind of work?"

Archer swallowed a bite of filet mignon. "I have a degree in art history with a certification in studio art."

Father stopped chewing for a moment. "Art history and studio art." He looked as though he'd tasted something sour.

Elsa felt a little defensive on Archer's behalf. "You should see the dioramas he paints, Father. They are such realistic landscapes for the animals that it's as much a science as it is art."

"Hey, next time you visit, I'll show you some of my finest work." Archer speared a lump of crabmeat and dipped it into a dish of melted butter. He closed his eyes in apparent bliss over what must be the most expensive option on the table. "My money's on this one for the main course."

A chuckle escaped Father. "You mean *my* money. But speaking of yours—"

"Julian, let's not be vulgar." Mother shot him a look, then apologized to Archer. "He works with money all day long on Wall Street, you understand, and forgets that it isn't a suitable topic for polite company."

Archer shrugged. "If it makes you feel any better, Mr. Reisner, I don't consider myself polite company. Go ahead."

Oh my. Elsa inwardly cringed. She could almost hear the clatter Archer made as he fell from the pedestal her parents likely placed him upon.

"Very good." Father leaned back in his chair, peering down his nose. "Do you intend to work at the museum long-term? And if not, what other employment does your education and experience qualify you for?"

"Father." Elsa didn't know what else to say. It wasn't that she hoped Archer would impress her parents, but neither did she want her friend humiliated by this line of questioning.

"It's okay. My own father has asked me the same thing, many times."

"So you've had time to practice your answer." Father smiled. "Do continue."

Archer laughed. "Yeah, you'd think. Well, the way I see it, I'm still young. I have lots of options. I like working at the museum and find it fulfilling. There are avenues of advancement there, so I may be looking at promotions in the future, which would come with an increase in salary. That's what you're getting at, isn't it, Mr. Reisner?"

"In part, yes."

"Naturally. But if I get tired of the museum or passed over for a position I've earned, I have no problem looking elsewhere. I'll cross that bridge when I get to it. But for now, I'm content where I am."

"You have investments, then?"

"Pardon me?"

Father sipped his coffee. "I know roughly what you make at the museum. You drive a Rolls-Royce, and the suit you're wearing costs at least four months of that pay. So I assume you've invested wisely to be able to afford the lifestyle that makes you so content."

"As a matter of fact, yes. Exactly. I invest wisely, and here I am. Content."

"Good for you, young man."

"Well, now that that's settled, I think we're ready for dessert,"

Elsa jumped in, as eager for tiramisu as she was for this interview to end.

The Caravellos' dessert was as divine as she had remembered from the engagement party last spring, and the unanimous winner from among the other options. Elsa tidied her notes and passed them to Mother, who would share them with Mrs. Caravello.

"All set to go, then?" Archer asked, rising from the table. "Coney Island awaits. Percy and Ivy took the subway there already. We'll take the Rolls. I'll get it."

After a round of handshakes with Mother and Father, he left.

"Interesting boy," Mother said. "You seem comfortable with him."

"We're only friends." Elsa pulled a silk scarf from her purse. "It was nice of you to invite him tonight, but don't think that just because we're going out again means we're some kind of item."

Mother lifted one eyebrow. "Does he know that?"

"I'm sure he does. I'm not his type." Preparing to ride in his convertible, she tied the scarf over her hair.

Father's expression grew serious. "Then what does he want? Why is he spending so much time with you when there are other young women he could pursue?"

"I'm surprised you didn't ask him while you had the chance." Elsa laughed, but the questions stung.

CHAPTER

15

It took an hour or more to drive to Coney Island, on the southwest corner of Long Island, but the time passed quickly. Elsa updated Archer on the plight of the Petrovics and the new Spalding relatives she'd met, and he shared about his quest to achieve independence from his father. He still hadn't moved out on his own, and as much as he joked about it, she could tell it bothered him.

"You'd have an easier time paying rent if you sold the Rolls," she suggested.

"And ride public transit with the masses? Not my style." He laughed, but Elsa suspected he wasn't kidding. "Besides, this auto was a gift from my father, remember? Not only would it be rude to sell it off, but the profit I'd gain would still be from my father since he gave the Rolls to me in the first place. So paying rent with that money would prove nothing. Savvy?"

"I get it." Elsa braced herself against the door as he took a turn too fast. "What about that suit you're wearing? Did it really cost you four months of paychecks?"

He squinted at her, though his hat brim blocked the lowering sun. "Listen, doll, don't worry about it. Didn't your mother teach you that talking about money was 'vulgar'?"

A retort sprang to mind, but the hard set to his jaw made her swallow it. She hadn't meant to pry, and she sensed he'd been pressed enough tonight.

By the time they parked and found Ivy and Percy at the appointed meeting place, however, he was all smiles and confidence again.

"Did you save any room for Nathan's?" Ivy hiked a thumb over her shoulder at Nathan's Famous Frankfurters and Soft Drink Stand, where hot dogs and root beer were only a nickel each. Situated on the corner of Stillwell and Surf Avenues, it was across the street from the subway station and always had a crowd.

Elsa put a hand to her stomach. "I'll definitely have room later. Let me walk off dinner first. Shall we?" Threading through couples and families, they headed south on Stillwell, toward the beach, the men leading the way.

"How did it go, by the way?" Percy hooked his thumbs into the pockets of his trousers.

"We sampled cuisine from four of the top caterers in Manhattan," Archer said. "How do you think it went?"

While the men chatted, Elsa explained to Ivy what her mother had arranged. "I wish I'd known about it ahead of time. It would have been so fun to have you there and cast your vote, too."

"You do know my favorite food is hot dogs, right?" Ivy spread her arms wide, emphasizing once more where they were. "Percy would have been a good judge, though. His palate is *quite* discerning."

Elsa lowered her voice. "Did you two get along all right while you were waiting for us?"

Ivy grinned. "I gave him some smashing ideas for that novel he's working on. You know something, for as different as he and I are, I'm more comfortable with him than I am with anyone at work, simply because I'm not trying to impress him. I don't think Percy is impressed by anyone or anything, which means there's no point in being anyone other than myself."

Elsa squeezed her friend's shoulder. Most of Ivy's colleagues at the New-York Historical Society were real blue bloods of old New York with roots going back to the Dutch families. From what Ivy had shared, they believed Ivy was less fit to work there due to her middle-class upbringing and the fact that she wasn't even from New York. She worked harder than any of them, though.

"Was Percy at least impressed with Nathan's?" Elsa asked, trying to keep the mood light.

"He didn't say so."

"Can't imagine he'd volunteer that. Let's ask." Elsa linked her arm through Ivy's and waited for a break in the men's conversation.

"Investments, I told him," Archer was saying, obviously rehashing her father's interview about his financial viability.

Percy burst out laughing. "That's what you call it now? Oh, that's rich." He swiped off his glasses to rub his eyes.

Archer slapped him on the back, but his head turned to follow an attractive young woman passing by. "He works on Wall Street. He gets it."

"And if that isn't a gamble, I don't know what is."

Elsa cut a glance to Ivy and saw her own concern reflected in her roommate's expression. Suddenly, she didn't care a hoot about whether Percy had enjoyed the hot dog.

"Ready to be amused?" Percy tossed over his shoulder as he put his glasses back on. "Ivy and I already explored Steeplechase Park, but we could hit Luna Park next."

"Why don't we start there?" Archer pointed to a giant contraption called Deno's Wonder Wheel. It stood almost fifteen stories high and looked like the Ferris wheel's unruly cousin. Elsa counted eight cars on the outside of the wheel, each of them holding six people. Then sixteen more cars swung from tracks in the interior of the wheel, sliding toward the hub and back out as the wheel turned.

Elsa's stomach turned just watching it. "I'd better give all that food a little more time to digest before I try that."

"No? The roller coaster, then. Thunderbolt opened last year," Archer said, but he was clearly distracted by all the beautiful women smiling in his direction. "What a crop of tomatoes here, eh, Percy?"

"Archer." Ivy cocked her head and snapped to get his attention. "If she isn't up for the Wonder Wheel yet, what makes you think she'd go on a roller coaster?"

Elsa's sentiments exactly, but Ivy's response was quicker.

"What? Oh." He shrugged again, and Elsa was beginning to understand why her elders had always called the gesture lazy. Truly, it was no substitute for words.

A man on stilts walked past them, wearing a straw boater and a sandwich board advertisement. "Don't miss Luna Park!" he bellowed, sweat streaking his ruddy face. "The heart of Coney Island!"

"It's a sign. A literal sign." Archer grinned. "How about it?"

The rest of the group agreed. Spying an approaching trolley, they hopped on and clattered down Surf Avenue beneath electric lights strung between poles on opposite sides of the street. Riding the breeze were the salty smells of sea and sweaty people. They disembarked outside Luna Park's elaborate white stone entryway and waited their turn to pay the dime-per-person fee. The name of the park was spelled out in electric bulbs that curved to fit inside giant crescent moon shapes.

Inside, the crowds moved at a shuffle pace. Barkers called out to steer tourists into their attractions. Popcorn and pretzels were sold on every corner, which explained the kernels crunching beneath Elsa's feet.

"Now what?" she murmured, barely hearing her own question.

"World Circus Sideshow!" a man called from his perch on

a stand outside a tent. "Step right up and be amazed by Armless Wonder, Spider Boy, a four-legged girl prodigy, the world's strongest man, and the ugliest woman alive! World Circus Show, ladies and gents."

Elsa shook her head and turned away, only to be confronted by more shouting men, each vying to be heard over the others.

"Get your thrills on the Toboggan, the roller coaster of the Alpines!"

"Fancy girls! Take a peep!"

Stepping over a puddle of spilled beer, Elsa pulled her friends to the edge of the sidewalk. "On second thought, this really isn't my scene." Cars full of shrieking children roared by on the wooden roller coaster. In a large window over Percy's shoulder, a woman was covered by strategically placed fans and nothing else. Heat rushed to Elsa's face.

"Come on, there's something for everyone here!" Archer protested.

As if to prove his point, another barker called, "Live babies! All the world loves a baby! Three pound babies, still alive!"

Elsa turned to find a huge sign that read *Incubator Babies*.

"I read an article about this," Ivy said. "Hospitals don't have these incubators, so prematurely born babies are cared for here in a hospital-like environment at no cost to their parents. The nurses, incubators, food, and medicine are all paid for by those who spend their dimes to see. I'd like to go in."

"Me too," Elsa said. "In fact, that is the only thing here I'm interested in. Other than that, I'd rather walk along the shore."

"You would?" Percy's necktie blew sideways in the wind, and he tucked it back into his vest. "Sorry, I'm surprised that would appeal to you."

Elsa frowned. "It appeals to millions. Not all at once, thank goodness, but the beach and boardwalk are the entire reason all of these amusement parks are even—"

"Yeah, I get it," Percy interrupted, "but I thought going for rides would be more your thing, given your condition."

"Change your mind about renting one of those rolling chairs?" Archer asked.

Irritation flared. Elsa bit her tongue, reminding herself that he could have no idea how the suggestion affected her. He didn't know she associated those chairs with shame and loss, and she would never tell him.

Ivy crossed her arms and glared. "And what are we going to do about *your* condition, boys?"

Now she had Archer's attention. "What condition is that?"

"Rudeness. It seems to be catching. Maybe you ought to go home and sleep it off."

Ivy's feisty spirit drew a smile to Elsa's lips. "All right. We don't have to all do the same thing. Why don't we part ways for the night? You and Percy can do all the rides you want and take the Rolls back afterward. Ivy and I will be fine on our own. We don't even mind taking public transit home."

Ivy nodded her agreement. "That sounds great."

Archer looked at Percy, and for a moment, Elsa thought he might push back about the idea of two unchaperoned young women in one of the busiest places in New York, especially during the last weekend of the season, with a subway ride ahead of them that would take at least ninety minutes including the transfers between lines. Darkness was already falling, though it was hardly noticeable with the lights blazing in Luna Park.

He didn't bring up any of that. He only looked at his watch and grinned.

"See you Monday, Archer." Elsa turned away, happy to spend time with Ivy alone instead. At least, as alone as they could be in this crowd of thousands.

Together, they crossed the street to stand in line for the Incubator Babies.

"Elsa? I thought that was you." Wesley Spalding caught up to her, and she made the introductions.

"Is your family with you?" she asked.

"Father is over there, working." He gestured down the street.

"He's working at the Circus Show?" Elsa asked.

"Yes, for the eugenics office. He really should have finished up before the last weekend of the season, but he's been preoccupied with Aunt Birdie's estate. He interviews the show people to get their family histories. You know, to see what led to their defects, so he can harp on how society cannot let this happen again. He even gets samples of their hair for the ERO."

The line moved forward. "And does he want to interview the parents of prematurely born babies for the same purpose?" Ivy asked.

"He tried, but Dr. Couney, the man in charge of this place, doesn't reveal the parents' identities." Wesley paused, jingling the coins in his pocket. "Aunt Birdie loved this place. In fact, before Uncle Linus died and his creditors came after her for his debts, she gave a huge Christmas donation to Dr. Couney for his Incubator Babies, and she did it in my father's name. You should have seen him when he found out. He was so mad, he was fit to blow a gasket." Wesley laughed. "Father's view has always been that the weaklings should be allowed to die. Natural selection and all that. He says that even if they did grow up, they would only reproduce more weaklings and lower the quality of the gene pool."

Elsa stiffened. "Do you agree?"

"Are you kidding me?" Wesley laughed again. "I barely agree with my father on anything. In fact, sometimes I'll take the opposite position, simply to defy him. Mother calls that diabolical, and maybe she's right. But if you had grown up with his hatred of weakness, as I have, you'd understand. He calls me weak for loving music even when it doesn't pay the bills. He's a machine, I tell you. He can admire a great musician's precision but has no appreciation for the emotion music is meant to evoke. I'll never forget the first time music moved me to tears. He—" Wesley's jaw clamped shut. "I'd better not get started on that score."

The line progressed again. Only ten or so more people stood between them and the entrance. "I'm sorry to hear that," Elsa told him.

"Yeah. Listen, I don't want to interrupt your evening, you two, so I'll get going. Elsa, I'm sorry you had to witness that family scene in the parlor yesterday."

"Never mind that," she said. "See you next week, if you'll be going back to Elmhurst."

"I will. I can't stay away from the piano, and the movers won't be picking it up for days." With a smile, he left them.

As Elsa watched him disappear into the teeming throng, she noticed one man across the street not moving. He was taller than the average man, made even taller by a brown bowler. He was staring directly at her.

A stilt-walker passed between them, and then the man in the bowler was gone.

Ten minutes after she and Ivy had entered the Incubator Babies building, Elsa was satisfied that the man had not followed them inside. Relaxing, she allowed herself to focus on the tiny miracles before her. The incubators were like metal ice boxes on stilts, except for the double doors made of glass. Each one held an impossibly small human life.

Nurses bustled between incubators. One approached Elsa and Ivy with a smile, then removed her wedding ring, opened the doors to the incubator, and slipped the ring over the infant's arm and back again to prove how small he was. Then, since the baby was too tiny to swallow, she used a special spoon to drip nourishment into each nostril.

"He will live," the nurse said with a smile. "He's a fighter. He has gained five ounces already."

No wonder Birdie loved this place. Birdie saw value and dignity where others didn't. Elsa could also imagine Mr. Spalding turning up his nose at these vulnerable little ones.

By the time they finished walking through the building, Elsa was ready for the hot dog she promised Ivy she'd eat. This time they walked the few blocks between Luna Park and Nathan's Famous, and Elsa was grateful to sit at one of the concrete tables while Ivy stood in line for her.

Seeing those tiny babies fighting to live had strengthened Elsa's resolve to fight, too. Not just for her own health and well-being, but for Danielle's, as well, at least as far as she had anything to do with it.

But that was the problem. What *did* she have to do with it? The nurses and Dr. Couney knew exactly what to do to give the babies their best chance at life, but Elsa remained at a loss. The aviary may never be found, and Tatiana and Danielle needed a new place to live and work in a matter of weeks. It wasn't Elsa's job to solve all of this, but if she didn't, who would?

She lifted her gaze to the Wonder Wheel, now lit up against the darkening sky. Thoughts spun through her mind, but like the cars on that wheel, they went nowhere.

A breeze picked up, blowing someone's cigarette smoke in her face. Turning away from it, she scanned the line still waiting to be served at the counter.

And there he was again, the man in the bowler and tweed suit. At least this time, he wasn't watching her. He pumped mustard onto a frankfurter like any other tourist.

"Here you go, hon." Ivy slid a paper basket across the table to Elsa and sat across from her. "And extra napkins, too."

"Thanks." Elsa glanced at the man and met his gaze. His expression immediately changed. He motioned her over to join him, as if she would do such a thing for a stranger. "Ivy, do you see that man standing by the condiments? Do we know him?"

"Never seen him before. But he sure is looking at you. What's his deal?"

"I don't think I care to find out." The idea of strolling along the boardwalk with a creep fixating on her didn't sound like a good one. Besides, the walking she'd already done had begun to catch up with her. If she was going to save some strength for the trip back to the Beresford, she ought not spend it all here. "Change of plans. Let's go home."

"I'm all for it. I don't like that man's vibe."

"He was watching me before we saw the Incubator Babies."

"Nope. Uh-uh. We don't stick around for that applesauce." Ivy scooped up Elsa's paper basket. "Hot dogs travel. Now where is a knight in a shining Rolls-Royce when you need one?"

Elsa spared no more than a moment scanning the crowd in the off-chance they'd see Percy or Archer. "My guess? Gambling, the both of them. I'd settle for Wesley Spalding, but I don't see him either. Let's go."

Zigzagging through the crowd, they crossed the intersection to the Stillwell Avenue station. The cacophony inside rattled Elsa, but Ivy took charge, navigating through the stream of people, all the while holding the garlic-flavored hot dog aloft. At the turnstiles, she paid the fares for both of them and guided Elsa through.

After a few glances over her shoulder, Elsa still didn't see the man. But he was tall. If he came looking, he'd find her as easily as Wesley had. Her limp made her stand out in any crowd.

Ivy looped an arm through Elsa's as they made their way to the right platform. "He could be harmless," Ivy said. "He might not even be following you, and even if he was, what could he do in front of all these other people?"

Elsa was about to concede the point when she spotted him. "There he is."

Ivy squeezed her arm tighter. "Never mind."

A blast of air whooshed over them, billowing their skirts and tugging the scarves that wrapped their hair. They walked away from the man in pursuit until the train doors opened and they could get on. They quickly slid onto a bench.

"Are you kidding me?" A fellow traveler gripped a leather strap from the ceiling and scowled at the aromatic hot dog. "You don't bring hot food on the train."

"Sorry." Ivy lifted her eyebrows at Elsa. "You hungry yet?"

Elsa took a bite, but she was too agitated to eat more.

"You sure?" Ivy proceeded to eat the rest herself in what felt like record time. "This is nothing," she told Elsa. "You should see the Fourth of July contest eaters. They eat dozens in a matter of minutes."

"Ivy," Elsa whispered. "Get up. He just got on at the other end of the car. He's coming this way. Or trying to." The car was so jammed with riders, his halting progress was slow.

Immediately, Ivy was on her feet and moving toward the still-open door, blocking Elsa from the man's view. They stuffed their scarves in their pocketbooks in case he was looking for the brightly colored head coverings.

"If we get off now, he'll chase us in the station," Elsa told her. "Wait until the doors start to close, and then we jump at the last second, before he has time to follow."

"Right. I'm ready." Seconds later, the doors began to shut, and Elsa and Ivy slipped through.

Safe on the platform, Elsa's heart thudded as she watched the train roll by. The man in the bowler slapped a hand to the window and shouted something she couldn't hear.

But she read his lips. A chill raced down her spine.

Ivy gasped. "Did he say, 'See you soon?' He was looking right at you."

Elsa's mouth went dry. She didn't know who he was, what he wanted, or if he would be waiting at some station along the way. She licked her lips. "We're taking a taxi home."

CHAPTER

16

Luke was alone when he picked up Elsa and her box of magazines Monday morning. He'd given Tom and Barney the day off for Labor Day, but not himself.

"What a nice boss you are." She accepted his hand as he helped her up into the truck, then closed the door. When he climbed into the driver's seat, she went on, "The American Museum of Natural History remains open on Labor Day, but even if it had been closed, I'd still be working. Mr. Chapman made it clear he wants the Elmhurst project wrapped up as soon as possible. I've already been here too long, according to him. He wants me to process specimen exchanges between our museum and a few willing institutions in London, Berlin, and Stockholm."

As Luke pulled back into traffic and began the journey to Tarrytown, she asked how his weekend had been. He'd spent Saturday at Elmhurst on his own, he told her. Sunday, he'd tried birding in Central Park. This time he'd brought Tom along. "Not nearly as fun—or successful—without you."

Elsa was sorry she'd missed him in both places and told him so. "Did you spy any interesting birds without me?"

"To tell you the truth, Tom got hung up on some pigeons, so we left early."

"Pigeons? Why—" She stopped herself, recalling what she'd read about homing pigeons serving during the war, ferrying messages through dangerous skies when radio equipment failed. "Do pigeons still remind him of the war?"

"Apparently."

She shook her head. "How awful. The city is full of them. But our urban birds aren't like the trained carrier ones."

"Close enough, I guess. Tom was part of the Lost Battalion over there." Briefly, Luke explained the plight of those men, isolated from reinforcements in the Argonne Forest, pinned down by enemy fire for days, unable to get food or water. They'd even been attacked from the air by friendly fire. "A pigeon named Cher Ami finally carried a message to the American base telling them their location and to stop the barrage upon them."

"I read about that little fellow," Elsa said quietly. The bird's name, in French, meant "dear friend." The pigeon survived his mission but lost his leg and was blinded in the process.

"Tom loved those homing pigeons. That ordeal in the Argonne was the most traumatic episode in his experience. And then about a year after the war, some bigwigs decided to make a film about the Lost Battalion, and they wanted to use the real soldiers. So they took Tom and some others right back to the place where it happened and made them relive it all over again so they could capture it on film." Luke's jaw set, and a muscle twitched near his eye.

Elsa gasped. "I can't imagine experiencing that ordeal once, let alone twice. Even if the veterans had a choice about participating in the filming, it still seems cruel."

"It set him back, but he's come a long way since then."

She allowed a few moments of silence as she looked out the window. Half a block of halting traffic later, she asked, "What about you, Luke?"

"Me? I don't need pigeons to remember the war, if that's what you're asking. All I need is a mirror."

She wished that wasn't true. "Do you still see the war in your reflection?"

"On occasion."

When he didn't say more, she figured it was easier for him to speak of Tom's experience than his own. "I'll never fully grasp what you went through."

"Good," he said, surprising her. "I wouldn't want you to. War is a soul-crushing evil. I found pockets of light and goodness during that time, but in general, I don't want you to know what it was like over there. That's a burden I refuse to lay on you." He glanced at her for only a moment before turning his gaze back to the road. But it was long enough for the sincerity in his eyes to strike her.

"All right, I won't ask about it," she said, "but I'm willing to listen if you ever want to talk."

He nodded. "I've done more than my share of talking this morning already. Your turn. How was your weekend?"

Well then. She hadn't planned on telling him *everything* that happened on Coney Island Saturday night, but he *did* ask.

When she reached the part of the story where Archer and Percy agreed to split from her and Ivy, his grip tightened on the steering wheel until his knuckles turned white.

But when she mentioned the man in the bowler, the look he shot her held a fierceness she knew was not intended for her. "Wait. I'm pulling over for this. And I think I need more coffee."

In the next two minutes, they'd stopped at a roadside café with a painted wooden sign. Luke purchased two paper cups of coffee and handed one to Elsa. Together, they sat on a bench outside in the shade.

She checked her watch. Luke didn't.

He drank what must have been half the cup at once. "Tell me everything."

As she did, he stretched his arm on the back of the bench behind her. His attention never wavered as he listened to the entire story. "I thought maybe I was overreacting, but at the end, I was sure that man said, 'See you soon.'"

Luke wrapped his hand around her shoulder. "Thank God you had the presence of mind to react the way you did."

She savored the coffee, pleased that he'd remembered that she took cream and no sugar. "Maybe I didn't read his lips right. Maybe he meant no harm."

"It would have been an unacceptable risk to stay and find out."

"Unacceptable to you?"

"Yes. To me."

The warmth from his hand radiated through her. He smelled of sawdust and clean, sun-dried cotton. It would be so easy for her to lean into him. It surprised her how much she wanted to. "You seem to be taking all of this very seriously."

"I take you seriously."

"So I noticed."

Hiding a rising blush, she finished the rest of her coffee, and they continued on their journey.

The closer they got to Tarrytown, the more the conversation centered on the Petrovics' plight.

"Danielle is vulnerable," she told Luke. "I have a feeling that if someone doesn't intervene, Mr. Spalding could do something terrible. He could separate her from Tatiana or worse."

Luke nodded. "When we deliver that box you brought, I'd like to hear if Tatiana has any updates. I can talk to her about moving that cottage off the grounds, too, if that's what she decides to do. But I'll need to inspect it first to see if it will hold together."

"I hadn't even considered that possibility. Thank you for thinking of it!" A measure of relief stole through her.

His lips tilted at one corner. "Don't thank me yet. I have no idea where she could park it, and that's if it doesn't fall apart on the way."

"I understand. But just knowing you care means a lot to me."

"I do care." Luke met her gaze for a moment before turning back to the road.

Elsa wondered if he'd meant those three small words for her. With a start, she realized she hoped he had.

Luke whistled low as they approached the mansion. "Haven't seen a Rolls here before. Looks like another relative has come to pick over what's left."

From the long drive up to the house, Elsa recognized Wesley's yellow Packard, along with a white convertible.

"That's no relative of the Van Tessels," she said, recognizing the license plate. "That auto belongs to Archer."

Luke tensed. "Why is he here?"

"Excellent question. Let's ask him."

As they reached the veranda, Archer exited the house. At least he was empty-handed.

"What are you doing here?" she asked without preamble.

Archer jumped back when he saw her, shock splayed across his face. "What are *you* doing here? You said, 'See you Monday.' Didn't that mean you were planning to stay at the museum today?"

"Hi, I'm Luke, and you're not supposed to be here. Allow me to see you off the property." Luke grabbed his arm and escorted Archer off the veranda and all the way to his Rolls.

Elsa followed them. "Change of plans. I decided to come here today instead of staying in Manhattan. You still haven't told us why you're here. Clearly it isn't to see me."

Archer jerked his arm out of Luke's grasp and rubbed the spot where he'd been gripped. "Gee, what happened to you? Cut yourself shaving?"

Elsa's temper burned, but Luke kept his cool. In fact, his expression turned stone cold.

"I was only trying to help. I wanted to surprise you." Archer threw up his hands. "So much for that."

"Surprise me how?"

"You said you wanted to find the aviary but haven't searched properly since you're here for work and shouldn't take the time. I met Wesley Spalding after I saw him talking to you at Luna Park. We hit it off. He told me where the estate was. I only wanted to help you look for it."

Luke glowered. "This isn't your concern."

"She's my concern. If it's important to her, it's important to me."

"Applesauce." Elsa didn't believe it. Not after his disregard for her on Coney Island.

"Consider it an olive branch after the way we parted Saturday night. Why don't you tell the guard dog here to leave us alone so we can talk?"

Elsa bristled. "No."

Luke looked from her to Archer. "Woof."

The air seemed to crackle with the tension radiating from Luke. Archer ran a finger inside his overstarched collar. "Well, I got the feeling after Percy and I left you and Ivy in Luna Park that maybe I should have made sure you made it home all right."

A muscle bunched in Luke's jaw. "*Maybe*? *Maybe* you should have made sure?"

"It was her idea," Archer insisted. "She didn't want to do the rides, so she suggested we go our separate ways. She said they'd take the subway home."

"And you had no problem walking away from her on a Saturday night in a place where all kinds of people congregate and make trouble. You decided it was better to hit the roller coasters than be a gentleman and enjoy her company while ensuring she was safe at all times from the unsavory elements. You figured two women walking between subway stations in the dark to make their transfers was an acceptable risk."

Archer spread his hands. "She's fine, isn't she? Ivy made it back all right, too, I guess?"

Luke opened the driver's side door and waited while Archer got inside before slamming it shut. "That risk was *not* acceptable." He crossed his arms over his chest. "Elsa, you want to add anything?"

"Only that we were followed by a strange man right onto the subway car, gave him the slip, and took a taxi home instead. Yes, I think that covers it."

As if he'd just heard this for the first time, tendons pulled taut in Luke's neck. He turned to Archer, who peeled away before Luke could say or do more, pebbles spraying behind the rear wheels.

Elsa stared after the dazzling convertible until it rolled out of view. "He didn't even say he was sorry," she murmured. "He was probably too afraid of your fists to stick around, but . . . I can't believe he just left like that after what I said."

"It's a good thing he did. I was ready to pound him." Luke shook his head and breathed deeply, expanding his already broad chest. "I've worked for years to control my temper. But so help me, if I see that rat again I don't know what I'll do." A lump shifted in his throat as he cleared it. "What exactly is the nature of your relationship with this Archer character?"

"He's a colleague. Up until now, I considered him a friend. Now I wonder if I can call him that. That isn't how you treat friends."

"No, it isn't. Do you believe he came here to make amends with you?"

A beat of quiet followed until Elsa admitted, "He came for the aviary. He said so himself."

"Do you trust he wants it for Danielle?"

She bit her lip. "I want to believe the best of people, but his behavior lately makes that a challenge. Hopefully your question is a moot point now. I don't think he'll be coming back."

"Not if I have anything to do with it." Luke took her hand in his calloused one. "I never asked how the walking went on Coney Island. How far did you go?"

"Far enough to do some good, I hope."

The steel in his eyes flashed with understanding. "Far enough to hurt." After she nodded, he pressed, "And your lungs? How did your breathing do?"

"We were only walking, no running this time. I promise." She smiled.

He didn't. "Tell me."

She inhaled the clean, pine-scented air as she recalled the hustle to the Stillwell station. "I was winded, but Ivy was with me."

His thumb circled the back of her hand. "I admire that you're pushing yourself to grow stronger. Just be reasonable about the pace you set for yourself, all right?"

A trio of Canada geese honked and soared overhead. "I want to fly, Luke," she told him. "Ever since I was a little girl confined to bed, told I may never walk again, I've wanted to know what it would feel like to be fast and light in the air, like all these birds I've spent my life studying. But I've decided to content myself with keeping both feet on the ground. I want to walk and not faint. What could be more reasonable than that?"

—————○—————

Elsa's body proved less than cooperative. After three trips to the second floor to bring the remaining birds down to the dining hall, both legs ached—the weak one from the pain, and the strong one from compensating for it. Pulse still throbbing, she stood at the table and unpacked the box she'd brought down.

The dining hall table was large enough to seat twenty people. Eating here must have felt lonely for the Van Tessels with all these empty chairs, but at the moment Elsa was grateful for the space. She spread the birds out in rows by color since that was how they'd been ordered when she collected them from the rooms. Now that her fresh ledger had been alphabetized, it would be a snap to find the entry and make a matching catalog tag for each bird.

"Now we're on the trolley," Elsa murmured once all three hundred birds were lined up and ready for proper identification at last. Circling the table to begin, she caught a glimpse of movement outside the window.

Tatiana and Danielle were coming this way from the direction of their cottage. A wicker basket swung from Tatiana's arm.

Elsa waved, but they didn't see her. Ignoring her body's protests, she walked to the corridor and outside to the covered veranda. "What a nice surprise! Please, come in!"

Tatiana smiled. "Thank you, dear, but we'd better not."

Danielle kicked at a pebble.

"The family isn't here right now," Elsa reassured them. Wesley's Packard remained parked in the drive, but neither he nor Jane were in the mansion at present.

"All the same. We've just come to bring you some refreshment in case you're hungry."

How on earth had Tatiana managed to think of that, when her own concerns were greater? Elsa was humbled by this woman. No wonder Birdie had cared for the Petrovics so much.

"That sounds wonderful," Elsa said. "I have some things to show Danielle, too. Why don't we visit in the courtyard?"

When Tatiana and Danielle agreed, Elsa convinced them to simply walk through the house to reach the courtyard behind it, rather than meandering all the way around.

"I need to pick something up from the dining hall. I'd be happy to show you what I'm working on right now, if you'd like to see it."

Danielle nodded. "I want to see."

Elsa drew a deep breath and hoped she hadn't made a mis-step with this offer. Danielle had been upset about the birds leaving the mansion before. Seeing them laid out might trigger more dismay. On the other hand, Danielle may feel better if she understood more about Elsa's work with the museum and saw them for herself one last time.

With a smile, she ushered them into the dining hall and prayed the Spalding siblings wouldn't return soon enough to interrupt them. "You're so good at classifying things, Danielle. Let me show you what I'm doing."

Tatiana rested the basket on the floor and stood back, hands folded, as if afraid to touch anything.

"They're still grouped by color," Danielle observed. "Miss Birdie did that for me. Red belongs with red, I told her. Blue with blue. Green with green. Yellows together, and blacks on their own. Every color should be separate."

Elsa smiled. She hadn't realized that Danielle was Birdie's interior decorating muse. "It's striking to see the colors together like that. May I show you how we order things for the museum?"

Danielle flicked a gaze at Elsa. "Yes."

Elsa explained the habitat groups inside the museum, with groups of birds based on geographic location. "But in the catalogs, like this one, they are alphabetized by their Latin names." She went on to explain that each bird would be assigned a number and a tag to match it to its field data.

Frowning, Danielle peered at the ledger Elsa showed her, and then at the rows of birds. "They don't match up. They're not in order."

"That's all right. I can look at the bird on the table and then locate it in the chart very easily by its name, now that this is alphabetized."

Tatiana brushed a loose thread from her skirt. "What will happen to the birds once they move into their new home?" she asked. "Will other children have the chance to see them, too?"

Elsa appreciated the thoughtful prompt. "Yes. Children come every day—and grown-ups, too—so they can see things they wouldn't normally. They will love Miss Birdie's collection, I'm sure."

"That is what she would have wanted. Isn't it, sweetheart?" Tatiana rested her hand on her daughter's shoulder. "This is why she wrote it in her will that the museum should have the birds. To share them with many, many others, so they wouldn't go to waste."

Danielle pursed her lips but didn't argue. She pulled a strand of hair around her finger and twisted it round and round.

"Ready to see what I brought you?" Elsa picked up her scrapbook and an issue of *Bird-Lore* and led the Petrovics outside to the courtyard.

She handed Danielle the magazine. "You already know so much about birds' scientific names and their migration patterns and songs. This magazine will tell you even more about the birds' personalities. What they do that makes them special."

"Like the bowerbirds, whose favorite color is blue."

"Exactly. I brought you an entire box of them to do with whatever you wish. You might simply read them, or you could cut them up and rearrange the illustrations or information any way you like." She opened her scrapbook on her lap. "I made this when I was a child. It kept me entertained for hours and hours."

"Oh, be careful, Danielle," Tatiana warned as the child began handling the pages.

But Danielle took care to turn them slowly, and from the outside corner only. Though she was quiet as she looked, her expression held an intense curiosity that proved her interest.

"That was so kind of you to bring these things, dear," Tatiana said. "Are you sure you want to part with an entire box of magazines?"

"I'm sure."

"What do you say, Danielle?"

"Thank you." She didn't look up, still focused on the magazine.

"You're very welcome. I'm delighted to share them with you."

The French door opened, and Luke stepped outside, shutting it behind him. "I thought I heard voices. It's good to see you both again."

Tatiana practically cheered at the sight of him, then dug into her basket, handing him and Elsa each a jar of honey. "I've had some busy bees this season," she explained.

The sound of shouting drew their attention toward the parlor.

"Where were you?" Jane asked her brother.

"Out. Same as you."

"Out treasure-hunting, you mean. I thought we agreed to search the outbuildings together. But as soon as I turned around, you were gone."

"Don't be droll . . ."

Elsa shook her head, wondering if they had gone so far as to search the Petrovics' cottage for the aviary. "Have they bothered you yet, Tatiana?" She kept her voice low.

"No. Not those two. We did have an unexpected visitor this morning, but it wasn't one of them."

A muscle clenched in Luke's jaw. "Was his name Archer?"

She shook her head. "He said his name was Hugh. He was keen to know where the aviary was. Thankfully, Danielle was out visiting the hummers when he stopped by."

Was Archer now giving a false name to hide who he was? Elsa didn't know what to think. "Whoever he was, he had no right and no business bothering you. Did he leave when you asked him to?"

"He did. But he saw the provenance for the aviary. I'd been looking at it this morning at the kitchen table, and it was still lying there when I opened the door and he pushed his way in. He spotted it right away and was convinced it was proof I must have the aviary, too. I denied it, but I have a feeling we may not have seen the last of him."

Oh no. The last thing Elsa had wanted to do was give anyone a reason to search Tatiana's house. But she could immediately see how they'd want to do just that, now that they knew she had the provenance document.

"I'll see what I can do about that," Luke said. "In fact, I'd like to go to your cottage now, if that's all right. I can deliver that box of magazines for you. If anyone else is there, I'll chase him off." He didn't mention checking the structure's integrity, but Elsa figured he didn't want to raise any false hope about being able to move the cottage elsewhere.

Tatiana sent him with her blessing. "I should be getting back soon, too," she added.

Piano music drifted out from the parlor, a sound much more welcome than the sibling spat of a few moments ago. "Can you spare another minute?" Elsa asked. "I just remembered something I wanted to show you, too."

When she agreed to wait, Elsa slipped back inside the mansion and retrieved five framed watercolors Birdie had painted of some of her favorite, if common, birds. As she passed back through the parlor, she paused to show them to Jane and Wesley. It smelled like smoke in there again, but she saw no cigarettes or ashtrays. Maybe Wesley had continued sprinkling ash into the carpet. Maybe he enjoyed angering his father that way.

Surely there were other methods, but Elsa wasn't there to give tips.

Near the fireplace, where he wrapped a crystal vase in linen, Crawford greeted Elsa with a polite nod.

"You're rather chummy with the gardener and her imbecile girl, aren't you?" Wesley spoke over the piano at her.

Crawford kept his head down, moving on to wrap a clock.

"She's no imbecile," Elsa said. "And they're about to go, anyway.

Look, these were painted by your great-aunt. Do either of you want them? Do you think your father or grandmother would?" she asked.

"Pish!" Jane waved a hand. "We've all seen those, and no, we don't want them. Get rid of them *and* those people in the court-yard, please, and then you must come back and tell me all your news. I'm dying for distraction."

"I've got to get back to work, Jane, but thank you for these. I'll see if the Petrovics would like them first."

Wesley stopped playing. "How curious. I cannot imagine what spell they've cast over you for you to moon over them so. Really, Elsa, I can't say it's dignified."

Nostrils flaring, Jane stood with fists trembling at her sides. "Those aren't supposed to go to them!"

"You said you didn't want them."

"I don't, but I'd rather they get destroyed when the county tears this old house down. Our family things are not to end up in the hands of servants—"

Uninterested in hearing the rest, Elsa ducked out and closed the door on Jane's tirade. With her back to the drama she hoped would not breach the house, she showed Tatiana and Danielle the paintings.

"Would you like to have these?" She spread them out flat on a bench.

Tatiana pressed a hand to her chest. "My, but aren't they beautiful."

"Please take your favorites," Elsa urged. "Take all of them, if you like."

"Yes." Danielle twirled her hair around one finger. "All of them."

Tatiana touched Elsa's elbow. "You're sure?"

"Of course. Here, you can use your basket to take them home with you." Elsa stacked the jars of honey in one elbow and a fresh loaf of bread wrapped in paper in the other. While Danielle carefully nested the watercolors in the basket, Elsa motioned Tatiana aside.

"Before you go, do you have any updates from those inquiries you've made seeking employment elsewhere?" she asked quietly.

"I wish I did."

"My parents know a lot of brownstone owners in Manhattan. Perhaps one of them needs a gardener. Would it be all right if I ask?"

A sad smile pinched Tatiana's eyes. "Bless you for offering, dear. Brownstones don't usually have gardeners' cottages on site, do they? So we'd have to find a home off the property. Even if we could find something affordable, Danielle and I aren't meant for city living."

Perhaps the New York Botanical Garden was hiring. But that was still in New York City. Even if Luke found that their cottage could be moved, any available lot near the Botanical Garden would be a far cry from the sprawling landscapes here on the Hudson River.

Elsa would have to keep thinking.

CHAPTER

17

S top!" Elsa deposited the honey and bread on the sideboard in the dining hall and rushed to the table.

Jane and Wesley each grabbed two more birds—one in each hand—and dropped them into various boxes Crawford was lining up on the floor. They weren't even wearing gloves.

"Please, stop!" Elsa repeated. "I wasn't finished with those, and they haven't been wrapped for transport. What are you doing?"

Jane stepped back from the table, hands up in surrender. "Don't have a kitten, darling. We only thought we'd help you pack. These are all going to the museum, correct?"

"Yes, but—"

Crawford stood back against the wall, looking between Jane and Elsa. She didn't blame him for doing only what he'd surely been ordered to do.

"You did seem to be rather occupied with non-work-related tasks." Wesley raised an eyebrow. "For once my sister and I agreed on something. You need a hand."

"If you are sincere, then I appreciate the sentiment. But these aren't ready to pack away yet. I need to write labels and tie them to each specimen before wrapping them in paper cones. And we don't dump them in boxes, even then." She pointed to the shallow trays she'd brought from the museum that stacked without touching the single layers of birds inside.

Wesley clucked his tongue, shaking his head. "My, my. You're further behind than we thought."

"I love having you here, Elsa," Jane added, "but truly, if you don't have time to chat with me, I don't see why you take breaks with those immigrants. Unless you're wheedling out of them the location of a certain valuable book? Great-Aunt Birdie wasn't in her right mind when she willed the aviary to that girl. Any judge will side with us on that."

Elsa gripped the back of a chair. "Why don't I get back to work?"

"Gee, why didn't I think of that?" Wesley winked, but his charm had worn off.

The faint smell of cigarette smoke lingered even after Crawford and the siblings left. She could at least be glad they hadn't smoked in here, spreading the odor to the birds, and possibly, heaven forbid, stray ashes.

Before Elsa had even pulled on her cotton gloves, a light tapping turned her head toward the door.

There stood Agnes Spalding, her hands folded atop her walking stick. "I apologize on behalf of my grandchildren."

Elsa glanced to the window and saw Mr. Spalding's Cadillac. She hadn't even heard him pull into the drive. "How much did you overhear?"

"Enough to know they suspect you may know where the aviary is, and that they resent your kindness to Tatiana and Danielle."

"I have no idea what happened to the aviary."

"I do."

Elsa blinked. "You do?"

Agnes looked over her shoulder, toward a crescendo of male voices. Mr. Spalding and Wesley were sparring again, and now a third voice joined in, which Elsa didn't recognize. "Let's get out of here," Agnes said. "I was hoping I'd find you here today to discuss it, but they don't deserve to hear this."

Boxes of birds needed to be unpacked, reordered, tagged, and wrapped. Elsa would stay late if she had to, as late as it took. Luke had already told her he'd stay busy until she was ready to leave. The birds could wait a little longer. Agnes's secrets may not.

Outside, Agnes set the pace and chose their path. They strolled to the Italianate garden built into the bluff by the river and sat together on a bench.

With a great sigh, she looked out over the river. "Linus took the aviary away from Birdie and hid it himself." She shook her head, as though ashamed of the confession.

Elsa's heart sank. "Why?"

Agnes leaned her walking stick against the bench and reached into a pocket in her skirt, withdrawing several letters. The return address on each envelope proved they were from Birdie. "He caught her showing the book to Danielle in the house. This was after the tea party incident. He'd already told Birdie he didn't want the gardener or her daughter in the mansion, but Birdie ignored him. He came home from a trip earlier than expected one day and saw them looking at the pages, turning them even. Linus blew up again, insisting Danielle would ruin the priceless treasure. It's all in that first letter you hold."

Elsa took the page from the envelope and scanned it. The story was exactly as Agnes had relayed.

He said he doesn't trust me with it anymore, and so he took it away to keep where I'll never find it. He said it was the only way he could be sure it would stay safe. I'll find it, though, if it's the last thing I do. And when I die, that book will belong to Danielle forever. She's special to me in a way he will never understand. He refuses to understand. But you know, don't you, dear Agnes?

"Birdie loved Danielle so much," Elsa murmured. "She had a mother's heart."

Agnes's thin eyebrows arched. "That she did."

Elsa swallowed. "I know about Sarah." She explained how she learned of the baby's birth and aftermath from Birdie's diary and from the Personal Analysis Card she'd found in Linus's secret office.

Agnes glowered at the mention of the card. "I'm not proud of my brother. But it didn't surprise me that after he retired from exploring and collecting, he took a summer course from the ERO so he could be a field agent, collecting personal and family histories. It was my son who inspired him to do it, though he didn't need much prompting. He'd always been interested in pedigrees. We called it genealogy decades ago, but his study took a more sinister bent. He was convinced that Sarah's cleft lip and palate were the result of some defect from Birdie's side of the family. His attitude when the baby died still makes my toes curl in fury."

Elsa's conversation with Wesley about his father's view of the Incubator Babies came back to her. "Let me guess. Did he think it was 'for the best' that she died?"

The older woman's lips pursed tight as a button. "He did. And Birdie grieved alone, though I did my level best to comfort her. But her grief doubled because he made sure that she would never bear another child. So she mourned the baby she had and lost, and she mourned babies she could never hope to meet. Now, whether that aim was accomplished through some kind of operation, or he just neglected her for the rest of their marriage, I don't know. But he told her it was their duty to society to never produce another child again. Linus had the nursery walls repainted and made it his bedroom while Birdie remained in the room across the hall, alone."

Elsa shook her head, unable to find words for what she felt.

"Things were never the same between Linus and me after that," Agnes went on. "I took up for Birdie, of course—she and I were friends even before she married into the family. There were times I wished I'd never introduced her to my controlling brother. I often visited her when he was away. I watched her affection for Danielle grow over the years, and I understood it. Danielle has never been the typical child. She had her own gifts and challenges, and still does. I think that made Birdie love her even more. Oh my, but she was so fiercely protective of her. I think she devoted herself to the girl in ways she wished she could have done for Sarah. She fought for the dignity of people who are different. Those two were so good for each other. Tatiana is the best mother the girl could have, and Birdie filled a grandmother's role."

Sniffing, Elsa cleaned her glasses. "She would be horrified if she knew her passing caused the Petrovics to be turned out with nothing. It isn't what she wanted."

"Birdie so rarely got what she wanted." Agnes's voice quavered. A breeze moved the black ostrich feathers sprouting from her hat band.

"Did she say anything else about the aviary after that?" Elsa asked.

"Oh yes, she had more to say." She handed Elsa another letter.

Agnes, I found it. Linus thinks I don't know about his secret room off the library, but of course I do. I've spent years more time in this house than he has. Yesterday I went inside his little den and found a package wrapped up in muslin and waxed paper, nested inside a box that hadn't been sealed up yet. I could tell by the weight of it this was the aviary. I unwrapped it—I was right. From the way it had been wrapped, I figured he was about to hide it somewhere else.

Elsa looked up. "Where would he hide such an old book without it deteriorating?"

"I doubt the condition of the manuscript was Linus's chief concern," Agnes said. "Even when we were children, he would rather risk destroying a coveted object than allow someone else to have it. I could tell you stories."

Elsa took her word for it and turned back to Birdie's letter.

I was so lucky to find it when I did. I found another book with similar dimensions and weight and swapped it for the aviary. I wrapped it up just as it had been. Now it's my turn to hide the aviary from him. I know what to do. Even if he discovers the switch, he'll never find it now. I must keep the aviary safe and close by. It won't be easy to show Danielle anymore, but it will be worth it. She'll have them soon enough, and forever.

This was amazing. Elsa withdrew the small notebook and pencil she had in her skirt pocket and took notes, paraphrasing most of the letter, but capturing word for word the last four sentences. Then she looked up at Agnes. "'Close by.' So it must be on the property somewhere." She glanced at the remaining letters Agnes held. "Did she ever tell you where?"

"The poor dear. Her memory was slipping even before Linus died, but after his death, her decline was much more rapid. See here." She withdrew another letter and pointed to one paragraph in particular.

I can't remember where I hid the aviary. I'm sure I'll find it. But at present, the location eludes me. My genius is a mystery even unto myself.

"That was around the time she gave her canary to Tatiana, too. She wrote about that in this same letter. Now look at this, from a few months later." Agnes presented another letter and tapped the page.

I haven't seen the aviary lately. Linus must have hidden it somewhere. I'll ask him about it when he returns, so long as his mood isn't foul.

Elsa looked at the date, confirming this had been written after Linus had died. "Oh no," she murmured. "Poor Birdie. Did she have to learn her husband had died, over and over again?"

Agnes gathered the letters and tucked them back into their envelopes before returning them to her pocket. "I was with her a couple of times when she remembered he'd died. She went through a painful mixture of emotions every time. Shock, embarrassment that she'd forgotten, grief over a lost life, relief that he'd never again control her, and an overriding dread about living the rest of her life alone. If it weren't for the Petrovics, she would have been lonely, indeed. I visited her whenever I could, but it got to the point where she would forget I'd been there before the sun set the same day."

The loneliness must have been haunting. Returning her notebook and pencil to her pocket, Elsa cast her gaze over the water to the blue-green hills on the other side. The land was beautiful here, but without a companion, she imagined the wind and storms could make this place feel desolate. Shuddering, she rubbed her arms. She couldn't imagine living in that mansion alone.

"And then," Agnes continued, "time seemed to loop back on itself for Birdie. During several of my visits, she would tell me she'd just had the nicest time with Danielle. 'We've been going through the aviary,' she said. When I asked where it was, Birdie became confused and upset, so I learned not to ask anymore. To let her be, let her dwell in the pleasant corners of her mind. I certainly didn't care about that illuminated manuscript for my own sake."

"But Birdie did. She cared a great deal."

"And she cared that it went to Danielle." Agnes's brows knitted together. "She didn't drive, so it must be on the property. The house has been searched. Do you suppose she hid it in an outbuilding?"

Elsa considered this. In addition to the pool building and gardener's cottage, there was the bowling alley, greenhouse, and laundry house. "Not if she was still lucid when she hid it. Those buildings are not friendly to centuries-old books. The temperatures are too extreme, the humidity volatile. If Birdie hid it as close as she says, I don't understand how we've missed it."

Agnes shook her head, then gripped her cane and stood. "I don't either. Now if you'll excuse me, it's high time I paid a visit to Tatiana and Danielle myself. I need to thank them for all they did for my brother's wife and tell them what we know about the book that rightfully belongs to them."

With admiration, Elsa watched Agnes head for the Petrovics' cottage, her black silk hem trailing the ground. She used her walking stick for support, and her pace was leisurely, but she held her head high and moved with purpose and grace.

Elsa could only hope to do the same despite her limp. With a final glance at the Hudson, she took the stairs out of the sunken garden and steered back toward the mansion. She hadn't planned to take such a long break from her work, but she'd make up for it. She would.

As soon as the house was in view, she also spied Luke striding toward her in that easy gait he had. Wind pushed his brown hair off his brow, revealing the one scar he daily attempted to hide. When he reached her, the wind shifted, and his hair fell back into place.

Before she could think to stop herself, she reached up and combed his hair back again with her fingers. "A haircut would look good on you. The more I can see of you, the better." She dropped her hand, wondering if she'd said too much. But she meant it, in more than one way.

Luke's presence strengthened and calmed her. Her experience with men was quite limited, given her boarding school years and then four years at the all-girls Vassar College. But being with Luke felt natural. She had not expected to find such a steadfast friend, but that was what he'd become.

Their time together would end, though, as soon as they finished their work at Elmhurst. He might have a few weeks left, but she had merely days. Surely he'd thought of this, too.

"What do you think about the cottage?" she asked. "Can it be moved?"

He offered his arm, and she took it as they continued to stroll toward the house. "No, it's far too rickety. One more good storm might blow the house down. It's not safe to live in as it is."

Disappointment fell like a stone to her gut. "So they'll have to start completely over somewhere else. It would have been such a comfort to be able to keep their familiar home. I appreciate you looking into it." She swallowed a swelling knot of frustration and shared what Agnes had told her.

"But if we haven't found the aviary yet," she went on, "I'm not sure we ever will. She or someone else could have moved the book after she hid it, and she simply might not have remembered that. It could be long gone."

"All is not lost." He covered her hand, and the warmth of his palm spread all the way through her. "I may not be able to recover the medieval manuscript, and the cottage is beyond repairing. But it's also small. I could construct a new one exactly like it."

Elsa stopped walking. "Are you serious?"

"As always." He winked. "With a crew to help me, we could build it in a matter of days, though they might not all be consecutive days. We'd have to work evenings and weekends. But we could build it in such a way that it could withstand being relocated wherever she and Danielle end up. Or we could wait and build it at their new location."

"And then we could give it fresh carpet and paper for the walls, but the exact match to what they have now so it still feels like home. Then move all their beloved furniture and knick-knacks right into it. Don't tease me now, because I am totally getting my hopes up for this."

"Let 'em soar. I'll get it done."

She believed him. Rising on her toes, she threw her arms around his neck and kissed his cheek. Before she could step away, his arm came around her waist, holding her to him for a moment before releasing her.

It wasn't long enough to be considered a true embrace. But it was long enough to remind her of what it had felt like when he'd carried her to the pool building in the rain. It felt like safety. It felt like all would be well.

"It will mean the world to them, you know," she said, "even if we can't solve everything. Sometimes knowing that someone is on your side makes all the difference."

He nodded. His hand cupped the side of her face. "I hope you know I'm on your side, too."

She smiled. "I'm beginning to get the picture."

A lump bobbed in his throat, and he drew her arm through his once more. Together, they crossed the uncut lawn. "I can't stop thinking about what happened on Coney Island. If anything had—"

Elsa gasped. "There he is!" Heading toward them at a brisk pace was the same man she'd seen Saturday night. He had just unfolded himself from a dark green Model T. "He's been here before."

Luke's arm tensed beneath her hand. His expression hardened into flint. "Stalking you? Here?"

"I wouldn't say that. A cousin arrived the day other museum staff were transporting artwork out of the mansion. Mr. Spalding argued with him in the drive, telling him he wasn't welcome in the mansion until the museums had been through it. He left before I could see his face, but that is definitely his auto."

Luke kept his eyes on the approaching man, shaded from the mansion behind him until he stepped out of the roofline-shaped shadows. As he neared, he doffed his bowler and extended a hand.

She didn't shake it, and neither did Luke.

"You were following her on Coney Island?" Luke asked.

"I'm sorry about that. I didn't mean to cause alarm, but . . ."

When he paused, Elsa finished for him. "You did. Explain yourself, please, and start from the beginning. You seem to already know who I am, but I don't even know your name."

"Dr. Hugh Geoffrey. I'm Guy's second cousin. My father was Linus's cousin. The two of them went on expeditions together when they were in their prime." He turned to Luke. "And you are?"

"With her," Luke said. The steel in his tone hadn't softened yet.

Dr. Geoffrey straightened the bow tie at his collar. "Clearly."

Only when Elsa nudged Luke did he offer his name and his role at Elmhurst. Up close like this, Dr. Geoffrey wasn't nearly as menacing as he'd seemed Saturday night. The tweed suit he wore, complete with elbow patches on the jacket, made him appear quite scholarly.

"Again, I apologize for my first impression. I didn't want to shout or draw attention, knowing Wesley and Guy were in the vicinity. I'm a professor of European history at the University of Pennsylvania, so my time up here is limited."

"Did you know I would be there, too?"

"No. I only went there because I'd been to Guy's home in Cold Spring Harbor, and his wife told me where he'd gone. As I said, my time here is limited before I need to return for the fall term, and Guy has been brushing me off. I went to Coney Island to talk to him about the aviary. While I was there, I spotted Wesley talking to you. I'd heard about your role here, and your friendship with the Petrovics. Forgive me, but I also heard you had a limp. It made you easy to recognize. I understand you have been looking for the aviary."

"Only to pass it along to its rightful owners if I find it."

"Rightful owners." He scoffed. "Linus van Tessel never concerned himself with rightful owners before."

"This isn't about Linus," Luke told him. "It's about honoring Mrs. Van Tessel's wishes as stated in a legal document."

Elsa reached back in her mind to what she'd read in the field notebooks and diaries. She'd read about a Geoffrey and assumed that was a given name, but it could have been a surname. "Was your father acting as Linus's assistant?"

Dr. Geoffrey said he was. "Guy said you read the field notebooks. I imagine you saw him mentioned there, but not to the extent that acknowledgment was due."

Oh dear. From what she'd read, Linus had not treated his cousin well. "I read enough to know that while Linus stayed at camp nursing blistered feet or a digestive ailment, your father did the hard work of hunting and collecting."

"That's right. Furthermore, when my father discovered a new species in the *Aratinga* genus, Linus stole credit and had it named for himself. Half the birds you are cataloguing here should belong to him. Or to me, rather, as his heir. Oh, don't worry, I'm not interested in those dusty specimens. But the aviary is another matter. A medieval illuminated manuscript has no business going to a gardener or her daughter. Neither does it belong to Guy or either of his kids. Don't think I don't know what's going on here. I saw Wesley talking to you in Luna Park. Maybe he's offered you something in exchange for the aviary."

"He has not."

"Then he's not as smart as I took him for. I know he's miserable in Morningside Heights, going to Columbia when Juilliard is right there in the same neighborhood, taunting him. If he finds the aviary, he'd have enough money to give up economics and live as an artist for years."

Elsa licked dry lips. "I told you I don't have it. Neither do the Petrovics, which I think you know, since you paid them a visit this morning, didn't you?"

"But she has the *provenance* document. Why would she have that unless she had the artifact, too?"

"I imagine she tried to explain that to you, but allow me to remind you." Elsa shared how that had come about.

"If we do find it," Luke added, "it will go straight to Tatiana and Danielle."

Dr. Geoffrey poked a finger in Luke's direction, then swung it toward Elsa. "There's where you're wrong. If you know where it is, and you don't tell me, I'll see to it that you lose your job. I'll tell your boss you're in possession of stolen goods."

"That's not true and will never be true," she sputtered. "You couldn't prove it."

"I don't have to. The scandal alone would ruin you."

"You're done here." Luke stepped forward, and Elsa let her hand drop from his arm. "She doesn't answer to you." He took another step forward, and Dr. Geoffrey stepped back. Luke lowered his voice so Elsa couldn't hear what he said.

Whatever it was, it was persuasive. The professor blanched, then pursed his lips and climbed back into his auto. He drove away beneath the dappled shade of the elms.

Elsa joined Luke on the drive, coughing in the exhaust fumes left behind. "That's the second time today you've chased someone off the property." Weeds had begun to sprout up through the pebbles. She fought the urge to reach down and uproot them.

"More importantly, that's the second time it was necessary. I don't like that."

"That makes two of us." She forced a laugh, but it was hollow. "Thank you." They stepped into the shadows of the carriage porch.

His brow creased, he pulled open the door and waited to enter after her. "The sooner we finish our work here and put Elmhurst behind us, the better."

"The sooner we find the aviary, the better," she countered. "Everyone wants it. Everyone is looking. And we're the only ones respecting Birdie's will."

But they both had mountains of work to tackle, and they both knew it. Mr. Chapman wouldn't fire her for allegedly possessing stolen property, but he'd be none too pleased if she neglected her duties for what he might call a wild goose chase.

Her heart heavy, she parted with Luke and braced herself for the boxes of mixed-up birds that awaited her in the dining hall.

Only, they weren't in boxes anymore. The birds had been lined up all along the table in neat rows once more. But this time they weren't grouped by color. *Who . . . ?*

She glanced out the window in time to see the back of Danielle. Frowning, Elsa turned her attention back to the birds.

They had been alphabetized by their scientific names.

Stunned, Elsa picked up her ledger and opened it. As her fingertip skimmed down the rows, she referred to the birds on the table. They matched up perfectly. Assigning catalog numbers and tags would be easy now.

Only Danielle could have done this. Only Danielle *would* have done this.

She must have overheard Elsa's heated conversation with Wesley and Jane over their careless handling of the specimens and then come inside once Elsa left with Agnes. She might even have done it because she felt compelled to create order for its own sake, not to make life easier for Elsa.

Regardless of the motive, Elsa was as grateful as she was in awe.

CHAPTER

18

NEW YORK CITY
WEDNESDAY, SEPTEMBER 8, 1926

Danielle was not all right.

The thought ran circles in Elsa's mind, even as she handed Mr. Miller dissection tools in the ornithology lab at the American Museum of Natural History. She did her job fine, but she couldn't stop thinking about her friends.

Yesterday, she had spent the morning at the museum assisting a researcher, so after arriving at Elmhurst after lunch, she'd worked late to tag and catalog another hundred birds. Luke and Tom had stayed, too, so they could give her a ride back to the city. Before they left the estate at dusk, they'd checked on the Petrovics.

Danielle had not been willing to see anyone, not even Barney. In itself, that would not have been cause for concern. What alarmed Elsa was the moaning and banging coming from inside her room.

"That's the rocking chair you hear hitting the wall, not her head, thank goodness," Tatiana had explained. "Mr. Field hasn't given us permission to stay. She didn't take the news well, but her moans have quieted, and she's replaced them with talking to herself, which is a good sign. It means she's trying to use her logic to help her emotions understand, as her tutor taught her to do. Still, such a difficult transition is a great deal for her to process." She spared only a few more moments with her visitors before begging leave to try again to console her daughter. From the looks of her, she'd been trying for some time.

As much as Elsa wished she could help, she hadn't been able to. During the ride back to Manhattan, she and Luke and Tom had put their heads together on what, if anything, they could possibly do for these vulnerable people Birdie had so wanted to take care of. Aside from building a new cottage when the time was right, and apart from finding the aviary before time ran out, all they could do was pray. And so they had, right there on Eighty-First Street, where Luke idled along the curb in front of the Beresford. The prayer was brief but sincere. Elsa had asked God for solutions to become clear. But remembering what Tatiana had said about God's presence in times of pain, she asked Him to be with the Petrovics, too.

Elsa still didn't have all the answers, but she was trying to trust the One who did.

"Miss Reisner," Mr. Miller prompted, and she handed him the scalpel.

Absently, she watched him work, her mind turning over the words Tatiana had left with her. *"All her life, I've tried to protect my daughter from things that upset her. But I can't protect her from change forever. Since we can't avoid it, I've got to find a way to help her overcome it instead."*

Elsa had carried that truth home with her and pondered it still. Change was inevitable, and even Jesus had said we'd have trouble in this world. She could not avoid it in her own life, either, as her weak leg reminded her every day. She couldn't avoid it. But what would it look like to overcome it? That was another riddle she still hadn't solved.

At last, the dissection ended. After cleaning the tools and storing them in the proper trays, Elsa returned to her own office.

To her surprise, Luke was already there, a paper cone in his hand. She was even more surprised by how glad she was to see him. She'd seen him last night, after all.

A small smile hooked into his cheek. "I found this little guy rolling around in the truck this morning." He handed her the cone.

Elsa peeked inside and found an indigo bunting. "Thank you for bringing him."

"Did you decide whether you're going back to Elmhurst tomorrow?"

She brushed a cat hair from her sleeve. "Yes, but not until after dinner, since this week is so busy here at the museum. I've convinced Ivy to go with me."

"Just the two of you?"

"Yes. She's been dying to see the place, and my work was so interrupted yesterday that I decided to return in the evening. I assume the family won't be there then. Mr. Spalding gave me a key before he left yesterday. We're going to make a night of it and sleep there. We'll bring our own sleeping bags and pillows, of course. I'll be able to get more done early in the morning, too, before any relatives come back."

Luke folded his arms, feet planted wide. "Elsa, are you serious?"

"It will be a grand adventure! Ivy gets to take some time off during the week since she's worked a few weekends with special events."

"It's in the middle of nowhere with no telephone service and no electricity."

"That's the adventure part. Ivy can't wait to pretend she's living in a historical era before all of that had even been invented." She leaned against her desk. If she had more than one chair in her office, she'd sit and invite him to do the same.

"How will you get there?"

"Train."

"So you won't even have an auto there. You'll be stranded with no way of communicating with the outside world."

"Exciting, right?" She couldn't help but laugh at the bewildered expression on his face.

"And you're determined to do this?"

"All joking aside, yes, I am. Mr. Chapman is putting the pressure on to finish up out there, and I'm almost done. Besides, Ivy and I can look for the aviary while we're there, too."

Luke raked his fingers through his hair. "I'm going with you. Camping. I'll bring Barney."

Elsa returned his determined gaze. "If you thought my plan was inappropriate before, you've just made it ten times more so."

"We won't be sleeping in the same room. In that house, we might not even be in the same county. But in all seriousness, I don't want you two there alone. You and Ivy can still have your roommate bonding time. I won't interfere with that. But I want to be there in case you need a hand with something or in case anyone decides to come harass you again. Besides, I have more work to do there, too, and, frankly, not enough time to do it, especially since I want to use the weekends to reconstruct the Petrovic cottage. I'll bring Tom, if he's game. We'll keep to ourselves unless you need us."

Elsa checked her watch. "I'm so sorry, but I have a meeting with my boss. Walk with me that direction?" She led him out of her office.

"I'll drive. We'll pick you up outside the Beresford. All right?" He nudged her with his elbow.

Elsa looped her hand through it. "If you're sure." The more she thought about it, the better his plan sounded.

"I am. Lean on me."

She looked up at Luke, softening at his earnest expression. "Is that a metaphor?"

One eyebrow lifted. "I suppose it is. It's also literal. When we walk together, I can tell you're trying not to press down on me, Elsa. But it's no burden to support you. I'm here because I want you to lean on me. Literally, metaphorically, consistently, perpetually. Also, voluntarily."

Releasing a sigh, she allowed herself to transfer more of her weight to him. "I volunteer."

———◯———

Elsa was still smiling when she knocked on the doorway to Mr. Chapman's office.

"Miss Reisner." He beckoned her inside. "Sit. Tell me how your work is coming along. Anything new to report?"

She eased into the chair and gave brief reports on the various projects he had her working on, from dissection assistance to skinning and stuffing birds to research assistance to processing the new inventory from Elmhurst. "I have an idea for something new," she added after all of that, surprising even herself.

"Because you don't have enough to do already?" he teased but bade her to continue.

She shared with him her experience last week as an informal birding guide in Central Park.

"I fail to see how this is relevant to the museum."

"Mr. Griscom wrote that article about bird-watching in Central Park, and it has clearly generated interest. Offering guided walks through the park is a service the museum could provide. I believe it could earn even more appreciation and drive foot traffic across the street to our museum so they could keep learning. Our location right by the park makes it a perfect setup."

"And am I to assume that you would be willing to be this bird guide yourself?"

Elsa's heart leapt at the opening. "Why, yes! I'd love to! If—"

"You." He interrupted her with a pointed look at where her skirt sloped over her leg brace.

Her mouth went dry. He didn't believe she could do it.

"Good heavens." Mr. Chapman closed the book on his desk and pushed it to the side. "You've become quite fanciful lately. If this is due to the goings-on at Elmhurst, the sooner you finish, the better."

The "goings-on at Elmhurst," as he put it, had breathed new life into a passion that had gone stagnant. At least, the episodes that involved people. The note-taking and record-making, whether here or there, fed her almost-compulsive drive for perfection. Bird-watching—and bird-teaching—shifted her focus onto that which couldn't and shouldn't be contained or controlled. Living birds inspired and delighted her again, as they had when she was a bedridden child.

"As I've told you before, I'll be finishing this week. And then I'll be back here full-time once again." Months and years stretched out ahead of Elsa. The vision played across her mind like a moving picture. She saw herself flaying skin away from flesh, cutting bones and wings, and cleaning blood off feathers with a fingernail file. She saw herself arranging and rearranging inventory and hunched over notebooks.

It didn't bring her half the joy she experienced watching birds with Tatiana and Danielle at Elmhurst or with Luke in Central Park. Finding Zeus had been more thrilling than stumbling upon the Spix's macaw in Birdie's dressing room. And leading the small band of people on an impromptu bird walk through the park had brought her more exhilaration than she'd known in any other aspect of her work.

"Your finishing at Elmhurst is what concerns me most." Leaning forward, he tented his hands over the open textbook splayed on his desk. "I'm not paying you to hunt down a manuscript that doesn't belong to you."

She blinked. "You mean the aviary?"

"Yes, I mean the aviary. When you're at Elmhurst, you're to be working for the museum. We are not paying you to do anything else. We certainly aren't paying you to make new friends or pick up lost causes."

Heat flared up her neck. Did the lost cause refer to the aviary or to her new friends? "Where is this coming from?"

"Dr. Hugh Geoffrey was here first thing this morning. He tells me you are spending an inordinate amount of time with the gardener and her daughter. Worse, he says you're meddling in the family's affairs by looking for an item that belongs to someone else."

"I've been looking for field notebooks and keeping my eyes open for the aviary at the same time, as requested by Mr. Spalding." She didn't need to mention the treasure hunt she planned for tomorrow evening since that would be on her own time.

"Dr. Geoffrey is concerned that if you find it, you'll keep it for yourself. I assured him that I know your character, and you would never do such a thing."

"Of course I wouldn't." She exhaled. "Thank you for that trust."

Mr. Chapman grunted. "I do not believe you would steal an object, Miss Reisner. But I take the theft of time just as seriously. You know how swamped we are here. You've been going to Elmhurst for three weeks now. You're done."

Elsa's heart dropped. "Sir, with all due respect, I have worked on that project on my own time to try to speed up my progress. I certainly haven't stolen time from the museum for personal pursuits. As far as I've come, I still have birds there. I need more time."

"I need you here. We have a full slate of researchers scheduled for tomorrow, and you need to bring them whichever specimens they request."

"Then let me have Friday at Elmhurst," she said. If they went

Thursday night, and slept over, she should be able to finish, as long as the relatives let her concentrate. Whatever she didn't get to, she could tag over the weekend at home, cramped though that would be.

"As I said, I need you in your position here. If you must return to Elmhurst, do so on your own time. You will be here by nine o'clock Friday morning, and you will have the last of the Hudson Collection with you by then. I tell you, Miss Reisner, you're done with Elmhurst, for good."

CHAPTER

19

S hopping after work was Mother's idea.

It wasn't Elsa's favorite activity, but it did push Mr. Chapman's reprimands to the back of her mind as she focused more on her mother than she did on any sale.

"I'm so glad you're here to help me, dear." Mother stood beside her on the wooden escalator. "I don't have a thing to wear to the next club luncheon, and I value your opinion."

Elsa smiled, and a chuckle broke free. Mother had never needed Elsa's input for her fashion choices before. And she must have remembered Elsa had previously suggested Macy's department store. She would never have chosen it for herself. Moreover, Mother's dressing room was already full of things she could wear to a luncheon.

So Elsa heard the sentiment for what it was: *"I value you,"* her mother had meant. *"I value time with you."* For that, Elsa dared to put her arm around Mother's straight shoulders. "I value you, too."

Mother's perfect posture softened. "Thank you." The earnest surprise in her tone touched something in Elsa's heart. Had her mother doubted such a simple statement? She didn't like to think so. Then again, when was the last time Elsa had truly tried to connect with Mother beyond manners and etiquette and what she assumed was expected of her?

It had been another long day. After her meeting with her boss, she'd skinned five more birds and processed more specimen exchanges with cooperating museums while entertaining an undercurrent of unease for the fate of Tatiana and Danielle. Her thoughts had run the gamut from the Petrovic mother and daughter to what Agnes had told her of Birdie, Sarah, and Linus. Elsa had been full to the brim lately with concern for mothers and daughters she couldn't help.

What about her relationship with her own mother?

Reaching the next floor, they stepped off the escalator in the handbags department, rounded the bend, and boarded another escalator on their journey to women's fashions.

"Are you sure you need a new outfit?" Elsa asked.

"Why? Do you need to go so soon?"

"Not at all. In fact, we can still shop if you'd like to. But there's an English tearoom on the seventh floor. Fancy a cuppa?" She grinned. "We could just keep going up an extra flight, and then be refreshed for the retail adventure ahead."

Mother smiled then, a real, imperfect smile. The skin near her eyes crinkled in a way she barely ever allowed. "Let's."

"Good."

On the sixth floor, they switched escalators one more time. Soft rays of sunshine fell through the atrium ceiling, tinting the white floors and walls a honeyed gold. The oak railing of this engineering marvel reflected the shine and felt as smooth as silk beneath Elsa's gloved hand.

And then they stopped. Elsa glanced around, waiting for the movement to restart.

"Is this part of the fun here at Macy's?" Mother whispered.

"It's never done this before."

"Well?" a shopper behind them called. "We have legs, don't we?"

Elsa dropped back a step to place herself single file behind her mother, allowing other patrons to climb past them on the left. She looked up and down, and judged they were a little more than halfway between the floors. But these escalator stairs were steep, and there were so many yet to go. Her heart thudded with dread.

"Shall we go on?" Mother asked, eyebrows lifted. "Like the middle class?" She winked, and Elsa couldn't help but laugh at the rare display of humor.

"I'm right behind you."

Mother climbed, and Elsa followed, her grip on the railing growing tighter. After ten steps, she couldn't keep up the pace.

Her pulse roared in her ears as she fell farther behind and more ladies swished by, knocking her with handbags swinging from their elbows. This shouldn't be so hard for her. Hadn't she been faithfully strengthening her muscles? Increasing her endurance? She'd been climbing the stairs at Elmhurst, but those weren't nearly so steep.

Sweat prickled her scalp beneath her cloche, then traced a thin trail down her temple. The ache was becoming unbearable. Her lungs labored in a way they hadn't, even in the stair tower of Elmhurst. Her glasses slipped, and she pushed them up again.

She had to get up these stairs. But her weak leg threatened not to hold her. *It's the end of the day*, she told herself. *I did too much already, that's all.* But she couldn't believe her own lie. It was true she'd walked a fair piece in the park before work, but she'd been sitting at the museum for most of the day. She ought to be fresh.

She felt faint.

Pausing to catch her breath, she glanced up the escalator and could no longer see her mother. Good. That meant Mother could not see her. Shame rushed to her face at the idea.

"What's the big idea, lady? If you haven't noticed, the escalator's on the fritz. You ain't gettin' nowheres fast."

Elsa grimaced at the shopper to prove that while she may be lame, she was not deaf.

She had to take it one step at a time. Using her good leg first, then pulling up the weak one to the same step. Over and over again. Right, together. Right, together. Like a toddler.

Only, she was pretty sure toddlers didn't sweat this much. The palms of her gloves were damp. Hair stuck to the back of her neck.

Breathe in. Breathe out.

Breathe.

When darkness crowded the edges of her vision, she leaned on the handrail and bent her head.

"Excuse me, pardon me, make way." From above, Mother's voice filtered down to Elsa. She was getting closer. "Out of my way, please."

"Listen, lady, you can't go down the up escalator."

"Watch me."

Elsa looked up just as Mother elbowed her way past one protesting shopper and shimmied around another, bumping a stranger aside with her hips.

Was she dreaming?

"Hello, darling." Mother shared the step with Elsa and slipped her arm around her waist. They were blocking everyone behind them. "Take your time. You tell me when you're ready, and we'll move."

The shoppers directly behind them kept quiet, but those farther back called up to complain about the holdup.

Mother ignored them. "I counted eleven more steps to the top, Elsa. You tell me what you want to do. Shall we go up for that spot of tea? Or shall we turn around and go back down? Never mind the crowd, we'll get past them if that's the route you want to take."

"As I live and breathe." One of the women who'd been griping called up. "Beryl? Beryl Reisner, is that you holding up all these people?"

Mother's grip on Elsa firmed. She looked over her shoulder. "I'm holding up my daughter, and that's all that matters to me. Oh, that's *you*, Mrs. Marshall. I beg your pardon. I didn't recognize you without your manners."

"Mother!" Elsa gasped.

Mother looked at her, with a set to her jaw and a fierce devotion in her eyes that Elsa didn't recall ever seeing before. "The lot behind us can jump ship for all I care. And how. Isn't that what you young folks say?"

Elsa laughed despite the scene she was causing, or perhaps because of it. Because for the first time in memory, Mother was causing her own. She was not embarrassed by Elsa. She was supporting her and even defending her.

"Let's go up," Elsa said.

Mother smiled. "Ready? Together now."

Yes, they were.

———

Once they were seated at a table in the tearoom, Elsa pulled a handkerchief from her handbag and dabbed her face and neck. Normally, she'd reserve such a task for the restroom but hadn't the energy to make the extra trip.

"Thank you for that, back there." She snapped her handkerchief away. "I've never seen you that way before. I rather enjoyed it."

Chuckling, Mother leaned forward. "So did I."

Elsa could barely contain her surprise long enough to place their order with the waiter. "Have you changed, Mother?" she asked once they were alone again. "Or have we not spent enough time together for me to notice this side of you?"

Her small sigh fluttered the lilies in the vase between them. "A bit of both, I think. Now, please, tell me what's going on. Your father told me you were feeling better. He said you'd been training to strengthen your body. Isn't that what you shared with him last weekend?"

"I did."

"And what have you *not* told us?"

"Wouldn't you rather talk about Lauren's wedding?" She pushed up a smile, but it wilted.

"I would rather hear about you." One eyebrow arched in a stern but caring command.

The waiter returned with the tea trays, giving Elsa time to think as she watched the steaming brew being poured into their cups. It didn't take long for her to decide on the truth.

"I saw Dr. Stanhope last week. In his office, that is. I made an appointment with him."

Mother blanched. "That man. There's a reason we discontinued his services partway through your boarding school years."

Elsa's cup rattled in its saucer. "Why do you say that?"

"Whenever I questioned his choices and predictions, he made me feel as though I were a fool. He was the doctor, he told me. I ought to let him do the thinking. My job, I suppose, was to ensure his payments were on time."

"What—what did you question, specifically?" Elsa looped her finger through the teacup handle. Heat from the cup burned her knuckle.

"Staying away from you when I knew you were sick at boarding school. He told me I would only teach you that pretending illness was the right way to get my attention."

"Did you think I was pretending?"

Mother shook her head, then hid a trembling chin behind her teacup as she sipped. "I didn't know what to think. The doctor told me not to try. I was too emotional. He was the one being paid to think on our behalf."

Too emotional? Before today, Elsa wouldn't have been able to picture Mother's emotions rippling beneath the surface, let alone breaking through. But now she had a glimpse of what lay underneath. Perhaps Mother had learned to suppress her feelings long ago. Perhaps she held her expressions as rigidly as her posture out of habit.

"You're allowed to have feelings, Mother. You're even allowed to show them."

She drew in a deep breath and nodded. "I was raised to believe otherwise. But tell me about your visit to Dr. Stanhope and I may not be able to hold them back."

Elsa told her everything, from the reasons for the visit to his accusations that her increasing weakness and pain was the result of a fresh bout of jealousy over her mother's attentions to Lauren. She told her about Luke, who supported her before the appointment and since.

"Supporting you how?"

"Literally, metaphorically, consistently, voluntarily." Not bothering to hide her smile, Elsa stirred cream into her tea and sipped again.

Light entered Mother's eyes. "I want to meet him. I want to hear more about him. But right now, we're talking about you. I don't believe you ever faked how you felt for attention. Regardless, if I have ever given you reason to feel I preferred your cousin over you, I profoundly apologize. It never entered my mind you could feel that way because the idea never entered my heart." She reached across the small square table and captured Elsa's hand. "How I wish I could have set you at ease about this long ago."

"Me too. But thank you." Elsa could have stopped there but decided to keep peeling back the layers of hurt and misunderstanding between them. "I've always thought you were embarrassed by what polio did to me."

"What? Where did you get that impression?"

"Well, we've never gone out shopping together before this summer. And last month, when you invited a bachelor to have dinner with us, he asked me about my leg, and you changed the subject immediately."

"Of course I did. There is so much more to you than your limp, darling, and I wanted him to have a chance to see that. I didn't want him to get hung up on polio."

"Really?" Elsa tried to recall exactly how that evening went. Had she gotten that all wrong?

"Yes, really. The fact that he hasn't called again proves how superficial he was, so good riddance to him. And as for shopping, I only wanted to make things easier for you, and I figured bringing clothes to you to try on at home was far more convenient."

A small apologetic smile edged Elsa's lips. "It certainly was."

She felt in her mother's grip a desperation to be heard and believed that spoke volumes. Could there be any more complicated a relationship than that between a mother and daughter? Was there any more significant in how that daughter saw herself and the world as she grew up?

"What else, dear?" Mother asked. "What else can I explain, or try to explain, or apologize for if I've done wrong?" The earnestness and humility in her plea made it easier to respond.

"I always thought you never had any more children after me because I turned out to be such a disappointment," Elsa confessed. "I wasn't what you were expecting. Rather than risk having another child who didn't fit the mold, you decided to give up the whole venture."

Tears glimmered in Mother's eyes and spilled over. "My darling girl, you were *never* a disappointment. I would have welcomed a sibling or two for you. But my sister and I shared in common a struggle that one simply doesn't speak of."

Elsa could barely grasp what she was saying. Aunt Goldie had struggled to conceive and then miscarried multiple babies. "Mother . . . Did you—did you lose . . . ?" She paused, aware of what a private thing she was asking. This was not a conversation for a department store.

"No. I have no babies in heaven if that's what you mean. You were the only baby God gave us. You had my whole heart, and still do, and always will." And then Mother—dear, repressed, tightly laced Mother—cried in earnest. Tears streaked her beautiful face. Shoulders bouncing with quiet sobs, she released Elsa to press a handkerchief over her mouth.

Elsa looked about the tearoom, confirming her suspicion that their table had become the center of attention. She didn't care. "It's all right, Mother. It's all right. I love you, too." Elsa left her chair and circled the table, stooping to hug her mother.

The sobs grew louder. They weren't refined little things, either, but halting, jerking convulsions that made Elsa both laugh and cry, as well.

When Mother began to quiet, Elsa returned to her seat and smiled. "That was beautiful," she teased, "and eloquent."

Mother dabbed her eyes and laughed. "I don't feel like shopping after this. What did *you* want to do this evening?"

"Honestly? Sit on a park bench and watch birds." She finally tasted a bite of her sandwich. "Want to come?"

———○———

Dusk in Central Park was always enchanting this time of year, but the fact that Elsa's mother shared a bench at the edge of the lake with her made it feel even more magical. They had never done this before, even though the Reisner house on Fifth Avenue bordered one side of the park, and Elsa's apartment building on Central Park West sat on the opposite side.

Before tonight, Elsa had never invited her mother to join her. It hadn't occurred to her she might want to.

The foliage was starting to change color, red and orange tipping the leaves. Fall migratory birds increased the bird population, and at this hour, they were active and easier to spot. Elsa pointed out the ones she identified, then marked them in the small notebook she always kept in her handbag.

"Is that a pigeon hawk?" Mother asked.

Elsa looked up and found a *Falco columbarius*, a feisty hawk the size of a pigeon. "It certainly is. Well done! How did you know that one?"

"When you were at Vassar, you sometimes mentioned birds you had seen on campus. I made a list of them. Your father and I brought the list, along with a field guide, here to the park to see if we could find them, too. I liked to think that we might see the same birds you did as they made their way south during fall migration. I knew it wasn't likely, but it brought me some peace to imagine it. It helped me feel closer to you during that dreadful time."

Elsa knew which time she referred to. "You—you never mentioned that. I didn't even know you missed me. We were so used to not living under the same roof by that point. You told me not to come home."

"For your own good, and in agreement with the Vassar College physician."

Elsa conceded that point. As soon as her first year began in September 1918, Vassar went into strict quarantine in an effort to protect the campus from the Spanish flu. Between their classes, Vassar students raised money for influenza relief work, made masks and layettes, and collected clothes and blankets for the Red Cross.

The idea of her parents sitting here, watching for birds she might have seen, touched her deeply.

"Did you see any?" she asked.

"A few." Mother smiled. "Our eyes are not so keen as yours."

Well, that was ironic, considering she was the only one in the family who wore spectacles. Elsa laughed. "Actually, it's easier to identify them by sound first, and then I know what I'm looking for."

"And what are you looking for?" It was Luke's voice, but when

Elsa turned toward him, it took her a moment to believe it was really him.

Standing, she greeted him, taking his hand. "I see you took my advice." Even though he wore a homburg, she could see he'd gotten a haircut. And heaven help her, it looked good on him. She only hoped he realized it, too. "You've never looked better. Would you like to meet my mother?"

"Absolutely."

Mother stood, and Luke shook her hand while introductions were made.

"Please, join us. I'd love to hear more about you and what you do." Mother beckoned Luke to sit with them, and the two immediately fell into conversation.

"And your parents?" Mother asked. "It sounds like we might run in the same circles. I wonder if we've met them."

Elsa held her breath, unsure if Luke would want to share about so painful a topic with someone he'd only just met. Then again, he'd shared with her already, and they hadn't known each other long.

"There you are." Father appeared from around the corner, looking dapper as always in a charcoal grey suit.

Elsa rose to greet him, and so did Mother and Luke. After introducing him to Luke, she asked, "How did you know where to find us?"

"Reeves came home after dropping you off. When he told me he was coming back to get you at an appointed time and place, I decided to come get you myself instead. Nice night for a walk, don't you think?"

"Lovely," Mother agreed. "We've been having a grand time getting to know Elsa's friend Luke. You were about to tell us about your parents, dear."

Elsa lifted an eyebrow at the endearment. Did she truly have an affection for Luke already? Not that anyone could blame her.

Luke was far and away more impressive than any of the bachelors her parents had tried to pair her with, including Archer Hamlin.

"Please, have a seat, sir." Luke gave up his spot on the bench and instead sat on a nearby boulder. He rested his elbows on his knees, hands clasped. "My parents are Helen and William Dupont. Mother doesn't get out much and hasn't since we lost my brother during the war. I work for Father in architectural salvage."

"Oh my heavens." Mother pressed a hand to her heart.

Father cleared his throat. "We are terribly sorry to hear of your brother's passing." A beat of respectful silence followed. "Your family business has done well, I understand. Dupont & Son is highly regarded. Several of my clients have used your services, in fact, and sing your praises. Was this always your ambition, or do you have others?"

"I hadn't planned on following in my father's footsteps until after my brother, Franklin, died. I studied architecture at Harvard and in Paris before the war. Back then, I considered using salvage in architecture and design as cheating. But now I see it as saving what's valuable even when everything else is crumbling down around it. The pieces that survive decay or destruction should not be discarded. It's not always better to start from scratch. It's better to preserve that which retains beauty and integrity whenever possible. To tell you the truth, working for my father has been a humbling experience that has taught me things I never learned at Harvard."

Elsa found nothing of the arrogant aspiring architect in this version of Luke Dupont. "Have you ever shared that with your father?"

His lips pressed flat. "Probably not."

"I think he'd really like to hear it," she said quietly.

Father agreed. "And is this your long-term plan?"

"One day I'd like to restore historic buildings, too," Luke said. "Instead of taking out the few pieces worth saving, it would be nice to save the entire structure when possible."

Mother smiled. "Any interest in designing Manhattan skyscrapers one day?"

"You're looking at the only Harvard-educated architect who isn't." Luke chuckled. "I'd rather preserve historic buildings in danger of being torn down and lost to us forever. Just because something is a little broken-down doesn't mean it isn't still precious and valuable."

"In your line of work," Father went on, "I suppose you've learned to place proper value on foundations and structural integrity, and not be so concerned with window dressing."

Elsa had a feeling Father was veering into the philosophical now. She wondered if he meant to imply that Elsa had a good foundation and integrity, even if she wasn't much to look at. But instead of taking offense, she smiled in amusement. She never felt unattractive around Luke. And more and more, she knew her parents loved her.

Soon, Mother stood and tugged Father up with her. "We really ought to be heading back home now," she said.

A crease appeared between Father's eyebrows. "Are you sure? I'm quite enjoying the company."

"I'm sure." Mother gave him a look that told him he ought to be, too. "Let the young people have some time before it gets too dark."

Understanding sparked in Father's eyes. "Quite right. Luke, will you see our daughter home?"

Luke shook Father's outstretched hand. "I will, sir. You can count on me."

Mother looped her delicate hand through Father's elbow. "I do believe we can."

"I'm glad you got to meet them," Elsa told Luke as soon as her parents had disappeared from view. "Thank you for putting up with all the questions."

"Putting up with them?" Luke laughed, and they resumed their seat on the bench. "Other than you, it's been a long time since anyone asked me so thoroughly about myself. It didn't feel intrusive. It felt like they cared, about me, but also about you. They wouldn't care who I was if not for my relationship with you." He stretched his arm out behind her.

She smiled. "That's true. They've surprised me lately. I had built them up in my mind as these formidable people who only cared about image and status. But I think I've gotten them all wrong. Or at least, if my perception was ever correct, it isn't anymore. Maybe they've changed, or maybe I'm just now seeing them as they really are." She told him about her father's apology last week and about the episode at Macy's with Mother earlier this evening.

"Are you all right?" he asked, clearly focusing on the part where she almost blacked out on the escalator.

"I feel fine right now. But sometimes I feel broken-down. And I'm not sure if anything can be done to restore me."

His fingers brushed her shoulder. "You are precious exactly the way you are."

She didn't know how to respond. She ought to have taken a few moments or just resolved not to say anything at all. Instead, words escaped without her permission. "To you?"

"To me." Luke's smile pushed back the scar in his cheek.

Elsa took his hand, her fingertips memorizing every crease and callous. "Earlier this evening, you asked what I was looking for. Funny thing about bird-watching. Sometimes you don't know what you want to see until it's right in front of you. Before I met you, I wasn't looking for you, either, Luke. But now that you're here, being with you is always the highlight of my day."

"Then you won't mind if I insist on seeing you even after our work at Elmhurst is through?"

A thrill uncurled inside her. "You mean, you might run into me in the park like this?"

"I mean to be a lot more intentional than that. But only if my pursuit would be welcome." He swallowed, and his expression showed the first glimpse of vulnerability she'd seen all evening.

Elsa squeezed his hand, when what she wanted to do was throw her arms around his neck. "You are welcome," she told him. "And how."

He chuckled. "I was hoping you'd say that." He brought her hand to his lips and pressed a kiss to her fingers. "Now let's get you home."

Leaving their bench, they walked hand in hand out of the wooded path and into the evening's last gentle rays of liquid gold.

CHAPTER

20

Sunshine filtered through the ash tree outside the Petrovics'
cottage. A threadbare tablecloth had been thrown over the
picnic table beneath it, and Elsa and Ivy distributed food
from the hamper they'd packed and brought with them for a
picnic dinner. Luke and Tom were there, too, along with Danielle,
who was busy petting Barney and feeding him slices of turkey
beneath the table. The little girl seemed much better off than
when they'd tried visiting her two nights ago.

Still, the peace that hovered seemed a fragile one, apt to break
with too much pressure. And the pressures upon the Petrovics
were never far away.

When everyone's plate was heaped with food, Tatiana led
them in a simple grace to bless the food.

"Danielle, I have you to thank for alphabetizing all the birds
in the dining hall, don't I?" Elsa asked.

The girl nodded. "It was easy. I don't know why you didn't
do that before."

Elsa smiled. "Me neither. It certainly makes my job go faster."

"Are you sure you'll be all done after tonight?" Tatiana asked.

"Barring unforeseen interruptions, yes." Elsa drank from a mason jar of lemonade Tatiana had provided. "It shouldn't take long now, especially with Ivy here to tie tags on the birds' legs and wrap them in paper cones." Anything left unfinished would be packed up and taken home to work on there, anyway.

"My goodness." Tatiana shook her head. "It's only been a few weeks since we met, but you've brought so much joy to us. We'll be so sad to see you go."

"You aren't that far from Manhattan," Elsa pointed out. "We could visit you."

"I'd like that very much, dear. Although I can't yet offer a forwarding address." Tatiana looked to Danielle and pursed her lips, as if wondering if she'd already said too much for her daughter.

"About that." Luke glanced at Tom, who nodded. "I wish I had more answers for you, but I can at least offer one piece to the puzzle of your next steps. Tom and I—and some other fellows I know—well, we'd like to build you a new cottage."

"I don't want a new cottage." Danielle rubbed between Barney's ears. "I want this one. Only this one."

"You're absolutely right," Luke told her. "This cottage is the best one there is, aside from the fact that it's about ready to fall down around you. It isn't safe. And that's to say nothing of the weather sweeping through it. Hard to stay healthy over the winter in a place like that."

"That's why we're going to build you one exactly like it," Tom said. The spoon in his right hand trembled until he stirred his food around on his plate, banishing the tremor once more. "And I mean down to the last nail. Luke and I are pretty good at building reproductions. We would like to build one for you."

Tatiana's eyes rounded. "You would do that for us?"

Tom grinned, clearly warming under her gratitude. "We would. To be fair, it was Luke's idea, but we're all in. What else do I have to do on weekends anyway?"

"I thought about trying to surprise you, but I figured this would be one less thing for you to worry about if you knew we could take care of it for you. Free of charge, by the way," Luke added.

Elsa had been closely watching the little girl, whose brow had begun to furrow. "How does that sound to you, Danielle?" Elsa asked. "A cottage that looks and feels exactly like this one. You can put all your same things inside it."

Danielle twirled a lock of her hair around her finger, then rubbed the strands with her thumb. Her gaze flickered from the dog to the people sitting around the table, and then back down again.

"Last spring," Tatiana began, "a robin built a nest inside the wreath hanging on our front door. It bothered her every time we opened and closed it, so finally she gave up on that nest. Do you remember, Danielle? She took the twigs from the nest and built another one in a safer place, right up there in the tree. She liked it there. That's where she had her babies. It felt like home to her anyway, even though she moved her nest. That's what we'll do, too. We'll just move our nest like the robin did."

Danielle made no reply, but the crimp in her expression wasn't quite so severe. Still, she looked worried. She would need time to get used to the idea.

Ivy smiled at her. "I've heard a lot about the birds around here, and about George in particular. Could you show me some of the things he's brought you? I'd love to see, when you're finished eating."

Conversation flowed easily around the table, right up until Ivy and Danielle left to go inspect the collection of George's gifts.

With a glance to her daughter, Tatiana leaned in and spoke in low tones. "Mr. Nigel Field came to the property with Mr. Spalding yesterday. He confirmed what I'd already heard, that he intends to turn the estate into a public park."

Luke leaned forward. "He'll need a team of groundskeepers and gardeners to maintain all this. Will he hire you on, even if we have to move your cottage?"

"I tried to convince him," Tatiana said. "I know this land better than anyone. I may not be as strong as I once was, but the county will hire all the strong backs they need, so that shouldn't matter. I waved my experience about as much as I dared. He wasn't making any hiring decisions yet, that's what he said to me. Something about weighing the options . . ." She shook her head. "Mr. Spalding pulled me aside after that exchange and told me not to get my hopes up. Mr. Field has been interviewing landscape architects already. It sounds like he may want to start with a clean slate. I doubt that would include retaining an aging gardener and child."

Elsa rested her folded arms on the table. "What did Mr. Spalding say, exactly?" She almost didn't want to know.

The tip of Tatiana's nose grew pink. "He said he felt it was his duty to make Mr. Field aware of Danielle's 'condition.' I overheard him myself. Mr. Spalding painted such a poor picture of my girl, focusing on her worst moments, predicting how such 'episodes' could affect park visitors. It was his recommendation to be done with us entirely. What could I possibly say to that? Mr. Field would never take my word over Spalding's. It's no use."

Dismay filled Elsa. She had no idea where the woman would find employment. But she did know one thing. The sooner Mr. Spalding and the Petrovics could part ways for good, the better. If Mr. Field had been receptive to the ominous warnings about Danielle, it was better for them to leave this place before he could threaten to have Danielle institutionalized.

"I'm so sorry," Elsa said.

"Whatever for, dear?" Tatiana patted Elsa's arm.

"I haven't found the aviary for you. I haven't helped you find employment."

"But that's not why you came to Elmhurst. Helping us was

never your job, or Luke's or Tom's. And you *have* helped us, you know. Just not in the ways you named."

The sun was sinking, and shadows stretched longer across the lawn. All that was left to do was say good-bye to Tatiana and Danielle.

———◯———

Luke and Tom had been in charge of bringing candles, matches, and kerosene lamps for their camping trip inside the mansion. Even so, Elsa and Ivy were determined to make full use of the remaining daylight to finish all the cataloguing and tagging they could.

"You'll see them again, you know," Ivy reminded Elsa. "This isn't the end of the story unless you want it to be."

"I don't."

"Then it's only the end of one chapter."

Agreeing, Elsa resolved to focus on work. She had failed the Petrovics, no matter what Tatiana said. She couldn't fail Mr. Chapman, too.

Minutes ticked by, and the room dimmed. Ivy fetched a kerosene lamp from Tom and placed it near Elsa on the table.

True to their word, Luke and Tom stayed away, presumably working in some other corner of the mansion. When the case clock struck nine o'clock, Ivy took the pencil from Elsa's hand.

"Enough work for tonight. This is my first sleepover in a Gothic mansion. The fact that we're so close to the legendary Sleepy Hollow makes it deliciously creepier. So come on, show me around, will you? I want to see everything."

Elsa rolled back her shoulders and stretched her neck from side to side. "I gave you the nickel tour as soon as we got here."

Ivy shook her head, her black bob swinging at her jawline. "Then give me the behind-the-scenes tour. Give me the heebie-jeebies."

Elsa laughed. "Would you like to look out over the Hudson River by moonlight? We can climb to the turret. There are windows on all sides up there, and the wind positively howls as it whips by. You can watch for bats and tell me ghost stories."

Ivy brightened. "Berries. Let's go."

By the time they reached the turret, Elsa's legs ached, and her lungs screwed tight from the effort of the climb, but the thrill of being caught up in Ivy's imagination made it worth it.

These windows didn't open, but they were clear enough to see out. From this height, they could see the river shine silver with moonlight beyond the trees along the bank. Much to Ivy's delight, bats darted through the night, their erratically beating wings easily distinguishing them from birds.

"There's your heebie-jeebies." Elsa shuddered.

"You don't like bats?" Ivy moved from one window to the next and, without waiting for a reply, launched into the Revolutionary War history of this area of New York. Apparently there was a lot to say. She didn't seem to notice when Elsa took the small kerosene lamp and examined the floorboards.

Minutes later, Ivy turned. "Let me guess. You're looking for the aviary."

"Only sort of." Elsa scanned the space. "The turret is empty, unless something has been tucked beneath the floor. But I don't see this as a good hiding place for a fragile manuscript. The climate in this room would fluctuate wildly between summer and winter, and the extreme temperatures and humidity levels would wreak havoc on the pages."

Ivy agreed. "Besides, I thought you said Birdie hid it somewhere close by. This turret is still part of the house, granted, but it wouldn't be close-at-hand for an aging woman who would have no other reason to come up here."

"I'm stymied," Elsa confessed. "It can't have vanished."

"Birdie hid it really, really well. We should keep looking. As long as we're here, and as long as no one else is but us . . ." Ivy angled back toward the window. "Wait a minute. I spoke too soon. Looks like we might have company."

Elsa gasped. "What kind of auto is it?"

"No idea. All I can see are the beams from the headlamps. They're coming down the county road and haven't yet turned into the drive. Who would be coming here at this hour?"

Elsa could name a few people. None of them would be happy to find her already here, even though Mr. Spalding had given her the spare key.

Did this visitor have one, too? If not, would that stop them from breaking and entering?

"They're slowing down," Ivy said. "They're definitely turning into the drive."

"Time to find Luke and Tom."

Nearly breathless, Elsa and Ivy found the men in the parlor moments later. "Someone's coming," Elsa said.

Luke's face hardened into granite lines. With his hair cut short, he was even more intimidating. Tom's knuckles went white around the flashlight he held. He shut off the beam.

A window shattered somewhere. The visitor had found a way in.

Luke nudged Elsa, then gestured toward the library. With pinched fingers, he turned his wrist, which Elsa took to mean she should lock the door once inside. She nodded her understanding.

With Ivy close at her heels, Elsa pushed on the panel beside the fireplace until it creaked open. They entered the secret room and locked the door behind them. "I'm sorry," Elsa whispered.

"Are you kidding me? This is the most fun I've had in a long time. Who do you think it is? What do you think our men will do to defend the castle?"

"I don't have either of those answers."

Ivy took off her sweater and pressed it against the small crack between the floor and the door. "We don't want our light to give us away."

"Good thinking." Elsa lifted the lamp and looked about the room. Mr. Spalding had taken every last book, folder, and paper from this place the day he learned this was where she'd found Linus's ERO files. It seemed to be the only room Spalding had been truly interested in.

"So this is the hiding place used for the Underground Railroad?" Ivy asked.

"That's our best guess," Elsa said quietly. "It even has a tunnel to the river."

"Are you serious?"

"Help me move this desk, and I'll show you." Setting the lamp on the floor, the women each took a side and moved the desk away from the wall. Then Ivy took up the light and held it while Elsa pried open the door. Just as before, damp air seeped into the room.

Ivy held the light closer. "Stairs!" She looked over her shoulder at the door. "What else are we going to do while we wait?"

"My thoughts exactly." Elsa's pulse pounded through her veins. "Luke tested the tunnel, but this could be the last chance to explore the path ourselves."

Ducking, they entered single file, Ivy leading with the light. "Easy does it," she said. "Take your time."

Cold humidity licked Elsa's skin. The steps were steep and the darkness so intense it crowded the air. She wasn't sure there was room for the dark and for oxygen, too. Still, a small light flickered inside the glass hurricane.

"Doing okay?" Ivy cast over her shoulder.

"Yes," Elsa breathed. "Just think about how the people must have felt who were running for their lives, trying to get north to freedom. I can't believe we're in the same tunnel now."

"I like how you think," Ivy said. "Except for the one small

detail that this space has changed a lot since then. Natural decay and deterioration must have taken place since the middle of last century."

That was true. The walls of the tunnel had been braced with wooden scaffolding at regular intervals, but the wood was soft and rotting now. Elsa guessed that the boards were originally set in place right up against the earth. Now there were gaps between the wooden supports and the crumbling wall behind it. Erosion added dirt to the path and caused the ceiling to feel lower. Elsa and Ivy both had to stoop.

The temperature dropped, and the air grew thicker. She felt the strain of stepping carefully in her good leg more than in her weak one.

"Ooph!" Ivy stopped short. "Watch out. The next few steps are so covered in mud it's like a drop-off of three feet to the next one. Good heavens, a body could break a leg on that if they aren't watching. Still game to go on?"

Elsa marveled at the length of that speech. Ivy seemed practically unaffected by the climate, while Elsa had to focus on drawing breath. It felt like she was sucking through a drinking straw when what she wanted more than anything was great big gulps of air. "Hang on." She steadied herself with fingertips against one of the weathered supports.

When she had chased Barney and climbed the escalator at Macy's, shadows had crowded the edges of her vision, a warning sign that she needed to stop. Would she notice such a sign here when all was darkness already? She doubted it.

This was foolhardy. She shouldn't be here. And she ought not be too proud to admit it.

"Elsa?" Ivy turned, holding the light so she could see her face. "What do you think?"

She thought it would require more courage to admit her limitations than to pretend she was fine and keep going. Luke's phrase *"unacceptable risk"* echoed in her mind. The bravest thing she could do was to be honest about what she could and could not do.

But she didn't have the wind to explain all that. Instead, she said, "I should go back."

"Good plan. You go in front of me so I can keep an eye on you. Here, you can carry the lamp—unless you'd rather I do it."

"Just hold it out to the side," Elsa suggested.

Ivy obeyed, and since she stayed right behind her, the light was enough for each step. Still, Elsa ran her hands lightly along the walls on either side of her. The splintered boards made for lousy railings, and she could feel mud collecting beneath her fingernails. But if she became dizzy, at least she'd be able to catch herself before crashing into Ivy and tumbling down the stairs.

There was no light coming from inside the den to beckon them upward, but the closer they got, the easier it was for Elsa to breathe again. The damp air didn't sit so heavily in her lungs, and the smell was not as rank. Besides, she'd been counting the steps on the way down. There were ten left to go up.

When the cobwebs cleared from her mind, she thought not only of the fugitives who had passed through here but also of Tom and all those men in the Great War who had had to live in darkness and tunnels, waiting to see if they would survive the next shelling or if they'd be sent over the top. No wonder Tom wanted nothing to do with this tunnel after that.

With seven steps left, the wooden supports ended, and her fingers grazed uninterrupted expanses of earth.

Until she touched something sticking out of the wall. Something that had corners.

"Ivy, hold the light over here." Elsa watched as the small amber glow illuminated what she'd found. Sliding her fingers in around all sides, it felt like a box wrapped in India rubber and coated with dirt.

"What is it?" Ivy asked.

"I don't even want to guess." Elsa pushed down the hope that flared to life inside her. It could be any number of objects. It could be the book Linus thought was the aviary, which Birdie had replaced with something else. Would Linus have actually buried what he thought was a medieval book inside a dirt wall? What a terrible idea!

Then again, Agnes had mentioned Linus would rather risk destroying a coveted object than allow someone else to have it.

If it wasn't the book Linus had buried, it had to be—*could be*—the aviary Birdie had swiped from Linus's den. She might have hid it here, right under his nose, so close to the room he thought she didn't know about.

Thank goodness the walls had eroded over time, revealing the edge. Elsa never would have thought to look here. She supposed that was the idea.

"Can you get it out?" Ivy asked. "Or will the whole wall come tumbling down?"

"Good question," Elsa agreed. "Luke would know."

"Gee, he's a handy fella to have around." Ivy's smile was obvious in her voice. "March on."

Gladly.

Moments later, Elsa pushed through the small door and back into the den, Ivy right behind her.

"Elsa! Ivy!" Luke pounded on the door as though he'd been trying to raise a response for some time. "I'm going to bust down the door if you don't answer me."

"We're here!" Ivy called. "Just a second!" She scrambled to the door and opened it while Elsa collapsed onto the desk chair.

"Why didn't you answer us?" Luke burst into the room, Tom following. Barney trotted to her and licked her filthy hands.

Elsa pointed to the door to the tunnel.

"We didn't go all the way down," Ivy explained. "We turned around at a three-foot drop-off."

"Thank goodness." Luke rubbed a muscle at the back of his neck.

"Are we alone again? Who was it who came?" Elsa figured Luke had chased whoever it was off the property but didn't want to risk sharing about her discovery if there was any chance someone else was in the house.

"We're alone again." Tom shook his head and laughed. "You won't believe who that was. Crawford!"

"Who's Crawford?" Ivy sat on top of the desk and crossed her ankles. Mud coated her Oxford heels.

Still recovering her breath, Elsa let Luke and Tom explain that Crawford was one of the Spaldings' servants who came to pack up the valuables Mrs. Spalding wanted.

"Did he come to search for the aviary, too?"

"He did," Tom said. "Gave us a sob story about needing it because he was in love with a woman above his station and would only ask her to marry him if he had the means to provide for her the way she had been raised."

Elsa's eyebrows raised. "Did he say who his sweetheart is? Is it Jane?"

Luke shook his head. "I didn't ask. I just reminded him that stealing is still against the law, which is what he had come here with every hope and intention of doing."

"And *I* reminded him," said Tom, "coming from a background of service myself, that he'd never be able to get another job in service if he had theft on his record. He replied that if he'd found the aviary, he wouldn't have to worry about working again for a long time. But we pointed out that was only if no one caught him. Which we already had."

"Well done," Elsa said, and Tom's smile unfurled. "And how about you, Barney? Did you have anything to tell Crawford?"

"Oh yes, he did." Luke chuckled. "Barney told him he was trespassing and ought to shake a leg before we decided to make a citizen's arrest and drive him to the Tarrytown police."

"That was magnanimous of you," Ivy told him. "I might have hauled him off myself."

"I'm pretty sure he learned his lesson," Luke said. "Besides, with so many people looking for the aviary, I doubt he would have had better luck."

Elsa cut a glance to Ivy before saying, "I don't want to jinx anything, but our luck may have turned." Oh, how she hoped it had.

CHAPTER

21

"Are you ready to open it?" Luke wiped his hands on his pants, then swiped a handkerchief over his brow. He had replaced the box with fresh wooden supports he'd made from materials he had in the truck. The fact that Tom had been willing to assist him while Ivy held up the light touched Elsa deeply, and she told him so.

"Ready." Elsa had thoroughly washed her hands while the others were in the tunnel. She nodded to her roommate, and Ivy removed the sheet of India rubber that had been wrapped around the box.

Beneath the rubber was a metal box sealed around the edges.

"Pitch and turpentine," Luke said. Using a blade, he cut through the seals and opened the box.

Nesting inside was another, this one made of teakwood and nailed shut, with more of the same sealant at the edges.

Again, Luke assisted, cutting through the seal and using a crowbar to open the lid.

"Whatever's inside, someone went to great pains to try to keep it safe." Elsa's heart beat harder. A metal box protected the package from insects. The wood box protected it from the rust and corrosion that may come from the metal.

"Your turn." Luke stepped back.

Elsa pulled on the cotton gloves she used for handling specimens and removed a package tightly wrapped in muslin, another
barrier intended to combat moisture. It was the shape and weight
of a large hardcover book, about nine inches wide and twelve
inches long.

With care, she unwrapped the muslin and found a layer of
waxed paper folded around the book.

Even Barney seemed to hold his breath.

Nerves tingling to her fingertips, she swept away the paper.

Her heart sank. The embossed cover read *Field Ornithology:
Manual of Instruction and a Checklist of the Birds of North America.*

Deflating, Elsa held it up, turning it so the others could see.

Tom scratched his head. "That doesn't look medieval to me."

"No, it definitely isn't," Elsa confirmed. She set it back down
and opened the front cover. This volume was published in 1874
by Elliott Coues. It was a rare find and would be valuable to
book collectors and ornithologists, but it wasn't what they'd all
been looking for.

"I don't understand," Ivy said.

Elsa tried to explain. "Linus took the aviary away from Birdie
to prevent her from sharing it with Danielle. One day when he
was out, Birdie entered his den and found a book wrapped in
waxed paper and muslin. It was nestled in the box but not nailed
shut yet. She rightly guessed it was the aviary and that he was
preparing it for a hiding place."

"Wait a minute, how do you know all this?" Tom asked.

"Birdie wrote about it in a letter to Agnes soon after it happened," Elsa told him. "She confided in Agnes that she switched
out the aviary, replacing it with a book of similar size and weight
in the hopes that he would box it up and hide it before he realized
what she'd done." She held up the field guide again. "Obviously
her plan worked. Linus never had a clue what he so carefully
preserved."

Ivy shook her head. "Clever girl. So we're no closer to finding the aviary than we ever were."

The small flame bobbed and leaned inside the kerosene lamp, casting light and shadow over four glum faces and one dog, who was now stretched out and snoring on the floor. There was nothing more to do here.

"Thanks, everyone, for your help unearthing this." Elsa cradled the book in one arm, ready to pack it with the rest of her things. Mr. Chapman, at least, would want to see it. "I don't know about the rest of you, but I'm exhausted and ready to retire for the night."

The weight of disappointment was tempered only by the knowledge that Birdie had succeeded in fooling Linus until his dying day.

If only Birdie hadn't fooled herself so thoroughly, too.

———————◯———————

FRIDAY, SEPTEMBER 10, 1926

Elsa shouldn't have expected she would sleep well in Birdie's bedroom. While Ivy's soft, regular breathing continued uninterrupted, Elsa's rest came only in snatches. The house creaked, and the wind moaned. Moonlight streamed through lace curtains, casting needlepoint patterns on the wall.

Elsa stared at the underside of the canopy above the bed and thought of the woman who had slept here, alone, her husband occupying the room across the hall. The one that once had been the nursery. Not for the first time, she wished she had known Birdie better while she still lived.

She wished she had been able to honor Birdie's wishes and hand the aviary to the Petrovics.

Regret made a terrible bedfellow.

Eventually giving up on sleep, Elsa wiggled out of her sleeping bag to make herself ready for the day. It was just after six o'clock, nearly time for dawn. She might as well go outside. This would likely be the only sunrise she'd ever spend at Elmhurst.

Careful not to disturb Luke and Tom, who slept in the parlor, Elsa let herself out the front door and took the paved stone path into the closest copse of trees. Dew beaded her shoes as she left the path and sat on a downed tree trunk. Bird vocalizations were much reduced from the spring songs that attracted mates and established territories. Still, enough made their presence known to bring a smile to Elsa's face.

She tugged her sweater tighter around her and inhaled the sharp woodsy scent. Slowly, the indigo sky faded, and a crimson ribbon on the horizon showed between the trees. Fallen leaves carpeted the ground. Twigs snapped, and Elsa turned to find Luke approaching with one hand held behind his back.

With any luck, he'd come to surprise her with coffee, but she'd pretend not to notice for now. "Did I wake you on my way out?" she asked.

"I was already up. Mind if I join you, or do you prefer to commune with nature alone?"

"Nature is better when shared." She patted the trunk next to her.

He paused a few feet away from her. "I brought you something. Close your eyes?"

She did so and could tell from the spicy smell of his shaving soap that he sat down beside her. Curiously, she did not smell any coffee.

She must have shivered, either from the chill in the air or from anticipation, because she felt him shift, and then he draped his jacket over her shoulders. It smelled of him and still held his warmth.

"You won't be cold without this?" she asked.

"Nope. Here, put your arms through."

Still not peeking, she obeyed and felt her body relax into the sudden comfort of being warm again. "Thank you. That's so much better."

"You're welcome. You can open your eyes, just don't look behind you yet, okay? First, I wanted to tell you that I took your advice. Yesterday morning I told my father what I told yours at the park about my changed perspective on salvage and restoration."

Her eyes widened. "And?"

"And I'm glad I did. So was he. Turns out, it meant more to him to hear that than I'd ever dreamed it would. All this time, he had been feeling like the family business was holding me back from bigger and better things."

"Oh my. Did you talk and sort that out?"

"We did talk. I'd been thinking about what you said about how you'd misinterpreted your parents for years. I wanted to know if I'd done the same thing, so I asked questions I wouldn't have otherwise. Once my mother joined the conversation, things slowly fell into place. At first, when I came to work for my father, he criticized me because, frankly, I deserved it. I had a lot to learn, and he was too raw from grief over losing Franklin to put a nice spin on the corrections I needed."

"I can understand that. Did your mother shed any light on things?"

He nodded. "She suggested the critical spirit became not only a habit but also a defense against bonding with me too much. They both expected me to leave them to make a name for myself as an architect. I guess Father thought losing his second son that way wouldn't hurt so much if we remained angry at each other most of the time."

Stunned, Elsa gripped his hand. "That was a big conversation. Huge!"

He chuckled. "I'm still exhausted from it. But I am so glad my parents opened up the way they did. If Mother hadn't chimed in,

I doubt Father and I would have gotten to the root of the issue. But we did, and I have you to thank for the prompt that started it. So thank you."

Her heart leapt. "I can't tell you how happy I am to hear all this. You may not recall that the first day we met, you asked a rhetorical question about whether people could be restored the same way old buildings could be. I think the answer is yes. People can be salvaged. Relationships can be restored. We can save the beautiful that remains and build upon that, can't we?"

His response was a smile that needed no words to improve it. "I also—I made you something. I hope you like it, and I really hope it doesn't hurt your feelings. My only intention with this is to give you something to remind you that you don't ever have to walk alone. I want to be the one you lean on, the one beside you. But for the times when we're apart, I'd like you to have this. To use or just to look at if you don't need it."

Elsa didn't know whether to be touched or nervous. She landed on both at once. "So it isn't coffee?"

He chuckled. "There will be a fresh-brewed pot waiting for us back at the house after this."

After reaching behind the trunk they sat upon, he handed her a long vertical carving of a dozen or so chickadees stacked on top of each other with the same branch winding around it beneath their feet.

"Luke," Elsa gasped. "It's gorgeous. Wherever did you find such a piece?"

"I started carving it for you the evening after you taught Danielle about the chickadees."

"You made this. For me?" She couldn't imagine the number of hours it had taken.

"Yes, chickadee, for you. Stand up, I want to see how the height is."

Not quite understanding what he meant, she stood anyway.

Still seated on the tree, he gently took her hand and placed it upon the round head of the bird at the top.

Understanding dawned as she let the opposite end rest on the ground. This was more than a stick repurposed into a work of art. It was a cane.

She was twenty-six years old, and he had given her a cane.

He had good reason to.

Tears fell faster than she could wipe them away. She felt herself teetering on the brink of something monumental. With the barest nudge, she could go either way. She could fall headlong into self-pity for the way her body refused to fully heal. Or she could, as she had done last night in the tunnel, accept that she had limitations but refuse the shame that had accompanied them in the past. She could rejoice that this man cared so well for her exactly the way she was. She could decide to enjoy this beautiful gift and the giver who valued her enough to make it.

"Elsa, what is it? What are you thinking right now?"

"It's perfect." She swiped the back of her hand over her cheek once more. "I don't deserve you."

"Funny, I've been thinking the same thing about you." Luke pulled her near.

When his arms came around her waist, she let the cane go and rested her hands on his shoulders. "Thank you, Luke." But what she felt for him was too big to be contained in those three syllables.

Without pausing to think about it, she pressed a kiss to the scar on his brow, then another to the scar on his cheek, lingering there while her stomach flipped in a somersault. His hand cupped the back of her neck, his fingers buried in her wavy hair.

She kissed the scar on his chin and felt him smile, his arm around her waist tightening. In the next moment, his lips were on hers in a kiss that left no room for doubting his feelings for her.

In fact, it left her nearly breathless. She leaned back.

"Are you okay?" he asked, alarm in his eyes and voice. "Did I—was that bad for your lungs?"

"Are you kidding?" She laughed. "It's not my lungs. It's my heart."

His frown deepened. "Is it okay?"

"Never better."

Luke's frown slowly curled into a smile instead. "Good."

"Very." Sunrise slanted through the branches in golden shafts that speared through mist rising from the ground. Elsa picked up the cane again. "It really is remarkable."

"Do you think you'll use it?"

"Yes," she decided. "I will, and proudly, too. I'll use it now, on my way to get that coffee you mentioned. We have some time before we need to head back, and there's a little more work to do."

Luke rose and walked beside her while she tested out the cane. "Will you be ready to leave in an hour or so?"

"In a manner of speaking." She allowed herself a sigh and told him what he surely already knew. She'd been so sure they'd found the aviary last night and so deeply disappointed to find she was wrong.

"It was still a worthy discovery, proving that Birdie was telling Agnes the truth with those letters. That has to mean the aviary is still around here, likely closer than we think."

After so much searching, the notion failed to bring comfort.

Luke motioned to the cane she'd been using along the path. "How does that feel?"

Eager to set her disappointment aside, she smiled up at him. "Like I'm on a field expedition," she answered, every word true. "Using this makes me feel like I'm on a grand adventure. Like *life* is a grand adventure, and I have all I need to enjoy it."

Pulling her close, he dropped a kiss on her hair.

CHAPTER

22

NEW YORK CITY
SATURDAY, SEPTEMBER 11, 1926

How ironic, Elsa mused, that the Gothic country estate where she had expected to be isolated had actually brought more friends into her life than she'd ever had before. She could scarcely believe her work at Elmhurst was over.

All day Friday, after she returned to the museum with the last of the tagged specimens, she carried on with her usual work in the ornithology department. But without the anticipation of the next visit to Tarrytown, her office felt more lonesome than usual.

So when Luke called her after dinner and asked if he and Tom could meet her at Central Park the next day, she didn't need to be asked twice.

Now the three of them sat on the steps of Bethesda Terrace, facing Bethesda Fountain. Ivy would have joined them but had to work on an upcoming event for another historical anniversary.

Barney stayed on a leash but remained alert as he watched other pedestrians. Many sat along the fountain's perimeter beneath the angel looking down from twenty-six feet above. Pigeons bobbed along the ground, their feathers iridescent in the sun.

"How about that view, Tom?" Luke extended an arm as though to encompass not just the fountain but the lake behind it and the sun-streaked sky. The heat of the day had mellowed to a golden haze over the city's most-beloved park. "And the jazz!"

At the bandshell a mere three hundred feet south of Bethesda Terrace, Fletcher Henderson and his orchestra performed his hit "Shanghai Shuffle." It was plenty loud enough to be heard without being in the concert audience. A couple sitting nearby tapped their toes to the beat.

But Tom's attention snagged on the pigeons. He pulled out a cigarette and lit it. With his other hand, he gave the dog a good scratch behind the ears.

With no other response forthcoming from Tom, Luke asked Elsa how work had been yesterday.

"Typical, for the most part," she started. "Although I did try to clear the air with Archer over his surprise visit to Elmhurst."

"Yeah? How'd that go?"

"He apologized for any misunderstanding but not for being there. When I asked him outright if he had been gambling, he admitted that he had. Percy was more of an influence on him than the other way around. Now he's cut Percy out and is pals with Wesley instead."

Luke took all this in with a single nod. "Nothing about that shocks me. Did you tell him anything about the aviary?"

"Only that we hadn't found it—and only because he asked." She glanced to Tom, who blew smoke from the side of his mouth but seemed to be following along. "Do you have any news from Elmhurst?"

A light wind feathered Elsa's skin, and geese and swans glided across the surface of the lake. From the opposite direction, Fletcher Henderson's orchestra played "The Stampede," a lively song she recognized from the radio. She felt very far away from the mansion indeed.

"We spoke to Mr. Spalding," Luke said. "He and his family have everything they want out of the house. The county has scheduled for it to be torn down on Friday."

Her stomach hollowed. She'd known from the start this day was coming, but now that it was upon them, the end seemed impossibly soon. She tried and failed to picture that piece of land on the Hudson without the turreted mansion upon it. "Did he say whether the Petrovics still had until the end of the month to stay in their cottage?"

"We confirmed that they do." Tom tugged at the brim of his straw boater. "We also finished taking all the measurements and photographs inside so we can build the new one."

"But there are still some elements we want to salvage before the mansion is bulldozed," Luke added. "Mostly doors and lighting fixtures. It will be a challenge to get it all out of there in time, so I'm afraid we won't see much of each other this coming week."

She told him she understood.

Even with the music in the background and children playing in the fountain, a heaviness seemed to surround both Luke and Tom.

"I wish we could find the aviary for Tatiana and Danielle," Tom said. "But . . ."

"I know," she said. "If we haven't found it by now, chances are really slim. And I know you won't have time to do anything but the job that brought you to Elmhurst to begin with."

He nodded, his face clouded with what looked a lot like defeat.

Luke regarded him, then turned to Elsa, a fresh sparkle in his eyes. "In the meantime, I can't think of a better way to spend Saturday night than wandering around in the woods looking for birds. If only we had someone to help us."

Beaming, Elsa accepted his hand to help her stand. With her other hand, she gripped the chickadee cane he'd carved for her. "Nothing would please me more." And she was pretty sure Luke knew that. He also knew bird-watching might help his younger friend decompress.

A laugh escaped Tom. "This has to be better than Luke's attempt last weekend."

Oh, how she loved that he'd tried.

———————◦———————

THURSDAY, SEPTEMBER 16, 1926

Days passed. Two evenings this week Elsa had spent with her mother visiting florists who were possible vendors for her cousin's wedding. The opposite evenings, she'd spent in Central Park, leading anyone who wished to go bird-watching with her. The Saturday evening expedition, which had begun with just Luke and Tom, had quickly picked up eager birders along the way. Guiding that little group had filled her with such satisfaction, she decided to repeat it, even without her friends. To her surprise, whenever she held her chickadee cane in the air and called out her offer to guide, people flocked to her. There were so many benches in the park, too, that it was easy to rest along the way. The thing about birding was that it involved being still and watching. She didn't always need to be moving, and when she did, a slow pace was better than fast.

Still, she thought about Elmhurst, the Petrovics, and the aviary. In her office at the museum, she gazed out her window over the trees changing color in the park. A pigeon alighted on her windowsill and looked at her sideways.

"Hello, you," Elsa greeted him absent-mindedly, and the pigeon flapped away.

Her gaze fell on the old book on field ornithology she'd found in the tunnel at Elmhurst. She'd suggested to Mr. Chapman that it be added to the departmental research library, and he'd agreed but insisted it be cleaned first. One of the conservators had put it on his schedule to remove the mold spots, but until that time, she kept it in her office.

Sliding it toward her, she started flipping through the pages, stopping when she found a card tucked into the table of contents with Birdie's handwriting.

Linus,

You never knew what true treasure was when you had it. And you'll never find what you're looking for unless you pick up all the pieces of my broken heart.

A chill slipped down Elsa's spine. She read it again. Surely the treasure she referred to was their daughter, Sarah. The second line had to be a clue as to the aviary's whereabouts. Linus would find what he was looking for if he grasped all the pieces of her broken heart.

"Oh, Birdie, what did you mean?" Elsa murmured.

She knew Birdie's heart had broken over Sarah. For a moment, she thought perhaps Birdie had buried the aviary at Sarah's final resting place, and then remembered that according to Agnes, Birdie didn't even know where that was. After Sarah died in the hospital due to complications from the surgery, Linus had never brought her home or given her a proper burial, instead allowing the hospital to "dispose" of the body. Birdie had no tombstone on which to lay flowers for her daughter, no resting spot where she could pin her grief.

Elsa recalled, then, the portraits of Sarah she'd found in the dressing room, both on the walls and in the bureau drawer. No wonder she had painted so many. With no grave to visit and a husband who wouldn't support her, painting must have been her way of mourning and remembering.

Elsa read Birdie's note to Linus once again.

Was she so confident that he wouldn't "pick up all the pieces" that she was simply taunting him, believing he'd never find the aviary? It did sound like an impossible task. Or did she *want* him to find it, after all? Was she trying to lead him to the pieces of her broken heart so that he would have to confront them himself?

Frustration buzzed through her. She was asking the wrong questions. All she needed to know was *where*. Tomorrow, the county would begin leveling the mansion, and all hope would be gone for finding the answer.

It was five o'clock. Maybe walking home would help clear her mind and get the gears turning better. Ivy wouldn't be joining her today, as she had an event with the New-York Historical Society commemorating the 150th anniversary of the British occupation of Manhattan. Lifting Birdie's card from the field guide, she tucked it into her satchel.

As she did so, her fingers brushed a few scraps of paper. She fished them out. They were a few old strips from the notebook she'd used when charting field data at Elmhurst. The notebook whose pages she'd ripped out, cut up, rearranged, and copied into a fresh ledger. Crumpling the strips, she tossed them into the waste bin, grasped her cane, and left her office.

Halfway to the elevators, she stopped, struck with a new idea.

Had Birdie done something similar to the aviary in order to hide it? Would she have cut out the pages, changing the shape of the treasure everyone sought?

Elsa leaned on her cane, mind swirling, then rummaged through her satchel until she found the small notebook she'd used to take notes when Agnes had shown her Birdie's letters. She skimmed to the exact quote she'd copied.

Even if he discovers the switch, he'll never find it now. I must keep the aviary safe and close by. It won't be easy to show

Danielle anymore, but it will be worth it. She'll have them soon enough, and forever.

Them she had written in that last sentence. Not *it*. That had struck her as odd when Elsa had first read it. Could it mean Birdie had cut out the pages and hidden them flat in many different places? The collection wouldn't be worth as much that way, but the individual pages would still be worth a small fortune.

And they could have been hidden almost anywhere. Tucked into books in the library would have been a reasonable option, so long as they were books Linus didn't actually read. If he wasn't interested in the subject matter, he certainly wouldn't be looking for his medieval aviary *inside* any other books.

Pulse galloping, Elsa continued walking to the elevators. At least Luke and Tom had removed all those books, and they were safely at the Dupont & Son warehouse, well out of harm's way when the mansion would come down tomorrow. That was a relief beyond words.

Inside the elevator, Elsa pushed the button for the lobby, then pulled out the card. She read it again and frowned. By the time the doors opened, she wasn't so sure Birdie would have hidden the pages in the library books after all.

Her cane tapping across the marble, she circled the giant meteor in Memorial Hall and stepped out into the sunshine. With every step down the stairs, she went deeper into her thoughts, deeper into everything she'd learned about Birdie and what was important to her.

When she landed on the sidewalk, she stopped again, vaguely aware of pedestrians parting and streaming around her, of traffic honking and pumping fumes into the air. *"Unless you pick up all the pieces of my broken heart."*

The pieces of Birdie's broken heart were not in random books in the library.

They were still in the house. Those paintings of Sarah were the expressions of Birdie's broken heart. The aviary pages were hidden behind the frames or mattes. It was the only answer that made sense.

And if Elsa didn't get there tonight and deliver them to the Petrovics, they would all be destroyed tomorrow.

TARRYTOWN

Elsa had left the spare key for Mr. Spalding when she left Elmhurst last Friday morning. But thanks to Crawford's breaking and entering, she knew exactly where she could get in without it if Spalding had still bothered to lock the mansion. She wished Ivy or Luke could be here with her, but both were occupied, and this wasn't an errand that could wait. She'd left a note for her roommate before catching the train to let her know she'd be back by nine o'clock. All she had to do was test her theory, and if she was right, gather up the paintings of Sarah and transfer them to the Petrovics' cottage. If Tatiana wanted Elsa to bring the paintings to Manhattan for safekeeping, she was prepared to do that, too.

The cab rolled to a stop in the circle drive, right behind a white Rolls-Royce Phantom, splattered by the country road. Elsa trapped a groan as Archer Hamlin got out of his auto, looking sharp in his grey suit and matching homburg. She paid her driver and asked him to come back for her at eight o'clock. That meant she had ninety minutes to do what she came here to do.

Archer wasn't part of her plan. And judging by the glint in his eyes, he hadn't factored her into his evening, either.

"I thought you were done here," Archer said. "Still hunting? One last chance before it's all torn down tomorrow?"

Elsa forced a smile, even as her palms began to sweat in their gloves. She tightened her grip on her cane. "I could ask you the same thing. My work here is done, yes. But I'm still allowed to visit the Petrovics."

Jane appeared on the veranda wearing a flaming orange sheath with handkerchief hem, black gloves to her elbows, and black feathers clipped in her hair. "Why, Elsa! Fancy meeting you here! If you had come twenty minutes ago you'd have seen Cousin Hugh. He spent all day poking around the estate but is finally going back to Pennsylvania. Wesley has dashed off to pick up some supplies for the party. I didn't know you'd be coming with Archer." She directed a pointed gaze at him.

"Oh! I came on my own. I'm sorry, I didn't intend to intrude on your plans. Don't let me bother you, I'm only here for a short visit to the Petrovics, anyway." Elsa's mind raced. If they saw her enter the house now, they'd want to know why. Could she possibly bring the paintings of Sarah to the Petrovics without arousing suspicion?

Not a chance. They would wonder what the Petrovics would want with dozens of paintings of a baby who wasn't related to them. They might not guess the aviary pages were hidden inside them at first, but they could figure it out. That wasn't a risk Elsa wanted to take.

Could she sneak in after the party started?

"You might as well come to the party, too," Jane crooned. "Only, there's going to be lots of music and dancing, and I don't want you to feel uncomfortable."

"Elsa doesn't dance," Archer said. "Believe me, I've tried."

Ignoring him, Elsa asked, "Is Wesley providing the music?"

"Oh no. The piano was taken away three days ago, but all his friends are musicians, most of them with instruments that travel. We're going to have a regular jazz band and plenty of gin to go with it. Father would *hate* it. He says jazz makes people disabled from the irregular rhythm." She laughed.

"If we trash the place, no one will have to clean it up. It all gets torn down tomorrow." Archer wiggled his eyebrows, clearly delighted at the lack of consequences for his upcoming actions.

"Gee, what fun." Elsa's sarcasm seemed lost on Archer and Jane. But actually, this all could play to her advantage. If the party was loud and the people were getting sozzled, it would be much easier for her to get in and out undetected. Depending on how many people were coming, and how many rooms they'd spill into.

"Chick-a-dee-dee."

Elsa turned toward the woods. That hadn't sounded like a bird. It had sounded like Danielle. Signaling danger?

"I'll leave you to it," she said, and headed for the Petrovics' cottage, where she planned to wait until the time was right.

"Not so fast, Els." Archer closed the gap and cupped his hand around her upper arm. "Before you go, I was hoping you could show me that secret room you told me about. The one used by the Underground Railroad? Jane here has no idea where that is, and it'll be gone tomorrow. I'd love to see it. Please?"

The way he gripped her, she knew there was only one answer. "Of course."

"You two have fun. I've got more to do before the guests arrive. Ta-ta, Elsa." She blew her a kiss, spun on her T-strap heels, and slipped back inside.

Alone with Archer, Elsa led the way to the library, or rather, the gutted room that once held the library. With all the woodwork, fireplaces, furnishings, and even chandeliers gone, it felt more like a tomb. Evening light slanted through windows whose coverings had also been removed.

Elsa pushed on the door beside where the fireplace stood. It was so much easier to spot now, Archer really could have found it himself. "Here it is." She stood in the doorway to the windowless room. "Not much to see if you don't have a candle or kerosene lamp."

"Fascinating." Archer stepped closer and inadvertently kicked

Elsa's cane out of her hand. It clattered as it fell to the floor in the secret den. "So sorry."

Elsa went to retrieve it, irritated that he hadn't done so himself. As soon as she bent, he shoved her farther into the room, slammed the door shut, and locked it from the other side.

"Archer!" Elsa gasped. "What are you doing?"

"I said I was sorry." His voice was muffled as it came through the door. "But honestly, Elsa, your timing is truly terrible. We need you to stay out of the way during the party."

"I promise I will!"

"Yeah, that's nice, but we need to make sure of it."

"Why, what on earth kind of party are you having, anyway?"

"The regular kind. But before that? A search party of the entire grounds. Didn't your grandmother ever tell you that many hands make light work?"

"Don't you dare go near the Petrovics' cottage," Elsa shouted. "You leave them alone, Archer, I mean it." If they found the provenance document there, or if Hugh had already told them Tatiana had it, would anything stop them from tearing the cottage apart to find the aviary? Danielle would not be able to cope with that. She shouldn't have to. Neither should Tatiana.

"We need you out of the way. It's for your own good, doll. Greed makes people grumpy and violent. If anyone thinks they're on to something and you swoop in and take it for that gardener, you're liable to get hurt. Wouldn't want your other leg to go gimpy, now, would we? And it isn't like we'll let you rot in here. Someone will let you out later."

"No, you let me out now," Elsa insisted, but receding footsteps told her he was already walking away.

———◦———

With no way to measure its passing, time had lost its meaning. All Elsa knew was that the search party must have ended because the jazz party had started about ten tunes ago, and still no one had come to let her out.

She had found the chair and dragged it close to the keyhole so she could sit while waiting. Her voice hoarse from competing with trumpets and trombones, she pounded the end of her cane against the door. She wasn't afraid of the dark. But being alone, cast aside and forgotten . . . well, she couldn't think of much worse. As a child, it had happened too many times not to leave a mark on her even as an adult.

She hadn't been chosen for teams because she couldn't help score points. She hadn't been chosen as a friend, either, usually. She was different, when she longed more than anything to be the same, to fit the mold everyone else seemed to have been made from. Different was not good enough. Different was wrong. And being wrong was shameful.

Elsewhere in the house, people her age were dancing the Charleston and King Tut Fox Trot. She could feel the music, hear their laughter, and smell their cigarette smoke. The house itself seemed to buzz with a frantic gaiety.

Elsa might as well have been miles away, here in this forgotten pocket of darkness. Though she couldn't see her hand in front of her face, she pulled off her glasses and cleaned them on a fold of her skirt, again and again. But this was applesauce. It didn't make her vision better or erase the terrible voices in her mind that told her to be better, *do* better, unless she wanted to be alone forever.

Elsa shook her head to dislodge those old feelings that threatened to twine around her. Shame was bondage, and right now, she needed to be free to think clearly. Grasping her cane, she felt in its grooves and curves the little birds Luke had carved to remind her she wasn't alone.

He wasn't here. But God was, or would be if she only asked. *Lord, draw near,* she prayed. *Be with me now. Clear my mind, and steady my nerves. Please send someone to open this door.*

She kept pounding her cane on the door to the library.

Had the taxi she'd requested to return for her already come and gone? Did anyone besides Archer know she was in here? She'd told Jane she was here to visit the Petrovics. Unless Archer told her otherwise, she'd have no reason to wonder where Elsa was.

Cool air touched her silk-stockinged ankles, a whisper from the gap under the door that led to the tunnel. Luke had made it all the way through and out the other side, but could she? Her lungs tightened just thinking about her last attempt.

Minutes stretched into what felt like hours. The music faded or stopped, or Elsa simply began losing her senses. Archer still didn't return, and neither did anyone else. For all Elsa knew, Archer could be passed out sozzled somewhere, or he could have forgotten her.

Well then. She was no longer a little girl playing hide-and-seek, waiting to be found by peers who couldn't be bothered to look for her.

Elsa would find her own way out. *Lord, be my light. Show me the path.*

CHAPTER

23

The tunnel was exactly how she remembered it, only darker. The air was thick and cold, and growing heavier in her lungs with every step. She wished she had conserved her energy instead of spending so much calling for help that never came.

Without the lamp, she proceeded slowly, using the cane to tell her where each step ended before taking another. Using her other hand, she felt the wall alternate from crumbling dirt to rotting wooden scaffolding.

She pressed on, controlling her breathing, counting every step. When she reached twenty-three, she sat on the floor and scooted to the edge of the drop-off. When she felt the ground three feet below with her cane, she stood on that solid ground and inched forward, always testing the terrain with the cane before trusting her next step.

It was exhausting. She ought to have asked Luke for more details about the tunnel. Was there another drop-off somewhere? How long was the passage, anyway? Did it ever get so narrow he'd had to squeeze through sideways?

That thought alone brought a sharp pain to her chest. Her leg didn't ache all that much right now, and she figured she had adrenaline to thank for that. But there wasn't much to be done about the fact that she was having trouble breathing. Going slower may calm her heart rate, but that meant spending more time underground. Going faster might get her out sooner, but only if she didn't pass out on the way.

A silent prayer on her lips, she kept going, kept counting her steps if only to assure herself she was moving forward. By the fiftieth step, her head pounded. By the sixtieth, she was fighting a rising tide of panic.

She was in too deep to turn around, even if she wanted to. She could only hope the end was near.

At some point after that, she forgot to keep counting.

Then she realized she'd stopped moving, too. She was sitting on the damp, cold ground. The only sounds were that of her labored breathing and a trickle of water somewhere.

Elsa had to carry on anyway. But if she could just close her eyes, sit still, and give her lungs a rest, she'd be better off in a moment. Cane still in one hand, she drew up her knees, wrapped her arms around them, and let her head drop forward.

Sweet relief.

The dark was a blanket, so heavy it pressed her down.

She surrendered.

With a jolt, Elsa awoke in pitch black, and felt a wet spot on her cheek. She swiped at it, and something licked her hand.

"Barney?" she gasped and threw her arms around his warm, furry body, shaking with the all-over wag of his tail.

The dog whined, nudging his cold nose at her face until she sat up. She had no idea how long she'd been out. Her thoughts felt slow to turn, but she knew she had to go. Using her cane to help her stand, and latching on to Barney's collar, she continued the slow trek through the miserable tunnel.

Barney tugged her along. His pace was impeccable—not enough to throw her off balance but enough to keep her progress steady. A couple of times, he stopped in front of her, and with her cane she realized he was blocking her from falling into a washed-out hole that could have twisted her ankle.

At last, they came to a door. A draft streamed around the warped wooden boards that no longer fit snugly in the frame. Elsa felt around for a handle, grasped it, and pulled it open. It hadn't been latched, so Barney must have pushed through when he'd come to find her, and then it swung back on its hinges. When a whoosh of clean air swept over her, she could have dropped to the ground right there to rest. But Barney pulled her forward and around a bend that ran parallel to the mighty Hudson River.

"Good boy," she said, kneeling to hug the animal again. "Good Barney, good boy." She'd prayed for someone to help her, and God had sent her a smelly, filthy, amazing, faithful dog. She had prayed for the locked door to open, but God, and Barney, had led her to a different one instead.

"Did Tom bring you? Did Luke?"

The German shepherd only grinned and panted. Either way, a friend had to be near. If she had the lung power to support it, she'd call out. Instead, she gave Barney a good scratch behind his ears and a pat on his rump. "Go find your master," she told him. "Get Luke, get Tom." Surely the dog would find one of them and bring him back to her.

Barney ran off, and Elsa filled her lungs, feeling them loosen and expand. *Thank you, God.* The breeze off the river ruffled through her hair and chilled the sweat on her skin. She pulled her sweater tight and rubbed her arms.

As her strength began to return, her thoughts raced ahead. Turning, she could see where she was in relation to the mansion. Up on the hill, its turret and fortress-like roofline loomed like the Gothic cathedral that had inspired it. It was a hike, but the slope was gentle, and she still had her cane.

A dim light glowed from the parlor, suggesting that someone was still there with a kerosene lamp or small fire in the hearth, or possibly wax-dripping candles. From here, it looked like the party was over. Finally, she could get inside and see if her hunch about the treasure was right.

———

The poor mansion. When Elsa entered through the door closest to the stair tower, the smells of bathtub gin and cigarette smoke clogged her throat. She held back a cough, careful not to alert whoever was still lounging in the parlor. Part of her wanted to check the library to see if the door to the secret den was still locked. Maybe someone had come for her after all and found her missing.

The larger part of her wasn't willing to waste another moment or take any more steps than she had to. The odors from the party were so strong all she wanted to do was find the aviary and leave. With her eyes so adjusted to the dark, she took the stairs to the second floor with only starlight to guide her.

Oh, those wretched stairs. Every one of them challenged her limits. Pain pulsed in her skull to the beat of her throbbing heart. Even her arms grew sore as she leaned harder on the railing and the cane, using every muscle she had to push herself to the second floor. She wondered if she'd be able to move tomorrow.

But tomorrow did not concern her. The next few moments held every hope she'd carried since learning Birdie had willed the aviary to Danielle.

Smoke stung her eyes and made them water. Taking care to avoid the floorboards that creaked, Elsa stole into Birdie's bedchamber and into the adjoining dressing room. She lifted the first painting off the wall and carried it to the desk by the window. A moonbeam fell across the gorgeous painting of a baby sleeping in the crook of her mother's arms.

This had to be what Birdie meant. These paintings, the pieces of her broken heart that Linus would never pick up.

Her throat tight and itching, Elsa turned the framed painting over, then took a letter opener and loosened the screws holding the frame in place. After wiping her hands the best she could on the inside of her hem, she removed the back panel from the frame. Then a layer of muslin, then a layer of waxed paper.

And there it was. Not just one gilded page from the aviary, but several, with waxed paper between each one.

She had found Birdie's treasures at last.

Tears rolled down Elsa's cheeks, and she wiped them away, surely streaking her face with mud. With her fingers dirty and her cotton gloves ruined, she wouldn't touch the medieval pages. Instead, she layered the muslin and waxed paper again, and rese-cured the frame. Then she went back into the dressing chamber for more.

There were so many. Eight hung on the walls, and there were more with mattes, but no frames, lying flat in the bottom drawer of a bureau. A quick check of those revealed that they, too, hid precious illuminated pages.

The cigarette smoke crawled into her lungs and triggered a cough she couldn't hold back. Whoever was still smoking down-stairs was sure to have heard her.

Elsa needed to hurry. Sweat filmed her skin. Her glasses slid down her nose, and she pushed them up again. What she needed was a pair of suitcases large enough to carry all of these at once. She'd seen a set in Linus's bedroom across the hall. She didn't need the light to find them.

When she stepped into the hall, however, the smoke was so thick and hot she jumped back into Birdie's room and slammed the door shut. A fresh wave of adrenaline pumped through her. Kneeling, she touched the floor and immediately drew back from its warmth.

The house was on fire beneath her.

She tore off her sweater and went to the water closet, intending to soak the fabric in water and hold it over her mouth and nose while she tried to find a way out.

No water. Of course they would have turned it off since they were tearing the house down tomorrow. She leaned on the sink and tried to think past the pounding in her head, the shaking in her limbs.

She could still get the aviary pages out through the window. The fire hadn't reached the second floor yet. It was only smoke, and smoke would rise to the ceiling, which meant if she stayed low, she could creep under it. She had to try.

Tying the sweater around her nose and mouth, she opened the door to the corridor once more and crouched as she crossed into Linus's room, grabbed the two suitcases from his dressing chamber, and hurried back into Birdie's room. Again, she slammed the door.

The sweater slipped down around her neck. She let it fall, gasping for air, though the quality even here was deteriorating. Asking God for another miraculous surge of strength, she threw open the suitcase, piled in the eight framed paintings, and stuffed a pillow on top to pad it. Into the other one went all the unframed paintings, along with the other pillow from Birdie's bed.

Elsa's throat began to close, and her lungs burned. She looked at the bed, wondering if she had time to pull off a sheet, thread it through the handles of the suitcases, and gently lower them down to the ground outside.

Black spots dotted her vision. Time was up. Her lungs would give out before the fire even reached her.

An incessant, repetitive noise filtered through her clouding consciousness. Barking. It was Barney, barking outside. Another voice pitched high cried, "Chick-a-dee-dee-dee-dee-dee! Chick-a-dee-dee-dee-dee-dee! Elsa! Elsa!"

Gasping for air, Elsa went to the window and leaned out to find Danielle and Tatiana with Barney between them. When Danielle saw Elsa, she moaned and flapped her arms. Wind from the fire whipped the child's hair and snapped her nightdress above her bare feet.

"Elsa!" Tatiana cried, her voice serrated with terror, her greying braid unraveled. "Get out now!" Flames from below crackled and rushed with the sound of a moving train. Glass shattered as windows exploded from heat.

Elsa threw her cane from the window so it landed well away from Tatiana and Danielle.

Then Luke ran into view, his face and clothes streaked with soot and soaked with sweat. "Elsa! I can't get to you without walking through fire. You have to jump." He held out his arms.

With no breath to explain, she lifted a suitcase and threw it out. He caught it and put it down before she tossed the second one, as well.

"Okay, chickadee, time to fly."

She knew he was right. She swung her legs over the windowsill, the heat at her back like an iron to her skin. All at once, the exertions of the night caught up with her, and she wasn't sure how far she could push off the ledge to jump down.

Luke moved so he was as directly beneath the window as he could get. "Just fall."

She did.

The next thing she knew, she was tangled in his arms and on the ground, on top of him. She'd clobbered him as he'd broken her fall. "I'm sorry," she rasped. "Did I hurt you?"

He sat up, cradling her against his chest. "Nearly." He covered her hair and face with kisses. Her lungs still burned, and her entire body hurt, but she was safe. And she wasn't alone. When he stood and lifted her in his arms, Elsa looked over his shoulder.

While flames reached the second floor in the mansion behind them, Tatiana picked up Elsa's cane and one suitcase, and Danielle picked up the other. They had no idea what they carried.

———◦———

If Elsa were to fall asleep now, she wasn't sure how many hours would pass before she could wake up. So when Luke brought her to Tatiana's couch and urged her to lie down, she refused.

"Drink." Tatiana pressed a full glass of water into Elsa's hand, and she gratefully sipped.

Luke sat beside her, and Danielle sat cross-legged on the floor, rubbing Barney's ears, her worried gaze darting to Elsa and back to Barney at intervals. "I knew you needed help," the child said, her tangled hair loose at her shoulders. "You were with that man who came here looking for the aviary. The one with hair the color of Sunny's feathers." She glanced toward Birdie's canary, quiet now in its cage.

"That doesn't describe Hugh Geoffrey," Luke said, voicing Elsa's thoughts as well.

Tatiana nodded. "They both came. First Dr. Geoffrey, then Archer."

"When you didn't come out after so long, I sent Barney to find you," Danielle said, giving the dog an extra scratch between his ears. "Mr. Luke let him stay here with us a few days this week, overnight and everything."

"He likes it here," Luke told her, and Elsa knew what he'd left unsaid. Barney calmed Danielle. The dog was good for her during this tumultuous time.

"Tom's been okay without Barney?" Elsa asked, wincing. Her throat still burned from the smoke, but she'd just have to push past that.

Luke smiled. "It was his idea."

A knock sounded. "Tatiana? It's Ivy. Tom's here, too."

Tatiana opened the door, and Ivy practically fell on top of Elsa in her rush to embrace her. "Are you okay? Mercy, what a

302

fright you gave us! What on earth were you doing? We saw the flames from the road, and I tried not to imagine the worst, but you know how that goes. . . ."

Luke took Elsa's water glass so she could hug her roommate with both arms. "I'm all right."

Ivy drew back, likely alarmed at the sound of Elsa's voice. "I want to hear your whole story, but it sounds like you ought to keep drinking that water for now."

Elsa agreed. "You tell me yours."

Ivy nodded. "I got home late from our event and saw your note. You hadn't come home by the time you expected, so I was worried. Naturally. There are no phones here, after all, and with all those other people after the aviary, too, I didn't know what to think. First I called the Tarrytown train station to see if the trains had been on schedule and ask if anyone had seen you boarding one for Manhattan. Those answers were yes, and no, respectively. So I rang up Luke and Tom, took a cab to their place, and together we hightailed it to Tarrytown. Let me tell you, those twenty-four miles never seemed so far."

Tatiana shuffled to the kitchen and returned with a fresh wash-rag and bowl of clean water. Elsa washed her hands and face while Tom picked up the story.

"We all agreed that maybe Wesley or Crawford or Dr. Geoffrey had been keeping you under duress and needed to be held accountable, but there would be no way of notifying police from Elmhurst." He pulled a pen from his pocket and flipped it between his fingers. "So Luke dropped off Ivy and me at the station to convince them to send out an officer. While we were doing that, Luke tore off to come straight here. We might not have persuaded anyone if a call hadn't come in from a motorist reporting a fire he'd seen while passing by Elmhurst. We just now hitched a ride on a fire engine to get here." Tom sat on the opposite side of Barney. Giving up on the pen, he sank his hand into the dog's fur. Sandwiched between two such attentive humans, the dog rolled to his back and practically grinned.

"When I arrived," Luke added, "the first floor of the mansion was on fire. Tatiana and Danielle met me on the lawn, and Danielle told me she'd seen Archer pull Elsa inside hours ago, and that Elsa hadn't been seen since."

"I figured you would come visit us after your business at the mansion," Tatiana said. "It seemed like a bad sign that you hadn't."

"I thought Barney could help," Danielle added. "He used to find people in the war. I thought Barney could help."

"He did." Elsa's heart squeezed at Danielle's obvious agitation. Elsa wanted nothing more than to put everyone at ease. "My turn," she said. "A short story."

With a stark economy of words, she told them why she had come this evening and what had happened to her since. "Luke, could you open that suitcase, please?"

He brought the suitcase into the living room and opened it on the coffee table. Discarding the pillow, he held up a framed painting of Sarah, questions in his eyes.

Elsa smiled. "Open the back of the frame."

As he did so, a mass of butterflies fluttered inside her stomach. When Luke drew away the waxed paper and layer of muslin, a collective gasp filled the room. Tom held on to Barney's collar so the curious dog couldn't get close enough to sniff at it.

"You found it!" Ivy cried.

"This is the aviary? She cut it to pieces in order to hide it?" Tatiana asked.

Elsa nodded. "I only checked a couple of frames before I had to pack them, but I suspect many, if not all, of these hide several pages of the aviary."

Danielle studied the page Luke had exposed. "Miss Birdie's book. I remember that. Miss Birdie's book."

"But . . . is it still valuable?" Tatiana asked.

"I'm sure it is." Luke replaced the layers and screwed the frame back together. "If you'd like, I can take these, along with the provenance, to get authenticated. The Metropolitan Museum of Art is currently curating a new museum that is exclusively for medieval art. I don't want to speak out of turn, but if you want to sell these, they'd likely make you an offer. If they don't, I know several private collectors who would."

Tatiana watched Danielle. The girl wasn't looking at Luke while he spoke, but she was clearly listening. "What do you think, Danielle? Birdie left this to you. Do you want to sell?"

"I want to keep one." She twisted and twisted the strand of hair. "My favorite."

Tatiana rubbed Danielle's back in a slow circle, and the child seemed to relax. "I don't know anything about how this works, but I don't see why you couldn't." She looked to Elsa, then to Luke. "What would it mean if we sell most of the pages?"

Luke smiled. "It would mean, Mrs. Petrovic, that you'd have enough money to purchase from the county the land your cottage is sitting on now. If they agree to sell it. And if they don't, you could buy a different plot in the area, I'm sure."

"It means you don't have to worry." Elsa's lungs and throat tightened again, but this time it had nothing to do with smoke. "Birdie is taking care of you, as she always intended to do."

CHAPTER

24

NEW YORK CITY
FRIDAY, SEPTEMBER 17, 1926

Elsa couldn't remember the last time she'd called in sick for work. But even before Ivy insisted she see a doctor today, she'd already decided to do so. Just because she'd had a terrible experience with Dr. Stanhope didn't mean she didn't need help after inhaling smoke and overexerting herself.

"Miss Reisner, is it? Am I saying that correctly?" Dr. Clay must see more than twenty patients a day at this walk-in clinic. The fact that he still cared enough to pronounce her name correctly made her hopeful he'd pay attention to other details, too.

"That's right." Elsa's throat still hurt, but not nearly as much as it had last night.

He scanned the notes the nurse had taken from Elsa moments ago, then looked her in the eyes. "Please tell me why you're here, and what I can do for you."

She licked her dry lips and briefly told him what had happened last night.

Dr. Clay turned to the water cooler in the corner of his office and gave her a glass to drink. "It says here you had polio as a child, with lasting effects on your leg and lungs."

"Yes." She sipped the cool water. "That's one of the reasons I thought I should come in. I didn't know if inhaling smoke might have made my lungs worse."

He nodded. "It's always wise to get checked out. Do your airways feel tight and swollen?"

She shook her head. She had only breathed in smoke for less than five minutes, although at the time it felt much longer.

"Let's take a listen." He used his stethoscope and asked her a series of questions.

"The good news is that the smoke inhalation wasn't prolonged or severe enough to warrant treatment, other than fresh air, plenty of fluids, and as much rest as your body calls for," he declared. "But let's talk about those other symptoms you mentioned. Your polio symptoms became worse this summer? Please tell me more."

She swallowed. This wasn't why she'd come, but she could really use a second opinion. "Do you think it's all in my head?"

Dr. Clay's eyebrows knit together. "I have no reason to believe that. In fact, I've seen this before in other patients. I'd like to hear your story and see how it compares to theirs. I'm collecting data on this previously unstudied phenomenon."

Elsa's jaw dropped open in shock. Mastering her composure, she quickly closed it again. She would never wish this condition on anyone else. But the idea that she wasn't alone in it brought an unlooked-for reassurance, somehow.

She told him everything. He took notes, asked questions, nodded, and generally made her feel heard and seen. "What do you think?" she asked at the end of it. "Am I like the others you know?"

"In what you have described, you're more alike than different."

Her heart beat faster. She wondered if she might ever meet these other patients. Would she recognize them by their limp if she saw them by chance on the street? Would the doctor consent to put them in touch with each other or perhaps facilitate some kind of group discussion? But those questions could wait.

Elsa took another drink of water, then asked the one that could not. "What will become of us?"

Dr. Clay set his clipboard and notebook aside. "I wish I could give you a clear answer. But we're now noticing a pattern emerging among some of our patients. It's too soon to be able to chart a trajectory."

"But you must have noticed something, anything, that you can share with me. Is what I'm experiencing a stage, or will this become normal? Will I—" She swallowed the catch in her throat. Her hand rested on her left knee, the hard edges of the leg brace sharp beneath her palm. "Will I get worse? Will I eventually need a brace for the other leg and crutches?"

The lines on his brow bespoke compassion. "I understand the compulsion to know what lies ahead. What we plan for, we can prepare for, yes? That's the idea, anyway. I'm sorry I cannot give you that. All I can offer is what I've seen in other patients whose cases are similar to yours."

She nodded. "Yes. Tell me."

"One of them has become far less mobile. He uses braces on both legs now and crutches since neither knee bends freely."

Tears welled in Elsa's eyes, not just from fear for herself but from genuine sadness for the other person. She could imagine what he was going through and figured not many other people truly could.

"But another patient is more like you. She has grown weaker but, so far, has not needed additional braces or crutches. In fact, she has held steady like this for three years."

Hope sparked. "Is it possible she could stay like she is forever? Could she even improve?"

A small smile touched the doctor's face. "As I said, at this point, we really don't know. I've only been tracking these patients for three years, myself. I can't say she won't eventually get worse. But neither can I rule out the possibility of improvement."

"Then maybe if I keep working at strengthening my body . . ." She trailed off when she noticed his expression change.

"Pushing your body to the brink of your ability isn't the answer," he told her. "That's only a path to breaking down faster."

She dropped her gaze to the gloved hands in her lap. That wasn't what she wanted to hear. But it rang true in a way her own wishful thinking never had. "Then what can I do to get better?" She had to get better. She must do something.

"Some ailments are of our own making, which means we can also unmake them. But this, Miss Reisner, isn't one of them. You didn't cause this. The minute I learn of something that you or I can do to improve your condition, I'll share that. The best advice I can give now is to pay attention to what your body is telling you. Push less, not more. And please schedule follow-up appointments so we can track how you're doing. Live within your limits instead of fighting against them."

During the cab ride home, Elsa considered what Dr. Clay had said.

She might stay at this level of weakness for years.

She might possibly improve, although he hadn't seen a precedent for that yet.

She might get worse. And there was nothing she could do about that, except possibly wear herself out quicker by being in denial of her true condition.

Elsa couldn't see the future. She was tempted to feel like she was in that locked dark room all over again, but she held up the light of the truth. She hadn't been abandoned by God in the secret den at Elmhurst, and she wasn't now, either. If one door in her life was locked closed, God would lead her on another path. He would be with her the entire way.

Just because she didn't know where it would lead didn't mean she couldn't trust Him. *Be my light,* she prayed again. *Show me the path.*

The first step was obvious. There was one question she needed to ask herself: Knowing her mobility may decrease in the future, how did she want to spend the time she had now?

———○———

By early afternoon, Elsa had made up her mind about what to do with the information Dr. Clay had given her. She needed to tell Ivy, Luke, and her parents. She also needed to talk to her boss.

She rose when she spied Mr. Chapman pushing through the revolving door to enter the Beresford lobby. She had called his office requesting a meeting, and he insisted they hold it here.

"Miss Reisner." He doffed his homburg. "Shall we sit?"

They moved to a pair of wing chairs, and she thanked him again for coming.

"After the ordeal you had last night, you should be resting. Having our conversation here is the least I can do."

The American Museum of Natural History was such a short distance from here, but he was right that she was too worn out for it, not to mention the long walk required to reach his office once inside the massive building. In fact, after this meeting, she planned to go back to bed and wouldn't mind staying there until tomorrow.

"You saw a doctor, I hope?" Mr. Chapman went on. "I must say I was shocked to hear you went back to Elmhurst after your work there was done. I'm sorry this happened at all, but I must ask, will you be blaming the museum for putting you there in the first place?"

"Not at all. I was there on my own time last night. My errand had nothing to do with work. If anything, Mr. Chapman, I owe you my gratitude for assigning me that project. It breathed new life into my passion for birds and people."

He leaned back in his chair, likely relieved not to have the museum involved in a scandal. If anyone was to blame for the danger she'd been in, it was Archer for locking her away. But she didn't have the energy to deal with him yet.

"Then what is this about?"

"My time. And my passion for birds and people." She felt as confident in her decision as her boss appeared bewildered. "I recently asked you if I might serve as the museum's guide for bird-watching groups in Central Park, and you said no. Would you reconsider?"

His eyelids flared, and his mustache twitched. "No. I still say no to that, Miss Reisner. I require your skills in skinning and dissecting birds and managing inventory."

She smiled. "I thought you'd say that. In that case, I'm giving you my notice that I need to reduce my hours with the department and only work part-time."

Color drained from his face. "Is this an ultimatum?"

"No, I promise you it isn't. It's the result of consultation with my doctor. I need to work fewer hours at the museum. I'll lead bird-watching groups on my own, as my health allows." She'd already been doing it.

But she couldn't keep working so hard at the museum and have energy left to do what she loved most. She had no idea how many months or years she had left before her mobility might be further compromised. She didn't want to spend all the time she had left in an office with dead birds. She wanted to be out with the living ones.

She had been asking God to *get* better, but He was showing her how to *live* better. The answer wasn't trying harder to do more and keep up with the razzle-dazzle, fast-paced city she lived in. It was doing less, to make room for what really mattered. She was placing her own priorities above any hope of promotion. She knew it. And she felt at perfect peace about it.

"Our department can scarcely keep up with the work as it is," he pleaded.

She hadn't expected him to place her health above the productivity of his department. That was *her* job. No one else could do that for her.

"Then hire another part-time worker, or even another full-time," she suggested. "Bring in a university student. You've said yourself you have stacks of applications sitting in your inbox. Handle it however you choose, but I'm choosing to only work twenty-five hours a week. That is, if you'll still have me on those terms."

He leaned forward, then back against the chair again, his gaze roaming the lobby. At last, he muttered, "For now. But if I find someone else with your skillset and expertise willing to work the full forty and then some, I may have to let you go. Are you willing to accept that?"

She took a deep breath. "I am."

CHAPTER

25

lsa paid the cab fare and leaned on her cane, relying on it more than usual after Thursday night's harrowing ordeal, even after resting for most of yesterday and all of today. She readjusted her cloche and climbed the eight steps, pausing for breath at the top before pushing through the brass revolving doors of The Plaza Hotel. It would take more than two days to recover from what she'd done at Elmhurst.

But Mother had sounded so excited when she'd invited Elsa here for their weekly dinner, she hadn't had the heart to cancel.

Elsa smiled as she entered the lobby. An enormous vase of lilies perfumed the air. Potted palm trees framed the entrance to the restaurant.

"Right this way." A man in a tuxedo led her into the spacious restaurant, lit by a glass ceiling stained with shades of blue, green, and gold. "Your party, miss." When he made to pull out her chair, he was interrupted by a bachelor her parents must have invited to join them.

This was one bachelor Elsa was thrilled to see.

"The honor is mine." He came around and seated her with a smile that warmed her to her toes. Luke Dupont in a crisp black suit was a vision she hadn't been prepared for. She had known he was strong and considered him handsome from the first time they'd met. But there was something about the way that jacket fit him that sent a little flip to her stomach. He was resplendent.

"And here I thought I was early." Elsa leaned her cane against the edge of the table. "Yet you three look like you've been deep in conversation."

Her father tented his hands on the white linen tablecloth. "We have."

Elsa raised her eyebrows, looking from one parent to the other. "And?"

Beside her, Mother's smile held nothing back, but it was Father who answered. "Your mother and I have decided to retire. From matchmaking."

"It would seem our services are no longer needed," Mother added. "And through no fault of our own."

Elsa coughed to hide a laugh.

"Do you agree?" Luke asked.

"I do." Elsa grinned. "Emphatically."

"Excellent." Father stood, and Mother slipped her hand in his as she rose, as well. "Then our work here is done. Enjoy yourselves."

Elsa glanced at the table and saw only two menus. "You don't have to go," she said. "Please, at least stay and have dinner. These reservations aren't easy to come by, after all."

"By all means, don't let us run you off," Luke echoed. "Join us."

"If you're sure, dears. I'd love nothing better." Mother returned to the chair beside Elsa's, and Father slid into the booth by Luke.

"We have a lot to catch up on," Elsa told her parents.

Father swallowed and shared a look with Mother before turning an affectionate gaze on Elsa once more. "That we do."

Dinner was soon ordered and served: crab cakes, grilled salmon, stuffed chicken, roast beef, and Yorkshire pudding. Over the course of the evening, Elsa told them she found the aviary pages for the Petrovics. She did not tell them she'd been locked in a dark room, had crawled through a tunnel, and jumped from a burning building. There was no point in upsetting her parents unnecessarily.

"I do have some good news on that score," Luke added. "I showed some of the pages to the curator of medieval art at the Metropolitan Museum of Art, and he's very interested. He'll have to bring it to the acquisitions board for official approval to extend an offer, of course. But he was impressed by the provenance, deemed all of it genuine, and is eager to move forward. Even if his offer ends up being on the lower end of the scale he mentioned to me, the Petrovics will have enough money to buy the land they want."

"And what is Tatiana's plan?" Mother asked. "If the county agrees to sell her some of the Elmhurst land, will she continue to work on the grounds?"

"I don't think they'd be able to stop her," Elsa said. "Even if she only does it as a volunteer, I have a feeling stewarding the land is all she wants to do."

"If the county has any sense," Luke added, "they'll consider her input when planning their landscape design. She has a wealth of experience with what grows on that land and what doesn't. I'm going with her when she meets with Mr. Field about all this. If he refuses to sell any of the land back to her, we'll connect with my real estate contact in the Hudson River valley. Even if her new home isn't right on Elmhurst grounds, we'll make sure it's on the same river."

"Would you? That would be so helpful," Elsa told him.

Mother smiled and folded her napkin, laying it beside her dinner plate. "And now, I think it would be most helpful for us older folks to take our leave and let you enjoy the rest of the evening."

Luke stood and shook Father's hand. Mother kissed Luke's

cheek. And Elsa marveled at the warmth already springing between them. Who were these parents of hers? And why had it taken so long for her to find them?

But people changed. Elsa was proof of that, as well.

Luke smiled at Elsa and took her hand, drawing her into the booth beside him. "Dessert?" he asked.

"I'd love to, but I couldn't possibly."

"Nice night for a walk in the park."

"One of the nicest. How about a carriage ride this time instead?" She was done ignoring her limits. It was time to be kind to herself instead.

Luke's smile broadened, pushing brackets into his cheeks. "Even better."

———

Clip-clopping hoofbeats made a soothing rhythm as the horse pulled the carriage through Central Park. To the left was the pond, its surface reflecting the cloud-tufted sky. Trees arched their branches overhead, releasing some leaves to swirl on the breeze. Elsa picked one off Luke's shoulder and rolled its stem between her fingers.

"What did they find out about the fire?" she asked, now that such questions wouldn't upset her parents. "Was it arson for a lark since they knew the house would be torn down the next day anyway?"

Luke shook his head. "I've spoken with the fire inspector in Tarrytown, and he didn't see signs of foul play. His best guess was that someone was careless with a cigarette right before leaving for the night, and it caused a fire, made worse by spills of whatever alcohol they brought in."

Elsa could believe it. "I still don't understand why Archer let me stay locked up for so long, even if he'd soured on our friendship. Was he being deliberately vengeful? Or am I truly that forgettable to him?"

"As it happens, I asked him the same thing yesterday morning. I went to his house before work."

She turned to look at him. "You did?"

"Of course I did. His parents were very interested in what I came to say and ask him. It was obvious he was suffering a headache from the night before, but I didn't let that stop me from speaking loud and clear. I would have hated for him to miss a word."

Elsa could picture it. "Did you go all scary face on him? I mean, scary is in the eye of the beholder. And behold, I don't think you're scary at all."

Luke chuckled. "He should have been scared. His parents looked horrified, but not because of me. Archer had to admit that he had locked you in that room and forgot about you. You should have seen their faces when I told them about the fire. I admit to waiting an extra beat before telling them you escaped. They needed to consider what could have happened. They needed to know you could have—" He swallowed and shook his head.

She laced her fingers with his. "But I didn't. It's over." After returning to her apartment in the wee hours of Friday morning, she'd fallen asleep only to wake with a start in the dark. It had taken her a few moments to reorient herself to her bedroom, as opposed to the pitch-black tunnel where she had been. Last night had been the same, waking with a surge of adrenaline as she had when Barney licked her awake in the tunnel. She told herself then what she told Luke now. "It's over. All is well."

"I haven't stopped thanking God for that." He put his arm around her, and she nestled into his side. "At any rate, from what Archer said—if we can believe the guy—he went back to let you out after you'd entered the tunnel. When he didn't see you in there, he figured someone else had let you out and had locked the door again after you left. When he drove home, he allegedly believed you'd left before him."

Resting her head on Luke's shoulder, Elsa pondered Archer's explanation as they rolled past Gapstow Bridge. The stone arch over the neck of the pond was mostly covered with vines that would soon turn bare for winter.

"Do you believe Archer's story?" Luke prodded.

She didn't answer right away. "It's easier to believe him than to think he'd intentionally leave me there when he left for the night. I can't believe he would be that cruel. No decent human being would do that, even to someone they didn't care for."

"Have you thought about pressing charges?" he asked. "Mr. and Mrs. Hamlin said they were ready to offer any sum to keep you from doing so, and from talking to the press about Archer's role. I'm surprised they haven't reached out to you already."

Elsa frowned. "Maybe they tried. Ivy kept the telephone off the hook today to make sure no ringing would wake me. No, I don't want to press charges or talk to the press, and I certainly don't need their money. The charges wouldn't stick, and I'd rather move on from the entire ordeal."

The carriage trundled by families and locals, past tourists smart enough not to come at the height of summer. When they came near enough to the Central Park Carousel to hear the organ music on the breeze, Elsa could picture the hand-painted horses going up and down on their poles, even though she couldn't see it from here.

She sat up straight and waved to a few folks she'd led in a bird-watching group before.

"Elsa!" One of them called to her. "When are you going birding again?"

"Soon! Monday twilight. Find me on Bow Bridge."

"I'll be there!"

Luke smiled at Elsa. "Is this going to be a habit now? Are you adding this to your job description as ornithologist at the museum?"

"Yes and no." She told him about her meeting with Mr. Chapman, and her decision to offer bird-guiding on her own.

"That's perfect. It suits you. I'm proud of you for recognizing what makes you happy and going after it."

"What about you?" She wondered if his work remained as satisfying as it had before.

He smiled at her. "I'm looking at what makes me happy. And I'm going after it, too."

A wave of heat rolled through her. She wrinkled her nose. "It?"

"You. I'm looking at you. I've spoken with your parents, because I want to do this right. So unless you object, I'm going after you." He bowed his head toward hers.

Elsa placed a hand on his chest, applying gentle pressure. "That does sound a tad proprietary and hostile though, doesn't it?" she teased.

He scratched his chin, feigning deep thought. "You're right. How about this: Thursday night, I thought I might lose you. The idea carved a hole inside me that I thought would swallow me up. And now you're here, and so am I, and I want nothing more than to be with you. I want to court you, Elsa. If you'll let me. I'm not perfect, and I might make mistakes along the way. But my heart is yours. Maybe not literally, but metaphorically, consistently, perpetually, and voluntarily."

Tears glazed her eyes. "That was so much better," she whispered and kissed him.

But her conscience tugged at her. She hadn't yet told him what Dr. Clay had said about her changing health. She needed to but wasn't quite sure how. Was it wrong for her to want to savor the moment without considering the challenges the future might hold?

The carriage rolled over mats of fallen leaves. When they passed the Sheep Meadow, Luke commented on the crowd gathered there. "Do you know what that's all about?"

"George Bernard Shaw's play *Man and Superman* is showing

until tomorrow night," Elsa said. "I read in the newspaper it's supposed to be a comedy of manners, but the underlying theme is the evolution of man into a superior version, as you can tell from the title."

"More eugenics claptrap," Luke muttered.

Elsa tightened her grip on the chickadee cane. Eugenics said she was weak and defective. It said the same of Tom, whose wartime experience left its mark on his spirit, and of Danielle, whose mind worked differently from her peers. Eugenics said Birdie's baby, Sarah, didn't deserve to live, and that neither did all of Dr. Couney's Incubator Babies.

"We are all made in the image of God," Luke reminded her. "All of us."

"Yes." Elsa squeezed his hand while she ordered her thoughts. Luke was so patient with her, so supportive. She agreed she'd been made in the image of God, but it was equally true that they lived in a fallen world inside bodies that broke down—some quicker than others. Hers quicker than his. He needed to consider what a future with her could look like. She had to tell him.

"Luke, I consulted with a different doctor yesterday. Ivy insisted I get checked out at a walk-in clinic after the ordeal at Elmhurst Thursday night."

He sat at attention. "Good. What did he say?"

"I didn't breathe smoke in long enough to require medical treatment. But that's not all we discussed." Briefly, she told him about their conversation.

"And? Please tell me he didn't say you were imagining your condition."

Elsa forged a small smile. "No. He was very interested. He has other patients who survived childhood polio, and some of them have reported similar symptoms. In all of us, our health started getting worse between fifteen and twenty years after first contracting the illness."

"So what does that mean? What did he prescribe?"

She drew in a breath. "It means my experience isn't an anomaly. The doctor—and colleagues with whom he has consulted—don't understand why, but some of us simply have long-term effects from polio that took years and years to show up. It may not get worse than it is now. But it could."

She thought of how when she exerted herself even her strong leg grew sore from compensating for her weak one. She didn't want that to happen to Luke. She didn't want the burden of her condition to wear him down. "I want you to think about what that means for us. What if—what if this is as good as it gets? Could you see yourself with me long-term—just as I am?"

His grey eyes misted. "Sweetheart, as far as I'm concerned, being with you *is* as good as it gets." He looked away for a moment, then captured her gaze with his once more. "You once told me you wanted to fly."

"Now we know how that ends," she said on a laugh. "In a heap, with bruises if not broken bones, for you and me both." He was lucky she hadn't truly hurt him when he broke her fall from Birdie's bedroom window.

He brushed a lock of her hair from her face, then let his hand linger on her neck. "What I mean is, I will always be your safe place to land. I can't give you wings, but I'll be your solid ground."

Her heart swelled at the tenderness in his voice and touch. "Even better," she said. "I don't need to fly. I just want to walk beside you."

Luke pressed a kiss to the back of her gloved hand, then to the skin on her wrist. He leaned closer, but she stopped him when a flutter of movement caught her eye.

Blue jays agitated around the top of an elm tree, leading her line of sight straight to Zeus, the Eurasian eagle-owl who had escaped the Central Park Menagerie. "He's still free!"

With a good-humored chuckle, Luke followed her gaze. "And he's still in the park."

"Maybe he'll never leave it," Elsa conceded. "Maybe he can't fly as far as other owls, or maybe he really likes where he is. And why not? It's a beautiful place to be. But he can still spread his wings, and obviously he's still managing to hunt and eat."

Luke squeezed her hand. The sun bronzed his profile as he peered up at Zeus from beneath the brim of his homburg. "He seems happy up there. He seems as free as he wants to be."

"I think he is," Elsa said.

And so was she.

AUTHOR'S NOTE

Thank you for journeying back to New York City, and to the Hudson River valley, with *The Hudson Collection*! Most of the characters in this novel are fictional with a few exceptions:

- Mr. Frank Chapman really was the head of the ornithology department at the American Museum of Natural History at the time. He left quite a legacy as longtime editor of *Bird-Lore* magazine and the creator of the Christmas Bird Count, a holiday tradition promoted by the Audubon Society to this day.
- The staff listed of the American Museum of Natural History were historical figures, as well as the Hudson Bay expedition members listed. Mr. Miller did dissect Galapagos penguins in 1926, and Mr. Griscom did publish an article on birding in Central Park, as well as a how-to guide for anyone who wanted to skin and transport birds properly.
- Johann Baptist von Spix did discover the Spix's macaw in 1819. The species became so rare that it almost went extinct. (The animated movie *Rio* was based on the plight of the Spix's macaw.) The American Museum of Natural History did acquire a Spix's macaw in 1926.
- Dr. Martin Couney, head of the Incubator Babies show on Coney Island, was a true innovator in caring for

premature babies at a time when hospitals were not equipped to help them. Dr. Couney's babies had an 85 percent survival rate.

- Fletcher Henderson was one of many popular jazz musicians performing in New York City at the time.

The Van Tessels' Elmhurst estate near Tarrytown, New York, is fictional but inspired by Lyndhurst, a historic mansion that is also outside Tarrytown. The house and grounds are open to the public. Several wealthy residents made their home in the beautiful Hudson River valley in the 1800s and early 1900s. As Ivy points out in the novel, the area is rich in history and folklore, including *The Legend of Sleepy Hollow*, which Washington Irving set near Tarrytown.

Luke Dupont's job as an architectural salvage dealer was based on that thriving trend among the elite to purchase entire rooms, as much for their history as for their aesthetic appeal. In the 1920s, museums across America were beginning to acquire period rooms, which represented a specific place and time in history. But wealthy private citizens were enamored with the same idea, making architectural salvage a booming business.

Cher Ami was a real homing pigeon who served heroically in World War I with the 77th Division. He died of his war wounds in 1919, and in 1921, his preserved body was presented to the Smithsonian Institution.

The eugenics movement peaked in the 1920s. All of the literature Elsa and Ivy read were direct quotes from historic documents of the times, including the material and score cards for the Better Babies contests held at fairs. Some historians believe the movement's popularity waned when soldiers returned from World War I with physical, mental, and emotional challenges. It became uncomfortable to call those brave heroes "defective" when held up to an "ideal" standard. While eugenics lost its grip in America, it became the precursor to the basic tenets of a "superior race" in Germany.

All of the projects Elsa worked on for the museum were taken from the annual report for the American Museum of Natural History for that year—with the exception of cataloging birds at Elmhurst. Her struggle with her polio symptoms reflects a phenomenon present in a percentage of polio survivors. Just as the second doctor tells Elsa near the end of the story, some patients develop a recurrence of symptoms fifteen to twenty years after first contracting the illness. More is known about this syndrome today, but in the 1920s, it had barely been studied.

In the novel, Danielle is never accurately diagnosed as being on the autism spectrum. Autism was not well understood in that era, which resulted in misdiagnoses and stigmas for those who had it, especially during a time when eugenics was so prized.

All of the Revolutionary War–related anniversaries Ivy celebrated were accurate, but I don't know how many of them the New-York Historical Society actually commemorated in 1926.

The experience described at Vassar College during the Spanish flu epidemic was true to what really happened. The college physician did forbid travel to help prevent the spread of the disease, and the students volunteered their time for Red Cross efforts when they could.

The Eurasian eagle-owl character named Zeus was based on a Eurasian eagle-owl named Flaco who really did escape his Central Park Zoo enclosure in February 2023, while I was writing this novel. Flaco surprised park officials by flying, hunting, eating, and surviving. At the time of this writing, he is still free. The analogy for this book was too good to pass up, so I readily admit to using the inspiration.

Visitors to New York City can still see many of the sites referenced in this novel, including several points of interest in Central Park, the American Museum of Natural History, The Plaza, and even the historic wooden escalator in Macy's. The Beresford hotel-complex where Elsa and Ivy live in the novel was originally built in 1889. The Beresford that you see today was rebuilt in 1929 and is an iconic part of the skyline view from Central Park. Visit Coney Island and walk the boardwalk, which opened in 1923. Try a hot dog from the original Nathan's Famous at the corner of Surf and Stillwell Avenues. They cost more than a nickel these days, but the restaurant still hosts the Fourth of July hot dog eating contests every year, now an international competition.

DISCUSSION QUESTIONS

1. Elsa's struggle with shame began when she was sick and recovering from polio. How has this issue affected her as an adult?

2. Ever since she was a child, Elsa dreamed of being an ornithologist with the American Museum of Natural History. She achieved this dream and then realized the job didn't bring her as much joy as she'd anticipated. Can you think of a time when a dream or goal didn't meet your expectations? What did you do?

3. Why do you think that Tatiana and Danielle were so important to Elsa? Why do you think she had such an interest in Birdie and her baby, Sarah?

4. Eugenics was a popular field in the 1920s but fell out of favor in the United States by the end of the decade. But do you still see traces of the quest for the "perfect human product" in today's culture? Explain.

5. Dr. Couney was a real person who saved hundreds of premature babies with his incubators on Coney Island. The money he charged people to see the babies went

toward funding their care. Do you think the Incubator Babies show exploited the preemies or valued them? Can you think of ways in which people make money off the most vulnerable in our society today?

6. In chapter 12, we learn that Elsa had prayed for healing before, and she still hadn't been healed the way she wanted to be. When you don't receive what you pray for, what is your typical response? Do you keep asking, stop praying altogether, or something in between?

7. In chapter 13, Tatiana admits that knowing God is sovereign isn't comforting but experiencing His presence in the midst of pain is. What do you think the difference is?

8. One of Elsa's biggest concerns is that she doesn't want her limitations to be a burden on other people. Have you experienced this fear? How has it affected your relationships?

9. In chapter 19, Luke says of architectural salvage, "I see it as saving what's valuable even when everything else is crumbling down around it." What parallels come to mind between architectural salvage and how we handle other areas of life?

10. In chapter 24, Elsa realizes, "The answer wasn't trying harder to do more and keep up with the razzle-dazzle, fast-paced city she lived in. It was doing less, to make room for what really mattered." Can you think of a time in your life when you felt prompted to do less, not more? How did that change things for you?

ACKNOWLEDGMENTS

My sincere gratitude and appreciation go to:

The multiple teams of talented people at Bethany House Publishers who are committed to bringing you quality fiction.

My agent, Tim Beals, of Credo Communications, for his unfailing support.

My friend Mindelynn Young Godbout, for touring Manhattan with me while I researched this series and for her enthusiastic support of these books!

Patrick Sheary, curator of Furnishings and Historic Interiors at the DAR Museum, for answering all my questions about period rooms and architectural salvage.

Paul Friedman, general research division, New York Public Library, for helping me navigate the myriad of research resources offered by NYPL.

Paul Sweet, collection manager, Department of Ornithology at the American Museum of Natural History, for answering my questions and directing me to the 1926 annual report of the AMNH.

Rachel Yutzy, middle school special education teacher, for answering all my questions about what would be likely for my fictional character on the autism spectrum.

My friend, fellow author, and brilliant speech-language pathologist Pepper Basham, who also lent wisdom gleaned from years of experience working with kids diagnosed with autism spectrum disorder. Thank you for going over Danielle's dialogue and behaviors with me! Any mistakes I made while writing the character are completely my own.

Rob, my husband, and our teens, Elsa and Ethan, for the grace and support through the multiple deadlines attached to every book. Special thanks to Elsa, my biology-loving daughter, for lending her name to the protagonist!

Everyone who prayed for me through the writing and editing of *The Hudson Collection*.

Most of all, thank you, Lord, for using story to reveal truth.

FOR MORE FROM

JOCELYN GREEN

read on for an excerpt from

The

METROPOLITAN
AFFAIR

With a notorious forger preying on New York's high
society, Metropolitan Museum of Art curator Lauren
Westlake is just the expert needed to track down the
criminal. As she and Detective Joe Caravello search for
the truth, the closer they get to discovering the forger's
identity, the more entangled they become in a web of
deception and crime.

Available now wherever books are sold.

D ead people were easy to talk to. It was the living ones that often gave Lauren trouble. Even her father.

No. Especially him.

Rolling her shoulders back, she headed toward the Central Park bench where he waited. At seventy years old, he'd diminished from the giant he'd been to her in childhood. And like the giants in her storybooks, her father had been just as fabled. Outsized in her heart and mind and not quite real.

Bridles jangled on a pair of horses pulling a carriage full of tourists. Lauren watched it pass, then crossed to the lawn spreading from the Egyptian obelisk erected by her employer, the Metropolitan Museum of Art.

Lawrence Westlake stood to greet her. "I wasn't sure you'd come."

She wouldn't stay long. "You said there was something specific you wanted to ask me?" She sat on the opposite end of the bench from him, near a barrel sprouting orange chrysanthemums. Behind the obelisk, trees flamed with autumn's glory beneath an azure sky.

He lowered himself to the bench. "There is. But first, how are you? How is your work?"

"Busy as ever. We're expecting another shipment of crates from the team in the field any day now." As assistant curator of Egyptian art, with the curator on an expedition, Lauren was doing the work of at least two people until the team's return next spring.

335

"Anything exciting?" Lawrence's eyes glinted. From a nearby pushcart, the smell of roasted pumpkin seeds and apple cider carried on the breeze.

After a quick glance at her watch, Lauren told him about the most recent mummy and coffin to arrive and felt herself relax. Lawrence Westlake might not have been the best father, but he'd been the one to instill in her a love for Egyptology. Aside from the curator, Albert Lythgoe, and the expedition director, Herbert Winlock, she couldn't think of anyone else who might share her enthusiasm for the nuances of ancient Egyptian artifacts.

"I'm proud of you." His smile brought a gentle tapping on the wall she'd built around her heart. Then he pulled a photograph from inside his jacket pocket. "Look what I found."

Lauren took it and stared at the little girl in the photo, standing as close to the man beside her as he would allow. It had been taken twenty-seven years ago. She'd been five years old.

"How small you were," Lawrence murmured. "Do you remember that day?"

"Of course." She recalled every detail. Someone from a geographical society had come to their home to photograph Lawrence before one of his many trips. Lauren had pestered to be in one of the photos, and they'd finally appeased her. She'd wanted to sit on her father's lap but hadn't been brave enough to do more than hold his hand.

She fingered the torn corner of the image. "Do you remember *this* day?"

He frowned. "When you tore off the corner? It was an accident. Out of character for you since you were always so careful with your things. You treated everything as though it were in a museum even then."

His expression held no hint that he remembered the circumstances. Lauren had been upset that he was leaving her behind again. Lawrence had tucked the photograph into the front pocket of her dress, saying that she was to keep the picture close, and in that way, they'd always be together.

Lauren had ripped the photo when she yanked it out of her pocket and thrust it back at him. She didn't want a piece of paper. She wanted him.

"I'm going on another trip," Lawrence announced above chittering sparrows. "To the field. Come with me."

Snapping the photo into her handbag, she thought of the times he'd said this to her before. There was always a reason she couldn't or shouldn't come after all. But all she said was, "I thought you'd given up traveling."

"I tried. Staying in one place won't stick." A sigh gusted from him as he leaned back against the bench. "How long do I need to do penance for missing your mother's death?"

But it was the *life* he missed that bothered her most, both before and after her mother died. He didn't understand that or didn't want to.

"You had your aunt and uncle and your cousin," he said. "You and your mother left Chicago to spend every Christmas vacation with them. Staying there after your mother died was best for everyone."

She hadn't said a thing about Mother, and still he argued, bringing up feelings and memories she'd rather leave buried. Was it any wonder she hadn't sought his company during the last four months he'd been living in Manhattan?

Wind teased a strand of hair from Lauren's chignon, and she tucked it behind her ear. "I don't want to do this today."

"It's time to make good on a promise I made to bring you with me."

A promise made and broken more than once. She was unwilling to argue with him anymore, and yet unable to agree.

"The only problem is, the board isn't convinced you ought to have a spot on the expedition team."

"Since I never asked for a spot, we're in perfect agreement." She plucked a petal from the chrysanthemums beside her.

"You're qualified to come. I know that, and you know that. But you need to prove it to the board. You know, with publications, that sort of thing."

Lauren stifled a dark laugh. She had proven herself to many people and institutions along the way to earning her doctorate in Egyptology and attaining this position at the Met. She most certainly did not need to prove anything for a role she hadn't looked for.

"I have no time to impress some nameless board," she began.

"Not nameless." He cut her off, handing her a business card: *Lawrence A. Westlake, executive board, Napoleon Society.* A phone number and Manhattan PO Box followed.

She'd heard of the society but hadn't known that her father was involved with it, let alone on the board. Still in a fledgling state, the organization was devoted to celebrating Egyptian history and culture, and was named for the man whose explorations in Egypt inspired so many others.

"Imagine what this could do for your career," Lawrence said.

Lauren had gotten further in a career in Egyptology than most women could ever dream of. Still, she couldn't deny the pull of the field.

"We've secured the perfect spot for our new office building and museum in Newport," he went on.

"Newport? That's a little out of the way, isn't it?"

"It's perfect!" he repeated. "New York already has the Met, and Boston has the Museum of Fine Arts. But Newport is where all those patrons spend the summers, and the Providence Athenaeum, a short drive from there, holds all twenty-three volumes of Napoleon's *Description de l'Egypte*. It's only fitting for the Napoleon Society to host a world-class collection nearby. I've been curating it for a few years now, and I expect it will be ready to open to the public in another two. Eighteen months if we're lucky."

"So this expedition is for that purpose?" she asked. "To discover and bring back artifacts for your new museum?"

"Precisely. We'll have to do some maneuvering around the new regulations over there, but that won't stop us. I'm inviting you to be part of that."

She broke from his dancing gaze and watched the wind move through the trees. Beyond those, Manhattan's skyscrapers needled the sky. *Far* beyond that lay an ancient land she'd been to as a tourist and then later as a student, but never as a professional.

As much as she'd like to believe this opportunity would work out, that she could uncover history herself, she knew better than to hope.

"No, thank you." Rising, she looked down at the white-haired man who had so often broken her heart. "But best wishes as you go about your business."

She tried to ignore the hurt etched on his face. She refused to feel guilty for rejecting the offer before he had a chance to take it away.

As he walked her back to the Met, she tried to talk to him of something else—anything else. But the conversation fell flat.

Little wonder. Egyptology was all they had in common.

"One more thing." Lawrence extended an engraved invitation. "The Napoleon Society's fundraising gala will be November 21. Please come and hear more of what we're all about."

She took it, and he tipped his hat to her. "Thank you for meeting with me today. I am sorry, you know. And I am proud of you. I would recruit you to this expedition even if you weren't my daughter. You're good enough to be on the team, Dr. Westlake."

Lauren hated that she didn't believe him. She hated that she wished she could.

THURSDAY, OCTOBER 15, 1925

Humming a melody from Verdi's *La Traviata*, Joe Caravello emerged from the subway station into the mottled dark of pre-dawn Lower Manhattan. The sky was a bruise, the sidewalk a series of cracks and broken pieces. He trod the final few blocks to work, eager to reach the place where his thoughts had been for more than an hour. Longer, if he counted thinking in his sleep.

At 240 Centre Street, the five-story granite and limestone police headquarters filled a wedge of land bordered by Grand, Centre, and Broome Streets. Streetlamps illuminated the columns and porticoes over the three arched doorways but failed to penetrate the shadows gathered in his mind.

The clock on the dome began chiming the five o'clock hour as he climbed the steps and entered. After passing through the marble reception room and into the detective bureau, he poured himself a cup of tar-black coffee and took it to his desk.

"Detective Caravello?" A lanky figure approached. His sleeves were a half inch too short. Must be fresh out of the Police Academy on the fourth floor. "Oscar McCormick." He shook Joe's hand with a firm grip. "We're neighbors now, so I thought I'd introduce myself." He jerked a thumb toward the desk across from Joe's. Up until two weeks ago, it had been Connor's.

"I heard about what happened with Connor Boyle," McCormick added.

"Yeah." Joe took another gulp of coffee, not minding the scald on the way down. "Not surprised."

"Right. Well, I'm real sorry things went down that way, and I wanted to tell you that straight off, but we don't have to talk about it again."

"Smart." Joe wasn't cutting the kid any slack, and he felt a twinge of guilt. If the new hire had come a month ago, Joe would have taken him for an espresso at Ferrara's. Ever curious, Joe would have asked for his story, what made him want to join the NYPD, and what his goals were on the force. He would have shared his own insights about the job and been the unofficial one-man welcoming committee. At thirty-five years old, Joe was a veteran, and if he could set an example for young officers, it might help them withstand corrupting influences.

What a joke. Joe couldn't even keep his own friend on the straight and narrow.

The young man shifted. "And I have no reason to believe what they're saying about you, either. I never judge a man based on rumor."

Joe studied McCormick's face, which had turned a ruddy shade to match his hair. "And those rumors are?" He figured he knew them all, but it wouldn't hurt to be sure.

"Oh, uh, just that you could have sprung Boyle from jail with your testimony but decided not to."

"I told the truth in my statement. That's it." Connor's story was that he thought the man Joe had been handcuffing during a speakeasy raid had a gun. Connor claimed he needed to neutralize the threat. The truth was that Wade Martin had been unarmed and already neutralized.

"Well, they say bullets were flying that night, and the one that killed Martin could have easily come from some other miscreant. If you'd kept quiet, maybe Boyle would still be free. They say you ought to have been more loyal to your friend."

"I'm loyal to the oath I took when I swore to serve and protect this city. My friend shot an unarmed man I had already subdued. Is anyone saying that Boyle simply shouldn't have taken the shot?"

McCormick kicked at the foot of Joe's desk, sending his coffee sloshing. "Well, me, for one. I say that."

With a nod of acknowledgment, Joe wiped up the coffee spill

with a napkin, then tossed the sodden wad into a nearby waste bin. If the kid had scruples, Joe could only pray he held on to them longer than Connor had. The man he'd shot left behind a young widow about to give birth to a fatherless child.

That senseless killing never should have happened.

Aware McCormick still stood there, Joe felt his mouth twitch at one corner in his best attempt to stop scowling. "Welcome to the force."

McCormick excused himself, and just in time. Joe had an appointment to keep.

At the doorway to his boss's office, he cleared his throat. "Inspector Murphy? I'm ready if you are."

After shoving a stack of files aside, the inspector in charge of investigations motioned Joe inside and gestured to the chair across from his desk.

Joe sat. "This isn't working," he began. He'd called this meeting and saw no sense in not getting straight to the point.

Murphy's blond eyebrows knit together. "After you tell me exactly what you're referring to, you'd better have a solution to propose."

Of course he did. Joe hadn't come here to whine. "Sir, every time we raid a speakeasy and padlock the door, violence breaks out, people get hurt, and five more speakeasies pop up within the week anyhow. I'm sure you read the commissioner's annual reports." In one year alone, the NYPD made ten thousand arrests on Prohibition-related charges. Only two hundred thirty-nine of those accused were convicted. Three thousand cases were dismissed, and the seven thousand remaining cases languished in the enormous backlog overwhelming state courts.

"Is this about Boyle?" Murphy's grey eyes narrowed.

Joe had expected that question. "It's not about what happened that night. But that does serve as one more example of the risks we take and the little reward we gain—if any—with these raids.

We aren't succeeding in shutting down the illegal sale of alcohol. We're only moving it around."

In truth, he'd been disillusioned about Prohibition enforcement almost since the Volstead Act went into effect more than five years ago. "This entire bootlegging underworld is a Hydra. Cut down one outfit and another one takes its place almost immediately. We're chasing our tails. Spinning our wheels. Pick your own metaphor, but you know what I mean."

Murphy folded his arms over his barrel chest. "Are you getting to the part where you tell me how to solve the problem of Prohibition in Manhattan?"

"You and I both know that's a problem that can't be solved completely. All I'm asking is that we try a different angle." Joe drew in a breath. "Egyptian art and forgeries."

"You're kidding." Murphy's expression suspended between amusement and the very opposite.

"Ever since King Tut's tomb was opened a few years ago, there's been a demand for all things Egypt. And since the Egyptian government closed off the exportation of antiquities, the demand for forgeries has gone up. Forgery is another form of money laundering, just like bootlegging."

"And you have proof this is happening?" The inspector lit a Chesterfield and sent a plume of smoke into the air.

"I have no proof that someone is going to get robbed tonight, but you and I both know it'll happen. Crime happens all the time, including forgeries, whether we're savvy to it or not."

"You didn't answer my question."

"Okay, how's this: two days ago, the antique dealer Reuben Feinstein made a call about his property getting egged. I went over there to check things out, and when I chatted with him, he mentioned that the restoration side of his dealership is slowing down because the specific supplies he needs are out of stock all over the tri-state area. I spent most of yesterday visiting his suppliers. Feinstein was right. Gold, turquoise, a certain kind of black paint—all consistent with Egyptian art—are in high demand." He paused to let Murphy absorb that.

"I couldn't get a list of his customers without a warrant," Joe continued, "but it doesn't take much math to put two and two together here. My gut tells me that if we find those involved in making or dealing forgeries, we'll find criminals who are guilty of other crimes. Racketeering, trafficking, and Prohibition violations. One crime leads to another."

The inspector tapped ash into a tray. "Even if what you say is true, you're forgetting one problem. Where are the victims, Caravello? When is the last time someone came to us to report that their artifact was forged?"

"I'm well aware of that dilemma. If it's a good enough forgery, they won't even know it's not genuine. If it's obviously fake, they wouldn't have acquired it in the first place. Or if they figure out it's fake after the purchase, they may be too embarrassed to report that they've been duped. That's why we go looking. You've told me yourself that purely reactive policing is bad policing. Here's a chance to be proactive."

Murphy took a deep breath, but Joe wasn't done speaking yet.

"Remember the oyster shell?" he asked. When Murphy didn't respond, Joe went on. "You read my report. When I was handcuffing Martin, I noticed he held a gilded oyster shell dripping with gin. There was an Egyptian carving on the inside of it. When I asked him about it, he claimed that Boyle had dropped it into his drink before the raid. Why? What does that shell have to do with anything?"

"It's not your job to find out. That's up to the investigators assigned to that case."

"But there's a connection there. And that's not all. I've been looking around at some art dealerships and antique stores. There's an undercurrent of Egyptian art flowing through Manhattan, and it's cloaked in secrecy. I'm telling you, it's worth looking into. Something is going on."

Murphy pinched the bridge of his nose. "I can't possibly sell this to the public, you know. Nor can I get funding from the Board of Aldermen or the Board of Estimates for this. More resources for murder investigations? Sure. Armed robberies? You bet. But to look into crimes that haven't even been reported . . ." He took a long drag and exhaled. "We've known each other a long time."

Joe nodded.

"So I know you have an appreciation for art that most cops on the force do not. I also know you have a thing about fakes. It's personal for you. Can you deny it?"

"Sir?"

"Scams. No one likes them, but you have more reason than most to crusade against them. I get that."

"This has nothing to do with my father, Inspector. It's a proactive avenue of investigation we haven't tried yet. What we've tried so far isn't working."

"You said that already."

"It bears repeating."

Murphy's mouth slanted in what Joe hoped was resignation.

"I wouldn't come to you with this proposal if I wasn't willing to do the work myself," Joe pressed.

A beat passed, and then another. The inspector blinked. "You're qualified to tell a fake from the real thing?"

"I know who is."

Jocelyn Green inspires faith and courage as the award-winning and bestselling author of numerous fiction and nonfiction books, including *A River between Us*, *The Mark of the King*, and THE WINDY CITY SAGA. Her books have garnered starred reviews from *Booklist* and *Publishers Weekly* and have been honored with the Christy Award, the gold medal from the Military Writers Society of America, and the Golden Scroll Award from the Advanced Writers & Speakers Association. She graduated from Taylor University in Upland, Indiana, and lives with her husband, Rob, and their two children in Cedar Falls, Iowa. She loves pie, hydrangeas, Yo-Yo Ma, the color red, *The Great British Baking Show*, and reading with a cup of tea. Visit her at JocelynGreen .com.

Sign Up for Jocelyn's Newsletter

Keep up to date with Jocelyn's latest news on book releases and events by signing up for her email list at the link below.

JocelynGreen.com

FOLLOW JOCELYN ON SOCIAL MEDIA

Author Jocelyn Green   @Author_Jocelyn_Green   @JocelynGreen77

More from Jocelyn Green

With a notorious forger preying on New York's high society, Metropolitan Museum of Art curator Lauren Westlake is just the expert needed to track down the criminal. As she and Detective Joe Caravello search for the truth, the closer they get to discovering the forger's identity, the more entangled they become in a web of deception and crime.

The Metropolitan Affair

In late nineteenth century Chicago, three women face life-changing tragedies during pivotal moments of history—from the Great Fire to the World's Fair to the capsizing of the SS Eastland. It will take all they have to unravel the truth and find peace while opening their hearts to unexpected love.

THE WINDY CITY SAGA:
Veiled in Smoke, Shadows of the White City, Drawn by the Current